PUBLICATIONS OF THE INSTITUTE
OF FRENCH STUDIES

G. L. VAN ROOSBROECK, Editor.

———

R. CAULFEILD—*The French Literature of Louisiana*... $ 1.50

J. L. GERIG—*Antoine Arlier and the Renaissance at Nîmes.* .... $ .75

R. A. SOTO—*Un olvidado Precursor del Modernismo Francés : Della Rocca de Vergalo* .... $ .25

E. M. LEBERT—*Le Masque de la Vie* .... $ .75

M. M. BARR—*A Bibliography of Writings on Voltaire (1825-1925)* .... $ 1.25

B. MATULKA—*A Defense of Romanticism* .... In Preparation

J. L. GERIG AND G. L. VAN ROOSBROECK --*Bibliography of Pierre Bayle* .... In Preparation

ADDRESS ORDERS TO :

> DR. G. L. VAN ROOSBROECK,
> 504, Philosophy Hall
> Columbia University
> New York, N. Y.
> U. S. A.

TO MY SISTER

ANNA CAULFEILD WINSTON

THE FRENCH LITERATURE

OF LOUISIANA

BY

RUBY VAN ALLEN CAULFEILD

INSTITUTE OF FRENCH STUDIES

A FIREBIRD PRESS BOOK

PELICAN PUBLISHING COMPANY
Gretna 1998

Manufactured in the United States of America

Published by Pelican Publishing Company, Inc.
1000 Burmaster Street, Gretna, Louisiana 70053

CONTENTS

PREFACE

Though almost a century and a quarter have passed since Louisiana was purchased from France by the United States in 1803, the French inhabitants of that state still love the language of their forefathers and are trying to keep it alive. Though active members of the American commonwealth, as they have proved in all the crises of American history, they are proud of their French origin, and the name of " creole " is dear to them.

This name they use in its original sense, not always remembered: " colonial ", " of pure European stock ", not mixed with Indian blood. Charles Gayarré says:[1] " The word " creole " was first invented by the Spaniards to distinguish their children, natives of their conquered colonial possessions ", from the original natives whom they found in those newly discovered regions of the earth. " Criollo " was derived from the word " criar " (breed, rear, educate) and used only to designate the Spanish-bred natives, who were not to be confounded with the aborigines... Therefore to be a " criollo " was to possess a sort of title of honor—a title which could only be the birthright of the superior white race. This word, by an easy transition becoming " creole " from the word " créer ", was adopted by the French for the same purpose—that is to mean or signify a white human being bred in their colonies of Africa and America—a native of European extraction, whose origin was known and whose superior Caucasian blood was never to be assimi-

---

[1] The *Creoles of History and the Creoles of Romance*, 1885.

lated to the baser liquid that ran in the veins of the Indian and African natives. This explains why one of the privileged class is to this day proud of calling himself a " creole " and clings to the appellation.

It is the literary work of these Creoles, with their efforts to keep their language alive, that is the subject of the study that follows. Several attempts along this line have already been made, and it is from them that I take my point of departure: The *Louisiana Studies* of the late Alcée Fortier and his brief article in the *Library of Southern Literature* (volume IV, pp. 1739-1750); the *Lettres françaises en Louisiane* of the late Edward Fortier and his article in the section on non-English writings of the *Cambridge History of American Literature* (volume IV, pp. 590-598). These are the only works that treat specifically of the literature in question.[2] Edward Fortier was planning to continue his researches at the time of his death in 1918. He left various notes which were kindly lent to me by Mrs. Fortier. Though containing mostly information already given in his *Lettres françaises en Louisiane,* they furnished some additional material. A few other books make occasional references to one or another of the Louisiana authors; I mention notably: *The South in Prose and Poetry* by Henry M. Gill; *The Louisiana Book, Selections from the Literature of the State* by Thomas M'Caleb; *The Living Writers of the South* by James Wood Davidson; *Southern Literature from 1759 to 1895,* by Louise Manly; and *Literature of the Louisiana Territory* by Alexander Nicolas De Menil. A comprehensive account of them has, however, not yet been written.

I had thought first of treating only writers actually born

---

[2] See Chapter IX for a discussion of these works.

in Louisiana; but on closer study, I believed that since so many of the authors, especially those of the early days and of most interest, were natives of France or San Domingo, they also should be included. I have therefore included not only those who went to Louisiana for various reasons and spent the remainder of their lives there but also some who went there, stayed several years, became identified with the state, and then, for reasons —not always known—left and were, in some cases, heard of no more.

I have used information furnished by Alcée Fortier and Edward Fortier and have tried to sharpen any outlines that they have left vague. I have been able to add the names of many writers and works not mentioned by them. I have made a special effort to obtain biographical information in order to present the authors both as men and as writers. Most of them were occupied chiefly with other pursuits and writing was only a pleasant recreation for them. This, no doubt, explains the fact that very few of them are known outside of Louisiana. Each one has, however, done his part toward creating a literature which, though still only a sectional literature, is the earnest, sincere, and heartfelt expression of the love of a people for the country, the language, the customs, and the traditions of its ancestors. Every form of writing was tried by the authors, and history, drama, fiction, and verse appeared in many separate volumes as well as in the newspapers and reviews of the time. Many who won distinction in prose have also written verse; many who produced dramas have also contributed lyric poems, while all contributed to the richness of the collection of this literature.

The names of these men and their works, together with the library where the works may be found, I have listed in the appendix. I have not treated the folk songs that have arisen in the dialect or patois mostly of negro origin. This phase of Louisiana literature has been discussed by several writers whose names and works I have included in the bibliography under " Works on Creole Dialect and Songs ".

In the preparation of this work I have used the Columbia University Library, the New York Public Library, the New York Historical Library, the Baton Rouge Public Library, and the Library at the State House in Baton Rouge. The bulk of my information, however, has come from the libraries and private collections in New Orleans. I desire to express gratitude to the following: the late William Beer, former librarian at the Howard Library, not only for help from the library but for aid from him personally and for the use of his private collection; R. J. Usher, the present librarian at the Howard Library, and all his assistants, especially Miss Marguerite Renshaw, who has been of inestimable aid to me; Miss Minnie Bell, librarian at Tulane University Library, and her assistants; Mrs. Mary Pohlman, custodian of the City Hall Archives, and her assistant, James Miller; Henry Lanauze of the City Board of Health; Miss Carrie Freret, librarian of the Louisiana Historical Library; John Ray, archivist of the St. Louis Cathedral; Father O'Brien, librarian of Loyola University; Henry P. Dart, President of the Louisiana Historical Museum and Editor of the *Louisiana Historical Quarterly;* E. A. Parsons, Mrs. T. P. Thompson, and Gaspar Cusachs of New Orleans, and L. B. Tarlton of Franklin, Louisiana, for access to their private libraries; Bussière Rouen, President of the Athénée Louisianais, for the many interviews and the great amount of information that he very generously gave me; Mrs. Frank Waddill for her great aid and many courtesies accorded to me; and all those who, either by interview or by letter, gave me information about the writers whom I have discussed.

I wish also to express my gratitude to those who have made valuable suggestions regarding the book—to Miss Katherine Galbreath Montgomery of the Mississipi State College for Women for her unfailing encouragement and her helpful criticisms; to Professor John L. Gerig of Columbia University for his great interest in the work and the generous use he allowed me to make of his private library; and especially to Professor Arthur Livingston of Columbia University, under whose guidance the study has been made, for his kind suggestions in all matters pertaining to the general plan of the book, and to Professor Gustave L. van Roosbroeck for his direction of the mechanical details, and the matter of publication.

CHAPTER I

EARLIEST WRITINGS

JOURNALS AND ACCOUNTS OF VOYAGES

The beginings of literature in Louisiana—it is not necessary to say French literature for, naturally, the beginnings were French—are, like those of any other country, identified with its history. La Salle's first expedition, his taking possession of Louisiana, his effort to find the Mississippi River on his return to France, Iberville's arrival, the efforts of Bienville to establish New Orleans, the struggles of the colonists with the Indians, their hardships in maintaining the colony, the venture of Anthony Crozat, and the Mississippi Bubble of John Law are described in the reports and journals of those connected with the early explorations and with the colony, or of travelers who came to Louisiana on official business. Chief of these journals were the ones by Henri Joutel, Henri Tonti, Father Hennepin, Father Charlevoix, Bernard de la Harpe, Le Page du Pratz, Jean Bernard-Bossu, Georges-Marie Butel-Dumont, and Jean Pénicaut.[1]

Joutel, Tonti, and Father Hennepin were at different times connected with La Salle's expeditions; Father Charlevoix, a Jesuit priest who had come out to visit the missions in Canada in 1720, made a journey through the

---

[1] See appendix for the titles of these journals and books of travel.

Louisiana Territory; Pénicaut came with Iberville in 1698 (he says in the beginning of his book) and stayed until 1722; Bernard de la Harpe, attempting to settle a colony on the Red River and making explorations in Texas and in the country of the Rio Colorado, remained in Louisiana from 1718 to 1723. He wrote his journal on his return to France.[2] Le Page du Pratz lived sixteen years in this vast country as overseer or director of the public plantations when they belonged to the crown. He strives in his writings to correct some wrong impressions.[3] What he tells is what he has seen on the spot, not conjecture. Captain Bossu, having studied the languages of the savages in order to learn their customs and to be able to question them better, relates what he has observed during the twelve years he traversed this region.[4] Butel-Dumont was an officer who resided for twenty-two years in this country.[5] Marie Madeleine Hachard, one of the Ursuline nuns who came to New Orleans in 1727, has given in letters to her father in Rouen an interesting account of the arrival of this group of women in Louisiana and of their first works among the colonists.[6]

The *Mémoire des négociants et habitants de la Louisiane sur l'événement du 29 octobre 1768*, attributed to Nicholas Chauvin de La Frénière, is so to speak, the *Oath of Strassburg* of Louisiana literature. This memorial sets forth the grievances of the citizens under the administration of Antonio Ulloa and defends their action in expelling

[2] B. F. French, *Historical Collections*, vol. 3, p. 9, note; F. X. Martin, *History of Louisiana*, pp. 143-150 (1882 ed.).

[3] Le Page du Pratz, *Histoire*, etc., *préface* p. vi and p. x, also Le Page du Pratz, *Histoire* (English Translation, preface, p. i).

[4] Bossu, *Voyages aux Indes*, preface.

[5] Le Page du Pratz, *Histoire*, English Translation, preface, p. i.

[6] M. M. Hachard, *Relation du voyage*, etc.

him. It also petitions Louis XV to win the colony back from Spain.

La Frénière was born in Louisiana about 1720.[7]   He was sent to France to be educated in law and returned to Louisiana to practice his profession. · He was always prominent in movements to maintain the rights of the colonists. As one of the leaders of the conspiracy against Ulloa in 1768, he was shot by the Spaniards in 1769.

POETRY, HISTORY, AND DRAMA

The Colonial and Territorial periods of Louisiana produced beginnings in poetry, history, and drama.

LA PRISE DU MORNE DU BATON ROUGE

During the American Revolution Spain declared war on England and issued a royal order authorizing her subjects in the Indies to take part. Bernardo de Gâlvez, who was then in command in Louisiana, marched on the English fort at Baton Rouge, directed his batteries against it, and two or three hours afterwards forced the English general to wave a flag of truce. Julien Poydras wrote a poem, " La Prise du Morne du Baton Rouge ", in honor of this battle and the taking of the Baton Rouge hill.

This poem was printed and circulated at the king's expense.[8]   It represents the god of the Mississippi River awakened by the noise of the cannon that makes his palace tremble and resound. He sends one of his nymphs to see what is the cause of the noise. Disguised as a mortal, she goes to the camp of the Spanish, sees the hero,

[7] Charles Gayarré, *History of Louisiana,* 1903 ed., p. 187 ff. ; F. X. Martin, *op, cit.,* p. 208.
[8] F. X. Martin, *op. cit.,* p. 227.

3

hears the joy of the army, and describes to the river god the hero, the lines of soldiers, the leader's words of encouragement to his men, the vain attempts of the English to withstand the guns, the surrender, and Gâlvez' praise of his army. The nymphs, the tritons, and the river god are overjoyed at the story and declare for the conqueror. They see happy times before them when diligent colonists will cover the plains with grain fields and flocks of sheep, and peace and abundance will reign in the land. The river god promises to bid the waters to moderate their floods and keep these plains ever fertile. There is general rejoicing among the nymphs.

Poydras, a native of Brittany, came to Louisiana about 1768. He spent a year in New Orleans but then left the city to trade in the country parishes. He was successful with his ventures and made a large sum of money. He finally settled in Pointe Coupée parish where he continued his business with the various posts in that section, increasing his territory and trading on a large scale. When he died in 1824, [9] he left legacies to charitable organizations in New Orleans and in Pointe Coupée parish.[10]

DU FOSSAT'S HISTORY

The first history of Louisiana was written by Guy Soniat du Fossat, a Frenchman who came to Louisiana with the marines in 1751 and settled in New Orleans. He was later sent on a government mission into Illinois to repair several forts there. He retired from active service in 1772. He was twice *alcalde* during the Span-

[9] See notice of his death in the *Courrier de la Louisiane*, June 30th, 1824.
[10] See Alcée Fortier's *Louisiana Studies*, p. 66 ff.

4

ish domination, appointed once by Governor Unzaga and once by Governor Miro. He died in New Orleans in 1794.

His history tells the story of the colony of Louisiana from its foundation to the end of the year 1791.[11]. It is a very short work. It confines itself to the main events of history and devotes at least half of its bulk to descriptions of Louisiana, of the Mississippi River and its tributaries, of Indian customs, and of the animals, birds, and reptiles to be found in the region. The author makes no mention of his sources; and his facts, on the whole, are so brief and general that it is difficult to determine what he owes to previous works, and what to his own personal experience and observation.

Du Fossat never printed this history; in fact, the Louisiana branch of his family did not know of the book's existence until 1900. In that year, Charles T. Soniat of New Orleans went to the Paris Exposition and while in France, visited relatives in the South of that country. He was shown one day into a spacious room full of family heirlooms, and among papers and letters from the American branch, he came upon Du Fossat's manuscript. He obtained permission to bring it home for a time and read excerpts from it to the Louisiana Historical Society. At their request he translated the whole work for publication in the *Historical Quarterly*. [12]. It appears that this interesting little book by a colonial officer of Louisiana has never been printed in the original French.

---

[11] *Synopsis of the History of Louisiana from the Founding of the Colony to the Year 1791.*

[12] See the biography of Du Fossat by Charles Soniat, preface to this translation, for the story of the finding of the manuscript as well as for biographical data.

The distinction of having written the first drama in Louisiana belongs to Paul Le Blanc de Villeneufve, whose *Fête du Petit-Blé* was first published in 1814 and reprinted in 1910. It transpires from the title page of the original edition that Villeneufve was one of a troop of soldiers from the French navy serving the government in Louisiana among the "Tchactas" from 1752 to 1758. In an attached letter, addressed to Madame de Laussat, wife of the last colonial prefect of Louisiana, he further explains that he was watching the movements of "a dangerous neighbor", who was trying to get these Indians to break with France. In his notice to the reader he confides that fate had brought him to Louisiana when he was quite young, and that in traversing the primeval forests, he had been favorably and hospitably received by the Indians. He passed seven of the happiest years of his life among the Choctaws and recalls them with pleasure. It is for this reason—he informs Madame de Laussat— that he had the idea of defending the aborigines of the New World from the false beliefs and unkind prejudices prevalent in Europe.

The theme of *La Fête du Petit-blé, ou l'héroïsme de Poucha-Houmma,* is a law of the Indians that every murder must be punished with death and that a father must die in place of a guilty son who runs away. Villeneufve offers his play as a true story of an incident that occurred in the execution of this law. It was told him by an Indian murderer whose father had died for him.[13]

Cala-bé, son of Poucha-Houmma, had killed a Tchacta Indian. At the celebration of the " Fête

[13] See preface to the drama.

du Petit-blé ", word is brought that the Tchactas
are coming to claim the murderer. The son and
his wife elect to stay and brave the enemy but the
father, who is determined to save his first born,
orders them to escape. After a long struggle with
his father, Cala-bé and his wife consent to depart.
The envoys from the Tchactas arrive. Poucha-
Houmma offers treasures in exchange for his son's
life, but the enemy demands that the law of retal-
iation be observed. Poucha-Houmma gives himself up for his son and is led away. Later Cala-bé
returns to submit to his punishment and is horri-
fied to find that his father has been put to death
in his stead.

La Fête du Petit-blé in five acts is written in Alexandrine verse. It is of value as a picture of Indian life and
customs. In the preface, in the stage directions, and in
notes at the end of the play, Villeneufve describes some
of the practices and superstitions of the Indians and
relates incidents of his own association with them. His
letter to Madame de Laussat solicits that lady's aid in
defence of the Indians. The author feels that his drama
will not be sufficient to defend them, and that the Indians
will need some one in Europe to be their advocate.

Le Blanc de Villeneufve died in New Orleans on
May 16th 1815 at the age of 81.[14]

OTHER WORKS IN THE COLONIAL PERIOD

In 1803 two books were published in Paris which
might be counted in the early literature of Louisiana: a
Recueil de poésies d'un colon de Saint-Domingue and a
Vue de la Colonie espagnole du Mississippi ou des pro-

[14] See record of his death in the St. Louis Cathedral archives,
New Orleans.

7

vinces de la Louisiane et Floride occidentale en l'année 1802 par un observateur résident sur les lieux. Both were the works of Berquin Duvallon, a refugee from San Domingo. All the poems save one in the collection relate to San Domingo and were no doubt written there. The " Colon voyageur, ode avec des notes composée l'an 1801 à la Louisiane " is an account of the author's voyage up the Mississippi River and his first sight of Louisiana and of sugar making. His *Vue de la colonie espagnole* has geographical chapters on various settlements in Louisiana, sketches of the houses in New Orleans, and descriptions of the flora and fauna of the colony. Duvallon seems to have liked the country better than he did the people. He accuses the latter of being hard and uncharitable to the refugees of San Domingo, and says that such guests were not long in shaking the dust of the colony from their feet.[15] Evidently Duvallon went too, for he has left no further trace of himself in Louisiana.

[15] See *Vue de la colonie,* p. 240.

CHAPTER II

HISTORY

FRANCIS XAVIER MARTIN'S HISTORY OF LOUISIANA

After the brief synopsis by Soniat du Fossat in the colonial period, the only history of Louisiana written for a number of years was the *History of Louisiana* by Francis Xavier Martin.[1] This splendid piece of work was written in English, but it must be discussed here because it was used by all the later historians of Louisiana who wrote in French.

Martin's *History* was first published in 1827 in two volumes. (A second edition in one volume appeared in 1882.) In the first edition Martin lists at the end of each chapter, the authors he has used (though he does not name the works themselves): Garcilaso de la Vega, Laet, Purchas, Charlevoix, Marshal, Robertson, Tonti, Hennepin, La Harpe, Vergennes, Du Pratz, Bossu, Hutchins; and archives, letters, and papers. A comparison of the history with the sources named[2] shows that Martin's

[1] *History of Louisiana from the Earliest Period,* New Orleans, 1827, 2 vols., Lyman.
[2] I base my comparison on the following works: Garcilaso de la Vega: *Histoire de la conquête de la Floride;* Charlevoix: *Histoire et déscription générale, etc.;* Tonti: *Voyage de M. de La Salle,* etc.; Hennepin: *Description de la Louisiane;* La

information for the very early events,—the discoveries of Columbus and De Soto,—came from Charlevoix and Garcilaso de la Vega, whose main line he follows, omitting a vast number of details. For La Salle's expedition he uses Charlevoix, Hennepin, Tonti, and also Joutel as quoted by Charlevoix. For the early days of the colony (after 1700) Charlevoix and La Harpe are supplemented with Le Page du Pratz, Bossu, and Vergennes. For the Spanish domination (after 1763), he refers to archives and letters.

For the second volume Martin names archives, letters, papers; Stoddard, Roman, Dwight, St.Mery, Clark, Wilkinson, Eaton, and Latour, but he is less dependent on such sources than in the first volume. His indebtedness to specific authors is not easy to detect. He carries the history through Jackson's victory at the Battle of New Orleans in 1815.

CHARLES GAYARRE'S HISTORIES

Charles Gayarré's *Essai historique sur la Louisiane* was the first history in French written after Louisiana had become a state. Gayarré belonged to a family which boasted of a long list of celebrated members[3]. His paternal ancestor, Don Estevan Gayarré, came to

Harpe: *Journal historique;* Vergennes: *Mémoire historique;* Du Pratz: *Histoire de la Louisiane;* Bossu: *Nouveaux voyages aux Indes;* Bossu: *Nouveaux voyages dans l'Amérique Septentrionale;* Major Amos Stoddard: *Sketches Historical and Descriptive of Louisiana;* Daniel Clark: *Proofs of the Corruption of Gen. James Wilkinson;* Gen. James Wilkinson: *Memoirs of My Own Times;* Arsene Lacarriere Latour: *Historical Memoir of the War;* John Henry Eaton: *Life of Major General Jackson.*

3 See the preface by Miss Grace King in the 1903 edition of his *History of Louisiana* for biographical information on Gayarré.

Louisiana as one of the Spanish commissioners with Ulloa when the latter took possession in 1766 and remained until 1771. Don Juan Antonio Gayarré, son of Don Estevan, remained in Louisiana in the service of the government. Don Juan was the grandfather of Charles Gayarré.

Gayarré's maternal ancestors were prominent among the French families of the state, and his grandfather, Etienne de Boré, is credited with having first succeeded in making sugar in Louisiana.

Born in 1805, Gayarré was brought up in a historic atmosphere. Not only were his ancestors and their brave deeds freguently discussed in his presence but his infancy and childhood were spent in the stirring times of the transfer of Louisiana to American domination, followed so closely by the great excitement of the battle of New Orleans. It is not strange therefore that he should later become one of the best known historians of his state.

He received his early education in New Orleans at the Collège d'Orléans. In 1826 he went to Philadelphia to study law and was admitted to the Pennsylvania bar in 1828. Not wishing to remain in Philadelphia, he returned to New Orleans in 1830. That same year he published his *Essai historique*. This *Essai* is in two volumes, the first extending from the discovery of America by Columbus through the appointment of Carondelet as governor in 1792, and the second extending from the administration of Carondelet to the election of Jackson as president in 1829. Gayarré says in his preface that he had read Martin's *History of Louisiana* and had thought that one written in French would be of interest to the French speaking population. He acknowledges his debt to Martin for the material he uses, and indeed he may, for at times his work is almost a translation of Martin's history.[4]

[4] F. X. Martin, *op. cit.,* p. 37:
" During the month of January, Muscoso employed carpenters in the construction of vessels to convey his men to Mexico. The neighboring caciques, apprehensive that his views in going thither were to appraise his coutrymen of the fertility of the land on the Mississippi and to solicit aid to return and subjugate Indians, leagued themselves for the purpose of raising a sufficient force to destroy the Spaniards or at least to set fire to the vessels they were building—The plot, however, became known to some Indian women, who attended the Spanish officers, and was disclosed to Muscoso— On the twenty-fourth of June, the vessels were launched and soon after, the army went on board, hides having been placed around the bows as a protection against the arrows of the Indians. Out of the twelve hundred and fifty men who were landed at the bay de Spiritu Santo, there remained now but three hundred and fifty, and the three hundred and fifty horses were reduced to thirty. On the second day after their departure, the Indian fleet hove in sight. "

Charles Gayarré, *Essai historique,* pp. 18-19:
" Pendant le mois de Janvier, Muscoso fit construire des embarcations capables de transporter son armée par mer à Mexico. Les caciques qui avaient surveillé ses travaux, craignant que son dessein ne fût d'aller avertir ses compatriotes de la fertilité des vallées du Mississippi et de les inviter à venir s'y établir et à l'aider à subjuguer les Indiens, résolurent de se liguer afin de réunir des forces suffisantes pour accabler les Espagnols, ou du moins pour brûler leurs barques... Cependant le complot fut découvert et avis en fut donné à Muscoso par des femmes indiennes qui s'étaient attachées à quelques-uns des officiers espagnols... Le 24 juin les Espagnols lancèrent leur flottille sur le Mississippi et l'armée s'embarqua. On avait eu la précaution de tendre des peaux autour des barques afin de se garantir contre les flêches. Des douze cents hommes qui avaient débarqué à la baie de Santo Spiritu, il n'en restait plus que trois cent cinquante, et des trois cent cinquante chevaux, il n'en restait plus que trente. Le second jour après leur départ les Espagnols aperçurent la flotte indienne. "

Martin, p. 96:
" The small fleet sailed on

Gayarré, p. 61:
" Cette petite flotte partit

12

Gayarré became active in the political affairs of the day and served his state for years as assistant attorney general and then as city judge in New Orleans. He was elected to the United States Senate in 1835 but resigned to go to Europe on account of illness. He there spent about eight years. During this time, whenever his health would permit, he examined the public documents in the department of the Navy and Colonies in Paris and in some private archives to which he gained access. The result of this study was the *Histoire de la Louisiane* which appeared after his return to Louisiana, the first volume in 1846, the second in 1847. He confesses that his earlier work was imperfect because of his youth at the time of writing it and because of his lack of materials. He acknowledges indebtedness in his new work to Martin's history, to the work of Garcilaso de la Vega, and to the documents in Paris. He explains that he wrote in French because he was trying to let the contemporaries

the twenty-fourth of September 1698 for Cape Francis in the island of St. Domingo, where it arrived after a passage of seventy-two days. Here it was joined by a fifty gun ship commanded by Chateaumorant. Leaving the cape on New Year's day, the ships cast anchor on the twenty-fifth of January before the island which bears the name of St. Rose... Iberville sent a boat to the main where Don Andres de la Riolle had a short time before led three hundred Spaniards, on the spot on which, in the time of De Soto, lay an Indian town of Anchusi. "

le 24 Septembre 1698 pour le Cap Français dans l'île de St. Domingue, où elle arriva après une traversée de soixante et douze jours. Là, elle fut renforcée par un vaisseau de cinquante-deux canons, commandé par Chateaumorant, et se remit en route le premier de l'an 1699. Le 25 Janvier, elle jeta l'ancre devant l'île qui porte aujourd'hui le nom de St. Rose, et Iberville envoya une députation à Don Andres de la Riolle qui venait de s'établir à Pensacola avec trois cents Espagnols, sur l'ancien site qu'occupait la ville des Anchusi, du temps de De Soto. "

themselves relate the history; because he saw Louisiana as it was under Louis XIV and Louis XV of France and Charles III of Spain; and because, knowing that the greater number of women of Louisiana read English very rarely, he hoped that they would be tempted to read his history if written in French.[5]

Gayarré used his *Essai historique sur la Louisiane* as an outline which he filled in for his new history. Many paragraphs from the earlier work are inserted word for word in the new, while others are considerably expanded. Like Martin, though much more extensively, Gayarré takes the part on De Soto's expedition (pp. 7-22) from De la Vega's account. Occasionally he translates a sentence almost directly, but usually he condenses several chapters into a short paragraph. As the work advances he derives his main events from the *History* of Martin and fills in with quotations from the reports given by different officials as he, no doubt, found them in the documents examined in France. The first volume ends with the appointment of the Marquis de Vaudreuil as governor in 1743. The first hundred pages of the second volume are devoted to the Indian wars and religious contentions endured by the colony between 1743 and 1763. The remainder of the volume—from page 100 to page 381—records the events between 1763 and 1770, and quotes the letters, memoirs, and official documents of the time.

This history is of great value to any one who wishes to refer to these documents. As one of Gayarré's contemporaries said, a better name for it would be "*Notes pour servir à l'histoire de la Louisiane*".[6]

---

[5] See *Histoire de la Louisiane, préface.*
[6] Charles Testut: *Portraits Littéraires,* p. 19.

14

After his return to Louisiana, Gayarré continued his political service to his state as a member of the legislature from 1844 to 1846. He was reelected in 1846, but having been appointed Secretary of State, accepted that position instead.

Financially ruined by the Civil War, Gayarré used his pen as a means of support in his later years and wrote for many magazines.[7] He died in New Orleans in February 1895.

VICTOR DE BOUCHEL'S HISTORY

An *Histoire de la Louisiane depuis les premières découvertes jusqu'en 1840*, written by Victor de Bouchel, appeared in 1841. De Bouchel was a Frenchman who came to Louisiana at the age of 19 years and settled in St. Bernard Parish. He founded a school there and taught until his marriage a few years later. He then bought a plantation in Plaquemine Parish. His interest in literature was such that he spent more time in writing than in managing his plantation, and as a consequence, his wife found it necessary to take charge of the business. De Bouchel's *Histoire* is a very brief work, leaving out, as the author says in the preface, all that might retard progress or discourage the reader. He felt that a history of Louisiana was needed in the schools. He asserts that he has examined all the sources available to him[8] but is indebted most of all to Judge Martin, whose book, while diffuse for certain events and brief

---

[7] See page xxxi of the preface to his History, 1903 edition, for a list of his writings in English.

[8] He mentions Barbé-Marbois, Bossu, Charlevoix, Garcilaso de la Vega, Chevalier, Gayarré, Martin, Le Page du Pratz, Robin, Roux de Rochelle, and Vergennes.

for others, is on the whole good authority. He adds that since Martin's *History* ends with the Battle of New Orleans and since he carries his through 1840, he has developed the causes leading to the financial crisis of the times through his own studies, and with what documents he could find. His *Histoire* is an outline rather than a history, and although very clear and concise, loses in interest because of its excessive briefness.

De Bouchel was a collaborator to the *Renaissance Louisanaise* in 1862. He died on his plantation in St. Bernard Parish in 1864.[9]

HENRI REMY'S HISTORY

In 1843, beginning May 8th, there had appeared in the *Courier de la Louisiane*, at first anonymously and later signed, several *Extraits inédits de l'histoire de la Louisiane*. These had continued for only a short while. They had been written by Henri Remy.

Remy was a Frenchman,[10] born at Agen about 1810. He received a good education in the schools of France. Impelled by his democratic views, he came to New Orleans in 1836 where he was employed as a private teacher. He studied law and was admitted to the bar in 1840. On January 3rd, 1844 he published a prospectus in which he offered an *Histoire de la Louisiane de la découverte jusqu'en 1844* for public subscription, and

[9] The biographical material on De Bouchel was obtained from Mrs. Octavia de Bouchel of New Orleans and from the death records in the Board of Health office at the City Hall.
[10] See Henry P. Dart: *Remy's Lost History, Louisiana Historical Quarterly*, Jan. 1922, vol. 5, no. 1, pp. 1-17, for the biographical material on Remy. Mr. Dart got his information from an interview with Dr. Pierre Armand Remy, son of Henri Remy.

stated that subscription lists could be found at New Orleans, Donaldsonville, Baton Rouge, Quebec, Montreal, New York, and Havana. The history, in four volumes in 8vo, would cost $10.00 for subscribers and $15.00 for non-subscribers. At the beginning of the prospectus, Remy quotes from Raynal's *Histoire Philosophique et politique, etc.* (volume 2, book 4, page 173) saying that in commencing this work, he has made a vow to be truthful, and he is not conscious of having broken it. He explains that he felt a desire to learn the manners and customs of the country in which he was going to live. He read and studied books lent him by friends, and made lengthy and conscientious researches. He confesses that the research was hardest for the period following the Louisiana purchase, for then he was facing contemporaries. He desired to be impartial, but the truth might stir up a storm. Frightened at first, he was tempted to stop; but having recovered his courage, he resolved to remain true to his motto. When it was necessary to criticise, he criticised the work, not the man. There were 148 signatures to the lists, names of men of prominence in New Orleans at the time. Some of the subscribers ordered two copies, making the number desired 160.[11] The history did not appear, and nothing more was heard about it for practically ten years.

In 1854 Remy established a weekly paper, the *St. Michel,* in St. James Parish and published it from February 1854 to 1856. His staunch democratic ideas and his fight against the Whigs made many enemies for his

[11] Two of these lists with the prospectus are in Mr. Dart's possession as are also the manuscripts mentioned below and the complete file of Remy's paper, *St. Michel,* all lent him by Dr. Remy. Mr. Dart allowed me to examine all of these, and it is from them as well as from his article that I obtained the information given.

little enterprise. He states in the issue for December 23rd, 1854 that hostilities against it will not succeed in destroying it. In the first issue of the *St. Michel* he began publishing a feuilleton *Découverte de la Louisiane* which he changed later to *Histoire de la Louisiane.* He continued printing these historical selections each week until June 2nd, 1855. On that date, part of chapter XVI appeared with the notice " La suite au prochain numéro ", but no more of it appeared. Alcée Fortier says in his *Louisiana Studies* (p. 26) that the history was published in the *St. Michel* in 1854 and was discontinued when the author had reached only 1731. Evidently Fortier had not seen the later issues of the *St. Michel,* for the events recorded in the part of Chapter XVI printed in June 1855 extend to 1750.

In the meantime the author had announced in the *St. Michel* for February 24th, 1855 that he would publish an *Histoire de la Louisiane depuis sa découverte jusqu'à la constitution de 1845,* in parts of 32 pages each every month, " imprimé avec luxe et enrichi de vignettes, de gravures, cartes, et plans ". The price of subscriptions was to be 50 cents per part and subscribers must pledge themselves to take the whole work. This plan must also have been unsuccessful, for when the paper was discontinued in February 1856, the advertisement was still appearing in it, and copies of the printed history have never been seen.

The author has left three manuscripts[12] of this history which show the care with which he worked. They are all written on the same sized paper, about 8 × 13, in a fine, neat handwriting, with a 2-inch margin on the right side and about 520 words to the page. The paper of

---

[12] These manuscripts are in the possession of Mr. H. P. Dart.

two of them is in fools' cap folio form with pages fastened together in the center. The third is on loose sheets. One of them, without doubt the first, has many lines crossed out and many sentences added in the margin. The paper is written on one side only, except where the author has inserted a long rewritten or additional paragraph on the left-hand page. On the first pages of this manuscript, he has very careful marginal references to authors from whom he has obtained his information, but as he advances, references to other works are rare. He has used the accounts of Hennepin, Du Pratz, Bossu, Charlevoix, Darby, Daniel, Cox, White, Stoddard, La Harpe[13], and La Fon. The authors most often referred to are Bossu, Hennepin, Charlevoix, and Stoddard, with mention of the journals of the Senate and the House of Representatives in 1814. The first manuscript bears the dates from June 1842 to October 1843. The author divides the French period into four books, the Spanish period into one book, and the American period into one book. The manuscript has 530 pages and ends with 1805. There is also a preface of 7 pages which discusses Louisiana Law as coming from the Roman law with French and Spanish modifications.

The next manuscript is not dated. It is very similar to the first and is evidently a reworked copy of it, for sentences and paragraphs that are added in the margin

[13] Of Remy's sources, I was able to find and examine the following: Hennepin, Stoddard, Du Pratz, Bossu, Charlevoix, La Harpe, Martin, and also: Wm. Darby, *Geographical description of the State of Louisiana*, New-York, Olmstead, 1814; Daniel Coxe, *Description of the English Province of Carolina, by the Spaniards called Florida and by the French La Louisiane, as also of the great and famous river Meschacébé or Mississippi*, London, Crowse, 1741; Joseph M. White, *New Collection of laws, charters, and local ordinances of government, etc.*, Philadelphia, Johnson, 1839.

of the other manuscript are inserted in the main body of this one. This is true through 1805, but after that time, the manuscript again has sentences and words crossed out and marginal corrections. This leads to the conclusion that the author revised the first work to this date and then added the remaining unrevised folios. Instead of dividing the French period into four books, he has combined the material into two books, the first from 1682 to 1717 and the second from 1717 to 1765. The Spanish period, as in the first manuscript, has only one book. The American period, likewise, has only one book and extends to 1815 instead of 1805.

The other manuscript, written on loose sheets, was used for the sixteen chapters printed in the *St. Michel.* No doubt the author was revising and shortening his work for the history that he advertised. This manuscript is not divided into books as are the two preceding ones. Its chapters follow each other with no break, and many details found in the others are either omitted entirely or condensed into a few paragraphs. It has 247 pages and 16 chapters which extend from 1682 to 1750. At the beginning of this manuscript Remy has inserted the quotation from Raynal already referred to in the prospectus.

The author has carried his record to 1815 instead of to 1845. Remy's style is simple and clear, and, while he has added no data not found in the preceding works, he has related his events in a more interesting manner and makes his characters seem more alive. The Louisiana Historical Society hopes some day to print a translation of this manuscript history.[14] Remy probably began to write his history over in English, for among the papers

[14] See H. P. Dart's article.

that Mr. Dart possesses, there is another very short manuscript of eight pages written in English in the same handwriting and showing the same care. It is not known whether he really had a plan to issue his work in an English version, nor why this work was interrupted. Remy died in 1867.

ALEXANDRE BARDE AND HIS
HISTOIRE DES COMITES DES ATTAKAPAS

Alexandre Barde was in Louisiana in 1844, first in New Orleans and then in the Attakapas section at St. Martinville.[15] In January 1845, poems by him began to appear in the *Courrier de la Louisiane* and also in the *Revue Louisianaise*. In 1848 he was teaching in New Orleans but left early that same year and returned to St. Martinville. The *Revue Louisianaise* of February 27th, 1848 (p. 528) laments the fact that he has departed and regrets that New Orleans did not retain so distinguished a professor. It speaks of him as being one of the editors of the *Créole,* a newspaper of St. Martinville.

In 1861, Barde published an *Histoire des comités de vigilance aux Attakapas,* a true story of crimes and thefts in the Attakapas section. They became so numerous that the law was powerless to combat them. The vigilantes took matters in their own hands and devoted themselves to freeing their country from these depredations. The author lists the names of the parishes having committees and quotes the campaign songs of some of them. This work is interesting as a sketch of sectional history.

[15] See the *Revue Louisianaise,* vol. 4, June 13th, 1847, p. 258, which speaks of him as having been driven from New Orleans in 1844 by fear of yellow fever, and of his having taken refuge in St. Martinville.

WOMEN WRITERS OF HISTORY

Besides the works mentioned, two little histories of Louisiana written by women deserve a place in the literature of the French people of that region. The first of these, *Histoire des Etats-Unis suivie de l'histoire de la Louisiane* was published in 1881 by Madame Marie Drivon Girard. Madame Girard was born in 1814. Her family belonged to Sainte Lucie, an island in the English Antilles. Her mother, on account of poor health, was forced to go to France to live and the child Marie was educated in Paris. They later returned to Sainte Lucie to their plantation. There Marie was married to Jean Marie Acquart who died two years after the marriage. She later married a cousin of hers, a Mr. Girard, who was managing her mother's plantation. This was a very unsuccessful marriage. Ruined financially by the abolition of slavery in the Antilles, Madame Drivon came with her family to Louisiana in 1843 and bought a plantation there. Later the family moved to New Orleans where Madame Girard began teaching in 1847. She died in 1913 at the age of 99.[16]

In her history, Madame Girard takes important dates, beginning with the discovery of America, and condenses the events into very short paragraphs. It is a little book of only 84 pages, rather an epitome or *résumé* than a real history.

The next year, 1882, the other little history appeared. It was called *Histoire de la Louisiane racontée aux enfants louisianais* and was written by Madame Laure Andry. Madame Andry, *née* Miss Bordelois, was born in Bordeaux in September 1829. She was educated in France

[16] See Grace King: *An old French Teacher of New Orleans, Yale-Review*, Jan. 1922, pp. 380-398, for the facts given above.

and came to America when a young woman. She spent the remainder of her life in New Orleans and died there in 1882.[17] Her little history is very much condensed, written in simple style and suited, as its title indicates, for children.

Neither Madame Andry nor Madame Girard mention any source for their information, and the simplicity of their treatment of the facts they record makes it impossible to ascertain any.

The publication of all of these historical works shows that the writing of history is one of the modes of expression chosen by the French writers to show their love for Louisiana and their interest in the record of her progress. The historians have not produced learned monuments of literature based on scientific investigation of the causes underlying the events, nor are they very seriously concerned about sources. Several of them, Martin and Gayarré, for example, mention that they had examined archives, but this is true only in very rare instances. They have, for the most part, based what they have to say on accounts given by travelers in the early colonial era, and have confined themselves almost entirely to giving a pleasing recital and a clear exposition of outstanding events either in narrative or outline form. History offered in such an interesting way easily inspired later writers to use it as a background for fiction.

[17] Information about her was obtained from her daughter, Mrs. Gus Durel of New Orleans.

CHAPTER III

HISTORY OF LOUISIANA
AS REFLECTED IN THE LITERATURE

Besides the histories of Louisiana that have been written in French by her sons and daughters, there are several works of fiction and a few poems which take for subjects some of the interesting epochs of her history.

MILA OU LA MORT DE LA SALLE

The earliest event which tempted the writers of fiction was the death of La Salle. Martin says in his *History of Louisiana* (p. 87) that there were two brothers by the name of Lancelot with La Salle when the latter's party started from Texas back to Canada. The younger Lancelot was ill and, not being able to travel rapidly enough, was asked to go back. The older brother wanted to return with him but La Salle, feeling that the loss of another man would leave the party too weak, refused his consent. The sick man, in fact, was killed by the Indians, and his brother, very resentful, threatened La Salle. The ill feeling seemed to have passed away, when one day Lancelot and several others, among them Liotot and Duhault, were sent with La Salle's nephew, Morangie, on a mission. A plot was hatched against Morangie and he died by the hand of Liotot. Anxious on account of Morangie's long absence, La Salle set out to

24

find him. It was on this trip that he was shot from ambush by Duhault.

In 1852 Charles Oscar Dugué published a drama, *Mila, ou la Mort de La Salle,* based on this episode. He follows history in the matter of having Liotot kill Morangie and of having Duhault kill La Salle. However, he makes love and jealousy the motives behind the two murders and introduces two women, one an Indian girl, Mila, and the other, a white woman, Rose, wife of Duhault. Liotot loves Mila and has killed Morangie, her fiancé, nephew of La Salle. In the first scene of the drama, he confesses the murder to her. Later, plans are made to marry Mila to La Salle in order to strengthen the bond of union between the Indian nation and the French explorers. On learning the news, Liotot is very much disturbed and fears that Mila will reveal the identity of Morangie's murderer to La Salle. To prevent this, Liotot makes Duhault drunk, tells him that La Salle is Rose's lover, and incites him to anger. When all are waiting at the church for La Salle to come for his wedding with Mila, a shot is heard. Duhault has killed La Salle. Brought on the stage by Indian warriors who witnessed the crime, Duhault confesses, but attributes the murder to the instigation of Liotot.

VEILLEES LOUISIANAISES—SAINT DENIS

In 1849 Charles Testut[1] edited a review called the *Veillées Louisianaises, série de romans historiques sur la Louisiane.* He planned (preface, p. v) to publish a series of novels based on all the epochs of Louisiana history. Without changing the facts, he would allow the imagina-

[1] See Chapter VI for information about Dugué and Testut.

tion to adorn the subjects with a poetical frame. In his opinion, the history of Louisiana, though not yet measured by centuries, was not sterile, but offered in its short and rapid course enough material to make volumes. Testut was not to be the only contributor to this anthology of historical prose; others were invited to submit their works also. All novels by others in the collection were to be signed; all unsigned ones were to be by the editor. In order of publication, historical chronology would be ignored.

Testut had evidently read the first part of Gayarré's history of Louisiana which had appeared in 1848. In an account of the expedition of the Chevalier of St. Denis into Mexico in 1714, Gayarré says: " I would recommend this expedition of St. Denis, and his adventures, to any one in search of a subject for literary composition ".[2] Thus Testus calls the first novel in his series *St. Denis*, derives his facts from history as he had planned, and allows his imagination full play for the rest. In the long journey of St. Denis to Mexico to arrange trade relations with the Spaniards, he encountered many adventures. He saves Fata, a young Indian girl, from a band of Red Skins, who are on the point of putting her to death because of her love for a pale face. Fata dresses in men's clothing and goes with St. Denis in order to find friends, but on the march dies of fever and is buried in a grave.

St. Denis reaches the Presidio del Norte near the Rio Grande and states his mission to Don Pedro de Villescas, the commander of the fort. Villescas can do nothing without the authority of the governor of Couais to whom word is sent. While waiting for a return message from Couais, St. Denis falls in love with Angelica,

[2] Gayarré, *op. cit.,* vol. 1, p. 166.

daughter of Villescas, and she returns his passion. The men from Couais arrive and, arresting St. Denis, take him back with them. Though greatly surprised, St. Denis submits. After several months he is released and returns to the Presidio del Norte. Villescas is having trouble with some of his Indians who are disgruntled and are threatening to desert him. St. Denis persuades the Indians not to depart, wins Villescas' gratitude, and is rewarded with Angelica's hand. Preparations for the marriage are in progress when Fata suddenly appears before St. Denis. She explains her resurrection. On the night of her burial, three men had been near, hiding behind the trees. They had stolen some diamonds and decided to hide them in Fata's grave with the idea that the booty would not be disturbed there. When they removed the earth from her body, she revived. Two of the robbers were frightened and ran away, but the third helped her to safety.

The arrival of Fata, who loves St. Denis passionately, complicates matters and arouses the jealousy of Angelica, who refuses to see St. Denis in spite of his entreaties. He is called away to fight in a war that has been declared against the Indians. Meanwhile Fata, jealous also, plans to kill Angelica and enters the latter's room with that purpose in view. She finds a letter in which St. Denis swears eternal loyalty to Angelica, affirming that he has never loved any one else and will die without her love. Realizing the hopelessness of her own passion, Fata kills herself. At the return of St. Denis all is made clear and the wedding takes place.

This is the main thread of the story; but Testut enlarges it with many digressions, particularly with stories told by the different characters. He gives many descriptions of the forests through which St. Denis and his men pass, and of many Indian customs. The author is present throughout the story. He speaks of " Notre héros ", interrupting the narration at very exciting moments with the explanation that he must abandon his hero in order to cast his eyes elsewhere. Then after long detours, he resumes his principal theme.

SOULIER ROUGE

In connection with the Choctaw and Chickasaw wars that took place between the years 1734 and 1748, Gayarré[2b] often mentions a certain Choctaw chief called " Red Shoe " who was a conspicuous leader in all transactions of the whites with the Indians. Edward Fortier speaks of a novel *Soulier Rouge* based on the history of these wars, written by " D'Artlys " and published in 1849 in a review, *La Violette*.[3]

Very little is known of this D'Artlys; in fact he was an enigmatic figure in his own day. He was in Louisiana in 1848 at which time he wrote the " Revue de la Semaine " in the *Revue Louisianaise* over the signature " *D'Artlys, ex-rédacteur du Corsaire* ". In the *Revue Louisianaise* of Feb. 13th, 1848 (vol. 5, p. 472) he speaks of the custom in France of signing articles with a *nom de plume* and adds that he is using the name that he had adopted in the papers and theatres of Paris. He calls himself a " fils d'un commandant de la garde impériale ". In the *Revue Louisianaise* for March 1848 (vol. 5, p. 623) he answers Placide Canonge who had evidently

[2b] *History*, vol. I, p. 460; vol. II, pp. 39-41.
[3] *Lettres françaises en Louisiane*, p. 16. I was unable to find the numbers of *La Violette* which contain this novel. The issues of this review which belonged to Gasper Cusachs and which he kept for a while in the Louisiana Historical Library are no longer there and no one knows what has become of them.

doubted the truth of his being " ex-rédacteur du *Cor-saire* ", expresses surprise that Canonge has not received him, a fellow dramatist, in a more friendly manner, and adds that perhaps Canonge does not know that he is the author of several plays published in Paris. The name D'Artlys, no doubt only a pen name, does not appear in the New Orleans directories for 1847 and 1849. The directory for 1848 is missing.

1763-1769.

The years between 1763 and 1769 in Louisiana history are full of dramatic material, for it was then that a vast country was given away by one king to another, a heart-broken people begged not to be thus bartered; ardent patriots participated in a bloodless revolution and planned a republic; and a new governor showed his authority by a stern condemnation.

The record tells us that France, feeling that she could not hold Louisiana any longer, ceded it to Spain by the treaty of Paris in 1763. Spain failed to claim her new possession at first and thereby raised hope among the colonists that France was not really going to abandon them. At a general meeting attended by noted planters and people of New Orleans, Nicholas Chauvin de La Frénière delivered an animated speech in which he suggested sending a representative to France to present an entreaty to Louis XV in person. In 1765 Jean Milhet, a wealthy merchant, went to Paris to place a set of resolutions before the king. By the aid of Bienville, then an old man, Milhet reached the Duke of Choiseul, minister to the king, but since the Duke had been the instigator of the transfer of Louisiana to Spain, he put Milhet off with promises, and never allowed him to see Louis XV.

At the end of two years, Charles III of Spain had not yet taken possession of his new country, and Aubry, the commander of the French troops, was still in power. This failure on the part of Spain encouraged the colonists to hope that the cession would be rescinded. The arrival of Don Antonio Ulloa in 1766 shattered their hope and Milhet's return from France in 1767 with the story of his reception at the French court reduced them to despair. Ulloa, waiting for more Spanish troops, had delayed taking possession officially and had made himself very unpopular. Another meeting was held in New Orleans in 1768, with La Frénière again as chief speaker. A petition was sent to the superior council of the colony asking that Ulloa and the provincial officers of the Spanish troops be sent away. Ulloa was ordered to produce his credentials from Spain or depart within a month.[4] He decided to depart. The night before his vessel was to sail, its cables were cut and it was set adrift.

Chief among the conspirators was a young Swiss, Pierre Marquis, who, after Ulloa's departure, planned to establish a republic similar to that of Switzerland.[5] His plan was doomed to failure, for the Spanish government was now aroused. Captain Alexander O'Reilly was sent as the new governor of Louisiana; he entered New Orleans on August 17th, 1769 with his entire fleet.[6] He was quite flattering to the representatives sent to him and promised forgiveness for all offenses. Notwithstanding this promise, on August 21st he had the chief conspirators arrested. One of them, Joseph Villeré, was on his plantation at the time, but, having received a letter

    [4] F. X. Martin, op. cit., p. 202.
    [5] E. J. Forstall, Analytical Index, p. 86.
    [6] Chevalier de Champigny, Memoir of the present State of Louisiana, p. 194.

of assurance from Aubrey advising him to return to the city, he came to New Orleans. He was arrested at the entrance gate, and killed in a struggle with a guard. The others were tried, found guilty of high treason, and condemned. Five of them, as chiefs and principal promoters of the conspiracy, were to be hanged; the other six were to be imprisoned—one for life, two for ten years, and three for six years. Villeré, although already dead, was not spared in the condemnation. O'Reilly's judgment reads: " As the late Joseph Villeré stands convicted likewise of having been one of the most obstinate promoters of the aforesaid conspiracy, I condemn, in the same manner, his memory to be held and reported for ever infamous. "[7]

The people, aroused, requested O'Reilly to remit or suspend the sentence until royal clemency could be secured, but the only result of the petition was that the prisoners should be shot and not hanged.[8] La Frénière, Jean Baptiste Noyan, Pierre Carrère, Pierre Marquis, and Joseph Milhet were shot; Joseph Petit, Balthasar Mazan, Jérome Julien Doucet, Pierre Hardy de Boisblanc, Jean Milhet, and Pierre Poupet were sent to Havana and imprisoned in Moro Castle.

LES MARTYRS DE LA LOUISIANE

Three of the French writers of Louisiana have chosen these events as a subject: two for dramas, and one for a novel. In 1839 Auguste Lussan[9] published *Les Martyrs*

---

[7] Charles Gayarré, *op. cit.,* vol. II, p. 338.
[8] F. X. Martin, *op. cit.,* p. 238. Charles Gayarré, *op. cit.,* p. 342, says that no executioner could be found, and that for that reason the sentence was changed.
[9] See chapter VI for information about Lussan.

de la Louisiane, a tragedy in five acts and in verse, dedicated to the descendants of the martyrs of 1769.[10] It is preceded by a prologue, which shows a meeting of the council in October 1768. Jean Milhet makes a report of his efforts to see the king during the two years of his stay at the French court. Villeré and La Frénière are firm in their belief that resistance is necessary.

The drama proper (the Villeré episode as related by Gayarré) opens in August 1769. Instead of having Aubrey's letter as the reason for Villeré's appearance in New Orleans, Lussan introduces an " Inconnu " who is hired by O'Reilly to bring Villeré to him. The scene is changed to the Villeré plantation and shows the " Inconnu " posing as a stranger in that section and asking hospitality. He relates what he pretends to have learned on the way: that O'Reilly has sent for the conspirators, and on their arrival at his office, has arrested them. The " Inconnu " adds that one of them, Villeré by name, has escaped and is being severely criticized. Villeré is aroused by this account and decides to go to the city. There he is arrested and carried on board a frigate.[11] Madame Villeré comes to the vessel, but her request to see her husband is denied. Hearing her voice, Villeré tries to reach her, and in a struggle with a soldier, is pierced by a bayonet. Before dying, he asks one of the sailors to give his handkerchief, dyed with his blood, to Madame Villeré.[12]

[10] *L'Abeille de la Nouvelle Orléans* for May 9th, 1839, contains a statement that the *Martyrs de la Louisiane* will be played on May 10th.

[11] Here the account again follows that of Gayarré, pp. 305-306, and of Martin, p. 207.

[12] Martin's account is different here. It tells that one of the sailors threw Villeré's bloody shirt into the boat where Mrs. Villeré was, thus notifying her of the death of her husband (p. 207).

The last act is placed in the prison on September 28th, 1769. The prisoners hear the news of Villeré's death and know that they too must die. An officer enters with a decree, and the drama ends.

LOUISIANA

In 1849, Armand Garreau's *Louisiana* appeared as one of the historical novels in Testut's *Veillées Louisianaises*. It is a rather long work, using the events of 1768 and 1769 for background. The author has taken much more liberty with the historical facts than Lussan did, inventing a love story with elements of hatred, jealousy, and vengeance. The story of Villeré and Madame Villeré, which constituted the whole drama in Lussan, is only an incident in Garreau's novel.[13]

This book is called *Louisiana* from the name of the heroine, Louisiana d'Iberville, a grand-niece of Bienville. Marquis, the hero of the conspiracy, is in love with Louisiana, and they are engaged to be married. Don Manuel, a protégé of Ulloa, loves her too, and his jealousy and desire for vengeance are the principal motivating forces of the story. When Ulloa and his men are withdrawing from New Orleans, Manuel jumps into the river, swims ashore, and remains in the city as a spy. By his craft, he discovers the plans of Marquis for setting up a republic and frustrates them. When O'Reilly arrives, Manuel reveals all that has happened and makes himself so serviceable to O'Reilly that he is appointed Secretary of the colony. He intercepts a letter from the Spanish minister to the governor containing orders that the prisoners are to be exiled, not killed. Manuel con-

[13] See Chapter VII for information about Garreau.

ceals these orders from O'Reilly. He goes to Louisiana and offers to save her lover if she will remain in New Orleans while Marquis is exiled. Her indignant refusal makes him swear further vengeance. He is the officer who arrests Villeré at the gate and taunts him until he resists. When Villeré in anger throws him down, Manuel rises and stabs Villeré several times. It is Manuel also who on the boat refuses to allow Madame Villeré to see her husband, and who finally kills Villeré when he insists on seeing her.

Manuel tries to get the negro, Jeannot, to be the executioner of the prisoners and offers him his freedom as a reward. In order not to be forced to decapitate the patriots, Jeannot cuts off his right hand.[14] Not to be foiled in his vengeance, Manuel puts on a mask on the day of the execution and takes the executioner's place. On the scaffold, he taunts Marquis until Marquis snatches off the mask and exposes him to the crowd. The people are so indignant that Manuel becomes frightened and runs away. For lack of an executioner, the sentence is changed to shooting.

Manuel has escaped to a launch in which two of his men are stationed. He plans with them to abduct Louisiana from the Ursuline Convent, where she has taken refuge, and to carry her off in the launch. In the meanwhile, Liza, the old negro mammy of Louisiana, has been weaving her net around Manuel, and before he can carry out his plans, she poisons him. The story ends with a realistic description of his death.

This novel is full of local color, giving street and place names. Marquis is made the leading person of the conspiracy and credited with a most noble character. La

[14] Gayarré, *op. cit.*, p. 341.

Frénière, Milhet, and Petit have minor places. Aubrey, who is usually portrayed as a tool of the Spanish officers, is represented by Garreau as having a conciliatory character which deserves all sympathy, and as having made efforts to bring harmony between the Spanish and the colonists.

FRANCE ET ESPAGNE

In 1850, the next year after this novel was published, *France et Espagne* or *La Louisiane en 1768 et 1769,* a drama in four acts and in prose by L. Placide Canonge, appeared. It resembles Garreau's *Louisiana* very closely and is evidently a dramatization of it. The heroine is named Léonie de Vaudreuil instead of Louisiana, and the villain is Don José instead of Don Manuel.[15] Disposed to be lenient towards the conspirators, O'Reilly is aroused to action by Don José who tells him that they have been slandering Madame O'Reilly. When they are invited by the governor to a masked ball, they go, although they are suspicious. Léonie enters and tells them the story of Villeré's death. She had been aboard the frigate with Madame Villeré and had witnessed the struggle in which Villeré was killed. She warns them to beware of the treachery of O'Reilly and urges them to avenge the treatment of Villeré. She gives them the bloody handkerchief to use as a banner. Before they can escape from the room, they are arrested and put in prison. Don José goes there himself and offers Marquis his freedom if he will leave at once and *alone* for France.

---

[15] Gayarré's *History* (vol. 2, p. 339) has Manuel José Urrutia as the second name signed to O'Reilly's letter with regard to the prisoners. This probably is responsible for the Manuel of one author and the José of the other.

This is a slight variation from the novel in which Manuel offers Marquis's freedom to Louisiana.

The final act of *France et Espagne* is quite different from the ending of *Louisiana*. In the drama, an Indian man, Tello, has the role the negro mammy plays in the novel. Don José comes to Léonie and, showing the King's letter, offers to give it to O'Reilly to save Marquis even this late if she will be his wife. Tello, seeing the grief of Léonie, stabs Don José, snatches the letter from him, and runs with it to O'Reilly, but returns in a little while still holding the letter. He arrived too late; the prisoners had been shot.

Louisiana and *France et Espagne* are much more romantic and much less true to history than *Les Martyrs de la Louisiane*, notwithstanding the fact that Garreau sometimes quotes almost word for word from Gayarré's account.

TWO POEMS CELEBRATING THE BATTLE OF NEW ORLEANS

In 1838, Tullius St. Céran published a volume of poems on a subject dear to the hearts of everyone in Louisiana, the Battle of New Orleans. He called the collection *Mil huit cent quatorze et mil huit cent quinze, ou les combats et la victoire des fils de la Louisiane.* He dedicated it to the soldiers who fought in the battle, and said that love of country was the inspiration of it. He divided it into two sections : the first dealing with the preliminary skirmish on the 23rd of December, 1814, and the second with the main engagements on January 8th, 1815. In the first account, the author tells of the arrival of the news that the enemy is coming, of the effect that it produced in the city, and of the departure of the troops

to meet the enemy. In the account of each of the con-
tests he describes the battle fields before the arrival of
the combatants, the fight itself, and the days after it is
over. The poem is written in the first person, and begins:
" Je comptais quatorze ans quand ce cri suprême ".

Quite different from the above is Urbain David's epic
poem, " *Les Anglais à la Louisiane en 1814 et 1815* ",
which appeared in 1845. Like St. Céran, David dedicates
his poem to the soldiers. One canto—there are ten in all—
recounts the pirate Lafitte's visit to Governor Claiborne
with the news that the English are on the way up the
river, and have tried to enlist his services against the
inhabitants. Another canto tells of the arrival of young
Villeré to report that the enemy's forces have reached
the plantation. The poet digresses here to relate the
story of Villeré's famous ancestor who was one of the
martyrs in 1769. Still another canto praises the women
of the city who spent their time in the church praying
for the soldiers while the battle was raging. David does
not tell of the preliminary battle in December. His
poem has a sustained martial note, while St. Céran's
gives the effect of reminiscences.[16]

[16] I was unable to find anything about David himself. There
is an Urbin David, druggist, in the New Orleans directories as
late as 1859. This name does not appear in 1860, but search
in the death records of that time failed to establish any dates
for his life. The copy of the poem bears on its title page
" Urbain David of Cette ". No town of that name could be
located in Louisiana.

CHAPTER IV

THE FRENCH NEWSPAPERS
AND THE LITERATURE

" The newspaper is the detailed index of daily life and the ledger of public life. What then, is not its power for the conservation and extension of the language, for the formation and influence of the literature? "[1]

This has certainly been true of the newspapers in Louisiana, for they have had great influence not only in preserving the French language, but also in forming the literature and encouraging the authors.

LE MONITEUR DE LA LOUISIANE

The *Moniteur de la Louisiane,* established in New Orleans in 1794, is usually spoken of as the first regular newspaper in Louisiana.[2] It did not have any literary influence, for it discussed only business matters. It is not known when the *Moniteur* suspended publica-

[1] " Le journal est le carnet détaillé de la vie quotidienne et le grand livre de la vie publique. Quel n'est donc pas son pouvoir pour la conservation et extension du langage, pour la formation et l'influence de la littérature? "—Charles ab der Halden: *Etudes de littérature canadienne-française, Introduction,* p. lxi.

[2] William Nelson: *Notes toward a History of the American News-paper* (p. 144) lists *Le Courrier du Vendredi* as established in 1786. I was unable to find any trace of this paper anywhere.

tion. The last copy in the archives in the City Hall in New Orleans bears the date of July 2nd, 1814. Papers in the file in the Cabildo, the museum of the Louisiana Historical Society, date from August 14th to November 26th, 1803; those at the City Hall, from October 1806 to July 2nd, 1814.

LE COURRIER DE LA LOUISIANE

The *Courrier de la Louisiane*, founded about 1807 and printed half in French and half in English, was devoted exclusively to business notices at first. Gradually articles of a literary nature began to appear and by 1840 the *Courrier* had quite a literary tenor. This continued for a short while and the verses of many local poets were published. Then again for several years no more poems appeared. In 1844 the paper changed owners and began to have a definite column, called either " feuilleton " or " variétés ", reserved for literature. In this column were seen from time to time articles and poems by Alexandre Barde, Adolphe Calongne, Charles Bléton, and other writers of Louisiana.

The *Courrier de la Louisiane* passed through a number of vicissitudes. The editor of the *Orléanais* says on September 21st, 1850 that the *Courrier* had not appeared the day before and that for some time its fall had been predicted. He believes that it will rise again. It reappeared on September 24th, 1850. On September 26th it offered a half page in order not to default the judicial notices, and expressed the hope of being able to resume regular publications as a morning, instead of as an afternoon, paper. Numbers from September 26th to October 1st, 1850 are lacking in the files. In the issue for October 1st the editors, Théard and Nicomède, allude

39

to misfortunes which have made it necessary for publication to cease. A syndicate was formed, however, and the *Courrier* continued to appear. In 1852 it was owned by Emile La Sère and in 1856, by Claiborne and Company. In 1859 issues for the months of July and August are missing, but on September 18th it began again as volume 1, number 1 with Emile Hiriart as editor. It was continuing on November 24th, 1860, the last number preserved in the archives at the City Hall. On January 1st, 1879 the *Comptes Rendus de l'Athénée Louisianais* (p. 236) announced that the old *Courrier de la Louisiane* had just reappeared bearing the subtitle, *Organe de la population créole américaine,* with Charles Bléton as one of the editors.[3] The files in the archives at the City Hall contain copies from July 1810 (vol. III) through November 24th, 1860 with a few numbers missing. The statement in *Biographical and Historical Memoirs of Louisiana* (vol. II, p. 155) that the *Courrier* passed to the city's newspaper graveyard May 29th, 1859 is a mistake.

L'ABEILLE DE LA NOUVELLE ORLEANS

L'Abeille de la Nouvelle Orléans, a political, commercial, and literary paper, was founded in 1827 by François Delaup who had come to New Orleans from San Domingo. In the beginning it appeared three times a week, but later became a daily except for occasional years. For example, in the issues of June 18th, 1829 and July 5th,

---

[3] I was unable to find any copies after this revival. According to the proceedings of the American Antiquarian Society (New Series, vol. 24, p. 405) Harvard University has copies for the following dates, October 23rd-30th 1807; May 9th-September 2nd, December 12th-23rd 1808. Wisconsin Historical Society Library has April 29th, 1808.

1842 the editors announced that owing to slackness in business, the *Abeille* would appear only three times a week during the summer months. On November 24th, 1827 a notice stated that because of numerous applications from English speaking people the paper would soon be published partly in English. This was done in December 1827. In 1829 a Spanish column was added because of the great number of refugees who had come to New Orleans from Mexico during the war between that country and Spain, and because of the important war news. This column was discontinued in 1830 after the refugees had departed.

In November 1827 there had appeared in the columns of the *Abeille* a letter complaining that the feuilleton never offered its readers any verse, and stating that the writer was sending a poem to be published. From that date on, the paper contained many poems, some signed and some unsigned. So many were published that the editor said on July 2nd, 1828 that a witty fellow had warned him to be careful because his paper was " plein de VERS ". In 1838 the editor tried to encourage contributions and called on his readers to send in selections. On September 11th he expressed his pleasure that several had responded. In the remaining numbers for that year (1838) and through 1839 the columns of the *Abeille* were crowded with poems, but most of the writers were either afraid or too modest to sign their names. The editor must have been displeased with this procedure after several years, for in the issue of September 29th, 1849 he stated that poetry, except election poems, was to be banished from his columns. In 1850 the feuilleton ran long continued works such as *Les Trois Mousquetaires* and *Le Comte de Monte Cristo* by Dumas; *Les Mémoires d'outre tombe* by Chateaubriand, and novels by Eugène

Sue. It did not limit itself, however, to these works from Europe for several local writers had their novels published in serial form.

On June 18th, 1872 the *Abeille* explained that after June 30th it would be published in French only because it was too expensive to keep two sides printed well enough to do justice to the patrons, and because the English papers had developed so well that it was no longer necessary to have the English section. It had derived its first support from the Franco-Louisianian population and it would continue to use the language of that group.

On May 3rd, 1914, in order to encourage the younger generation to write in French, the new administration of the *Abeille* offered to receive articles by all who would send them in. Each one would be allowed to choose his own subjects and might use a *nom de plume*. Contributions found sufficiently interesting would be published in the Sunday edition, and a prize was offered for the best during the year. If the articles merited it, a prize would be given at the end of six months and the winner of half year prizes might try for the annual prizes. The editor desired several articles a month and, if possible, one a week.[4] This same issue stated that as the conservation and propagation of the French language was one of the prime objects of the new editors, the paper would contain graduated exercises every day from Berlitz' work, accompanied by explanatory notes with English equivalents. In this way Americans would be able to study French for seventy-five cents a month. These lessons continued for about six months.

The *Abeille* later had great trouble in maintaining itself

[4] I was not able to find out whether any of these articles ever appeared.

and changed owners several times. In an article, *L'Abeille de la Nouvelle Orléans*, printed in the *Louisiana Historical Quarterly* for October 1925 (p. 587), Bussière Rouen said that the *Times Picayune* had bought the *Abeille* in 1921. Everything possible was done to prevent its collapse, but it ceased publication on December 27th, 1923. Files of it beginning with volume 1, September 1827, are in the Historical Library at the Cabildo; copies from January 1831 through 1888—with the years 1832, 1838, 1839, and 1887 lacking—are in the City Hall.

L'ORLEANAIS

L'Orléanais, a political, commercial, and literary daily paper published partly in French and partly in English, was founded in New Orleans in 1847. It had a section devoted to literature and its feuilleton often contained works by Louisiana writers. In the issue for April 18th, 1858 the editors explained that they were going to suspend operations because they were located too far from the post office, the court house, the telephone office, and other commercial centers.

MISCELLANEOUS PAPERS AND WHERE TO FIND THEM

Many other newspapers which contributed during their existence either toward developing literary tastes and efforts or toward preserving the French language, were founded and published for a short time. The date of their initial appearance can be learned or deduced from the copies preserved, but very rarely is mention made of their suspension nor reason given for it. Charles

Testut states in the *Semaine de la Nouvelle Orléans* of April 11th, 1852 that very few of the French papers, or those partly in French, lived twelve months without " accidents "; many were not able to live six months; many, not even three months; and if their existence were counted by weeks, the greater number would be included. He attributes the cause of so many failures to lack of ability on the part of the editors or publishers, to bad management, or to indifference. The papers, especially those that were able to live for any length of time, are known from the bound files kept at the Cabildo and in the archives at the City Hall; some have come down only as a name from mention made by other papers of the time; while others are known through several copies —sometimes only a single copy—which have been saved.

PAPERS IN THE CABILDO

Gaspar Cusachs of New Orleans has kept many of these papers, and several from his collection are in the Cabildo, either in the cases in the museum or in a file with other unbound papers in the Historical Library. In this file are the following: *Le Télégraphe,* volume VI, March 11th, 1809, a tri-weekly;[5] *Le Renard Démocrate,* number 13, June 26th, 1834, a bi-weekly with no volume number given; *l'Ane,* no volume number stated, number 3, July 16th, 1835, weekly; *l'Ecureuil,* volume 1, number 1, November 19th, 1837, bi-weekly; *l'Echo National,* volume 1, number 28, July 18th, 1847, bi-weekly; *le Moniteur du Sud,* volume 1, number 1, August 5th, 1849, with a notice that it plans to be a tri-weekly but

[5] The American Antiquarian Society has the *Télégraphe* for December 17th 1803 ; Library of Congress has copies for October 19th, 22nd, 1807 ; Wisconsin Historical Society Library has May 7th, 1808.

that during the slack business season it will be a weekly until November; *l'Indépendant,* volume 2, number 30, October 17th, 185 (a blur here has erased the date), bi-weekly; *le National,* volume 2, number 21, October 24th, 1856, which promises that an English side will be added as soon as the number of subscribers warrants it;[6] *la Renaissance,* volume 1, number 35, June 28th, 1862, daily except Sunday;[7] *l'Avenir,* volume 1, number (torn off), May 26th, 1867, weekly; *l'Epoque,* volume 4, number 32, April 18th, 1869, weekly; *le Sud, journal de la conciliation publié sous le patronage de membres éminents du parti républicain à la Nouvelle Orléans,* volume 1, number 6, August 14th, 1873, weekly; *le Moustique dévoué aux intérêts et à l'amusement du public,* volume 1, number 1, September 14th, 1892, weekly.

The following are exhibited in the museum at the Cabildo: *le Corsaire Louisianais,* volume 1, number 5, February 8th, 1834, weekly; *le Moqueur,* volume 1, number 31, September 10th, 1837, weekly; *le Vrai Républicain,* volume 1, number 59, December 28th, 1837, tri-weekly; *la Créole,* volume 1, number 15, December 31st, 1837, bi-weekly; *le Patriote,* volume 1, number 13, May 27th, 1838, daily except Monday; *le Figaro,* (no volume, no number), July 3rd, 1838, daily; *le Bon Sens,* volume 1, number 19, August 14, 1842; *le Grelot,* volume 1, number 1, July 5th, 1846, bi-weekly; *le Journal de tout le monde,* volume 1, number 1, February 24th, 1848, bi-weekly; *l'Union,* volume 2, number 135, May 12th,

---

[6] This was the last copy I was able to find hence I do not know whether the English part was ever added. Copies from October 1st, 1855, volume 1, number 1, through June 1856 are preserved in the archives at the City Hall.

[7] The Wisconsin Historical Society Library has scattered copies of the *Renaissance* from May to July 1862.

1864; and *la Lorgnette,* volume 2, number 41, November 13th, 1842, bi-weekly.

PAPERS IN THE HOWARD LIBRARY

Copies of the following are preserved in the Howard Library: *le Franc-Parleur* (no date, no statement of volume and number); *le Moniteur de la Louisiane,* August 16th, 1804; *la Réforme,* volume 1, number 65, March 29th, 1846, bi-weekly; *le Passe-Tems,* July 30th, 1827-January 1829; *la Lorgnette,* January 6th, 1843—April 2nd, 1843; *le Dimanche,* September 8th, 1861; *le Courrier de la Louisiane,* August 6th, 1854, January 10th—13th, 1855; *l'Orléanais,* January 10th, 1852, November 19th, 1852, September 15th, 1857, November 4th, 1857; *la République,* volume 1, number 5, February 1st, 1863, daily; *le Courrier Français,* volume 1, number 1, February 9th, 1864, daily; *le Carillon,* volume 2, number 40, August 3rd, 1873, weekly; *la Semaine de la Nouvelle Orléans,* volume 1, number 51, April 11th, 1852, weekly; *le Diamant,* February 5th, 1887—August 1887.

In 1857 the *Spiritualiste,* a monthly magazine containing articles on spiritualism, was published by the "Spiritualistes de la Nouvelle Orléans". The first issue, January 1857, asserts that it will continue at least a year and longer it favorably received. According to the number for February 1857 it was well received. The issue for December 1857 promises that it will continue to appear. In December 1858, however, an announcement states that the number of subscribers has not been sufficient to cover expenses, and that issue will be the last. The articles in the *Spiritualiste* are written, through mediums in seances, by persons from the spirit world, such as Bossuet, Madame de Staël, Pope Leo X, Vincent de

46

Paul, Fénelon, and others. In one of his articles, Fénelon makes observations on the education of the young
girls of the time (1857) and says (March 1857, p. 74)
that the subject occupies him as much as it did when he
was on earth, and that his views have become modified.
Copies of this paper from January 1857 through December 1858 are in the Howard Library.

PAPERS IN THE CITY HALL ARCHIVES

The papers in the archives at the City Hall all had at
least one year of existence. The *Louisiana Gazette,*
established July 27th 1804 was the first newspaper in
New Orleans in the English language.[8] It continued to
be issued in English alone until after April 15th, 1817,
when a French section was added. On January 17th,
1826, its name was changed to *Gazette de l'Etat.* The
Gazette had such a checkered existence and " changed
places of residence so often that business men finally fell
into the habit of sending out a clerk every morning or
two to find where the Gazette's office was located ".[8]
It was able to live for a numbers of years, however,
since, with the exception of occasional missing copies,
files of it from 1804 through November 1826 are
preserved in the City Hall. In 1826 the two languages
were still being used.

The first copy of the *Ami des Lois* found in New Orleans bears the date June 1st, 1813 and is numbered
volume IV. (The Wisconsin Historical Society Library
has the issue of January 18th, 1810, volume 1, number 25.) In 1816 it became *l'Ami des Lois et Journal
du Soir;* on February 22nd, 1819 it was called *l'Ami des
Lois et Journal du Commerce.* On September 20th,

[8] *Biographical and Historical Memoirs of Louisiana,* volume II,
p. 154.

1822 the name *le Louisianais* was adopted and added to
that of *l'Ami des Lois*. In April 1824 the *Argus* was
established and took over the *Louisianais et l'Ami des
Lois*. Its first number bears the date April 19th, 1824.
On August 7th, 1834 the name was changed to *Républicain de la Louisiane* with the English section called
the *Louisiana Whig*. The files include copies from
June 1813 through December 1834 with occasional years
lacking.

In 1864 *l'Union*, which was devoted to the interests
of the negro, was purchased and a new paper, the *Tribune de la Nouvelle Orléans* was established. The *Tribune* from its first copy, July 21st, 1864, through December 1867—the copies for the year 1866 are missing
—is in the archives at the City Hall. It was a tri-weekly
at first, but after October 4th, 1864 it appeared daily
except Mondays. The issue for December 31st, 1867
states that, according to custom, there would be no paper
on January 1st. It adds that none would be published on
January 2nd either. It probably did not appear again.

Another *Union*, altogether different from the one mentioned above in connection with the *Tribune de la Nouvelle Orléans*, is preserved from its first number on February 1st, 1857 through October 31st, 1857. It was a
daily and was entirely in French.

The T. P. Thompson private collection contains several issues of the *Semaine Littéraire*, published in New
Orleans in 1850. It has a subtitle, *Revue franco-américaine des principaux romans et feuilletons nouveaux*,
and contains novels by Balzac and Alexandre Dumas, but
none by local writers. This is true of a great many of
these short-lived papers; their columns offer stories by
Europeans only, such as Emile Souvestre, Paul Féval,
and Alexandre Dumas. A notable exception to this was

l'Epoque, in which a novel, *Hénoch Jédésias,* by Dr. Mercier appeared.

Of the majority of papers nothing but the few copies preserved has been discovered. Of a few of them, however, mention is made later in other periodicals. Several copies of *la Réforme*—the last one, number 87—are in the Cabildo. It did not exist long, for the *Grelot* of July 30th, 1846 (in the Howard Library) speaks of it as " feu *la Réforme* ". *L'Avenir* was more fortunate and was still in existence in 1875, for the city directory of that year mentions Charles Bléton as its editor. The *Revue Louisianaise* (volume 5, number 10) September 5th, 1847 has a notice of the uniting of the *Echo National* with the *Revue Louisianaise* and the *Echo National* for April 23rd, 1846 calls itself an *Annexe de la Revue Louisianaise.* The *Grelot* on July 30th, 1846 boasts of being published by an association because individuals have so often failed. Nothing was found to tell how long the *Grelot* existed or whether the association was any more successful than individuals had been.

Having explained, as quoted above (p. 43), the causes of the failure of many of the newspapers, Charles Testut defends his new venture, *la Semaine de la Nouvelle Orléans.* On April 11th, 1852 he says that he has not urged that subscriptions be paid in advance because he knew that many subscribers were no doubt skeptical of his success. Now that his paper has been appearing for a year and has proved that it is able to exist, he must insist that payments be made three months in advance. He will erase from his books the name of any one who has not confidence for at least three months. He speaks of having undertaken a long local work, *Les Mystères de la Nouvelle Orléans,* the first volume of which is finished and the second volume of which is on its way to publica-

49

5

tion.   He has done this to lend more interest to his paper, and has doubled the number of subscribers thereby.[9]

PAPERS OF WHICH NO COPIES WERE FOUND

There are a number of papers mentioned by other reviews and publications of their day but no copies seem to exist in the libraries of New Orleans.

On July 27th, 1841 the *Courrier de la Louisiane* announces for " about August 1st " a new paper with the name l'*Ami du Peuple* and on August 5th, the *Courrier* states that the *Ami du Peuple* had made its appearance on August 4th, that it is in French only, and that it will be issued three times a week until after October, when it will become a daily.

The *Revue Louisianaise* for November 15th, 1846 (volume II, p. 172) in speaking of a new bi-weekly, l'*Eventail,* says that it was to have made its appearance that day but was delayed because the engraver had not finished the vignette that was to adorn it as a frontispiece.

The *Franco-Américain* must have been intermittent in its publications because the *Revue Louisianaise* on July 9th, 1848 (p. 360) mentions that some one has asked whether the subscribers of the *Franco-Américain* pay for interruptions in its publications.   It must have aroused enmity among the literary men of the day, for Charles Testut says (*Portraits Littéraires,* p. 109) that when it was founded it was to absorb all the other papers, but has absorbed only the money of the stockholders.   Testut

[9] I could find no copy of this novel nor of the *Semaine de la Nouvelle Orléans* after April 11th, 1858.   The catalogue of the Louisiana Historical Society Library has a card for *Les Mystères de la Nouvelle Orléans,* but the librarian was unable to find the book.

adds (p. 111) that the editor, Masson, thinks himself a
" Hercules of journalism ", and the *Revue Louisianaise*
for August 13th, 1848 (p. 476) accuses the editor of the
Franco-Américain of believing himself more important in
the community than he really is and charges him with
copying his editorials from the newspapers of France
instead of writing original ones.

The *Orléanais* of December 4th, 1850 announces that
Placide Canonge is to publish a paper, *l'Entr'acte,* which
will deal with everything pertaining to literature and fine
arts. According to the issue of the *Orléanais* on December 7th, the *Entr'acte* appeared on Thursday, December 5th, and was enthusiastically received by the public.

The *Comptes Rendus de l'Athénée Louisianais* in May
1879 (p. 267) mention a new paper which had just appeared under the name of the *Petit Journal* with Charles
Bléton as editor.

The *Renaissance Louisianaise* of November 6th, 1864
(p. 4) quotes the *Propagateur Catholique* as saying that
it would commence its 45th volume the next week, that it
was then passing through hard times, that it was a
Catholic paper, and that it ought to be supported by all
Catholics. There are varying accounts of the *Propagateur Catholique.* The *Catalogue of Newspaper Files in
the Library of the Wisconsin State Historical Society*
(p. 78) calls it the oldest French paper in the United
States and sets the dates of its existence from 1810 to
1888. The *Newspaper and Periodical Press* of 1884
(p. 255) records 1842 as the date of its establishment.
The statement of the *Renaissance Louisianaise* that it
would begin its 45th volume in 1864 infers that it was
established about 1819. According to the *Biographical
and Historical Memoirs of Louisiana* (vol. II, p. 137) it
was founded in 1844 by the Abbé Perché and survived

his death in 1883 only a few years. Its publication, like
that of many of the other papers, was probably intermittent, which would account for a variation in dates. The
Wisconsin Historical Society Library has the following
copies: November 1842—May 1843; January 1861—
March 1862; and April—December 1862.

NEWSPAPERS IN OTHER TOWNS

Besides the many papers in New Orleans there were
successful ones in smaller places. The *Gazette de Baton
Rouge* was published partly in English and partly in
French. It contains anecdotes and poems, but very few
of them are by local writers. On several occasions it
contains poems by Auguste Lussan and Alexandre Latil
of New Orleans copied from the New Orleans papers.
After May 13th, 1845 the French part ceased to exist
except for announcements, advertisements, and special
notices. The editor says that money earned on the English side has been lost on the French side, which has
been a dead expense to him. Copies from March 3rd,
1827, which is volume IX, through 1847 are preserved
in the University of Louisiana Library at Baton Rouge.
Copies from February 8th, 1826 through December 17th,
1827 are in the Library of Congress.[10]

The *Gazette des Attakapas* of St. Martinville was very
influential in its day. The *Revue Louisianaise* on June
6th, 1847 (volume IV, p. 231) speaks of it as the oldest
of all the country papers. The New Orleans *Item* of
April 20th, 1924, in an article entitled " *Louisiana News-*

[10] See *Checklist of American Newspapers in the Library of
Congress,* compiled 1901, p. 73-76.

papers of 100 Years Ago " by Mary Wyman Bryant, contains a picture of the title portion of the *Gazette*. This bears the date April 18th, 1829 and is volume V, number 20. Along with the *Gazette* the *Revue Louisianaise* mentions another paper at St. Martinville, *Le Créole*, founded in 1837 and composed mostly of clippings from the important papers of New Orleans.

The *Vigilant* of Donaldsonville, volume 1, number 1 of which appeared on September 28th, 1845,[11] seems to have had a hard struggle in its early days. The *Revue Louisianaise* for February 27th, 1848 (volume 5, p. 524) speaks of it as having once been a poor little paper which everybody expected to see disappear at any moment, but calls it now a " superb paper, very successful and filled with talent ". It is not known when it ceased to exist. The *Comptes Rendus de l'Athénée Louisianais* in July 1877 (p. 82) refers to a new paper, *le Vigilant*, just started in Donaldsonville, whose editor deplores the state of abandonment in which the French language had been found for so many years, and the inability of a number of the older citizens to keep informed on questions of the day because of not being able to read English. It is not known whether this new paper was really a revival of the old *Vigilant* or whether it was an altogether different venture under the old name.[12]

Le Messager was published at Bringier in St. James Parish. One copy of it, volume 1, number 20, dated December 4th, 1846 is included in the file of unbound papers in the Historical Library at the Cabildo.

The *Pionnier de l'Assomption* was established at Napoleonville in September 1850 by Eugene Supervielle. At

[11] This date was obtained from notes left by Edward Fortier.
[12] I was unable to get copies of the *Gazette des Attakapas, Le Créole* and *Le Vigilant*.

first it was entirely in French except the judicial and commercial advertisements. In about 1857 it was issued half in French and half in English under the ownership of Charles Dupaty. In 1893 the *Pionnier* was bought by a stock company, the Pioneer Publishing Company, and the French part was discontinued. The paper is still being published with E. D. Gionelloni as editor and manager.[13]   One copy, April 13th, 1858, volume 8, number 26, is in the file in the Louisiana Historical Library.

The *Meschacébé* was published in St. John Baptist Parish. According to the *Comptes Rendus de l'Athénée Louisianais*, November 1878 (p. 205) which speak of the death of Eugène Dumez who had been editor of it for twenty years, the paper disappeared with its editor and left a vacancy in the Franco-American press. It must have been quickly revived by some one else, because a copy dated April 23rd, 1904 bears the statement, " 52nd year ". Two issues of the *Meschacébé* are in the unbound file in the Historical Library, April 23th, 1904, volume 52, number 17; and December 16th, 1905, volume 53, number 50. It is still being published at Lucy, Louisiana, by John D. Reynaud who says that " it still is and has always been the official journal of St. John Baptist Parish ". It is now almost wholly English with only an occasional article in French. The French part was gradually discontinued because all the inhabitants of the parish now speak English.[14]

The *Foyer Créole* was published in Convent, Louisiana. It was established in 1880, by a political group, and printed in both French and English. In a lottery fight

[13] The information about the *Pionnier de l'Assomption* was furnished me by Mr. Gionelloni.
[14] The information about the *Meschacébé* in recent years was furnished me by Mr. Reynaud.

the editor, F. B. Dicharry, was on the side opposite to the one taken by the group, and the paper was stopped. The editor, enjoined from publishing it in 1888, founded that same year another paper which he called the *Intérim*. He later won his suit and could have continued under the old name, but did not change back. The French section was discontinued during the World War, because there was very little demand for it, and the space was needed for war news. The editor now has a few requests for a French column, but not enough to justify one.[15] Issues of the *Foyer Créole,* beginning March 16th, 1881, volume 1, number 13, are preserved in the printing office at Convent. They contain, besides the news and official announcements of the parish, charades, proverbs, and occasional poems, most of them unsigned or signed with a *nom de plume* as " Une Créole ". It was at Convent that Henri Remy established his paper, *St. Michel,* in which he began to publish his *Histoire de la Louisiane.*[16] Here also Jean Gentil published *Le Louisianais.*

L'Observateur of Reserve, St. Johns Parish, has now reached volume XV. It still has a French section in which continued stories appear. It is issued every Saturday by Wallace Lasseigne.[17]

THE REVIEWS AND THEIR IMPORTANCE

More important, perhaps, than the daily or weekly papers, were the *Revues* that were organized for purely literary and artistic purposes. *La Violette,* a musical and

[15] The information about the *Foyer Créole* was given me by B. J. Dicharry, the present editor of the *Intérim* at Convent.
[16] See the account given in Chapter II.
[17] This information was furnished me by Mr. Lasseigne who also sent me a copy of his paper.

literary review founded in 1849, published several novels and a great many poems by local writers. It was issued monthly and, according to its title page, was published under the patronage of the ladies of Louisiana. The T. P. Thompson Collection contains several copies of it. The issue for March 1849 constitutes volume 1, number 1. The *Comptes Rendus de l'Athénée Louisianais* for November 1899 (p. 581) have an article on *La Violette* and quote from its last copy, February 1850, where the editor says: " La Violette va mourir ".

In 1849 also Charles Testut was director of a review, *Les Veillées Louisianaises,* which appeared every Sunday and had for its special object the publication of a series of novels based on interesting facts of Louisiana history (preface p. v). *Louisiana* by Armand Garreau and *St. Denis* and *Calisto* by Charles Testut, appeared in this review. It was published in two volumes a year, each volume containing twenty-six numbers. Volumes I and II are in the T. P. Thompson Collection, and volume I is also in the Howard Library. It existed, without doubt, no longer than one year, and these two volumes were probably the only two published, for in 1850 Testut left New Orleans and went to Mobile. The *Orléanais* of August 14th, 1850 contains an article, " *Chronique de la Mobile* " written by him, and on October 4th, 1850 speaks of a new French and English paper, the *Alabama-Courrier* which is about to be started in Mobile by Charles Testut.

The *Revue Louisianaise,* also a weekly magazine, was more successful and had a great share in cultivating things Louisianian in Louisiana. In it Madame Emilie Evershed published a great many of her poems before having them printed in book form, and Placide Canonge published some of his plays and stories. Interesting news items from abroad and from local sections appeared in its " Revue de la Semaine ". There were two volumes each year with twenty-six numbers to a volume. Issues extending from volume I, number I, April 5th, 1846 through volume 7, number 14, December 1848—except volume III and number 10 of volume V which are missing—are in the Howard Library. It is not known whether it continued to be published after December 1848.

The *Renaissance Louisianaise,* another weekly review, was called the *Organ of the Franco-American population of the South.* The number for June 15th, 1862 constitutes number 24 of volume II. Published, as it was, during the Civil War, it contains more political and war news than literary material. It has stories also, but very rarely are these by local writers. Hégissippe Moreau and Arsène Houssaye offer the favorite serials. Armand Garreau's *L'Idiote,* which appeared as a feuilleton in 1864, is the only story in it written by a local author. A copy of the *Renaissance Louisianaise* for June 15th, 1862 is in the glass case in the museum at the Cabildo and copies for the year 1864, volume IV, are in the Howard Library. No copies later than 1864 could be found.

Another magazine—published monthly— which had great influence in aiding the cause of the French language and the French people of Louisiana, was the *Observateur Louisianais.* It existed from January 1892 through December 1897. Many articles appeared in it, most of them unsigned. Those contributed by François Tujague deserve a place in the literature of the time.[18] When Placide Louis Chapelle was made Archbishop of New Orleans, in December 1897, a notice in the *Observateur* explained that, now that a Frenchman had been made Archbishop, there was no further need for the

[18] See Chapter VII for special treatment of François Tujague.

existence of the magazine. It had been established for the purpose of defending the French language and the French people when the former Archbishops, and the Catholic press of the country seemed to want to destroy all that was left of French culture in Louisiana.

In March 1895 a new magazine, *La Revue,* which promised to appear every Saturday, was established with Miss Marie Roussel as owner and director. Number 1 of volume 1 is dated March 30th, 1895. It contains a prospectus, as it were, written by François Tujague, who, deploring the decrease in the use of French, states that this review is added to the French publications with the definite and loudly proclaimed aim of contributing toward maintaining the use of this language in Louisiana. In the March and May numbers, 1895—the two copies in the Howard Library—there are articles from various papers in Europe, notices of local interest both political and religious, and a few stories. In the issue for May 1895 (p. 119) there is an announcement that Miss Roussel will marry the Count of Calcinara on June 1st, but that she will continue to be director of the paper. No other copies of this paper are preserved and it is not known how much longer it continued to exist.

MEDICAL JOURNALS

Several medical journals were also issued in New Orleans in French. In 1852 Dr. Charles Deléry edited a monthly review called *L'Union Médicale de la Louisiane.* The number for February 12th, 1852 (Howard Library) constitutes number 2. In the prospectus in this number the editor expresses his feeling that, in a city with as many French people as New Orleans, a medical journal in French will fill a vacancy and be of use. It will be a means of propaganda for the medical body and

will give, at intervals, reports on public health. Dr. Deléry plans to have articles from medical publications in
England, France, and Italy, in order to keep his associ-
ates in the profession in New Orleans in touch with
medical science in Europe. As only one copy of this
journal could be discovered, the length of its existence
is not known.

*Le Practicien homéopathe, journal de médecine homéo-
pathique,* published by Louis Caboche, began its existence on November 15th, 1857. It contains articles telling the merits and advantages of homeopathy, and long
discussions on its efficacy in yellow fever. Copies of
this magazine from November 15th, 1857 through October 1858—with the April and June number missing—
are in the Howard Library. On May 1st, 1859, *L'Homoïon, organe de la doctrine Hahnémannienne* appeared,
edited by Dr. Louis Taxil. The review continued under
this name until May 1860 when, on beginning volume II,
the subtitle became *Revue de la doctrine homéopathi-
que dans le pur esprit de la lettre Hahnémannienne* and
the statement is made that it will appear at irregular
intervals, at least once a month.[19] On April 10th, 1861
*L'Homoïon, journal de la société Hahnémannienne de
la Nouvelle Orléans* began volume I, number 1. It
stated that a Homeopathic Society had just been founded
in New Orleans. This number (in the Howard Library)
was the only one found after the beginning of the new
volume. *L'Homoïon* contains abstracts of articles from
such papers as the *Homeopathic Review of America.* In
a column called " vous et nous ", the editors often refer
to differences between their ideas and those of the Medical Society of New Orleans.

[19] The file of this journal in the Howard Library extends
through December 1860.

In July 1859, the Medical Society of New Orleans began to publish a magazine, the *Journal de la Société Médicale de la Nouvelle Orléans*. In a preface, the editors explain that this review has been founded by the Medical Society in order to have an organ of publicity in which the discussions, observations, and studies made in the meetings of the society, could be made known; it will also be a link between the city and country physicians; it will discuss the question of yellow fever and will review recent publications. Three copies of it, July 1859, and July and September 1860, are in the Howard Library. In these are recorded some of the discussions of yellow fever between Dr. Charles Faget and Dr. Charles Deléry.[20]

When the literary reviews were discontinued, and the stimulation to produce novels and poetry was removed, the interest in literature was not so great, and the production gradually decreased. *L'Abeille de la Nouvelle Orléans, Le Courrier de la Louisiane,* and *L'Orléanais* were still existing and were doing their part. As literature, however, was not their first interest, and as political questions were becoming more important, their columns were filled with news of the day. This was true also of the *Guêpe* founded in 1902 by J. G. de Baroncelli, for very little poetry and very few stories appear in it. The *Guêpe* bears the slogan: " The only French Newspaper published in Louisiana ", and has just celebrated its 25th anniversary.

As the authors who contributed works to these papers were seldom writers by profession, very few of them have published their works in book form.[21]

---

[20] See Chapter IX.
[21] The information that I have given about the newspapers

was obtained from examining the files of the papers themselves, except in the cases where I have referred to statements about them in other papers of the time.

In naming the copies available, I have added numbers listed in the files of Harvard Library, the Library of Congress, the Wisconsin Historical Society Library, and the American Antiquarian Society whenever these numbers were earlier than the copies preserved in New Orleans. Papers of which no copies were found and to which no references were made in other papers are in the following libraries:

Wisconsin Historical Library:
> *Echo du Commerce,* September 28th, 1808.
> *Estafette du Sud,* May-December 1862.
> *Lanterne Magique,* November 20th, 1808.

Yale University:
> *Gazette des Opélousas,* August 16th, 1828.

Library of Congress
> *Courrier des Natchitoches,* May 2nd—September 1825; March 13—December 12th, 1826.
> *Gazette de l'Etat de la Louisiane,* January 3rd—December 6th, 1826.

After concluding the above chapter, I found a *Histoire de la Presse Franco-Américaine* by Alexandre Bélisle, which contained a table of French Newspapers in Louisiana (pp. 380-384). Bélisle got a great many of the names on his list from Baroncelli's *Colonie Française en Louisiane.* The papers listed by him, and of which I was unable to find copies, are the following:

Outside of New Orleans:
> *l'Autochtone*
> *la Gazette, le Rappel Louisianais,* Convent
> *la Ruche Louisianaise, la Voix du Peuple, la Jeune Amérique,* St. John Baptist Parish
> *l'Avant Coureur,* Bonnet Carré
> *l'Ami des Planteurs,* Donaldsonville
> *le Journal,* Pointe Coupée Parish
> *la Vallée du Thêche, la Sentinelle des Attakapas, l'Union,* Breaux Bridge
> *l'Organe Central, le Pélican,* Avoyelles
> *la Sentinelle,* Thibodeau; *l'Echo,* Lake Charles
> *le Courrier, le Journal, St. Landry Progress,* Opelousas
> *la Sentinelle,* Lafourche; *Iberville South,* Plaquemine
> *le Méridionial, Cotton Hall, Lafayette Advertiser,* Vermillonville
> *Courrier de la Thêche, l'Echo, l'Evangile, le Reveil,* St. Martinville.

61

> *l'Etoile, le Journal,* Louisiana *Sugar Bowl,* New Iberia
> *le Courrier,* Houma ; *Review,* Marksville
> *le Progrès, Advocate,* Terrebone ; *le Kaplan Times,*
> Neville

In New Orleans :

> *l'Ami des Noirs; le Tintamare; la Démocratie Française;
> la Guêpe* (1817) ; *le Charivari; Country Visitor; le Cétacé; l'Opinion; le Franco-Louisianais; l'Omnibus; la
> Démocrate; le Réveil.*

Bélisle mentions also *le Trait d'Union.* I found a copy of
this paper in the Cabildo but it was printed in Mexico, hence
I did not include it in my list. Besides the reviews that I have
treated and which he does not list, I have the following names
not mentioned by him :

> *l'Ami du Peuple; l'Avenir; le Bon Sens; la Créole;
> l'Echo National; l'Ecureuil; le Franco-Américain; la
> Gazette des Attakapas; le Grelot; l'Indépendent; le Moniteur du Sud; le Moqueur; le Moustique; le National;
> l'Observateur; la Réforme; la République; le Sud;
> l'Union.*

CHAPTER V

FRENCH ORGANIZATIONS IN NEW ORLEANS

French societies in New Orleans have been numerous, and the purposes for which they have been organized many and varied. All of them have contributed to the preservation of the French language and spirit. As regards literature particularly, the *Athénée Louisianais* has had the most appreciable influence.

When Louisiana was ceded to the United States in 1803, the inhabitants of the colony and their descendants continued to use their own language. In the reconstruction days of 1868, however, a legislative decree was issued declaring that laws and public documents should be preserved and published in English only.[1] It was also forbidden to teach French in the elementary schools, nor was the teaching of it in the high schools looked upon with great favor. This decree was a severe blow to the French speaking population, and great indignation was expressed against it. In 1879 one of the delegates from New Orleans succeeded in having an amendment to the constitution passed. This amendment suppressed the word " only "[2] and added a clause stating that the legislature might allow the publication of documents in French, and that laws and judicial announcements in

[1] Acts of the State of Louisiana, 1868, p. 10, Act. 8, sec. 10.
[2] *L'Abeille de la Nouvelle Orléans,* July 4th, and July 10th, 1879.

certain towns and villages would be inserted in French.[3] A vote of the convention also authorized the teaching of French in the parishes where the French language predominated.[4]

THE ATHENEE LOUISIANAIS

In the meanwhile, however, a small group of men, fearing that the French language would die out, and wishing to prevent this, met and discussed plans whereby interest in this question might be aroused and maintained. The result of these discussions was the formation of the *Athénée Louisianais* in January 1876.[5] The credit of having conceived the plan is given to Dr. Alfred Mercier. The purpose of the organization was threefold: to perpetuate the French language in Louisiana; to devote itself to scientific, literary, and artistic works; and to organize itself into an Association of Mutual Assistance. The third purpose was never attained. The first was the principal one.

There were twelve charter members, six of whom were physicians. It is therefore not surprising that the first numbers of the *Comptes Rendus* contained articles of a scientific, rather than of a literary, nature. In the beginning this magazine appeared every two months, but after 1902 every three months. It records the minutes of the business sessions and contains all lectures and articles read at the meetings. At first the members were men only, but in 1905, women were allowed to join.

Believing that in devoting its efforts to the preservation

[3] Constitution of 1879, Article 154.
[4] Constitution of 1879, Article 226.
[5] Information for this account was obtained from different numbers of the *Comptes Rendus de l'Athénée Louisianais* from 1876 to 1925, and from the president, Bussière Rouen.

of the French language in Louisiana, it was working for the good of the people of Louisiana, and wishing to give these efforts a practical form, the *Athénée* announced in 1878 that it would have a literary contest. Wishing to make itself known to the public at large which was not being reached by its magazine, the *Athénée* announced that it would have an annual open meeting when the prize essays would be read, and the prizes awarded. The conditions of the contest were stated clearly. Anybody living in Louisiana could compete; the language, of course, was to be French; the manuscript was to be sent in with a symbol rather than with the writer's name; the name was to be enclosed in an envelope bearing the symbol; the manuscript was not to be returned to the owner; and no one having obtained the prize once was to be allowed to try again. At the first contest, the subject of which was: " De la puissance de l'éducation et de la nécessité du travail dans toutes les conditions de la vie ", nineteen manuscripts were submitted. The prize article was read to the assembly and received with great applause. The acclaim grew still louder when the name of the winner, Alcée Fortier, was announced.[6]

For some time two prizes were given, one for men and another for women, but in 1893 this distinction of sex was abolished, and only one prize, a gold medal and $50.00, was established. Each year since this contest was organized, a medal has been offered, but nine times the committee for awarding it has found no manuscript entirely satisfactory, and has refused to give it to a mediocre one. Two medals have been awarded occasionally. This was true at the last contest in 1926, when one was awarded to Gladys Renshaw and one to Marga-

[6] See chapter IX for a full account of Alcée Fortier.

rita Gutiérrez-Nájera for essays on the subject, *Ronsard, poète lyrique.*

This contest has not only furthered the first purpose of the *Athénée*, the preservation of the French language, but has also furthered the second: an interest in literary works. These manuscripts, published in the *Comptes Rendus*, form a part of the French literature of Louisiana, and have in some cases—discouragingly few in number, says the president of the organization—aroused their authors to further productions which have also become of importance as literature.[7]

The *Athénée* was especially interested in having repealed the Republican order of reconstruction days, which had abolished the teaching of French in the elementary schools. In 1878 its members addressed a petition to the directors of the public schools asking that French be put back in the primary grades. In 1893 the president of the *Athénée* was influential in persuading the director of the Normal College at Natchitoches that candidates for teaching should have a chance to study French. To increase enthusiasm in the study of this language, the *Athénée* offered prizes for the best work in French done by the pupils of the two high schools in the city of New Orleans, as well as in the schools of the French Union and of the Society of the 14th of July.

Wishing to awaken still greater interest in the French language and literature, the *Athénée* has been instrumental, through the *Alliance Française*, in bringing to New Orleans French speakers such as Henri de Regnier, Firmin Roz, Eugène Brieux, Hugues Le Roux, and many others.

---

[7] See the appendix—list of Louisiana writers—in which each one who has won the medal given by the *Athénée Louisianais* is included.

Mr. Rouen, the president, said at the meeting in January 1921 that several years before this date, realizing that the copies of the works of the old French authors of Louisiana were getting rare, he had decided to republish them. Three of the old dramas were reprinted: *Mila, ou la mort de la Salle,* by C. O. Dugué, in 1907; *Poucha-Houmma* by Le Blanc de Villeneufve in 1909; and *Les Martyrs de la Louisiane* by Auguste Lussan in 1912.

The *Athénée Louisianais* is the official group of the *Fédération de l'Alliance Française aux Etats-Unis et au Canada.* It celebrated its 50th anniversary in February 1927. On the occasion of the celebration, Mr. Maurice de Simonin, the Consul General of France at New Orleans, presented to the society, in the name of the *Institut de France* a " Médaille de vermeil " as a recompense for its work.

THE CAUSERIES DU LUNDI

The *Causeries du Lundi,* like the *Athénée Louisianais,* is affiliated with the *Fédération de l'Alliance Française aux Etats-Unis.* In 1912 a number of prominent women who were interested in literature and in the French language, met and after several informal meetings, definitely organized the *Causeries du Lundi*[8] with the purpose of " encouraging and maintaining the French language in New Orleans ". Madame Alfred Le Blanc was the first president and remained in that office until her death.

The meetings were held twice a month and the number of members was limited to one hundred. In 1926 the number was enlarged to one hundred fifty, but even then,

[8] Information about the *Causeries* was obtained from the secretary, Mrs. Pinckney Galbreath.

not all the applicants for membership could be admitted. Both men and women are eligible. There are ten meetings of the club during the year, beginning the first Monday in December and ending the third Monday in April. The programs consist of lectures, readings, and music.

Madame Le Blanc personally gave a prize each year to the student at Newcomb College who submitted the best French essay on a subject chosen by the department of French at that college. After Madame Le Blanc's death, the *Causeries du Lundi* continued to give a prize and, since 1923, have been giving in memory of her a medal which is known as the " Jane Stewart Le Blanc Medal ". Madame Thomas Sloo is now president.

TWO SOCIETIES PRIOR TO THE ATHENEE

Before the founding of the *Athénée Louisianais,* there were already formed two French organizations which are still in existence today. The *Société Française de Bienfaisance et d'Assistance Mutuelle* was organized in 1843. Its purpose was to help needy Frenchmen, either those living in New Orleans or those passing through the city. It is the largest French society in New Orleans, and maintains an asylum for the aged and infirm.[9]

The *Union Française* was organized in 1872, inspired by feelings of benevolence toward the natives of Alsace and Lorraine who might come over to Louisiana. J. Passama Domenech was its first president. Not many Frenchmen came from these provinces, but the *Union* continued to exist.[9] In about 1882 it organized an Eve-

---

[9] *Biographical and Historical Memoirs of Louisiana,* pp. 186-188. Aslo an article in *L'Abeille* on May 19th, 1913.

ning School for Boys, and in November 1886, François Tujague, who was then president, announced the establishment of a school for girls, of which Miss Ermance Robert was the first director.[10] This school is being successfully carried on today under the guidance of Miss Marie Dumestre. Georges Legrand is now the president of the *Union*.

OTHER SOCIETIES

Les Enfants de la France, 1892, and *La France,* 1894 are both mutual and benevolent associations.

In 1882 some public-spirited French patriots residing in Louisiana decided to have a commemoration of the fall of the Bastille. A committee was appointed and this celebration was held. The day was celebrated each year thereafter until 1889, the hundreath anniversary of this national day, when an association was formed. In 1890, a constitution was drawn up and the name *Société de la Fête du Quatorze Juillet* was adopted. The festival of the 14th of July is a celebration by the subjects of France who reside in Louisiana, many of whom are connected with the consulate in New Orleans. Natives of Louisiana participate in it as guests.[11] A. de Chateauneuf is president of this society. It maintains a school for boys.

The *Alliance Franco-Louisianaise* was founded in 1908 for the purpose of having French taught in the public schools. J. N. Vergnolle is president.

The *Comité France-Amérique de la Nouvelle Orléans*

[10] *Comptes Rendus de l'Athénée Louisianais,* January 1887, pp. 290-291.
[11] *Comptes Rendus de l'Athénée Louisianais,* March 1883, p. 319 ff.

of which André Lafargue[12] is acting president, is a branch of the *Comité France-Amérique* of Paris. It was organized in order to foster strong ties of friendship between America and France. It strives to do this through scholarships, lectures, and receptions.

THE LOUIS BUSH MEDAL AND ALCEE FORTIER MEMORIAL PRIZE

Two prizes given at Tulane University in New Orleans also help to preserve a keen interest in the French language. The Louis Bush Medal founded in 1882 by Louis Bush consists of a gold medal given for the best essay in the French language. Students in all the French classes of the University may compete for this prize. The other is very fittingly called the Alcée Fortier Memorial Prize, and is given for proficiency in the classes of the Colleges of Arts and Sciences and Engineering. In 1923, the contributions to the Fortier Memorial Fund were given to the University by the Executive Committee of the Alumni Association and the prize was established.[13]

Although not all of these organizations have turned their efforts directly toward literary production in Louisiana, each has contributed its part in preserving the French language, thus making possible a literature in French.

[12] I am indebted to Mr. Lafargue for the information I have given above about the present officers of these organizations.

[13] *Bulletin of Tulane University, Colleges of Arts and Sciences.*

CHAPTER VI

POETRY

Although there were many writers of French poetry in Louisiana, especially between the years of 1825 and 1855, these poets were not connected with one another. Occasionally one of them would address a poem to another, but usually they worked independently. They did not try to establish a school of poetry, nor did they try to create a tradition. They seemed content to write in imitation of the Romantic poets of France, and many of them, either in prefaces or in poems, acknowledge that their inspiration is due to Hugo, Lamartine, De Musset, or to some other of the poets of that time. Julien Poydras and Berquin Duvallon had made beginnings in poetry in the territorial period, but it seemed for several years after the purchase of Louisiana by the United States that poetic inspiration was dead, for no poetry was produced.

However, on November 13th, 1827 the editor of the *Abeille* received a letter signed " Un Amateur de Poésie " which complained that the columns of this paper never offered any poetry to its readers. The writer enclosed a poem to be printed. This poem was about the Battle of New Orleans and had as title " *Dédié au Général Jackson* ". It was signed " Un invalide (de corps et d'esprit) ". The author praises Jackson and names him as

71

his choice of the candidates for the presidency of the United States.

Je chante ce guerrier qui sauva notre ville
Son grand nom est Jackson, toujours brave et civile,
Il battit les Criques, il battait les Anglais
Il nous rendait heureux contre vents et marais'
. . . .
. . . .
Nous avons deux partis, les uns sont Jacksonistes,
Les uns du bon côté, les autres Adamistes,
Je suis républicain, mon vote est pour Jackson,
En tout temps, et pour lui, ce sera ma chanson ;
Vous serez président, pour vous est la victoire,
En dépit des jaloux, nous vous couvrons de gloire.

In spite of the efforts of this poet to remain unknown, he was recognized as Jean Duperron. He continued writing poems in favor of Jackson's candidacy. These were eagerly received, and the editor of the *Abeille* says on June 17th, 1828 : " Nous considérons toujours comme une obligation de livrer à l'avidité du public tous les produits de cette imagination poétique et chevaleresque quand on nous fait la haute faveur de nous les communiquer ".

Following his example, other anonymous writers sent in poems, some praising, some criticizing Duperron. Duperron answered his critics and was at times quite caustic in his replies. He boasted of the regularity of his Alexandrine lines, thereby calling forth the following pun in the *Abeille* for June 23rd, 1828 : " Un certain poète en " on " assurait qu'il ne faisait jamais que des vers de douze pieds. Ah ! vous avez trop de modestie, dit un plaisant, laissons donc, ce sont des vers à mille pattes ".

Duperron then turned from political poems and in the *Abeille,* July 29th, 1828, produced a hymn of love singing of the beauties and charms of Zizine.

Dédié à une aimable beauté.

. . . .
Quand tu parus vers moi je fus des plus heureux.
. . . .
Je te vis mainte fois souvent rire, pleurer
Lorsque je dis soudain oui, je veux t'adorer;
Oui, céleste Zizine, à Vénus comparable,
Tu créas dans mon âme une plaie incurable;
Tu fais naître à la fois les plaisirs, les chagrins,
L'âge d'or et de fer dans le cœur des humains.
. . . .

The election of Jackson inspired him to write another long poem " *Dédié au Général Jackson* " which appeared in the *Abeille* on March 5th, 1829. It is composed of thirty Alexandrine lines and closes thus:

Etant sans cesse aimé, te voilà Président
Tu seras bien heureux, tout le monde est content.

On June 25th, 1828 a notice in the *Abeille* stated that the *Recueil Complet des poésies fugitives, érotiques et politiques* of M. D..... would soon appear.[1] In 1830 and 1831 no poems were published by Duperron. Every one was wondering about his silence, and verses such as the following were asking

Qu'est-ce donc Duperron? d'où vient ton silence?
. . . .
Ah! de ce changement je veux savoir la cause,
Et tu me répondras, soit en vers, soit en prose.

Finally in October 1832, the editor of the *Abeille* announced that the Louisiana Bard had taken his lyre again to answer a Parisian poet who in his poem had proposed

[1] I could not find a copy of this. All the poems I was able to find by Duperron were those which appeared in the *Abeille* as mentioned above.

to make the Bard "sortir de son sommeil". Duperron answers in the *Abeille* of October 18th, 1832 with a poem called " *Ma réponse* " :

> J'obéis... mais depuis quarante et demi mois
> Mon pégase Coco paît en paix dans les bois.
> . . . .
> Pour te répondre ami, je suis donc sans monture ;
> Mais mes vers vers Paris dirigés en droiture,
> Arriveront, j'espère . . . .

Although time has made Zizine wrinkled and gray, he loves her still.

> Que ton ton est touchant, en parlant de Zizine
> A plus forte raison, si sa mine divine
> Eût frappé tes regards, quand elle avait quinze ans !
> Mais que ne peut sur nous l'inexorable temps ?
> Rien ne peut arrêter le cours de ses outrages,
> Et sa main sur Zizine a fait bien des ravages !
> Il a ridé son front, a blanchi ses cheveux...
> Je l'aime bien toujours . . . .

Jackson holds firm as a rock in spite of his enemies :

> J'ai célébré Jackson, ce vrai républicain
> Et je crois que mes vers ont produit quelque bien,
> En prouvant clairement à notre république,
> Que lui seul a sauvé du pouvoir britannique
> Notre Mississippi, nos femmes et nos droits.
> . . . .
> Il a des ennemis dans sa propre patrie
> Qui peu reconnaissans, mûs par la jalousie,
> Le traitent de tyran, voudraient le renverser ;
> Mais il tient aussi fort que tient un dur rocher
> Car c'est l'ami du peuple . . . .

The author adds the following postscript :

> Lis et relis mes vers ; ils sont tous de mesure ;
> Car ils ont douze pieds, ainsi que la césure ;

74

Et pour m'en assurer, je les ai mainte fois
Comptés et recomptés sur le bout de mes doigts.

Duperron was elected to a place in the Académie
Royale in France in 1832.[2] He was a Frenchman who
had come to New Orleans and taught for many years.
He died there in 1836.[3]

This complaint of Duperron of the lack of poetry in
the columns of the *Abeille* and his own example in producing poems must have been of influence in the development of verse. Many collections of it appeared after
this challenge. The subjects treated in these volumes
were varied—love of Louisiana, love of solitude, love of
humanity, yearning toward God, sadness in suffering,
patriotism, humor, and satire.

POEMS EXPRESSING LOVE FOR LOUISIANA

It is not surprising to find that many of the verses
produced are filled with praise of Louisiana and expressions of love for the landscapes. One of the most
important writers of poems on this subject was Dominique Rouquette.

Rouquette[4] was a native of Louisiana, born at Bayou

[2] " Il est de notoriété publique que M. J. Duperron, sur-
nommé le Barde Louisianais, a reçu dernièrement par les soins
d'un passager venant de Paris, chargé de cette mission par le
président de l'Académie Royale, un diplôme en règle, signé des
principaux membres de cette illustre société et contre-signé par
le ministre de l'intérieur, par lequel il appert qu'il a été élu
et nommé à la dernière place vacante à la dite société par la
mort d'un homme de lettres. " *L'Abeille de la Nouvelle Orléans*,
December 1st, 1832.
[3] See the earliest directories of New Orleans and his death
record in the Cathedral archives of that city.
[4] See the baptismal and death records at the Cathedral and
J. A. Reinecke's article in the *Comptes Rendus de l'Athénée
Louisianais*, January 1920.

Lacombe in January 1810. His family was wealthy and he was sent to France to study at the Collège Royal de Nantes. On his return to America, he went to Philadelphia to study law, but soon abandoned it. His poetic nature was too restless to be confined in a law office.

In 1836 he was in Paris for a short while but returned to Louisiana the next year. Again in 1838 he was in Paris. His first volume of poems, *Les Meschacébéennes,* was published there in 1839. Fearing that he might die far from the Mississippi he loved so well, he felt the need of leaving these poems as a souvenir to his family and friends. He also wanted to inspire in the young poets of France a desire to visit the forests of Louisiana, a land of sadness and poetry.[5] The verses of this volume are expressions of his love for his native state and its scenery. He calls the first poem " *Exil et Patrie* " and expresses the desire to have others see his beloved river and pine trees.

Qu'un autre, ingrat enfant, vieux fleuve, te blasphème,
Moi, je chanterai, Michasippi — je t'aime.
Je chanterai toujours, lorsque l'on te maudit,
Tes savanes, tes bois, où le bison bondit.
A toute âme, aspirant aux émotions neuves,
Je dirai: " Venez voir le plus grand de nos fleuves,
Ce vieux Nil des déserts où Chateaubriand but,
Et les mille affluents qui lui portent tribut...

Viens voir les Indiens, dans nos pinières vertes,
En cercle, insoucieux, couchés sur leurs couvertes;
Viens voir le nègre heureux pêchant au bord de l'eau;
. . . .
Sous la hutte de pin, oh! viens, comme Pavie
Retrouver dans nos bois l'indépendante vie,

[5] See *Les Meschacébéennes,* preface.

76

Et chanter, tour à tour, dans ta mâle fierté,
Dieu, la grande nature, avec la liberté.[6]

This same love and longing is expressed in nearly all of
the thirty-three poems in this volume, all written in
1836, 1837, and 1838.

Oui, je pars ; il me faut la solitude immense !
Quand je vois ma forêt, alors je recommence
A revivre, à rêver sous mes pins toujours verts,
A m'égarer pensif, à composer des vers.
Quelle est donc, réponds-moi, ta puissance secrète
O solitude sainte, ô mère du poète.[7]

They are addressed to different friends and members
of his family and record many incidents of his life. He
expressed disappointment in his love for a young creole
girl, his renunciation of this dream of love, and his desire
to live in solitude :

Oh ! puisque pour toujours, enfin, j'ai renoncé
A ce rêve d'amour qui m'a longtemps bercé,
A cet ange divin, ma créole inconnue...
. . . .
Oh ! désormais, je puis vivre content de peu,
Et plus sage aujourd'hui, je ne forme qu'un vœu :
C'est de m'ensevelir dans une solitude
. . . .
Je suis, je suis toujours l'enfant de la savane.[8]

In another he addresses his mother who had reproached
him for giving up the study of law, and for going to the
plains to stay, and tells her that he lives like Robinson
Crusoe because he is a poet :

Si votre enfant aimé vit comme Robinson
Oh ! c'est qu'il est poète et que son cœur est bon.[9]

[6-9] *Les Meschacébéennes*, p. 8-9 ; 65 ; 10-13 ; 20.

In another he records his grief at his mother's death and his rebelliousness toward God:

Mon Dieu, je t'ai maudit, et tu m'as pardonné;

and in still another, he speaks of his dread of being buried in Paris and begs Anatole, to whom the poem is addressed, and Adrien, to have him buried in his creole forests:

Loin du lac Pontchartrain reposera ma cendre.
Au sol de l'étranger, sous quelque tertre nu,
Le créole, exilé va dormir inconnu.
. . . .
A vous, poètes donc, Adrien, Anatole,
Le soin de me choisir, dans la forêt créole,
. . . .
Le tertre du repos, le tumulaire abri.[10]

His fear of death is seen also in

Pontchartrain, lac sacré, recevez du poète
Le solennel adieu!
Je meurs, je vais enfin d'une vie inquiète
Me reposer en Dieu.[11]

Rouquette returned to Louisiana in 1839 and spent his days reading under the trees of his loved forests and smoking pipes with the Choctaw Indians. In 1846 he married, and realizing that his life of dreaming had to cease, he went to Arkansas, where he tried to support his family, first by teaching and then in the grocery business. He was not successful and soon returned to Louisiana where he wrote poetry again.

In 1856 he published his *Fleurs d'Amérique,* a volume much larger than his first publication. It contains 107 poems written between 1839 and 1856. There are four

[10-11] *Les Meschacébéennes*, p. 104-105 ; 107.

sections: the first has no title, the second bears the title
" *Chansons et Chants divers* ", the third " *Chants Patriotiques* ", and the fourth " *Chants Religieux* ". A poem
at the beginning is addressed to Hugo, Béranger, Barthélemy, E. Deschamps, and Berthaud, and speaks of
the author's care-free existence under the pine trees.
He asks these poets to listen to his verses from America
as they had once listened to those from France   The
poems in this collection, though still showing his love
for his home, are now more varied in subject matter and
are not so melancholy.   Happy in his forests, the poet
thinks of his friends in Brittany, wonders what they are
doing, and expresses willingness to live there if he could
not remain in his Louisiana:

O Bretagne! Bretagne! ô pays des grands cœurs!
Beau pays des landiers et des genêts en fleurs!
Vieux sol armoricain, vieille terre celtique!
S'il me fallait jamais quitter mon Amérique,
S'il me fallait jamais, banni du Pontchartrain,
Fuir mon beau ciel natal pour quelque ciel lointain;
. . . .
Je volerais aux lieux où dort Chateaubriand.
. . . .
J'irais te demander, ô Bretagne, un asile.[12]

His love for his pipe is seen in several places in these
verses:

Oh! comme avec bonheur dans ma vieille cabane,
Le front ceint des flocons de la nicotiane,
En relisant le Dante, et Milton, et Soumet,
Nous fumerons tous deux, frère, le calumet.[13]

. . . .
Assis près du foyer noirci par la boucane,
J'aspirais la vapeur de la nicotiane.[14]

[12] *Les Fleurs d'Amérique,* p. 94.
[13] *Les Fleurs d'Amérique,* p. 102.
[14] *Les Fleurs d'Amérique,* p. 67.

His longing for solitude made him very unhappy during his stay in the city:

> Qu'a-t-il été faire à la ville
> Naïf poète, enfant des bois,
> Parmi cette foule servile?
> Il était heureux autrefois![15]
>
> Qui me rendra mon ermitage
> Mon banc de bois près du tison?
> Oiseau que l'on retient en cage,
> Oh! que je maudis ma prison![16]
>
> Rendez-moi ce que je regrette
> Ma cabane, le coin du feu,
> La paix, le bonheur, la retraite,
> La solitude avec Dieu.[17]

He uses Alexandrine metre more often than any other in both collections of poems, but the *chansons* of the second volume, written to be sung to various melodies, are nearly all in eight-line stanzas with an alternation of eight and nine syllables.

Rouquette's fear of death in his youth was a groundless one, for he lived to an advanced age and is still remembered by many people of New Orleans. He died there in 1890.

No less ardent in his love for Louisiana was Adrien Rouquette, brother of Dominique. Adrien was born in New Orleans in February 1813. He received his early education in his native city, and was sent to Transylvania College in Kentucky. He went later to Philadelphia to study. At the age of sixteen he was sent to France where he attended the Collège Royal de Nantes. After a visit home, he went back to France to study law, but, like

---

[15] *Les Fleurs d'Amérique,* p. 86.
[16-17] *Les Fleurs d'Amérique,* p. 82; 84.

his brother Dominique, having no taste for it, he soon gave it up. In 1840 he published in Paris his first book of Poems, *Les Savanes, poésies américaines.* In his preface he maintains that only an Americain can paint the scenes of America, and praises the *Meschacébéennes* of his brother.

Adrien attributes his inspiration to God, to his family, and to his country. His poems, like those of Dominique, breathe a fervent love for the forests and for solitude, but they have not the sad note found in Dominique's. His stay in Kentucky aroused in him great admiration for Daniel Boone, and he expresses a desire to exile himself in a desert as Boone had done. He varies the subjects of his verses, expressing in one of them regrets for Paris, a literary Paris which appeals to him,

Paris, où chaque coin est marqué d'un libraire.

Two of the poems of this collection are narrative in character. " *Le premier voyage de Colomb* " and " *Saint Paphnuce et Sainte Thaïs l'Egyptienne* ". All of these save one or two are written in Alexandrine verse. The later ones show more and more the religious fervor which finally impelled him to study for the priesthood.

He began studying in 1841 and was ordained in 1845. He labored first in the parish of the St. Louis Cathedral, but, inspired by his love for the Indians, he went as a missionary to the Choctaws with whom he worked for about twenty years. He died in New Orleans in 1887.[18]

In 1847 a volume of poems, *Essais Poétiques,* was published by Charles Oscar Dugué. The preface of the collection was written by Adrien Rouquette, who praises

[18] See baptismal and death records at the Cathedral, and C. R. A. L., July 1920, article by J. A. Reinecke.

Dugué's verses very highly. He asserts that they are
spontaneous. He had often heard Dugué say that he
always waited for inspiration, and received before he
gave.

It is very fitting that Adrien Rouquette should have
written the preface to this volume, for there is a great
similarity between the two poets—the same love of Louisiana, the same longing for her when absent, the same
love of solitude, and the same religious fervor. Such
poems as *A M. C. A.* which begins:

> Oh! viens visiter ma chère Louisiane;

" *Souvenirs de la Louisiane* "; " *Souvenirs du désert* ";
" *Le chant du départ* ", with its

> Je suis un enfant des forêts
> Et ne veux pas d'autre patrie,
> Que toi, Louisiane chérie,
> Objet de tant d'amers regrets;

" *Le Meschacébé et ses bords* "; and " *Les bois de Bara-
taria* " show the ardent passion of the young poet for his
native land. Many of his verses are addressed to his
family and friends. In one to his brother, "*A M. H. D.*",
he confesses that he dreams of a brilliant future. Several
are entitled " *A M. A. R.* " and " *A M. D. R.* " and
show his great admiration for the Rouquette brothers. In
the last poem of the collection, " *Aux détracteurs de la
poésie* ", Dugué rises almost to sublime heights in his
defense of poetry. Its enemies had said that the lyre
brings no good to the State; and the poet disputes this
statement. He thinks that the lyre revives the flame of
patriotism and enthusiasm in time of war, and fills the
home with sweet songs in time of peace. In the olden
days the poet was the interpreter of the gods and had a

place of great honor. The king's courage was roused by his words, and the poet was crowned with laurel like an athlete.

Dugué was born in Jefferson Parish, Louisiana, in 1821. He too was sent to France to be educated. On his return to Louisiana in 1843, he elected journalism as his career and contributed articles to the *Orléanais* and to the *Propagateur Catholique*. During the year 1850 he was editor in chief of the French part of the *Orléanais*. He studied law with his father and practiced for a while. He then accepted the position of President of Jefferson College in St. James Parish, and labored there until the Civil War. During his leisure moments he wrote poetry. A great many of the poems in his *Essais Poétiques* bear the date of 1840, and betray that they are the work of a young man to whom form means very little.

In 1872, Dugué decided to go to Paris to have his *Homo, poème philosophique*, published. His health which was poor when he left home, failed him and he died in Paris in 1872.[19]

Erato, published in 1840, is a collection of short poems by Dr. Alfred Mercier. Most of them express the author's personal feeling toward his native land and his joy in his return to it. The storm on the sea in " *Sur Mer* " only retards his course in reaching his real subject,— his river, his forests, and his old servants. " *Patrie* " is his joy in his return :

> Après huit ans écoulés dans l'absence,
> Je viens revoir le ciel de mes aïeux.
> . . . .
> Voici mon fleuve aux vagues solennelles;
> . . . .

[19] Facts about him were given me by his niece, Mrs Gil Toboada of New Orleans.

Après huit ans écoulés dans l'absence,
Fidèle oiseau, je reviens à mon nid.
Le Souvenir vaut parfois l'espérance;
C'est un doux songe où l'âme rajeunit.

" *L'Incendie du Temple* " expresses the feeling awakened in all the spectators by the burning of the old St. Louis Hotel; and " *La lune des fleurs à la Louisiane* " is a picture of revelry on April 1st with all the young girls under a balcony.[20]

Tullius St. Céran has made Louisiana and Louisianians the subject of a great many poems, but he has not shown such passionate love for the State as have the Rouquette Brothers, Dugué, and Dr. Mercier. St. Céran expresses his admiration for his fellow countrymen in general in " *Le Louisianais* " and in " *La Poésie; les Créoles essentiellement poètes* " and for certain ones in particular in verses addressed to them, as " *Souvenir d'enfance, à mon ami Charles Bayon* ", " *Sur le capitaine Arnaud* " and " *A M. Lepouzé* ". His " *Ancien Collège d'Orléans* " shows his tender feeling for the old college where he was educated.

These, with a number of other poems, were published in a volume entitled *Rien ou Moi* in 1837. This collection is furnished with a great amount of explanatory material such as notes, dedication, and preface by the author, in which he explains fully his title and his ideas. On the title page he even makes the statement that the price is $5.00 and that the printing and binding of it had cost him $1000.00. He dedicates it " Aux hommes de lettres ignorés dont la pénurie pécuniaire s'oppose à la publication de leurs œuvres ".

His title is literally the " To be or not to be " of

---

[20] See Chapter VII, part II for information about Dr. Mercier.

Shakespeare, for he must be himself or else cease to be. His language is to paint his sensations and be the mirror of his heart, which he offers to the view of the reader (preface VII). He does not believe in polishing and re-polishing his work before giving it to the printer and does not wish the advice of men who are subject to error just as he is, although a little more correct, perhaps, in the matter of shades of phrasing. He does not yield to any one in the matter of thought and enthusiasm which are, to him, the two most important characteristics of the poet. If, in the heat of composing, he has failed to make a participle agree, he does not want proof readers to correct his mistake; he prefers to let the reader's good sense act as his intercessor. He boasts that he has never appropriated the thoughts of others although, with his knowledge of three languages and with his good memory, he could easily have done it so well that no one would have recognized it. Whenever he borrows the thought of some one else, he gives full credit by admitting that he is imitating. He concludes this rather long preface by bidding disenchanting prose, whose yoke is tiring to him, to be gone; and inviting his favorite language, poetry, to come.

The poems in this collection are written in various metres from Alexandrine down to one-syllable lines. These latter appear in a composition whose sole merit, the author says in a statement at the beginning of the poem, consists in the difficulty conquered, for verses of one syllable are like a lute with one string, there is no harmony possible. For his longest poems and the ones on which he evidently concentrated most thought, he uses Alexandrine verse. His rhymes are sometimes mere play on words.

The subjects of these poems are practically the same as

the ideas which the author sets forth in his preface. In the first stanza of the dedication to " Mes souscripteurs ", he speaks of the rapacious printer who makes genius crowd back into the heart of authors; and in the last ones, he explains his title. Other poems are " *Mon indifférence pour la critique ou la louange* "; and " *Un volume de poésies où j'ai découvert des phrases entières de Bossuet* ".

In 1840 he published another collection which he called *Les Louisianaises*. He speaks again of the high cost of printing and adds that this expense, together with the limited number of subscribers, forces him to divide his verses—three thousand in number— into two volumes, the second of which will appear when " *Plutus le voudra* ". He is happy over his choice of a title which will add to his immortality, for there is no Creole so indifferent as not to want to know these *Louisianaises,* and none so lacking in chivalry as not to be willing to defend them.

The poems in this collection resemble the ones in *Rien ou Moi* in form, but there is a great difference in tone. The author is still very personal and the longest of the poems, " *La Havane en 1819 et 1839; ou plutôt moi-même à ces deux époques* ", is filled with incidents relating to his own life and to the death of his brother. He has lost his wife too[21] and seems to be broken in spirit. He does not vaunt his powers and talents as in the earlier collection. The greater part of the poems are without other title than an address to some of his friends, as " *A M. P. Pérennes* ", " *A M. Alexandre Latil* "; and several poems written by his friends to him are inserted in the collection.

[21] See the poem " *Mon Réveil* " page 87 of *Les Louisianaises* in which he speaks of " deux tombeaux " and explains that they are those of his wife and brother.

St. Céran published another volume of verse entitled *Chansons*. This may be the one that he was going to publish when " *Plutus le voudra* ", but there is no way of ascertaining the date of the publication. The title page, preface—if it had one—and first poem are missing in the copy in the Howard Library. A great many of these *Chansons* had already been printed in the *Abeille* during the years 1831 and 1836. They are set to familiar airs and are usually for special occasions such as banquets of the " Tirailleurs d'Orléans "; anniversaries of the Battle of New Orleans; the anniversary or death of friends, or similar occasions, and are generally quite short.

St. Céran was born in 1800. He was educated at the Collège d'Orléans and shortly after finishing school, established a private school in New Orleans in which he made a specialty of teaching languages. This was in 1825.[22] He died in New Orleans on May 26th, 1855 at the age of fifty-five.[23]

In a collection of poems called *Esquisses Poétiques* by Madame Emilie Evershed there is a group called " *Dix Louisianais* ", for which Louisiana serves as a background. The " *Magnolia* " is a very pretty picture of the magnolia with the different people who come to rest under its shade:

> Toi, du sol Louisianais
> L'armement et la parure;
> Toi qui grandis sans culture
> Dans ses immenses forêts,
> . . . .

[22] See *Les Louisianaises,* p. 36, l. 9, for the statement that he was born in 1800; p. 24 of *Rien ou Moi* for his youth at the Collège d'Orléans; and the *Louisiana Gazette,* June 23rd, 1825 for the establishing of his school.

[23] See a notice of his death in the *Louisiana Courier* for May 27th, 1855 (found in the City Hall Archives).

Beau magnolia centenaire,
Combien as-tu vu d'amans,
Entendu de doux sermens
Et protégé le mystère?
. . . .
Dis-moi combien de doux noms,
Confiés à tes fleurs blanches,
Et balancés sur tes branches
Sont tombés sur les gazons?

Fraîche oasis de feuillage
As-tu vu le voyageur,
Quand il s'arrêtait penseur
Sous ton vert et frais ombrage?

" *La Savane* " is filled with the gladness of children
playing and dancing, with the fragrance of flowers, with
the song of the birds, and with the joy of young lovers:

Sous la fraîche brise,
Dès le grand matin,
Sous le ciel sérein,
Quelle est la surprise,
Des enfants joyeux,
Dont les blonds cheveux,
Longs anneaux de soie,
Que le vent déploie
En les caressant,

Quand dans la savane
L'herbe sous leurs pieds
A peine se fane
Tant ils sont légers.
Et dans la savane
Les mille senteurs
Des nouvelles fleurs,
Dont l'air diaphane
Est tout saturé
. . . .

Sol louisianais
Tes vertes savanes
Ont des caravanes
Venant des forêts,
Des lointains rivages
Ces hôtes d'un jour
Ont, dans leurs ramages,
Des notes d'amour ;
. . . .
Puis on voit là-bas
Sous le saule souple,
Un bien jeune couple
Qui parle bien bas.
. . . .
Adieu donc savane
Que rien ne te fane,
Que ta grande voix
Des villes, parfois,
Porte à ton silence
Douce souvenance,
Des enfans joyeux
Que tu fis heureux !

" *L'Oranger* " shows young girls dreaming under the
orange branch, of the time when they will have a wreath
of its blossoms ; and " *Le Lac* " sings the charm of Lake
Pontchartrain with young girls and boys on it.

Beau lac, ton onde unie
Est charmante le soir
. . . .
Beau lac, tes fraîches lames
Qui caressent, les soirs,
Ces frêles jeunes femmes
Et leurs cheveux noirs
En longs anneaux, en tresses,
Se jouant sur tes flots,
De ces trésors si beaux
Qu'avec loisir tu presses,
Tes flots sont-ils jaloux,
Quand des regards bien doux

De jeunes hommes viennent
Comme les aspirer?
Quand tes flots les amènent
Plus près pour adorer?

Madame Evershed was a native of France, but it is not known when she came to Louisiana. All of her works, though published in Paris, bear on the title page " Emilie Evershed de la Nouvelle Orléans ". She died in New Orleans in January 1879 at the age of 79. She was before her marriage Emilie Gabrielle Poullant de Gelbois.[24]

A great number of the poems of Jules Choppin were inspired by the natural scenery around him. In " *Au Bayou St. Jean* ", " *Assis au bord du Bayou St. Jean* ", and " *Encore le vieux bayou* ", he expresses the thoughts that come to him as, seated on the bank smoking, he sees the moon rise and the stars appear. " *Toujours le vieux bayou* ", " *Les cloches au bayou* ", and " *Le retour des oiseaux* ", show the strong fascination that the Bayou has for him, for everything is connected with it in his mind. " *Le chêne de Bienville* " and " *L'Arbre du grand-père* " exhibit his sensitiveness to the old trees that have a story to tell.

Choppin was born in St. James Parish, Louisiana, in 1830, the son of August Choppin and Marie Le Bon, both of France. He was educated at Georgetown College in Washington and later occupied the chair of Latin and Greek there. Returning to his native state, he opened a day school in New Orleans. He taught French and English in private schools of that city and also at Tulane University. He was a great lover of literature and wrote a number of poems, many of which were lost to the

[24] See a record of her death in the Board of Health office.

outside world on account of his modesty and dread of publicity. He died in New Orleans in 1914.[25]

The scenes of Louisiana are the inspiration also of several poems by Georges Dessommes. His " *Mandeville, Paysage Louisianais* " is dedicated to friends in France and pictures the beauties of the oak trees with the long moss that covers them. What the poet loves about this landscape is its tranquillity, its distance from the noise of the world. To him the only thing lacking is a chain of mountains. " *Un soir à Jackson Square* " and " *Afternoon* " describe very forcefully two of the favorite places of New Orleans. Jackson Square is filled with workmen who go there every evening, and among whom the writer likes to be. He recounts several incidents that occur one evening as he takes his usual walk. " *Afternoon* " is a picture of Canal Street " couverte de monde " and enlivened by a gay crowd of shoppers.

Dessommes was born in New Orleans in 1855. In 1860 his family went to France where he was placed in school in the Lycée Louis le Grand. In 1870 he returned with his parents to Louisiana. Dessommes began writing poetry early, and in 1876 some of his verses were published in the *Comptes Rendus de l'Athénée Louisianais*. He continued writing for the *Athénée* and his published poems can be found in its magazine between 1876 and 1894.

He was a close observer of nature as is shown in " *L'Orage* ", a good word picture of the gathering of a storm, of a proud pine tree standing haughtily, waiting for the storm to break in its fury, and of a forest struggling with the wind. A long poem by Dessommes, " *L'Ob-*

[25] Facts about Choppin were obtained from his son, Ernest Choppin of New Orleans. His poems were published in the *Comptes Rendus de l'Athénée Louisianais* from 1896 to 1905.

session " portrays the drama in a young man's soul when, hearing a voice calling to him, he departs in order to follow where the voice leads. He feels his love for his sweetheart die in his heart on comparing it with the love that he feels for nature. However, when his sweetheart finally leaves him, he realizes his great love for her and feels that no consolation remains to him. A little poem by Dessommes, " *Berceuse* ", so impressed the *Athénée Louisianais* by its musical quality, that this group offered a prize to the one who would write the best music for it.

Although endowed with genuine poetic talent and having dreams of a life devoted to literary pursuits, Dessommes had to resign himself to the inevitable, and follow a calling which would better enable him to support his family. He is now engaged in business in Montreal, Canada.[26].

A splendid picture of the New Orleans carnival is shown in a little poem. " *Mon Pays* ", by Madame Gabrielle Shoenfeld. It appeared in a collection of ten poems and three short stories called *Poésies et Nouvelles*.

Madame Shoenfeld (née Hockersmith) was born in New Orleans and has always made her home there. She was educated in the Orleans Institute. She is now at the head of the Southern College of Music in New Orleans. She began writing, for her own pleasure, poetry that was published in the *Abeille* and that was highly praised by the editor of the paper. Other works by her were published by the *Athénée Louisianais*. When Mlle Jennie Allard of the Opéra Français was in New Orleans, she read some of Madame Shoenfeld's verses to her audiences. This appreciation, together with the encour-

[26] Facts about his life were given me by Mr. Dessommes himself.

agement of her friends, induced Madame Shoenfeld to publish her works in book form.[27]

In " *La Toussaint de la Nouvelle Orléans* ", Auguste de Chatillon gives an account of the custom of covering all the graves with flowers on All Saints' Day. He represents a voice from a tomb asking that a flower be thrown on the grave of a stranger, buried there and without a family. In " *A Mon ami Eugène Chassaignac* ", de Chatillon expresses great praise of the talent of Eugène Chassaignac, memories of whom were awakened in him by the sound of an organ; and in " *L'Eglise* " he exalts the mission of the church. His artistic interests are seen clearly in his poem " *Michel Ange* " in which he describes his conception of Michel Angelo. In the opinion of the poet, Michel Angelo was lonely in the midst of his grandeur, and would rather have been loved than have painted the " Last Judgment ".

The verses by De Chatillon were all published in the papers of New Orleans after his arrival there. He was a native of Haut-Rhin in France. He came to New Orleans about 1846, and lived there until his death on August 4th, 1859, at the age of 45.[28]

Madame W. J. Sheldon's " *A Travers les siècles* " is a long poem in Alexandrine verse in which the author records the history of Louisiana from the discovery of America by Columbus to its cession to the United States. She expresses her love for her native city in " *Loin* " where she says:

La cité du croissant où naquit ma famille
. . . .
C'est là que je suis née, où je voudrais mourir.

[27] Facts about her were obtained from a personal interview.
[28] See the New Orleans directory of 1846 for the first ap-

Poems like " *Le groupe des barques* ", " *Avril* ", and
" *Réflexion* " are more spontaneous in their expression.
" *La barque vide* " was inspired by the sadness of the
famine sufferers in Brittany.

The majority of her poems are sonnets for special occasions, as for instance, " *A un artiste* " which is an
expression of praise for the pianist, Joseph Lhevinne.
Another sonnet is dedicated to François Coppée and sings
his praise. " *Réponse à l'auteur de Jérusalem* " is a
reproof to Pierre Loti for seeking Jesus in the Holy Land,
for

C'est au tréfonds du cœur qu'on retrouve la Foi
Ce n'est pas dans un lieu, ce n'est pas dans les cho-
[ses.

" *Guynémer* " was written on the occasion of the death
of that hero, and " *Chant en l'honneur de Virgile* "
praises Virgil for his pastorals but especially for his
Aeneid. Her " *Echo des Pêcheurs de lune* ", which
opens

C'est dans le rêve bleu que les pêcheurs de lune
Jettent tous leurs filets, flottant sur les roseaux—,

shows best the powers of her imagination and the lyric
quality of her style.

Madame Sheldon (*née* Roche-Lauve) wrote under the
nom de plume of " Ulla " and many poems by her were
published by the *Athénée Louisianais.* She is now living
in Mexico[29]

POEMS OF PATRIOTISM—LOUISIANA

This great love for Louisiana manifested itself also in a
great number of patriotic poems. The earliest of these

pearence of his name. See his death record in the Board of
Health office at the City Hall.

[29] See the *Comptes Rendus de l'Athénée Louisianais,* January

were Julien Poydras'[30] " *Prise du Morne du Baton Rouge* " in 1779; Tullius St. Céran's " *Mil huit cent quatorze et mil huit cent quinze* " in 1838; and Urbain David's " *Les Anglais à la Louisiane en 1814 et 1815* " in 1845.

Louis Allard wrote one short poem, " *Les Anglais à la Louisiane* ", 1815, describing very briefly but clearly the arrival of the English at New Orleans and their defeat. This was published in Allard's collection called *Les Epaves*.

During the Civil War, Dr. Charles Deléry showed his ardent patriotism by using his pen in favor of his country. Besides being a collaborator of the *Renaissance Louisianais* which gave him an opportunity to write in that paper, he published a poem, " *Les Némésiennes Confédérées* " in 1863, and an article " *Les Yankées fondateurs de l'esclavage aux Etats-Unis et initiateurs du droit de Sécession* " in 1864.[31] The titles of these works show obviously that they were bitter towards the Federals. This bitterness is seen also in a pamphlet written in 1868, *Le Spectre noir ou le radicalisme à la Nouvelle Orléans*. The war was responsible for Deléry's writing a poem that was not political in tenor, called " *Le dernier chant du guerrier orateur* ". It was dedicated to one of the heroes of the South, Colonel C. D. Dreux. Dreux had enlisted at the first cry of war and was killed at the very beginning. The poet recounted his patriotic words to his comrades before leaving home. Instead of returning

1922, p. 22 for the little that I was able to find out about Madame Sheldon besides what she tells in her poems.

[30] See chapter I for a discussion of Poydras' poem and chapter III for St. Céran's and David's.

[31] I was unable to find these. Alcée Fortier mentions them on pages 45 and 63 of his *Louisiana Studies*.

triumphant to relate his experience to his friends, he
was brought back home to be buried.[32]

Placide Canonge wrote several patriotic poems that
were set to music and sung during the Civil War. One
of these is " *La Louisianaise, chant patriotique sur l'air de
la Marseillaise* ", published in 1861. It is patterned very
closely after the " *Marseillaise* ", being at times only an
adaptation of it.

> Entendez-vous ce cri terrible
> La république est en danger,
> Cri puissant d'un peuple invincible
> Que Caïn voudrait égorger (*bis*)
> Le fratricide en sa furie
> Pour frapper n'hésite jamais,
> C'est une ivresse de forfaits,
> C'est le délire de l'impie
> Aux armes citoyens !
> Debout ! mousquet en main.
> Marchons ! Marchons !
> La Liberté
> Nous montre le chemin !

Another, written later in the war, in 1864 is " *Brise du
Sud* ". This was set to music by Eugene Chassaignac
and sung both in the original and in its translated form
entitled " *Exiled* ".

POEMS OF HERO WORSHIP—NAPOLEON

That France was present, too, in the minds of these
writers of poetry, is shown in the great number of verses
that extol Napoleon as a hero greatly to be loved.

In 1841 *Les Impériales* by Auguste Lussan, author of
Les Martyrs de la Louisiane, was published. The book
derived its name from four poems in the collection that
have Napoleon as their subject. " *Les noms immortels* "

---

[32] See chapter IX for information about Deléry.

praises the brave soldiers of Napoleon and lists his battles; " *Vœu* " expresses joy that the body of Napoleon is back in France; " *Au roi sur la translation des cendres de l'empereur* " thanks the king for having Napoleon's body brought to France, and adds that posterity will unite the two names, that of the king and that of the emperor; and " *Les trois journées du grenadier de Ste. Hélène* " depicts the love of an old soldier for his general. The old grenadier, watching over Napoleon's grave in Saint Helena, is ever looking toward the sea for the sight of the tricolor on a ship that would take his master home. After many years of faithful watching and waiting, the sound of cannons is heard, a troop arrives from the ship, and in answer to the old man's " Qui vive " the leader says:

> France et cortège d'honneur,
> Chargé de rapporter le corps de l'empereur.

The old soldier is overjoyed and addresses his former general:

> Sire, vous l'entendez, votre cendre sacrée
> Va reposer enfin sous la voûte dorée;
> Votre vieux grenadier, sire, l'y conduira.

The other poems in the collection have various titles. " *Comment est-il tombé ?* " treats of the funeral of Marshall Ney and praises him as a glorious soldier; " *Un combat en Afrique* " is fashioned after Hugo's " *Djinns* "; " *A la Nouvelle Orléans* " represents New Orleans as holding the scepter of the world with her commerce; " *A mon père, mort à l'Hôtel des Invalides* " tells of the service of the father of the author in war; and " *L'Histoire et la Victoire du 8 janvier 1815* " is a dialogue between Victory and History in which Victory asks History to reward the heroes of the battle of New Orleans with immortality.

c.

8

Lussan spent several years in New Orleans. It is said that he was an actor. He died there in poverty in 1842.[33]

Napoleon is the subject of a poem by Charles Testut in his second collection, *Les Fleurs d'été,* which appeared in 1851. Testut says that most of the poems in *Les Echos,* his first collection, were the work of different periods long past, and had no connection and no order. This new volume is the work of a riper age, and religious feeling and love of goodness are the bases of it. He has dedicated each poem to some one to whom he wanted to render homage, sometimes as a sign of gratitude and sometimes as a sign of sympathy or esteem.[34]

After a dedicatory ode " *A mes fleurs d'été* ", Testut has a poem, " *Sainte Hélène* ", which shows his great admiration for Napoleon and his deeds of valor. To the poet, St. Helena is still a sacred place, for

Sa cendre n'est plus là, mais les branches du saule
    Pleurent encore sur son tombeau.[35]

Jules Choppin's poems with Napoleon as subject present effective contrasts. " *Le berceau—la tombe* " describes the different feelings of this hero; in Corsica he thinks of the great deeds he would like to do; and in St. Helena he is like Prometheus bound to a rock and unable to accomplish anything. " *Elle et lui* " is a good example of antithesis. This time it is Napoleon and Josephine who are seen just before his departure for

[33] See the New Orleans directories of 1841 and 1842. A pencil note beneath his name in the copy of *Les Impériales* in the Howard Library says that he was an actor. Armand Lanusse tells in his preface to *Les Cenelles,* p. 12, of meeting the funeral procession of the author of *Les Martyrs de la Louisiane* a few years before. It was on its way to the potter's field where the body was to be buried.

[34] Preface of *Les Fleurs d'été,* p. x, xiv.

[35] See *Fleurs d'été,* p. 33.

his second marriage. The wife, who had adored him for his heart and not for his genius, is depicted as broken-hearted.

A poem, " *Le retour de Napoléon* ", written by Victor Séjour,[36] one of the collaborators of a collection called *Les Cenelles,* is filled with sympathy for Napoleon. The author blames France for leaving her great man in St. Helena during his lifetime when he had yearned so ardently to see France and had cried:

> Mon Dieu, je donnerais mon âme,
> Pour le revoir encore.

Now that he is dead and cannot enjoy his return, he is brought back amid great pomp and splendor.

Napoleon was greatly admired also by P. Pérennes, who expresses his feeling toward this hero in his " *Funérailles de Napoléon.* " He describes the dead Napoleon as a great person still feared by his enemies, for his

> ......*cercueil fait trembler leurs trônes.*

Pérennes also shows himself a hero worshiper of two other heroes. In his " *Conquête du Mexique* " he furnishes a good picture of Montezuma and his power over his people. The poem ends with the sight of the victorious Spaniards. Montezuma's era is over and his army is dead. It is to Victor Hugo, however, that Pérennes sings the greatest praise. In his " *A Victor Hugo sur*

[36] James Wood Davidson in his *Living Writers of the South,* p. 501, says that Séjour was born in New Orleans in 1809 " although M. Vapereau in his *Dictionnaire Universel des Contemporains* states that he was born in Paris towards 1816 ». I looked for Séjour in Larousse's *Grand Dictionnaire Universel* and found a statement that he was born in Paris in 1821. This is the same Victor Séjour of whom Davidson speaks, for each article lists his dramas, and the titles are the same. I was unable to find Séjour's baptismal registry at the Cathedral or at the City Hall.

son désir d'être admis à l'Institut ", the author expresses
his great love for Hugo and classes him with Homer and
Virgil :

> Jamais l'antiquité sous sa couronne épique
> Rome virgilienne et la Grèce homérique
> N'ont poussé de plus nobles chants.
> . . . .
> Et toi, grand comme Homère et roi par le génie ;
> . . . .
> Hugo, tu tiens tout dans tes mains ;

No one could give comfort as Hugo could :

> . . . . aucun d'une main sûre
> N'a su même adoucir nos pleurs ;
> Toi seul tu soutiens l'homme ou relèves la femme,
> Et Christ harmonieux, tu jettes de ton âme
> Un chant d'amour à nos douleurs ;

Now that he desires a place among the " Immortels ",
he should not have to wait on the threshold until he gains
entrance to the Academy.   This body should be only
too glad to receive him as a member :

> Pour cueillir ses honneurs dois-tu courber l'épaule
> Attends que l'Institut ait haussé sa coupole,
> Géant, pour te laisser passer.
> Radieux et puissant, n'incline pas la tête ;
> On t'a vu comme un chêne affronter la tempête ;
> Quand ton ciel rit, pourquoi fléchir ?
> Règne enfin, tu le peux, courtisan débonnaire,
> Ton laurier qui fascine un corps retardataire
> Doit s'imposer et non s'offrir.

Hugo is joined in the author's mind with Napoleon,
and the poems ends :

> Monte à ton tour, poète, et bondis par la terre,
> Va, comme allait Napoléon.

After spending some time in the deserts of Mexico, Pérennes, a Frenchman, came to New Orleans where for several years, until 1843, he kept a private school.[37] During his stay in New Orleans he published various poems in the *Abeille* and the *Courrier de la Louisiane*.

HERO WORSHIP—ROMANTIC POETS OF FRANCE

Other writers have followed the example of Pérennes in choosing the romantic poets of France as objects of admiration. Georges Dessommes in a sonnet, " *Mes Poètes* ", praises Hugo highly. For Dessommes, Gautier was too careful of the plastic side, Lamartine had too much soft laughter, and De Musset had too much poison in his flowers. Only Hugo could awaken the hope of the poor disillusioned child.

Charles Testut expresses his love for the poetry of Lamartine in his " *A Lamartine* ". A collection of Lamartine's poems was Testut's first book. He was proud of the volume and would take it into the garden with him in order to feast on the thoughts, the songs of love, and the rhymes found in it. Testut puts all this information in the poem itself. Another one, " *A Béranger* ", shows his ardent admiration for the verses on liberty written by Béranger.

---

[37] See page 7 of the introduction of *Guatimozin*, a drama by Pérennes, in which he states that " absent de France depuis plusieurs années, je vivais dans un désert du Mexique " and page vi where he calls himself a " pélerin froissé des orages du Mexique " whom the people of Louisiana received with indulgence. See the New Orleans directories for 1841 and 1842. It is not known when he left Louisiana.

POEMS OF SADNESS

Not only did the works of Charles Testut express admiration for Lamartine and for Béranger, but they are also filled with sadness because of the unfortunate experiences of his life. He came with his wife and child to New Orleans in 1843, fleeing from the great earthquake which had just occurred in Guadeloupe in February. Impressed by the hospitality accorded him in his trouble by the people of New Orleans, he settled there.[38]

In 1849 he published a volume of poems *Les Echos,* " whose sweet voice chased away his despair ".[39] The first poem, " *La Guadeloupe* ", describes the tropical beauty of the little town of Point-à-Pitre and the earthquake that came to destroy all its loveliness. It is filled with pathos and expresses the sadness of the refugees, their lack of hope, their search for a place to go. His having to leave home had a deep effect on the poet, and many of his verses are lamentations of exile. " *L'Exilé* " and " *Le chant de l'exilé* " show very clearly this feeling in him. The latter is similar to Chateaubriand's " *L'Exilé* " and is at times almost an adaption of it, as in the following lines :

> Las ! quand reverrai-je ma plaine
> Et mon torrent et mon grand chêne,
> Le pays et ma jeune sœur
> Qu'à peine
> Je vis naître avec bonheur
> Au cœur !

In his various poems, Testut has shown himself very versatile in the use of meters. He employs the long and the short verse with equal success. His poetry is correct in form without that studied effect so often found.

[38] See a letter from him printed in the *Abeille* for March 15th, 1843 for an account of his fleeing from Guadeloupe and his reception in New Orleans.

[39] See *Les Echos,* p. 204.

With him, form and subject matter are of equal importance.

Testut left New Orleans and went to Mobile in 1850. In the *Orléanais* of August 14th, 1850, he wrote a *Chronique de la Mobile*. This same paper on October 4th, 1850, announced that Charles Testut was going to publish a French-English paper, *The Alabama Courrier* in Mobile, on November 5th, 1850. No record can be found of how long Testut remained in Mobile. No doubt he did not stay very long, for he published his *Fleurs d'été* in New Orleans in 1851, and in April of that year he founded *La Semaine de la Nouvelle Orléans*.

On May 3rd, 1855, the *Abeille* published a letter from Testut in which he states that he has been ill for six months, has twice been near death, and is not yet out of danger. He has composed, during his illness, some poems that he plans to publish under the title of *Cahier Poétique*. It is to be a pamphlet of about sixteen pages and will cost twenty-five cents. He feels that time and illness have not injured his faculties. He says he is very poor and is doing everything that he can to keep his " head above the water ". On June 4th, 1885, he explains in the *Abeille* that he did not have the *Cahier Poétique* printed in time, and intends to make it a part of the monthly publication, *L'Album Poétique de la Louisiane,* which he is planning. Each number is to have sixteen pages and will cost twenty-five cents. He calls on the poets of Louisiana, especially the unknown ones, and asks them to send him their best work so that he may include it in his *Album*. He does not know when he will begin, but he will announce it. He calls attention to the novels and poems which he has published, and to his efforts to propagate and preserve the French language in Louisiana. On July 11th, 1855, he asks those

who wish to help him to publish the *Album* to leave
their names at the office of the *Abeille*. He has enough
contributions ready for six months of printing. He
hopes that the first number will appear at the beginning
of the next month. This notice is still appearing in the
Abeille on August 21st, 1855. It does not occur after
that date and diligent searching failed to discover any
other notice of his collection, or of its ever having been
published.[40]

Charles Oscar Dugué also shows a tendency to melancholy thoughts in " *Désanchantement* " when he says:

Mais, j'ai vu se ternir le beau ciel de ma vie,
De mes illusions la coupe s'est tarie...

also in such poems as " *A Gilbert* " when he envies Gilbert his early death; and " *Le Génie des savanes* " when
he represents the *génie* as appearing to him, rebuking
him for his thoughts of suicide, and leading him away
from the abyss.

Sadness is the keynote of *Les Ephémères* of Alexandre
Latil. He was a native of New Orleans, born October
6th, 1816.[41] His life was a sad one and full of suffering
for he was stricken with leprosy when quite young. For
twelve years before his death in 1851 he was confined
to his bed. Seeing his future broken and being chained
to a bed of illness with no illusions and no hopes left to
him, he takes consolation in literature. He tells that he
had always passionately loved the works of Béranger,
Barthélemy, and C. Delavigne, but he had never felt
the desire awaken in him of acquiring a literary reputa-

[40] Testut's name does not occur in the New Orleans directories after 1892. I was unable to find any record of his
death.
[41] See his baptismal record at the Cathedral, his death
record at the City Hall, and a notice of his death in the *Orléanais*, March 18th, 1851.

tion for himself. He published some of his poems in the newspapers and received great praise, but he had no idea of publishing a volume of them until he was so urgently solicited to do so by men of superior worth, that he consented. He wanted to leave his friends and relatives a souvenir.[42]

The result of this solicitation was the collection he published in 1841 called *Les Ephémères,* comprising twenty poems dedicated " A mon père et à ma mère ". The prevailing metre in this collection is the twelve-syllable verse arranged in stanzas of six lines. The majority of the poems are impregnated with Latil's sufferings. " *Amour et Douleur* " tells the story of his love for a young girl and his grief at not being able to offer her anything, because there was nothing on the horizon for him. In " *Déception et Tristesse* ", he thought for a moment that he saw happiness shining but it was a delusion, and he was tempted to suicide. " *Le Désir* ", is a cry of pain, and " *Désenchantement* " is full of melancholy, for he had long hoped to recover. He now realizes his hopeless condition; and his lyre is broken. Other poems with this same sadness are " *Le Départ* ", " *Mélancolie* ", and " *Prière à elle* ". There are several, however, that are more joyful in character as: " *Epithalame pour le mariage de ma sœur* ", " *Ode à Béranger* ", " *A Barthélemy* ", and " *A mon grand-père* ". The last of these four has almost a joyful tone when the poet tells how his old grandfather, who had retired after fifty years of life as a sailor, used to delight his grandchildren with the wonderful tales of his voyages. These show the same care about form as the others do, but they lack the fire and appeal of the author's personality.

[42] See *Les Ephémères,* preface, p. viii.

POEMS OF LOVE

The thoughts expressed in most of the love poems are quite different from the feeling of hopelessness of Alexandre Latil. In 1847, two volumes of such verse, *Les Cenelles* and *Les Epaves* appeared.

Les Cenelles, choix de poésies indigènes is dedicated " Au beau sexe Louisianais ". The first poem is a " *Chant d'Amour* " and most of the others are love poems also, for with very few exceptions, each one of the sixteen authors who contributed to this collection sang praises of some lady-love. Some of the verses are mere exercises in rhyming and have no claim to be called poetry.

Armand Lanusse seems to have been the chief agent in the publication of this volume. He wrote the dedication and the introduction, and contributed sixteen poems to it, more than any other single poet. They have such titles as " *A Elora* ", " *Le Dépit* ", " *Les Amans Consolés* ", " *La jeune fille au Bal* ", and " *Le Portrait* ". None of them has any great value. Lanusse was born in New Orleans and spent his life there as a teacher. He died in 1861 at the age of 55.[43].

The most striking of the verses by Camille Thierry in this collection is " *L'Amante du Corsaire* " in which he depicts very effectively the anxiety of a young girl for her absent lover. While some of the poems by Thierry are rather uneven and " jerky " in meter, most are in regular four-line stanzas with alternation of twelve-syllable lines and six-syllable lines.

Thierry was born in New Orleans in 1814.[44] Educated

[43] For information about him see the city directories and his death record at the City Board of Health office.
[44] For information see the *Comptes Rendus de l'Athénée Louisianais,* January 1878, p. 134. There is in the Howard Library

in France, he returned to New Orleans for a short time but later went to France to live. In 1855 he settled in Bordeaux and lived there until his death in 1875. The poems he contributed to *Les Cenelles* and a few which were published in the *Orléanais* in 1850 represent his work done while in Louisiana. In France he published a collection of verse, *Les Vagabondes,* which contained some of the poems already printed in Louisiana.

Pierre Dalcour ranks next to Lanusse and Thierry in so far as the number of poems contributed to this collection is concerned, but most of Dalcour's are acrostics or a play on words. Though born in New Orleans, he was reared and educated in France. On a return visit to New Orleans he wrote the verses he published in *Les Cenelles.* He returned to France to live and spent the remainder of his life there.[45]

The poems of note which Mirtil Ferdinand Liotau contributed to this volume are " *Mon vieux chapeau* " and " *Un condamné à mort* ". The first expresses a spirit of *badinage,* and the second has a religious tone. Liotau was a native of New Orleans, and died there in 1847.[46]

What the other collaborators donated to *Les Cenelles*

in New Orleans a volume of poems which has no title page and no name of the author. The late Mr. Beer, former librarian at Howard Library had written in pencil on the front, Thierry's name as author. It is a long poem in six cantos treating of the Crimean war. Several works are listed on the back of this volume with the statement: " Du même auteur ". The titles are :

> *Fleurs et débris, poème intime*
> *Les océanides, poésies maritimes*
> *Les Créoles, poésies d'outre-mer*
> *L'Empire et ses gloires ou le passé,*
> *le présent, l'Avenir, poésies nationales.*
> *Odes, Chants et Poésies diverses.*

[45] See Desdunes : *Nos Hommes et notre Histoire,* p. 47.
[46] See his death record at the St. Louis Cathedral.

is so small—for the most part, one poem each—that judgment as to their value can hardly be rendered.

The second volume of poems, *Les Epaves,* was published under the name of " Un Louisianais ". The editors claim that the manuscript was found in a trunk left on the banks of the Mississippi river after the wreck of the boat *Hecla*. It was rescued from the old trunk together with some other objects which caused them to recognize Louis Allard as the author. Since Allard denied that the work was his, the editors published it under the title *Les Epaves*. They quote from the preface in which the author explains what he intends to treat in his work. Part I is to tell of " l'amour, encore, de l'amour, l'éternel amour, ce dieu si vieux et pourtant si jeune et si nouveau ". Part II is to contain free translation in verse from the epigrams of Martial.[47]

The first of the original poems, " *Epitre A——,* " sixteen pages long, is in lines of ten syllables with no definite rhyme scheme. The poet shows his classical knowledge throughout. He compares himself with so many of the gods, and tries in so many ways to gain the favor of his love, that the reader is in a maze before the end is reached. The other long poems in the collection: " *Le Lit* ", an elegy; " *Phèdre* ", an *épitre* to one of the actresses of the French theatre of New Orleans; " *L'Immortalité* "; and " *Le Message* ", written the day of President Adams' speech at the opening of Congress, December 1827, are all labored and heavy in tone. Several of Allard's short poems, as " *Au moqueur* ", in which he describes the effect on him of the mocking bird's song; " *Niagara* ", in which he wishes he could engrave his beloved's face on the rock beside Niagara

[47] Preface, pp. i, ii, iii, v.

so that there might be two wonders to look at instead of one; and " *L'Amour enfant* " are somewhat lyrical in nature, but they leave the reader with the feeling that the poet's heart is not very much affected by the sentiments he tries to express.

Louis Allard of New Orleans was born about 1877. He was educated in Europe and lived there for several years. He came to Louisiana and lived on his plantation on Bayou St. John. During the last seven or eight years of his life, he was ill and his plantation had to be sold at a forced sale.[48] It was bought by John McDonogh[49] who, at his death, bequeathed it to New Orleans. It is now a part of City Park.[50] By special agreement with John McDonogh, Allard continued to live there, and in accordance with his dying wish, was allowed to be buried there when he died in May 1847 at the age of 70.[51]

Dr. Alfred Mercier uses nature as an introduction to a short love poem, " *Le Matin* " which opens with a picture of the dew, the birds singing their morning songs, and the freshness pervading everything. Then a young girl appears at the window and recites verses to her lover. Other poems of his which are merely descriptive of young girls are " *Lolotte* " *and* " *Gentille Suzette* ".

[48] For information see his death record in the City Board of Health office and a notice of his death in the *Courrier de la Louisiane*, May 18th, 1847.

[49] See record 38 (January 23rd, 1845 to May 18th, 1846) in the Conveyance Office at the Court House in New Orleans which says that there was a seizure sale of his property in the name of the Consolidated Association of the Planters of Louisiana on June 11th, 1845. This record says that his plantation on Bayou St. John, measuring 18 arpents front by 43 arpents in depth, together with buildings, etc., also 19 slaves, 10 horses and mules, and 40 head of cattle were sold to John McDonogh for the sum of forty thousand five hundred dollars.

[50] See the " *History of New Orleans City Park* " compiled by Alfred Wellborn.

[51] See J. S. Kendall's *History of New Orleans*, vol. ii, p. 683.

Madame Shoenfeld's *Le Vase de Sèvres* is a charming little poem of only five stanzas, perhaps on the motive of Sully-Prudhomme's famous poem. The love of the couple on the vase is broken with the vase.

> Sur un vase de Sèvres
> Je vois un couple heureux
> Qui se donne des lèvres
> Un baiser d'amoureux.
>
> Depuis plus d'une année
> Ils s'aiment sans bouger
> Sur l'ample cheminée
> De ma salle à manger.
>
> Là, leur pose suprême,
> Leur immobilité,
> Me révèlent l'emblème
> De la fidélité.
>
> Mais d'éternelle extase
> Le doux et long baiser
> Sont morts avec le vase
> Que je viens de briser.
>
> Ainsi fuit la constance,
> Ainsi finit l'amour ;
> Les cœurs et l'espérance,
> Tout se brise en un jour.

This was one of the poems read by Mlle. Allard (p. 92).

" *Elmina* " by Onésime de Bouchel is a love poem which tells of the death of a young girl when autumn comes, and pictures her lover's grief over the loss. In " *Rêverie* " the effect of a spring twilight is seen on the soul of the poet, making him forget the world and its cares and think only of love to which all the world bows its head.

De Bouchel was the son of Victor de Bouchel who

wrote a history of Louisiana. He was born on a plantation in Plaquemine Parish, educated at the Jesuits' College in New Orleans, and after graduation, made his
home in that city. He liked traveling and visited many
of the principal cities of the United States, Canada, and
Europe. Like his father, he was very fond of literature
and of writing poetry. He published some of his verses
in the *Comptes Rendus de l'Athénée Louisianais*.

His poems bear the mark of youth, yet they show that
he had talent which would, no doubt, have been seen
more clearly when age and experience had ripened him.
This opportunity was denied him, for he died on August
16th, 1880 at the age of 33.[52]

RELIGIOUS AND MORALIZING POEMS

A long hermitic poem, " *L'Antoniade ou la solitude
avec Dieu* ", written by Adrien Rouquette, belongs in a
group of poems showing faith in God. " *L'Antoniade* "
consists of several parts. Part I contains a series of
short poems which the author calls *Preludes*, and most
of which are in praise of solitude. He makes them very
effective by titles in which he employs antitheses as
" *Les Royautés et la République Américaine* ", " *Les
hommes d'action et les hommes de prière* ", " *Le Pape
et les souverains temporels* ", and " *L'Indien et la Robe-
noire* ". Part II, *Poèmes Patriotiques,* is full of
patriotism and love of America. Part III contains two
sections, " *Le Conciliabule Infernal* " in which the " demon of the city " and the " demon of the desert " take a
prominent part ; and " *Les deux esprits lutins* " in which
the domestic ass and the wild ass express pity for each

[52] Information about his was obtained from Mrs. Octavia de
Bouchel of New Orleans and from his death record at the City
Board of Health office.

other. The wild ass prefers the swarm of mosquitos in the forests to the hu man swarm of jealous brothers. Part IV, " *Le nid d'aigle* ", is another exaltation of solitude.

All of this is an introduction, so to speak, to what follows, a volume in itself. It treats of three stages in the religious life: conversion, the choice between the world and the desert, and finally God alone. Then follows an epilogue stating that the poet has dreamed of this book for a long time in his woods and if it helps some soul in its struggle upward, he will bless the spirit that inspired it.

This poem is so long that it defeats its own purpose, for very few ever read through it, to reach the epilogue and learn of the poet's ardent hopes.

Charles Testut expresses his religious faith in such poems as " *A de jeunes filles qui venaient de faire leur première communion* "; " *Le 8 juin 1850, jour de la mort de ma fille* "; " *l'Athée et le Croyant* ", a dialogue on the goodness of God and on life after death; " *Stabat Mater Dolorosa* "; and " *Le Cimetière* ". In poems like " *Le Jour des Morts* ", " *Mystère* ", " *Dies Dolorosa* ", and " *Le Jour des Rois* ", he exhibits a deep religious yearning and resignation. His love of humanity is clear in " *Donnez* ", a long poem in which he exhorts the rich to help the poor; in " *La peine de mort* ", a poem against capital punishment; and in " *Le Convoi du pauvre* ".

Jules Choppin's religious fervor is embodied in " *Qu'est-ce que l'âme* ", in " *N'en doutez pas* ", in " *Jésus sur la Croix* ", in " *La Résignation* ", in " *Le Signe de la Croix* ", in " *Une Trinité* ", and even in " *La Défense de l'âne* " when he points out that this was the animal Jesus chose to ride for his triumphal entry.

" *Homo* " by Charles Dugué is a long poem in Alexandrine verse consisting of seven cantos. The first canto is a dialogue between A Voice (God) and Man. In the other six cantos the Voice alone speaks. Man is doubtful of his right to any pardon or mercy on account of his many sins which he enumerates. The Voice convinces him and he surrenders himself. The Voice announces that it is by the force of his will that man reaches heaven and if he does not succeed, it is because he has not wanted to do so. The human will alone, however, is not enough; divine help is needed, and sacrifice is necessary here below. Duty fulfilled is the germ of happiness. Power, beauty, honors, riches, all leave sadness in the heart. Even knowledge gives a desire we never attain. Faith and Reason agree. Faith is Reason surrounding itself with mystery. A great man is necessary, but one must be careful not to consider the charlatan and ignoble flatterer of as much worth as the real orator. These are some of the many ideas crowded by the author into " *Homo* "—" Poème philosophique " as he calls it. " *Homo* " is didactic in tone and contains a great amount of repetition.

A didactic trend is seen also in many of the shorter poems in *Poésies Diverses* of Madame Evershed's collection. " *Douleur* " mentions various griefs; but none is so poignant as that of a mother whose son, for whom she has sacrificed her all, drives her from his heart; " *Pauvre Femme* " has the same idea: that of a woman grown old who feels that she is not wanted and thinks there is no pity for her. However, she will stifle her sobs in the bottom of her heart and no one shall see her grief. At times, Madame Evershed tries to be philosophical, as in " *Les joujoux* ", in which she says that each one has his plaything although different in nature: the child has the doll, the financier has his money, the warrior has his

113

weapons, and the poet has his verses. In " *Le Rideau* "
she maintains that each one wears a curtain before his
face at times; and there are some who would not want to
be seen without this curtain; in " *Le Miroir* " she philoso-
phizes on the different messages of the mirror according
to whether one is twenty, thirty, thirty-five, or forty.

Dr. Alfred Mercier, published in 1890 " *Réditus et
Ascalaphos* ", a long philosophical poem written in
Alexandrine verse and describing the efforts of Réditus
to find solitude for his work because he realizes that:

> La vie est un naufrage; et l'étude est le port
> Où l'homme qui se sauve attend la douce mort

In some of his other writings Dr. Mercier displays a
tendency toward moralizing.

Nature is the subject of many of them. In " *Les Soleils* " and " *La Nuit* ", he personifies these two. The
suns boast of being conquerors of the night and owners
of the infinite expanse. The night disputes this and says
that her dark abysses extend far beyond the distances
where the sun's rays fall. Dr. Mercier often presents a
description of nature and draws a moral from it. " *La
Houle* " opens with the sea in perfect calm suddenly
aroused and transformed by a gigantic swell; so, in the
sorrowing heart, grief sleeps for a while and calm is
believed to reign when, suddenly, a bitter memory arises
and changes all. In " *Soleil Couchant* ", nature is only
a pretext for reminiscences which easily lead to moralizing. The thought expressed is usually superior to the
form of expression in Dr. Mercier's work.

This tendency to moralize is seen in several of the
other poets also. Léona Queyrouze in her descriptions
of nature quickly turns from the scene that she is describing in order to moralize. " *Vision* " describes a cemetery

with its calming effect on the tired, wounded soul. The
poèt's thought passes to the future and she emphasizes
the idea that time breaks and destroys the ripening plans,
the ideals, and the hopes; and pride, ambition, and
pleasure all pass. In " *A ma mère* ", a falling star causes
the poet to wonder what the star can be. She lists a
series of fancies that come to her as possibilities: perhaps
it is a jewel taken from the neck of a fairy and thrown
down by a goblin; perhaps it is a kiss; perhaps, the soul
of a child; perhaps, the skate of a fairy; perhaps, a germ
of love falling from heaven for some poor arid soul; or
perhaps, the star has merely become bored with shining
and falls. Like the star, everything on earth grows pale
and is extinguished.

Léona Queyrouze was born in New Orleans where she
still lives. She has written several articles and many
poems, which have been published in the *Comptes Rendus de l'Athénée Louisianais*. This magazine printed in
its issue for September 1885 (p. 230), a letter written to
her by François Combes, president of the Academy of
Science and Letters of Bordeaux, which praised her
verses. He had read them before the Academy and this
body wished to congratulate her. Under the pen name
of " Constant Beauvais ", she published a number of
poems in the *Abeille* from time to time.[53]

She has written a great many sonnets for various occasions. One of these " *Palpitans* " is dedicated to François Combes; one is in response to some lines written to
her by a friend; one is " *Au Docteur Charles Turpin* ";
and one is " *Exil* ", a farewell to one's native land. Her
" *Fantôme d'Occident* " is dedicated to Lafcadio Hearn.

[53] Information about her was obtained from Mr. Rouen and
from the *Comptes Rendus de l'Athénée Louisianais*, March 1887,
p. 322.

She has written two very pretty descriptive poems, " *Idylle* " which tells of a grandmother's fête, and " *La lyre brisée* " which pictures a lyre that once belonged to a poet.

In her sonnets, " Constant Beauvais " uses the conventional rhyme scheme of French sonnets with variations in the last three lines only. In her poems, her meter is quite varied, but she has some very poor rhymes, as when she uses the same word with different meanings in both verses.

In " *Amaranthin* " Auguste de Chatillon describes a certain young man and draws a moral from his description. A handsome young fellow—" Il était bien beau, le bel Amaranthin "—only son of a butcher, thinks himself irresistible and believes that everyone is in love with him. He is kind-hearted and adopts a boy and girl whom he educates. Then follows the moral of the poet:

> On ignore, on suppose, et toute erreur abonde,
> Et voilà comme on dit du mal de tout le monde.

Pérennes' " *Une Fleur au désert* " opens with a description of a desert in its calmness and joy. A lonely rock had been sad and grieved until a light wind brought a flower seed which cast roots and bloomed in the shadow of the rock. The description changes to a storm in the desert. The rock protects the little flower. The poet is led to moralize on the fraility and the short life of the flower, and the strength of the rock.

Onésime de Bouchel uses two short poems in fable form to teach morals. " *Le Chien et ses amis* " pictures a dog, who so long as his master lived, had plenty and entertained his friends. After his master's death, the dog is in want, he seeks the aid of his friends, but finds them deaf to his appeals.

Morale.

Si fortune vous favorise
Vous aurez tout, amis, honneurs;
Mais si misère vous maîtrise
Vous serez seul dans vos malheurs

"*La Louve et la brebis*" has for its moral " Do unto others as you would have them do unto you ". A wolf, who had stolen many lambs from an old sheep, returns one day to find that her cub has been stolen. To her cries of grief, the old sheep says:

A vous donc maintenant d'être blessée au cœur;
Malheureuse, apprenez à plaindre le malheur.

POEMS SOCIALISTIC, POLITICAL, AND SATIRIC

Les Lazaréenes, a collection of poems by Joseph Dé-jacque, was published in sections in 1857. A short intro-ductory poem explains the name *Lazaréenes* which comes from Lazarus, who represents poor, suffering, humanity waiting on the threshold of opulence, claiming a place at the festive board, and crying " Equality ". These poems appeared for the first time in Paris in 1851 but lawsuits and seizures prevented their sale except clandestinely. Later some of those that had escaped were printed in pa-pers in Belgium, England, and the United States. The author asks his readers to read to the end before judging his work.[54]

This collection has for subtitle *Fables et Chansons, poé-sies sociales.* Most of the poems are fables showing from the beginning general socialistic tendencies in the author. " *Le Minotaure* " pictures the minotaur as killed by Theseus and shows that the oppressors of nations, always devoured by thirst for carnage, and choking out every effort of democracy, are the minotaurs which socialism, like Theseus, will have to kill. "*L'Architecte*"

[54] See *Les Lazaréennes,* preface.

tells of a man who built his mill on the foundation of an old castle which soon crumbled away. The architects of society are trying to do the same thing. In the " *Bûche et Scie* ", the people are the trees cut down by the scepter of the arbitrary, who are the law. Several poems bearing the date of " Ponton le Triton 1848 " tell of the course of the refugees of 1848, of whom Déjacque was evidently one. " *La Famille du Transporté, épisode de Juin 1848* " tells of a man dragged away from his home and wife and child; " *Aux ouvriers de Cherbourg, en réponse à un meeting en faveur des transportés* " thanks all of those who, when near prisons, fraternize with the prisoners; " *Prononcé sur la tombe d'un proscrit le 24 Juin 1852* " tells of the death of one of the refugees and bears the date, London 1852. The dates of some of the poems are Jersey 1853, and New Orleans 1856. In all of them the author pays attention only to content, and is not concerned much about form.

When *Les Lazaréenes* began to be published, the outside cover stated that they would appear every week beginning Sunday, January 4th, 1857; the price of the complete work would be two dollars, and the price of each number would be twenty-five cents. The series ends after the appearance of the eleventh part.

Déjacque was a Frenchman who came to New Orleans about 1855. In February and April 1856, short poems by him began to appear in the papers there. It is not known what became of the author,—whether he continued in exile, or whether he had returned to France. He seems to have departed from New Orleans about 1858.[55]

Political questions were oftentimes the subject of Jules Gentil's poems. The Boer War was the source of

[55] See the New Orleans directories for 1857 and 1858.

inspiration for many of them. " *Ils sont morts* " deals with that subject; " *Honte et Gloire* " blames the conqueror, England, and glorifies the conquered Boer; " *Anarchisme* " shows keen disapproval of England; " *L'Inde meurt de faim* " is filled with praise of Victoria but regrets the condition of her subjects in India; " *Or, sang, et crime* " and " *Kruger* " deal with the Boer War again. " *Elle* ", which mourns the death of a little girl; " *Dolor* ", which shows weariness with life; and " *Le moqueur* ", which is full of praise for the mocking bird that he loves, portray a less militant side of the poet's nature. His favorite metre is the four-line stanza with six syllables to a line.

Gentil was born in Blois, France, on August 15th, 1825, and educated at the Collège de Blois. He went to Louisiana in 1853 and served on the faculty of Jefferson College at Convent as professor of French and Spanish. He wrote articles for *L'Abeille de la Nouvelle Orléans* and for *La Démocratie Française* of New Orleans, for *L'Intérim* of Convent, and for *Le Meschacébé* of St. John parish.

He became the proprietor of the *Louisianais* of Convent and took an active part in the politics of his day. He was an able writer and always fearless of public opinion. He was a great lover of literature and wrote poems as well as political articles. Many of the former were also published in the *Abeille*. Gentil spent all of his life, after coming to America, in the little town of Convent, and died there in 1911.[56]

Félix de Courmont caused a literary battle to ensue in New Orleans when the first numbers of his *Taenarion* appeared. After the prospectus—a long poem declaring

[56] Facts about him were obtained from his daughter, Miss Blanche Gentil of Convent, Louisiana.

its purpose and explaining its name—a satire against Cupidity was published. The editor of the *Revue Louisianaise,* on August 18th, 1846 (p. 462), speaks of its " biting verses " and its " pitiless scourging " as well as its interesting subject. He seems to feel that the first two enhance its richness. He recommends it to his readers. Again in a later number, September 13th, 1846 (p. 585), he recommends these satires as possessing energy and conciseness and an expression always exact. He warns the author, however, not to be personal and spoil the effect. Others evidently did not have the same opinion as this editor, for in the *Courrier de la Louisiane* for September 24th-25th, there was a long article called *Les Satires de Félix de Courmont* signed " Anti-Taenarion ". After a short complimentary paragraph, Anti-Taenarion began to criticize de Courmont's satires. One might think oneself back in the days of the appearance of Du Bellay's *Défence et Illustration de la Langue Française,* so bitter was this attack on De Courmont on somewhat the same grounds as those on Du Bellay. This anonymous writer attacked De Courmont's grammar, his syntax, his rhyme, his figures of speech, and finally the title. De Courmont had said that the temple Taenarion was near the Parthenon, but his critic takes issue with him and says that only in De Courmont's verses are these two near each other, for in reality they are at the two extremes of Greece.

De Courmont answered in the *Courrier de la Louisiane,* the next week, October 2nd, 1846. His poem is very sarcastic and accuses all his enemies of being leagued against him and of saying, " Il succombera ". He assures them that he will not succumb but will continue his satires. He quotes Corneille, Crébillon, and La Fontaine as having taken poetical license with grammatical constructions and uses their example to defend himself. He assumes the role of martyr and declares that his enemies wish to place a crown of thorns on his brow. They may accomplish this, but still he will not succumb.

Anti-Taenarion answers again in the same paper on October 7th, 1846, ridicules the defense of De Courmont, and reiterates what he said before. He accuses De Courmont of trying to play the role of Barthélemy, but assures him that Barthélemy's mantle is too big for him and that he stumbles in its great folds.

The editor of the *Revue Louisianaise* on October 11th, 1846 (p. 50) speaks of this literary war and expresses the hope that De Courmont will continue his publications. Evidently he did, for the *Courrier de la Louisiane* on April 16th, 1847 has a notice of the *Recueil de douze livraisons* of the *Taenarion* and gives a review of it by " Philo-Taenarion ", who is very frank in his admiration of the work. He speaks of the rare boldness of thoughts and images, and of the " picturesquely incorrect style ". He says that the critics have missed the point and that the mistakes were part of the sarcasm and irony of de Courmont's talent. These poems had appeared at different times and were now collected, and published with the addition of some new ones. Of the twelve poems— thirteen, including the prospectus—two, " *La Cupidité* " and " *Les Solliciteurs* ", are the most important because of their subject matter.

De Courmont was an attorney in New Orleans at the time of the publication of his satires. Whether they brought him unpopularity or not is not definitely known, but no trace of him can be found in New Orleans after 1848.[57]

[57] His name occurs in the New Orleans directory for 1841 and

NARRATIVE POETRY

The narrative poetry of the French literature of Louisiana finds its best representative in Madame Emilie Evershed. In 1843, she published a collection of poems under the title *Essais Poétiques*, consisting of two distinct parts: two long narrative poems, " *Une Faute* " and " *Le Château désert* ", and a collection of short poems called *Poésies Diverses*. The two long poems are both written in Alexandrine verse in five cantos each. " *Une Faute* " tells the story of a young girl, Néida, whom her father has reared in all simplicity and who is the pride of his heart. She grows up into a charming girl, meets Léon, the young lord of the manor, loves him, and is betrayed by him. The old father dies of grief, and Néida, in despair, listens to the old curate who persuades her to become a sister of charity and nurse the sick of the country. She finds great comfort in her service to others until one day her peace is disturbed by the arrival of Léon who is brought in unconscious and in a serious condition. She nurses him three days until he is out of danger and does not reveal herself to him. She conquers any tender feeling left for him and puts earthly love out of her heart altogether.

The second of the long poems, " *Le Château Désert* ", relates a tale of a lonely old castle of long ago. The lovely bride is brought there by her husband who becomes so cruel to her that all gladness is gone from her life, and she is relieved when he goes away on long journeys to spend months and even years. One day while visiting relatives in town, she meets a cousin who falls in love with her. She returns his affection but

the years following. It does not appear in 1849. No record of his death could be found.

keeps all knowledge of it from him. Before his departure for the war, he goes to the old castle to bid her farewell. While he is there, fate wills that the husband should return. Knowing his wicked nature, the wife hides the young man in the oratory of her apartments. The husband, suspicious and crafty, guesses that some one is in there, and in order to be avenged, has the door, the only opening to the oratory, walled up by stone masons, so that the young man smothers to death. The husband remains at home several weeks to torture his wife and finally leaves her while she is dying. She leaves a will giving all of her possessions to the poor, and ordering that the castle be left abandoned and isolated with no human trace to profane it. In this poem the descriptions of the lonely castle, the conjectures of the people about it, and the stories of ghosts in it are very vividly narrated. The scene between the wife and husband when the door is being sealed is very realistic in its cruelty.

Madame Evershed is at her best in narrative poetry since she does not display the spontaneity and verve necessary for a more lyric type. She evidently recognized this herself, for in other volumes that she published, she had long narrative poems forming the first portion. In 1846 she published another collection called *Esquisses Poétiques.* The long poem here is called " *Arthur* " and is written in Alexandrine verse and in eight cantos. A young nobleman, Arthur, loves a poor girl, but marries a girl in his own station in life in order to please his father. Unhappiness results when the wife realizes that her husband loves another, and she commits suicide. In the meanwhile, Arthur's father confesses what he has long wanted to confess, that is, that Lucie, the poor young girl, is his daughter and Arthur's sister. Grief at his wife's suicide and at his father's revelation causes Arthur to lose his mind. The father, in remorse, follows him from place to place, and Lucie devotes her life to caring for the two. The plot is well developed here but the writer is prone to be didactic.

In *Une Couronne Blanche* published in 1859, Madame Evershed follows her usual plan of a narrative poem and *Poésies Diverses*. In this volume, however, the narrative is given in a series of shorter poems each of which, when taken separately, tells a story of its own. The first, " *Une Couronne Blanche* ", gives the name to the group and is like those of the other collections in that it pictures the unfaithful husband, the long-suffering wife, and the child of the husband and his mistress. Here the child is a little blind girl, Rosita, whom the wife takes and rears with her own little girl, Bianca. The story of the death of this blind child's mother as told in the poem " *Rosita, l'aveugle* " in one of the best works that Madame Evershed has produced. It is full of feeling and more natural than most of her poems.

Of the *Poésies diverses* in this collection " *Le Laurier Rose* " and " *Sa Robe nuptiale* " are short narratives showing the power of superstition. In the former, the mother warns her daughter not to dream under the pink laurel, for according to a saying, all dreams dreamt under this bush are deceiving. The young girl does not heed her warning but lingers there, speaking aloud her love for a young priest whom she has seen. An Indian who loves her, hears her, and in jealousy, stabs her. In " *La Robe nuptiale* ", a young girl, in spite of the superstition that it is bad luck to display a wedding dress before the wedding ceremony, shows hers to her friends. Her marriage is unhappy, her crown is that of a martyr, but she wears it with a smile.

" *L'Amazone* ", by Charles Testut, is a narrative poem

of a young Amazone who, on the day of her betrothal to one whom she does not love, flees to join her lover and never returns to the manor. This story is written in eight-syllable lines which are in accord with the brisk movement of the young girl in flight.

Amadéo Morel published in 1858 a long poem in Alexandrine verse, " *Récit sur l'ouragan de la Dernière Isle* ". This recital is very poor poetry but has a fine description of a storm. The author pictures very vividly the fright and excitement of the people when the storm is predicted and when it appears, as well as the destruction it leaves in its wake. There are two parts to the poem —the author promised a third later if his subscriptions warranted it—and each part is an account of the suffering of people floating in the water on tables and planks, and tortured by hunger, until they are finally rescued by two men in a boat. The third part was never finished.

Morel was born in New Orleans in 1813. He left his native city and went ot Napoleonville, Louisiana, where he continued to reside until his death in 1867.[58]

Alexandre Barde has written two narratives of a ballad nature, " *Isabelle de Victor* ", 1846, and " *Peppa* ", 1848. The first is a story which the author says was often told him by the old men of the country. A knight, lover of the rich Countess Isabelle, tells her that for love of her he would defy God. At this boast, the lightning flashes and the castle becomes a mass of ruins. Later a hermit passing sees the words " Ave Maria " imprinted on it. Where the marble manor once was there now

[58] See his birth record in the Cathedral Archives, and a letter to Mr. Beer, former librarian at the Howard Library, from Mrs. Oscar Dugas, president of the Napoleonville Circulating Library, saying that he died in Napoleonville on November 15th, 1867, before he finished the poem, with part III. This letter is pasted in the copy of the *Récit* in the Howard Library.

stands an old tree under which merry children are often seen dancing rounds. The second selection shows a proud courtesan telling the story of a young Cuban girl who walked the shore unafraid with a dagger at her belt. A young corsair came to woo her and offered her his brig and all he had. She accepted and became queen of the brig. The superb courtesan ends the story thus:

> Veux-tu connaître cette femme?
> C'est celle dont l'œil de flamme
> S'entr'ouvre et rayonne sur toi.

Barde has not collected his poems in a volume but many of them appeared separately in the newspapers of New Orleans. The shorter ones show a diversity of subjects. " *Romance* " is a lover's lament that his beloved has married another man; "*Chant de Noces* " wishes happiness to a young bride and groom; " *Impressions* " records a change in the soul of the poet brought about by " Le jour des morts " and his walk in the " Champs des morts " on that day; " *A Rachel malade* " is in honor of the actress Rachel who was ill at the time in Havana; and " *Journal d'un Candidat* " with its three divisions, *Avant, Pendant,* and *Après,* is a very clear description of the feelings of a candidate during the different stages of the election. While these short poems show the talent and versatility of the author, he is at his best in the narrative ones. His poetry is full of inspiration but he is not always careful of its form. Charles Testut, one of his contemporaries, said of him: " Alexandre Barde est pour nous l'écrivain le plus poète qui ait jamais écrit en Louisiane ".[59]

Georges Dessommes has contributed to narrative poetry his " *Geoffrey le Troubadour* ", a long poem in easy,

[59] See *Portraits Littéraires,* p. 16, published 1850.

simple verse with songs inserted. It is a ballad of one of the knights of old in the court of love, when the gallant troubadour sang his songs to the ladies of the court. Geoffrey had been left, when a baby, on the banks of a stream and had been picked up by passers-by. At the age of sixteen, he hears an old traveler tell of the lovely Princess Bertha in a far-away country. She is just Geoffrey's age and is also a poet. He feels a longing in his heart and departs. After long, weary wandering, he arrives at the capital, where he finds a contest in progress. Bertha is to bestow her hand on the victor. Geoffrey breathes forth his soul in his song and is crowned the winner, but worn and exhausted from his long journey, he can not stand the strain, and falls back dying in the arms of the princess.

This poem is very much like Edmond Rostand's drama, *La Princesse Lointaine,* and is based on the story of Geoffroi Rudel and the Countess of Tripoli.

Dr. Alfred Mercier began his literary production with narrative poetry. In 1842 he published in Paris " *La Rose de Smyrne* ", and " *L'Ermite de Niagara* ". He calls " *La Rose de Smyrne* " a *Nouvelle Poétique en trois chants* and gives a picture of Oriental life with its sad condition of women. Hatidla, sold by her father to old Aroun, laments her fate in very touching words. A young Greek comes, they meet, and love each other. Their love is discovered by Aroun and the Greek is killed. The faithless wife is dragged before the judge and condemned to be stoned. The other poem, " *L'Ermite de Niagara* " tells the old story of a wounded pale face who comes to as Indian hut, sees an Indian girl, loves her, and is killed by the jealous Indian lover. It is really a drama in verse in five acts. The third acts is, to a certain extent, a digression from the story. The young lover, Elfrida, has jumped into the falls of Niagara. The remainder of the act gives his experiences under the falls. The nymphs are singing, in chorus, the praises of Niagara. When the Genius of the falls tries to make Elfrida promise obedience, the Father of Waters intercedes in his behalf and he is allowed to go. He is met by the goddess of vengeance and hatred who tells him that his race is pursued because of its actions toward the Indians. As Dr. Mercier's talent for narration is greater than his skill in verse, he is more successful in writing narratives in prose than in poetic form.[60]

HUMOROUS POEMS

Humor is used more skillfully by Edgar Grima than by any other of the poets of Louisiana. Many of his verses are very light and witty. The first he published, " *Pour un nickel* ", tells the story of a young man who chivalrously offered to pay the car fare for a young girl when she discovers she has no money. Much to his surprise, he finds that he has none either, and is about to rush out of the car, when he remembers that he wears a nickel on his watch chain as a good luck charm. He takes it, pays the fare, and, in the course of time, marries the girl. " *Une défaite en amour* " describes a humiliating accident that occurred to a young lover. Just as he was about to receive a kiss from his sweetheart, his heel turned and he fell into the water. " *Mon premier testament* ", is a very amusing picture of a young man who had pretensions to being a notary, and who went through wind and rain one night to the home of a dying man in order to draw up his will. He was deeply angered when he found that the

[60] See Chapter VII for further information about him and his novels.

man possessed a horse, five pigs, a skiff, six turkeys, and his dilapidated furniture which he wanted equally divided among his eight nephews and ten nieces. This poem ends with the young man's advice.

> ......écoutez mes leçons
> Soyez planteurs, docteurs, avocats, militaires,
> Prêtres, hommes d'états, constructeurs ou maçons,
> Mais, surtout, croyez-moi, ne soyez pas notaires.

His " *Chantecler fils* " is a clever discussion between two mother hens of the foolish ambitions of new born chickens, and their disdain of Chantecler Junior, who enters with his " air de petit prince. "

This humorus turn of Grima is seen even in poems of a more serious nature, in which he shows sad scenes which he quickly relieves by a swift turn of the picture. In contrast to the grief of the young girl over the pet bird that she has lost, he gives the complacency of the cat who has eaten it, in " *La Veille de Noël* ". The tenderness of a mother's love is shown in the poems " *Le baiser* ", " *Les Deux Siècles* ", and " *Sans Mère* ". The poet's love of nature and the religious feelings awakened in him by the quiet and tranquillity of the wood are seen in " *Au bois* ".

Grima furnishes a revised edition, as it were, of the old fable " *La Cigale et la fourmi* ". He makes of " Madame Cigale " a person who has moved from the country to the city and has taken a garret to live in. Bored by having to care for her large family, she seeks places of amusement where one does nothing except adorn oneself and dance. Thinking that this is liberty, she forgets all about her children. " Madame Fourmi " lives in the same building and in her usual way has worked diligently and stored up food for the winter. The remainder of the fable is in accordance with the old version. It is addressed to mothers and fathers whom pleasures draw away from home duties. Grima's favorite metre is the twelve-syllable line with alternate masculine and feminine rhymes. His style is easy and clear and shows a remarkable spontaneity.

Grima was born in New Orleans and has lived there all of his life. He was educated at Jefferson Academy and Tulane University, where he studied law. He is now one of the leading notaries of New Orleans. He has a thorough knowledge of French and English and is a great reader and lover of literature.[61] He is one of those who have contributed most to the French literature of Louisiana in recent years. His work has been published chiefly in the *Comptes Rendus de l'Athénée Louisianais*. He has written articles for the French papers of New Orleans, but it is his poems that show best his versatility.

Madame Evershed has one poem, " *Les Bonnets de Nuit* ", of a humorous nature. She describes the dainty night caps worn by young girls and compares them with the hideous cotton ones worn by men.

" *Mon premier coq* " is very different in spirit from all the other poems of Jules Choppin. Here the author goes back to childhood days and pictures his cock ruling the barnyard and waking all with his clarion call. His plume waved like that of the great king of France. This cock was called Bayard and he died " sans peur et sans reproche ".

TRANSLATIONS

Besides their many original verses, Louis Allard and Constant Lepouzé made poetic translations of several classical poems.

---

[61] Facts about him were obtained from *Biographical and Historical Memoirs of Louisiana,* vol. i, p. 453, and also from a personal interview.

The second and greater part of Louis Allard's *Les Epaves* is filled with epigrams of Martial. As a preface to the section, the author presents a short poem in which the editor argues with him about the suitability of some of Martial's epigrams for ladies to read, for the women of America have ears different from those of the Roman ladies. The author promises to leave out the immodest ones, and adds that any girl will allow her mother to read those he will choose. He feels that the prose translations of Martial are not satisfactory because a poet can be translated only into verse. He confesses that he has oftentimes altered the sense in order to get a French meaning, and has given—rarely however—his own thoughts instead of those of Martial in passages where there has always been doubt among the commentators as to Martial's meaning.[62] Allard quotes two hundred of Martial's epigrams in their original form and places his own poetic translation beside them.

The poems offered by Constant Lepouzé's *Poésies diverses*, are mostly translations from Latin poets. The author says in the preface (p. iv) that he had always loved the Latin lyrics and had amused himself for many years translating the odes which pleased him most. Then the idea came to him to publish them in a volume. The difficulty he had in the selection awakened in him the desire to translate them all at some future date. He has published in this volume thirty odes, two epodes, and one satire from Horace; the " *Discourse of Ajax* ", and the " *Discourse of Ulysses* " in their dispute over the arms of Achilles; and the " *Death of Ajax* " from Ovid. They are nearly all in verses of twelve syllables or of eight syllables with an occasional blending of the two.

[62] See preface, pages i, ii, iii, v.

On the whole the verses are accurate, but sometimes the author has difficulty in rounding out his line.

To these translations, Lepouzé has added thirteen poems of his own. Three of these are odes, " *Sur la mort du Général Foy* ", " *Sur la mort de Thomas Jefferson* ", and " *Sur les trois journées* "; two are addressed " Au Barde Louisianais " (Jean Duperron) and express great admiration for the work of this author; one is in praise of Tullius St. Céran whom Lepouzé calls the " Béranger of the Mississippi " and several are love poems. His " *Couplets sur les trois Journées* " and " *L'Exil* ", both express his love for his native France and the sadness he sometimes feels at the thought of being absent from home.

Lepouzé came to Louisiana about 1818 and taught there for many years.[63] In 1838 he published his *Poésies Diverses*. He says in the preface that this little volume belongs to the literature of Louisiana because he has been living in New Orleans for more than twenty years and has passed the best part of his life there.

Thus we see that the poetic production in French in Louisiana has been abundant and varied. This form of writing seems to have been the one favored most by the authors, perhaps because it furnished the easiest and shortest means for self-expression. The newspapers were ready and willing to publish poems and encouraged poetic production. The greater part of the poetry is subjective and represents a cry of distress, of love, of sadness, of patriotism, and of veneration for the great names of history and of literature, of love of humanity, and of longing for God.

[63] His name is in the New Orleans directories for 1822 and following years. It does not appear in the one for 1838. Search among the death records for the date of his death was unsuccessful.

CHAPTER VII

THE NOVEL AND THE SHORT STORY

I

STORIES WITH LOUISIANA AS A BACKGROUND

Not only did the French authors of Louisiana fill their poems with incidents from her history and descriptions of her wild beauty, but also the writers of fiction produced many pictures of her people, her customs, and her landscapes.

A NOVEL OF EARLY LOUISIANA—CALISTO

In the second volume of his review *Veillées Louisianaises,* in 1849, Charles Testut produced *Calisto,* a story based on Russian history during the time of Alexis, son of Peter the Great. The opening scene is on board a vessel bound for Louisiana. After presenting the people on the ship, the author goes back many years to tell their history. The heroine, Sophie de Wolfenbuttel, wife of Alexis is escaping to America on account of his cruelty. Her life in Russia; the dreadful treatment endured at the hands of her husband; her supposed death and burial; and her escape to France and then to America, are described in detail.

With some of her followers, Sophie falls in with the German immigrants in 1721, and lives quietly in Carrolton, now a part of New Orleans. After the death of

Alexis, she is happily married to d'Olban, a Frenchman whom she meets in New Orleans. Later, she returns with her husband and daughter to France, where friends recognize her and try to persuade her to return to her own land in order to resume her rank. She has been so happy as a simple woman that she refuses to become a princess again.

There are many digressions and sub-plots to this novel, and the author, with no care for arrangement or sequence, shifts the scene from Louisiana to Russia, and from the past to the present and back again, to suit his fancy. He also introduces a great deal of nature description, and depicts hurricanes, fires, and adventures with Indians.

Testut evidently based his novel on Gayarré's romantic account (*History of Louisiana* vol. i, pp. 263-272), for at times, he interrupts his own narrative to say: " Laissons parler l'historien pendant quelques instants ", and quotes Gayarré. This is especially true in his descriptions of the expeditions of the time against the Indians. According to Gayarré, the Frenchman d'Olban (or d'Aubant) had been in the guard of Sophie's father, and had loved her before her marriage to Alexis. As soon as the princess reaches Louisiana, she seeks him out, and they are married the day following her arrival. Testut has her make d'Olban's acquaintance first in New Orleans and marry him only after hearing of the death of Alexis. Gayarré states (p. 272) that the " particulars of this adventure are found in many memoirs of the epoch ". His record is like that of Bossu in his *Voyage dans l'Amérique Septentrionale* (pp. 38-48). Martin (*History of Louisiana*, p. 140), calls Sophie a female adventurer who had been one of the maids of the princess and who now poses as the princess herself. Bossu adds (p. 47) that D'Arens-

bourg, who had been the leader of the German immigrants in 1721, would only say that a German woman,
whom they thought to be the princess, had come at the
beginning of the settling of his immigrants in Louisiana.[1]

TWO NOVELS PICTURING SLAVERY

Another novel by Testut, written in 1858 and published
in 1872, is *le Vieux Salomon,* a picture of slavery days in
Guadeloupe and in Louisiana   The first scenes take place
in Guadeloupe and show Salomon, a man one hundred
years old, who had been a slave up to the age of eighty
and had then been freed.   He is considered a sage by the
whites and a wizard by the negroes.   All of the slaves
come to him for advice.   During the course of the novel
Salomon tells his own story and describes the earthquake
of 1843.

The story proper revolves around two young negroes,
Casimir and his wife Rose, sold in a slave market by
their kind master and mistress, Mr. and Mrs. Lambert,
who are now too poor to keep them.   They are bought
by Captain Jackson of New Orleans and carried there.
Jackson and his wife are very kind to them but, after
Jackson's death, Rose and Casimir fall into the hands of
a cruel master by the name of Roque.   His treatment
causes them to run away on several occasions, but each
time they are caught and punished.   At last they are able
to escape and make their way back to Guadeloupe.
There they are joyfully received by Old Salomon, who
dies a few days later.

This novel, though long and loosely knit together like

---

[1] Further discussion of the different opinions of the story of
this princess of Brunswick would be too much of a digression
here.   If any one wishes to examine further the various stories
current of her, he can find a short bibliography in Edward Fortier's *Lettres françaises en Louisiane,* p. 14.

Testut's other narratives, does not have the usual number of sub-plots. While his presentation of the cruel slave master is very realistic, he also portrays the first two owners, who were kind to their slaves and concerned over their welfare.[2]

Dr. Alfred Mercier in his *L'Habitation St. Ybars* (1881) presents a picture of slavery also. The first scene shows a slave market in New Orleans as seen by Anthony Pelasge, a young Frenchman who, fleeing from his own country in 1851 because of his political opinions, has just arrived in Louisiana. He is very much interested in the sale. St. Ybars has come in from his plantation to buy some slaves. He meets Pelasge whom he engages as a tutor to his young son. Pelasge returns with St. Ybars to the country, is introduced to life on a big plantation with a large number of slaves, and brought into close contact with all of the sorrows and heart-aches found among such a large group of people. The war comes in 1861, and scatters all except a few old servants, who are faithful to the end. Dr. Mercier has added interest to this work by filling several chapters with *patois* spoken by the negroes to their masters and among themselves.

A NOVEL OF PIRACY

Alexander Barde's *Michel Peyroux, ou les Pirates de la Louisiane* is an unfinished novel on a very interesting subject. Barde explains in a letter to the editors of the *Revue Louisianaise* for May 28th, 1848 (vol. V, pp. 193-197), that he had been writing it the preceding summer

[2] Alcée and Edward Fortier mention another novel, *Les Filles de Monte Cristo,* written by Testut. Edward Fortier says in notes left by him that it was published in the *Semaine Littéraire de la Nouvelle Orléans;* but in spite of searching in every collection of books to which I was given access, I was unable to find it.

in the country quite near the Gulf of Mexico, but had not intended to present it to the public. He had wished to write it at his leisure and use it as a trial composition before starting a larger work on the famous Jean Lafitte, but the editors of the *Revue Louisianaise* had finally persuaded him to publish it in serial form. He has had to modify his plan because of the haste of the publishers, and feels that his novel will lose some of its value thereby. He warns the reader that installments will appear intermittently because he cannot devote all of his time to collaboration to the *Revue Louisianaise*. There will be three or four volumes—he has only a few chapters ready—and the action will become local only in the third or fourth. He objects to the subtitle *Pirates de la Louisiane* added by the editors. He explains his objections to the name and sets forth his reason for calling it simply *Michel Peyroux*. He was living at the time in the Attakapas section of Louisiana, a region which was the richest of all, perhaps, in tales of the pirates, Lafitte and Dominique You. He had carefully collected and preserved all the available stories of these sea robbers. Realizing that the accounts furnished material for a good book, Barde began thinking of writing one. He felt incapable, however, of producing anything worthy of the subject, and putting his notes away, thought no more of the pirates. One day in St. Martinville, he met Michel Peyroux coming out of a tavern, drunk. Barde's companion addressed the old man and asked him about his last voyage. Peyroux related an adventure of piracy so bold that Barde thought it a creation of the old man's drunken imagination. Several weeks later, a report of this same adventure was published in the *Abeille de la Nouvelle Orléans* with no names disclosed. Barde's interest was aroused in Peyroux as a " man of energy and of greater gran-

deur " than he had thought, and he sought other meetings
with him at the tavern. Peyroux told him the story of
his life, which Barde decided to write down exactly as
Peyroux told it. Peyroux was the hero of it, and the
historical pirates of Louisiana were not to appear in it,
for this novel was to be the prologue to a later work on
Lafitte. For this reason, says Barde in the letter, he had
called it *Michel Peyroux*.

Michel Peyroux begins in the *Revue Louisianaise* for
April 30th, 1848 (vol. VI, pp. 97-105). There are two
chapters with the scene in St. Martinville. The first
relates Barde's meeting with Michel Peyroux on Easter
Sunday 1846, and presents a clear portrait of the old
man; the second pictures the tavern where Peyroux tells
the author the story. In the chapters that appear in
the following numbers, Peyroux himself speaks of his
birth in Toulouse in 1777 and of the events of the first
sixteen years of his life. In the issue of the *Revue Louisianaise* for June 18th, 1848 (p. 288), the editors say
that the publication of this story will have to be suspended
for a while, because the manuscript sent by Barde was
lost or stolen on the boat, and it will not be possible to
procure another copy before two weeks. On August 20th,
1848 (p. 504), they speak of resuming its publication, but
no other chapters appear, and no explanation is given for
their non-appearance.

A RELIGIOUS NOVEL—LA NOUVELLE ATALA

Adrien Rouquette published in 1879 his *Nouvelle Atala*
or *La fille de l'esprit*. The author shows his admiration
for Chateaubriand in having the father and mother call
their daughter Atala because of their love for Chateaubriand's novel. Atala has been educated in a convent

138

and has returned home. There she finds no joy in the pleasures suited to her age, but loves solitude and communion with nature. She envies the Indians in their freedom. Advised by the doctors, the parents take her to the country, where she is lost one day in the woods and never found. She lives in the forests, communing with nature, and only her confessor knows where she is. She is joined by an Indian girl, Lossima, and later by Rosalie, a negress who had been her childhood companion.

Atala spends her time in prayer, asking to be released from this life. A Frenchmen, a friend of Lossima's brother, comes to see Atala, is attracted by her, and declares his love for her. She utters a cry and faints. Nature is in such accord with her that the sky turns black, rumbles of thunder are heard, and the lightning flashes at the sacrilege of speaking of love to the daughter of the Spirit. Atala's prayer is answered and she dies immediately after Rose has disclosed the secret that Atala is the daughter of the Frenchman who had been so strongly drawn to her. About twenty years before, on his first visit to Louisiana, he had fallen in love with a young Indian widow, Pakanli. He had adopted the Indian name Hopoyouksa and had married Pakanli. Her family had been very much opposed to the marriage, and had refused to allow her the custody of her son and daughter. While Hopoyouksa was absent from home one day, his wife and baby were spirited away by Pakanli's relatives, and he had never been able to find them. He learns from Rosalie's story that Pakanli, when dying of yellow fever, had entrusted her baby to a kind French couple who changed her name to Atala and reared her as their own child. On hearing this recital, Lossima and her brother realize that Atala is their half-sister.

In an appendix, Rouquette has given some " Pensées et

impressions de Marie-Atala ", in which the young girl expresses her love of nature and the mysterious influence that its scenes of dawn, of twilight, and of night have over her, and her distaste for the tumult and strife of the world and society. Just as Chateaubriand wrote *Les Martyrs* to show in novel form what he tried to say in his *Génie du Christianisme,* so Rouquette seems to have written *Atala* to set forth in different form his ideas expressed in *L'Antoniade ou la solitude avec Dieu.* It is written in poetic prose and reveals at once the same author as the *Savanes.*[3]

MADAME SIDONIE DE LA HOUSSAYE
AND
NOVELS OF THE ACADIAN COUNTRY

Madame Sidonie de la Houssaye (*née* Perret) was born on Bellvue Plantation near Franklin, Louisiana, in 1820. She was married at the age of thirteen to Pelletier de la Houssaye, lived for a while in St. Martinville, but soon moved to Franklin. Her school days were ended by her early marriage, but being a great reader, she taught herself. Having had success with herself as pupil, she established a fashionable French school in Franklin, where she taught as late as 1874. The principal people of the community were educated there. She died on February 18th, 1894.[4]

Madame de la Houssaye has written a number of stories both short and long on different subjects as " *Le Mari de Marguerite* ", " *La fauvette et le poète* ", " *Charles et Ella* ", " *Amis et Fortune* ", " *Pouponne et Bal-*

[3] See Chapter VI.
[4] Facts about her were obtained from her grandson, L. B. Tarlton of Franklin, La., and from her great grandson, Arthur de la Houssaye of New Orleans.

thasar ", but her novels dealing with the Acadians in her section of Louisiana are her best.

In " *Pouponne et Balthasar* " (1888), the author relates a story she had heard from her grandmother who, in turn, had heard it from her mother, — a narrative of the early days of the Acadians who came down from Canada. Old Father Jacques, the priest who came with these refugees, relates the events of the first part of the story: the love of Pouponne, the prettiest maiden in Grand Pré, for Balthasar; their plans to marry on her next birthday; the departure of Balthasar on a mission for his father; the coming of the English shortly after his departure; and the cruel separation of families. The narrative proper begins with the arrival of Pouponne, her young brother, and Balthasar's father in Louisiana. The natives of Louisiana become very much interested in these refugees, especially in Pouponne, and are very kind to them. Later in the story, Balthasar tells of his return to Canada after fulfilling his mission and of his surprise at finding his father and his sweetheart gone. After many unpleasant experiences while searching for them, he comes to Louisiana, hoping to find them. He is overjoyed at seeing them again. The old father, however, is ill and dies soon after Balthasar's return. Pouponne and Balthasar are happy in their plans for the future. The friends of the young people, both the Acadians and the Louisianians, devote themselves to preparing a magnificent wedding feast for them. The account of this feast offers a very interesting picture of the manners and customs of the people, and of the wholesome joy shown in the songs, partly in verse and partly in prose, sung by the guests.

In 1893, Mme. de la Houssaye published *Amis et Fortune, roman louisianais*. The scene is laid on the shore of Bayou Têche in St. Mary's parish, but otherwise the story has nothing typical of Louisiana. It tells of a wealthy young girl, who, fearing that her unknown relatives are making advances to her only on account of her money, changes places with her companion and pretends to be very poor. She has several unpleasant experiences which show her who her real friends are. She becomes the good fairy of the whole neighborhood when her identity is finally disclosed.

Les Quarteronnes de la Nouvelle Orléans was published in 1894, signed by " Louise Raymond ", the *nom de plume* of Madame de la Houssaye. In the introduction, the author tells that in 1878 she found, in a trunk of old papers belonging to her grandmother, a roll tied with ribbon, bearing the inscription " Les Quarteronnes de la Nouvelle Órléans de 1800 à 1830 ". After reading the manuscript, she found that the work was merely a sketch, and that she would have to do some research before giving the story to the public. She spent about three years obtaining the necessary information. Since she owes the story to her grandmother, Madame de la Houssaye lets her tell it in her own words. It is divided into distinct parts, each one the portrait of quadroons who were famous at different times in New Orleans.

Madame de la Houssaye had a wonderful imagination and wrote quite a number of " marvelous cure " tales for patent medicine men. She also helped George Washington Cable to collect material for some of his novels. In his " Strange True Stories of Louisiana ", in the part called " How I Got Them ", he speaks of Madame de la Houssaye and of the help she gave him.

Besides the authors of long novels who wrote of Louisiana, there were many who chose to call their stories
nouvelles louisianaises.

Georges Dessommes, though better known for his
poems, produced a novel in 1888, *La Tante Cydette,* to
which he adds the subtitle *Nouvelle Louisianaise.* The
scene is laid in New Orleans, and the first chapter pictures that city on Easter morning. The chief characters
are introduced to the reader as they return from church.
Tante Cydette has refused two offers of marriage, and
has waited in vain for a third. Resigned to being an
old maid, she acquires a passion for getting other people
married. She lives with her brother, whose daughter
Ermence, she has reared. The marriage of this girl is
her single aim now. When Henri de Fallex, a young
Frenchman, arrives in the city, Tante Cydette begins
scheming to make him the husband of Ermence. At
first, the young man prefers Louise, a poor cousin of the
family, causing Tante Cydette to bend her energies more
and more toward winning him for Ermence. Though not
sentimental by nature, De Fallex feels the influence of
the Louisiana climate, and is easily caught in Tante
Cydette's net. The story is well told and the interest
as to which of the girls Henri will marry, is sustained
throughout.

In 1851 Charles Lemaître issued a novel, *Rodolphe de
Branchelièvre.* Although the scene is laid in New Orleans, the events might have happened in any other local-
ity, for the author has made use of local color only in
place names. The story is poorly constructed and is full
of episodes which bear very little relation to one another:
murders, attemps at poisoning, and the discovery of unknown relatives. Lemaître was born in New Orleans on

January 25th, 1824, son of Carlos Lemaître, a native of
San Domingo. He died in New Orleans on February 9th,
1895.[5]

Adolphe Lemercier Du Quesnay was born at Kingston,
Jamaica, in May 1839. His family, originally from
France, had gone to San Domingo to settle. Having to
flee because of the rebellions, they went to Jamaica
where they spent several years. They returned to
France when Adolphe was still a boy. He received his
education at Versailles and at Paris. He was a brilliant
musician, a pupil of Malandan. About 1860, his father
brought all his family to New Orleans where Adolphe
became a music teacher. While on a visit to Paris in
1892, he published a volume called *Essais littéraires et
dramatiques,* which is his sole literary attempt. He died
in New Orleans in 1901.[6]

This volume includes three *nouvelles* written in very
poetical prose. The scenes of two of them are laid
in Louisiana: *Un été à la Grand'Ile,* which appeared also
in the *Abeille* on September 25th, 1898, and *Le Chant
d'Ipomoea* or *Légende créole.* Both contain fine descriptions of Louisiana scenery, and portray the pleasure that
the inhabitants of the state derive from its woods and
lakes.

In 1886 and 1887, John L. Peytavin published in the
Comptes Rendus de l'Athénée Louisianais a story which
he called *Albert Dupont* with the addition, *Nouvelle Louisianaise.* This work portrays Louisiana life in St. James
and Iberville Parishes in the early fifties of the
nineteenth century. The plot is a simple one of misun-

[5] Facts obtained from his baptismal record at the St. Louis
Cathedral and from his death record at the City Board of
Health office.
[6] Facts about him were obtained from his brother, Albert
Lemercier Du Quesnay of New Orleans.

derstandings in love, with a happy ending. Peytavin was a native of Louisiana and was educated by private tutors until he entered Jefferson College at Convent. He was graduated from there in 1879 with the degree of A. B. After attending the law school at Tulane University (then known as the Louisiana University), he was admitted to the bar in 1882. That same year he received the M. A. degree from Jefferson College. From 1882 until 1924, he resided in New Orleans, where he practiced his profession. He spent his summers at his country home, " Ancient Domain " and while there, conceived the idea of doing something for the cause of education in the community. In 1891, he was instrumental in perfecting plans for the organization and maintenance of a good high school. He still has an office in New Orleans, but since 1924 he has been residing at " Ancient Domain ".[7]

François Tujague has related several incidents of life in Louisiana. *Les forêts de la Louisiane; une aventure tragique* and *Les prairies tremblantes de la Louisiane* both show the intense suffering of men lost in the dense forests. In the former sketch the man is found dead, holding in his hand a diary which contains a record of his experiences; in the latter, the man is rescued by friends to whom he recounts his adventures. *Les Chasseurs de crocodiles* describes the sport of crocodile-hunting, and *Sous les chênes verts* depicts one of the many duels fought under the duelling oaks of City Park. Under the title of *Chroniques Louisianaises,* Tujague has furnished three short sketches: *Lafrénière*, a history of one of the patriots and martyrs of 1769, and two chronicles partly true and partly legendary, of the pirate Lafitte. *Le Pirate*

[7] Information about him was obtained from *Biographical and Historical Memoirs of Louisiana*, p. 119, and from Mr. Peytavin himself.

Lafitte relates Jean Lafitte's part in the Battle of New Orleans, the continuance of his piracy on the Gulf of Mexico, and the legend of his disappearance after he had returned to Louisiana secretly to bury his fortune in her soil. *Le Navire " Le Charles "* is an account of the indignation of the citizens of New Orleans when news was brought that the *Charles* had been found abandoned at the mouth of the river. Its decks were filled with blood, but no dead bodies were found. The story ran that pirates had killed all on board the ship and had thrown their remains into the sea. A group of citizens formed an expedition and started down the river. They saw a campfire on the shore and, being sure that they had found the pirates, opened fire on the supposed enemy. When the citizens reached the camp, they found only two frightened men, and one other whom their shot had killed—poor fishermen who thought themselves captured by pirates. Saddened by the experience, the expedition returned to New Orleans. It was learned later, from sailors in New York, that the *Charles* had run aground and had been abandoned. Before leaving, the members of the crew had killed many chickens in order to take a supply with them. This solved the mystery of the bloody decks.

Tujague was a native of southern France who came to Louisiana in 1836 at the age of fifteen. He was always greatly interested in France and in making her known abroad. He was one of the founders of the *Union Française* and was its president from 1879 to 1892. It was he who conceived the idea of a competitive contest of the *Athénée Louisianais* in order to promote writing in French. He was a contributor to several of the papers of New Orleans and, from 1892 to 1894,[8] wrote the

[8] See *L'Abeille,* March and April 1896, Sunday editions.

146

" Causeries " regularly in the *Observateur Louisianais*. At his death in December 1896, this paper said: " il laisse un grand vide dans la colonie française."[9]

Among the contributions by Madame Louise Fortier to the *Comptes Rendus de l'Athénée Louisianais* are several short sketches of Civil War days. They are all in the form of reminiscences of old people who tell their experiences to children in the family. The best example of these stories is *Chroniques de vieux temps*, which has two sections: " *La folie aux roses* " and " *Un Incident de la Guerre Confédérée* ". *Le bon vieux temps* is another example.

Madame Fortier (*née* Augustin) belonged to a very literary family. Her ancestors originally came from Marseilles, France. They went first to San Domingo, and later to New Orleans. Madame Fortier was born in New Orleans, was educated there, and was prominent in the educational work of the city. She taught for thirty-five years in what is now the John McDonogh High School, and died on February 29th, 1924 at the age of seventy-four.[10]

Ulisse Marinoni is greatly interested in the ancient creoles of Louisiana and has written some charming stories about them. *Tante Louise* is full of local color and presents a picture of the decoration of graves on All Saints' Day. An old aunt, who is the head of the family, is busy during the week preceding All Saints' Day in gathering her relatives together to go to the cemetery.

[9] Facts about him were obtained from the *Observateur Louisianais* issued at the time of his death in December 1896, and from *Comptes Rendus de l'Athénée Louisianais* for January 1897, pp. 9-11.

[10] Facts about her were obtained from her nephew, L. A. Augustin, and her sister, Marie Augustin of New Orleans, and from death records at the City Board of Health office.

After the decoration ceremony is over, and the others have gone back to their homes, she remains for a while among the tombs recalling memories. In *Mon Oncle Jacques,* a typical picture is seen of an old man, who, poor now, comes down to the river every afternoon to think of the days that are gone. In his dream he sees his home and its activities. His childhood and his youth pass before him; the war comes, bringing the Federal army; then the war ends, leaving destruction and ruin everywhere.

Marinoni was born in New Orleans in 1869. He received his education in that city, and was graduated from the law department of Tulane University in 1890 He is a busy lawyer, but finds time to take an active part in the *Athénée Louisianais* and to write for its *Comptes Rendus.*[11]

II

STORIES ON OTHER SUBJECTS

Besides the historical novels and those for which Louisiana serves as a background, there are many stories that treat of other countries and other subjects.

LONG NOVELS

Prominent among the writers of novels is Dr. Alfred Mercier, who not only produced romantic works like *Le Fou de Palerme,* and *Lidia,* and short stories like *Le Banquet* and *Emile des Ormiers,* but also *romans à thèse* like *La Fille du Prêtre, Johnelle,* and *Hénoch Jédésias.*

Mercier was born at McDonogh, Louisiana, in 1816.[12]

[11] Facts about him were obtained from a personal interview.
[12] Facts about his life were obtained from a eulogy on him at the time of his death. It was given by Alcée Fortier at a spe-

At the age of fourteen, he was sent to France to be educated at the Collège Louis le Grand. His first ambition was to be a lawyer and he studied for a while in Paris. His interest in literature, however, was so strong that he did not finish his law course. His first writings were two volumes of poems which he published in Paris in 1842.[13] After these two productions, he traveled extensively in France, Spain, Belgium, Italy, and England. He decided to give up writing as a profession, began the study of medicine, received his medical diploma in 1855, and went to Louisiana where he practiced for several years. He was in France again in 1859 and spent three years in Normandy. After the Civil War, he returned to New Orleans.

Mercier produced no other literary works until 1873, when *Fou de Palerme,* his first novel, was offered to the public. It shows, in a very marked degree, the effect of the author's travels in Italy and Sicily. It is very romantic with its gypsies, its poisoned daggers, and its masked balls. A young man, Angiolo, seen wandering in the garden of the Duke di Falco, arouses the attention of everyone; it is his story as told by one of his friends, that Mercier relates. Angiolo had been studying music in Paris for many years. Shortly after his return home, a band of gypsies makes its appearance in the city. They are not favorably received and, to all appearances, depart. Instead of going, however, they hide in the tombs. At a masked ball given by the duke, Maniska, a lovely gypsy girl, appears in the crowd and causes many conjectures as to her identity. Angiolo falls in love with her and she returns his love. When she tries to slip away from the

cial session of the *Athénée Louisianais* in May 1894. See the *Comptes Rendus,* July 1894, pp. 97-108.

[13] See Chapter VI, p. 127.

149

ball before the time for unmasking arrives, he follows her home. A jealous gypsy boy kills her. Then Angiolo, through the intensity of his passion and the bitterness of his grief, loses his mind and spends his time wandering around the duke's garden.

To Dr. Mercier is attributed the idea of founding the *Athénée Louisianais* in 1876,[14] and many poems, articles, and stories by him have been published in its *Comptes Rendus*. He did not confine himself to this magazine, however, and between 1877 and his death in 1894, he produced several other volumes. *La fille du prêtre* (1877), is really three novels in one, for each of its three parts—" Fausse Route ", " Expiation ", and " Réhabilitation "—is a novel in itself. It is a *roman à thèse* attacking the celibacy of the priests. The author inserts in the narrative a great deal of the history of Europe: the wars of Garibaldi, the siege of Paris, and the Commune. The characters are fairly well drawn but some of them are too nearly angelic to be real.

In that same year, 1877, Mercier produced in the May number of the *Comptes Rendus* a short fantastic sketch called the *Banquet*. A laborer, weary and worn with the weight of his toil, falls asleep by the road-side and dreams of a great banquet where many guests are assembled, and where a spectre enters and beckons to them to follow him. It is clear that the banquet represents life and the spectre death. The laborer awakens with his courage revived and is ready to continue his toil.

In 1887, Dr. Mercier wrote *Lidia* which he calls a sort of idyll in prose, and in which the reader is conducted to Paris and incidentally to Sicily. The author says (in his preface) that the facts of this story were told by him

[14] See the *Comptes Rendus de l'Athénée Louisianais,* July 1894, p. 102.

to a group of friends who insisted that he write them down. He did this and read the result to the same group. One of those present was a writer who at that time was directing a daily paper. He asked permission to print the work under the title of *Lidia*. It was published anonymously. Years afterward, in looking over the papers, the author found *Lidia* again. The editor had died shortly after the publication of the novel, and his paper had been discontinued.[15] The author revised it somewhat, and now offers it, as it were, in a second edition. Most of those who had heard the story before were gone, hence it would probably be new for the majority of people. This time Mercier signs his name to the preface. *Lidia* is rather simply written. It shows how fondness for music brought two young people together and awakened love in their hearts, although they might not have been attracted to each other if they had met in a more formal manner. The author pictures the joy and contentment which the peasant classes of both France and Sicily find in their work.

Dr. Mercier published in 1891, *Johnelle,* a novel attacking infanticide, and *Emile des Ormiers,* a short record of the grief, sadness, and ultimate suicide of a young painter in Paris.

While in Paris in 1848, Dr. Mercier wrote a novel, *Hénoch Jédésias,* which was to have appeared in the *Réforme*. The manuscript was lost, however, when the offices of the *Réforme* were pillaged.[16] Mercier later rewrote it from memory, and published it in the *Comptes Rendus de l'Athénée Louisianais* in 1892 and 1893. *Hé-*

[15] I was unable to find any paper containing this story, nor was I able to discover who this editor was. *Lidia* in book form is in the Howard Library.

[16] See *Comptes Rendus de l'Athénée Louisianais,* July 1894, p. 104, for this story and for other information about Dr. Mercier.

noch Jédésias is a gruesome, unpleasant story of a young man who allows love of money to stifle every feeling in his heart, until he slays his wife, robs his father's tomb, kills his friend, and shuts himself off from all human intercourse except for lending money at exorbitant rates of interest. Thieves finally enter his house, subject him to terrible torture, steal his money, and leave him to die. The development of Hénoch's character as he descends to miserliness is realistically given; his love of money is, however, too suddenly disclosed to be in keeping with the picture first presented of him.

Dr. Mercier died in New Orleans in 1894.

While Madame Emilie Evershed is known chiefly for her poetry, she wrote a novel, *Eglantine; ou le Secret,* in 1843. According to the introduction, the events of the story are real and the author has changed only the names of the characters. It is very much like the long narrative poems that Madame Evershed included in her collections of poetry. Eglantine de Lespin, a young girl—extremely good, like all of Madame Evershed's women—is reared by M. d'Ormeuil, her grandfather. Her father is still living, but she feels an aversion for him, and fears him. She is devoted to Madame de Sinval, a neighbor. These two feelings of Eglantine are so greatly stressed that the reader knows the secret long before the end of the story is reached, when it is disclosed that Eglantine is not the daughter of M. de Lespin, but of Mme. de Sinval. The latter had married Jules d'Ormeuil, who had gone away to war and had not communicated with his family for many years. She had thought her marriage illegal. Wishing to give her child every advantage, she had persuaded the nurse to exchange children when Clara d'Ormeuil, M. de Lespin's wife, had died. Clara's child was very frail and had lived only a short time. No one knew of the substitution, and Eglantine was reared as de Lespin's child, while her mother, assuming the name of Mme. Sinval, moved near her daughter and won her love.

Madame Evershed says that truth would seem less real than fiction and for this reason, instead of portraying all the tenderness and devotion of the young mother, she has diminished her real ills and even her virtues in order to create a more probable character. In spite of this statement, the sacrifice of Mme. Sinval produces the effect of being exaggerated, and all of the characters are too virtuous to be natural.

Jacques de Roquigny (C. de la Bretonne), usually known as Jacques de R., was well known in the world of journalism in New Orleans, and his name is found in many of the papers of his day. In 1849, he conducted a column in the *Violette,* and in 1855 and 1856, signed the " Revue de la Semaine " in the *National.* In 1873, he was on the editorial staff of the *Sud,* and in that same year became editor of the *Avenir.* Jacques de R. was his pen name. He later became a teacher in New Orleans. He must have left that city about 1875, for in 1876, he was a corresponding member of the *Athénée Louisianais.* The issue of January 1879 (p. 231) of the *Comptes Rendus* of that organization speaks of the death of Jacques de Roquigny in July 1876 and calls him Charles de la Bretonne.[17] In 1854 he published a novel, *Les Amours d'Hélène* or *Deux cœurs brisés.* He claims that it is a true story. Alexis, the hero, returns home after an absence of five years. He finds that his sweetheart has married, that his old friends do not recognize him, and also that his uncle has died. A

[17] Facts about him were obtained from the city directories for 1873, 1874 and 1875, and from the *Abeille* of August 27th, 1872.

servant delivers to him a letter written by the uncle just before his death, expressing a desire that Alexis marry Hélène, a niece of the old man who has been living in his home for several years. The uncle was very shrewd, for he has ordered that the terms of his will be kept secret for a year after his death, or until the marriage of either Hélène or Alexis. In the meanwhile, a preliminary document is read before the assembled relatives. It orders that the chateau and grounds go to Alexis; that all of the heirs live together in the chateau until a year has expired; that Hélène receive nothing if she marries one of her cousins; and that she receive a dowry of 50,000 francs if she marries some one else.

Hélène loves Alexis but conceals her love, because she has heard one of the cousins say that it is the château, and not Alexis, that she wants.

The year passes. The heirs, assembled to hear the reading of the will, are hilariously happy over the large sums of money they receive. Only Alexis and Hélène show a feeling of indifference. The old notary has watched all the heirs closely and, after a short pause, begins reading again, this time a codicil which revokes all the legacies given, and leaves the bulk of the fortune to Hélène and a goodly sum to Alexis. To each of the other relatives, the old uncle leaves a portrait of himself and 3,000 francs.

The love element is very poor. When it seems to be settled that Hélène and Alexis will marry, Hélène receives a great shock and dies of heart trouble. Alexis, greatly grieved, finally leaves France and is heard of no more. The redeeming feature of the story is the description of the heirs, their assurance of receiving big legacies, their plans for spending the money, and their final disappointment and chagrin at receiving the portrait.

Edward Dessommes, author of several novels, was born in New Orleans in 1845. He was sent to Paris in 1859 and was educated at the College Sainte Barbe, where he was a brilliant pupil and showed great artistic and literary talent. After graduation from college, he studied medicine. His love of literature and painting was so strong that he devoted a part of his time to these arts. In 1869 he published a short novel called *Femme et Statue*, dedicated to Venus de Milo, and telling how the author conceived the origin of that statue of Venus. Hipparque, a young sculptor in Milo, makes a statue using his mistress, Daphne, as a model. Shutting out his friends, and after a time, his mistress, he works so intently that Daphne becomes jealous. In truth, his admiration and love for his work know no bounds.

Later the Huns come down, ravage the country, and take the town. The Hun priestess decrees that the most beautiful woman there must be sacrificed. One of the Hun soldiers had formerly been a slave in Milo and knows that Daphne is more beautiful than anyone else. He tells this fact to the priestess, and she demands that Daphne be brought forth for the sacrifice. Hipparque, now a prisoner, is forced to lead the Huns to his home. They do not find Daphne, for she has been hidden in a subterranean place of safety. They find the statue, however, and bringing it out of its niche, begin to smash it. When they have broken off the arms, Hipparque can endure it no longer, and, in order to save his beloved work, betrays the hiding place of Daphne. She is led away to the priestess and sacrificed.

Help soon arrives, the Huns are driven from the country, and Hipparque is freed. He takes possession of Daphne's body and returns to his home. Wishing to assure his statue against further mutilation, he chisels its broken arms so that they may seem to have been cut off, and then, with the aid of friends, buries it. When this deed is done and the friends depart, Hipparque kills himself beside Daphne's body.

In 1870, Dessommes published a second novel, *Jacques Morel,* in Paris.[18] When the War of 1870 began, Dessommes' family, which had gone to Paris in 1860, returned to America; he remained in Paris to continue his medical studies. When he had finished everything except his thesis, his love of art proved too strong for him, and he began landscape painting. As he did not possess the self-assurance necessary to interest newspaper men and art critics in his literature and art, he was not successful in his chosen fields. Somewhat disillusioned, he returned to New Orleans in about 1887. From 1891 to 1894, he taught in the High School of Tulane University in that city, but finally retired to Mandeville, Louisiana, where he built a small cottage and lived alone like a philosopher. He indulged his artistic talent in cultivating around his home a beautiful flower garden which he filled with hundreds of rose bushes; in the spring it was a landscape in itself. He died in Mandeville in 1908.[19]

After his return to America, two of his stories, *Madeleine et Berthe* and *Artiste et Virtuose,* appeared in the *Comptes Rendus de l'Athénée Louisianais.* In *Madeleine et Berthe,* the husband of Madeleine is killed in a duel defending her honor. After his death he sees a marble statue coming to him, the statue of Bertha Rucellai, before which he used to sit in the church of San Lorenzo at Florence. Bertha confesses that she had loved him as

[18] I have been unable to find a copy of this novel.
[19] Information about him was obtained from his brother, Georges Dessommes.

he sat before her tomb, and has been waiting for his death. She invites him to come with her and fill a niche in the chapel of San Lorenzo. She adds that Heaven makes beautiful statues of the dead whom it loves and allows them to return to life at night. If he will come to San Lorenzo, she will put an arrow into the wound in his breast and will call him St. Sebastian. He feels himself turned to marble, and Bertha takes him away with her.

Artiste et Virtuose relates a fantastic tale of a young nightingale, Ernest, who, having read Schopenhauer, becomes very skeptical, scorns the advice given him by his father, and elopes with his cousin Sophie, the lark. They journey to various lands and see many interesting sites and people. Ernest finally tires of Sophie and, having heard some picknickers talk of eating boneless lark of Pithiviers, he goes to Pithiviers in order to have her killed and made a " boneless lark ". Sophie escapes this plot against her life, but later sacrifices herself before a hunter's gun to save Ernest. He changes his name to Ernestski and, pretending to be Polish, seeks other adventures. This story has a charm of narration which recalls very strongly Alfred de Musset's *Merle Blanc.*

All these three works by Dessommes show a combination of artist and writer and have a fascination that can be derived only from such a union. They show clearly that the thought of a medical career must have been a bitter one for the author.

Alcée Fortier made one attempt at fiction, *Gabriel d'Ennérich,* 1886, to which he affixes the explanation, *Histoire d'un cadet de famille au dix-huitième siècle.* In this novel Henri, the older son, is heir to the inheritance and title, while Gabriel, the younger, has no chance of a profession except that of priest, a calling very distasteful to him.

The two brothers are at enmity with each other not only because of the title but also because both love the same girl. Henri is represented as haughty, overbearing, cruel, and hated by every one on his father's estate; Gabriel is kind, friendly, and loved by both young and old. The *dénouement* is easily seen: Henri is killed by an enraged subject and Gabriel wins both the inheritance and the girl. Fortier, no doubt, realized that fiction was not his field, for he did not produce any other novel.

In 1892 Marie Augustin published a novel *Le Macandal* which she signs " Tante Marie ", and dedicates to her young nephews and nieces. Its subtitle is *Episodes de l'insurrection des noirs à San Domingue, 1793.* It relates some harrowing incidents. M. de Villeneuve has three slaves, Macandal, his wife Wamba, and their young son. Macandal runs away from his master, commits many deeds of violence, and is finally caught and burned. The negroes believe that he will return some day. His son, Dominique, grows to be very much like him. Wamba also runs away and, with Dominique and others, plans an insurrection. These negroes are suspected by Philippe Duverney, who decides to follow Dominique one evening. He witnesses a meeting of the plotters, sees their horrible orgies and hears their incantations. Agains the negroes he seeks the aid of Toussaint, who is a rival of Dominique for supremacy. The insurrection takes place, a horrible battle is fought, and the whites are put to flight. Philippe rallies the refugees until help arrives from Toussaint. In a second combat, Dominique is killed and his mad followers are dispersed. De Villeneuve departs with his family to New Orleans in order to escape further troubles. The descriptions in this novel are very vivid and realistic, especially that of the orgies witnessed by Duverney. The assurance that

Macandal will return, and the belief that Wamba has supernatural powers, are superstitions typical of the negroes.

Mademoiselle Augustin is a native of New Orleans and a member of one of its most literary families. Her immediate ancestors came to Louisiana from San Domingo. She began her career as a teacher at the age of eighteen in the school of Miss Meta Huger. She was a teacher of French at Newcomb College in New Orleans from 1891, until she was pensioned by the Carnegie Foundation.[20]

SHORT STORIES

Louis Placide Canonge, although primarily a dramatist, has also written some short stories which appeared in the papers of New Orleans. In the *Revue Louisianaise* of August 23rd, 1846, he published *Rires et Pleurs,* a story with two parts and an epilogue. In *Rires,* the author and a group of young men are assembled in a room where they revel until two o'clock in the morning. In *Pleurs,* on his return home that morning, the author passes a house where a child is dead, and hears an old woman sobbing with grief. In the " Epilogue ", struck by the contrast between this sorrow and the hilarity he has just left, the writer tells his friends on the next day what he has witnessed. They are touched by the recital, and one of them suggests that it is a fine subject for the imagination, and that each one produce something: the painter, the musicians, the two journalists, and the author. This little story is the author's contribution.

[20] Facts about her were obtained from her nephew, L. A. Augustin of New Orleans and from an interview with her.

Canonge published another story, *La Première et la dernière nuit de Nourrit,* in the *Violette* in March 1849. Part I describes the great success obtained by an actor, Nourrit, on the night of his first appearance in Paris, in the role of Pylade in *Iphigénie en Tauride.* Part II presents Nourrit again after eighteen years of continued success. He now finds himself out of favor and displaced by younger artists. Against his will, he is persuaded to appear on the stage in Naples. He distinguishes hisses among the applause during the performance, and is broken-hearted. Unable to endure his sorrow, and thinking of the sad fates of Gilbert, Chatterton, and Chénier, he commits suicide.

In 1864, Armand Garreau published *L'Idiote* in the *Renaissance Louisianaise.* This title refers to Françoise, the sister of M. Laurent, a rich man of the country. He had hated her, had wanted her share of the inheritance, and had so mistreated her that her mind had become unbalanced. She now lives in a hovel, and is keeper of her brother's sheep. Jules, the hero of the story and the betrothed of Blanche Laurent, sees Françoise one day and hears her muttering curses against someone. His interest is aroused and he learns her story from the innkeeper. Jules resolves that, when he becomes a member of the family, she shall receive better treatment. For many years Françoise has awaited her opportunity for vengeance, and on the day set for Blanche's wedding, she locks Laurent and his daughter in an upstairs room, and sets fire to the house. Jules, riding along on the road, and seeing the flames, hurries on at a mad pace. He arrives, seizes a ladder, climbs to the window, gropes his way through the smoke, feels a woman's hair, rushes with her back to the window, and climbs out with his precious burden just as the floor falls through. When he reaches the ground, he faints on finding that he has saved the idiot, Françoise, instead of his fiancée, Blanche. This story, in spite of its unpleasent character, is well told, for the elements of surprise and suspense are successfully employed.

Garreau was a Frenchman who came to New Orleans in about 1843. There for several years he conducted a classical institution for boys and girls. He is doubtless the " Armand G. " who signs the " Revue de la semaine " in the *Revue Louisianaise* in 1848.[21]

Among those who have written stories in the last half of the nineteenth century is Gustave Daussin. Several by him were published in the *Comptes Rendus de l'Athénée Louisianais*. *Le Talisman de Gérard* (1886) told with naturalness and simplicity, is the account of a young lover, who, too proud to ask the girl whom he loves to marry him when she is rich and he is poor, goes to Arizona to make his fortune. In the desert, he and his friends are attacked by Indians. Gérard is shot, but a medallion, in which he wears a flower given him by his sweetheart, turns aside the bullet, and saves his life. He returns home, finds the girl poor and teaching for a living, and persuades her to marry him. After the wedding, they return to Arizona where they make a fortune together. In 1887-1888, Daussin produced: *Camma,* an incident from the history of the Gauls and Parthians in which the element of suspense is skilfully used; *la Sirène,* a

[21] His name first appears in the city directory for 1843, and he is listed as a teacher. His name is omitted from the directory in the early fifties but it is back again in 1859. A pencil note above his « Louisiana » in *Les Veillées Louisianaises,* Howard Library, says that he died in 1864. The name of A. Garreau is in the city directory of 1876, and a Widow Garreau is in the one for 1877. In spite of my search in the death records for 1864 and 1876, I was unable to find any account of his death.

tale of the heroism of one of the many French corsairs fighting against the English in 1795; and *La Soirée du Colonel,* a very short and amusing skit.

Bussière Rouen is vitally interested in everything that will preserve the French language and literature in Louisiana. He won the medal at the *Athénée* contest in 1883, and since that time has published several articles in the *Comptes Rendus.* His *Rayon de Soleil* relates a simple story of an old grandfather who, having exhausted his supply of tales because of the many demands of his grandchildren, tells of finding his wife and happiness because of a ray of sunshine. *L'Enfant et l'image* also possesses the charm of simplicity. Two little girls, aged ten and nine, are admiring the pictures in a store. Marie selects one which portrays a happy couple going down a flowery path while another girl, in tears, watches them pass. Anna chooses a picture of two turtle-doves, soon grows tired of it, and destroys it. Several years later, they both love the same man, but Marie keeps her love a secret. Anna marries the man and is happy. Later Marie finds the picture which she had bought when she was a child, and recognizes the similitary between it and her own life.

Rouen was born in New Orleans in 1861. His father was principal of the first Boys' School in that city; the great architect, De Pouilly, so well known in New Orleans, was an ancestor of his. Rouen was, for a short time, art critic for the *Abeille.* He was vice-president of the *Athénée Louisianais* for many years and has been its president since 1914.[22]

Felix Voorhies devoted much of his time to literature and wrote several tales relating incidents of the Civil

[22] Information about him was obtained from a personal interview.

War. They are very short and humorous and tell of the author's own experiences. In *Un cochon de lait féroce*, a soldier, caught by his Major in the act of foraging and killing a pig, explains that the pig had attacked him, and that he had killed it in self-defense. Another of the same type is *Une nuit parmi les Jayhawkers*.

The fame of Voorhies is due chiefly to a little book, *Acadian Reminiscences*, which he published in English. It contains the true story of Evangeline, called in real life, Emmaline Labiche.

Voorhies was a member of one of the most prominent families of Southwest Louisiana. His ancestors came to America from Holland about 1600, and settled in New Jersey. Some members of the family went to Louisiana and settled in St. Martinville. It was there that Felix was born in 1839. He was educated at Spring Hill, Alabama, and at the Jesuits' College in New Orleans. He studied law in his home town and was there admitted to the bar in 1860. He saw active service during the Civil War. Later he served his parish in the state legislature. He died on August 21st, 1919.[23]

These writers of French novels in Louisiana have no doubt proved that story-telling has formed a prominent element in Louisiana literature.

[23] Facts about him were obtained from *Southwest Louisiana Biographical and Historical,* Gulf Publishing Co., New Orleans, 1891, pp. 349-350, and also from André Olivier of St. Martinville.

CHAPTER VIII

THE DRAMA

Of all the literary *genres* in Louisiana the drama was the least developed. Several plays by Louis Placide Canonge; those with a historical background that have already been discussed (chapter III); one attempt, *Fortunia* by Dr. Alfred Mercier; *Sara la Juive* and *La famille créole* by Auguste Lussan; *Guatimozin, ou le dernier jour de l'Empire mexicain* by P. Pérennes; and a few comedies by Marie Augustin, Felix Voorhies, and Dr. Charles Deléry comprise the total of dramatic works produced.

LOUIS PLACIDE CANONGE AND HIS SUCCESS AS A DRAMATIST

Louis Placide Canonge was perhaps the most versatile of all the French writers of Louisiana. Although he devoted his talent principally to the drama, he also wrote verse, short stories, and criticisms, both literary and musical.

Canonge was born in New Orleans in June 1822.[1] When very young, he was sent to Paris to be educated at the Collège Louis le Grand. In 1839 he returned

---

[1] See the baptismal record in the Cathedral; the article by Charles Patton Dimitry in the *Times Democrat,* Jan. 22nd, 1893; the one in the *Times-Picayune,* Feb. 6th, 1927, by his great-nephew, George William Nott, and the papers already mentioned, for information about Canonge.

to New Orleans and began writing for the *Abeille*. Two
short stories by him, *Les Fantômes* and *Christophe*, appeared as serials in the feuilleton column of the *Abeille*
in February and in October 1839. Both show strong
influence of the Romantic School. During that same
year, he produced a sketch, *Le Maudit Passeport*, a vaudeville in one act, having a subtitle, *Les infortunes
d'une drogue*. On May 16th, 1840, a notice in the
Abeille stated that there would be a special performance
on May 17th at the Théâtre d'Orléans for the benefit
of the orphans; it would be an evening of amateurs and
artists, and the drama, *Gaston de St. Elme* by Placide
Canonge, would be presented.[2] After the performance,
the *Abeille* for May 19th, commenting on the play, spoke
of its beautiful scenes.

On May 17th, 1846 the *Courrier de la Louisiane* announced in the program of the Théâtre d'Orléans for
that evening, the *Comte de Monte Cristo*, a drama by
Placide Canonge. Canonge apparently took the story
told by Alexandre Dumas and arranged it for the stage.
He followed the original story rather closely in some
respects, but introduced quite a change in the story
of Fernand de Morcerf. In Dumas' novel, Mercedes is
finally convinced of Edmond Dantes' death and weds
Morcerf. Their son, Albert Morcerf, is one of the important characters in the later chapters of the story. Morcerf kills himself. In the drama of Canonge, Dantes
finds, on his return, that Mercedes has died without ever
having married, and it is Dantes who kills Morcerf. On
bending over the dead body of his victim, he finds a medallion, which he opens. From this he learns that Morcerf is the son of the Abbé Faria, who had been his fel-

---

[2] I have been unable to find a copy of this drama.

low prisoner. Canonge does not introduce the character of Haidée at all. Instead, just before Dantes dies from poison that he has taken, he confesses to Valentine that he loves her.

Canonge began his drama with a prologue describing the events of Dantes' life before his imprisonment in the Chateau d'If. Act I of the drama proper begins with Dantes and the Abbé Faria in prison. Act II tells of the sensation created by the appearance of Monte Cristo with all his wealth. The other three acts treat of his plans of vengeance and their success. The *Comte de Monte Cristo* was published by the *Revue Louisianaise* on May 17th and May 24th, 1846.

On May 20th, 1849, the *Courrier de la Louisiane* announced another drama by Canonge, *Juan ou une histoire sous Charles-Quint,* which was to be performed at the Théâtre Français of New Orleans. This drama was staged, but it was never published. In this same year, Canonge wrote a comedy, *Qui perd gagne,* which he dedicated to Alfred de Musset. It gives a charming account of a young wife's strategy to keep her husband at home one evening. It shows the author's admiration for de Musset, since it resembles de Musset's comedies, especially *Il faut qu'une porte soit ouverte ou fermée.* The *Courrier de la Louisiane* announces *Qui perd gagne* on the same bill with *Juan* for May 7th, and again for May 20th at the Théâtre d'Orléans. On May 12th, this same paper speaks of the great success of this comedy, and on May 21st, of the double success that Canonge had achieved on the previous evening, as editor and actor. In 1850 his *France et Espagne* appeared. In 1851, another drama of his, *Un Grand d'Espagne,* was

[3] See Chapter III.

published in the April numbers of the *Orléanais*. It had been played in New Orleans in 1847 (the *Courrier de la Louisiane* announced it in the theatre program for May 30th and again for June 5th) but had not been published before. *Un Grand d'Espagne* is a story of bandits, abductions, and murders. The characters are taken from various stations of life and are well represented. In the final scene, the grandee is killed and is about to be thrown into the water, when Mateo, one of the murderers, shows his practical side by exclaiming:

" A l'eau le Grand d'Espagne; (regardant le pourpoint)! mais sauvons l'enveloppe ".

The *Comte de Carmagnola* by Canonge was played in 1852 (the *Courrier de la Louisiane* announced it in the program for June 6th) and published in 1856. Edward Fortier, in his *Lettres Françaises en Louisiane* (p. 8) states that in this drama, Canonge was too greatly influenced by Manzoni. A close examination of the two plays shows that the Louisiana author and Manzoni have given entirely different pictures of Carmagnola. The latter dramatist treats him as a soldier only, and places the scenes in the camp or in the senate chamber at Venice. Carmagnola is seen as a proud, haughty, fiery general, who has many enemies among the leaders of the army. The story of his life is told only from the time that the council at Venice deliberates on making him general. Discussions in this council give the reader the information that Carmagnola had been in the service of the Duke of Milan, that they had quarreled, and that an effort had been made by the envoys of Milan in Venice to kill Carmagnola. In the same drama he is represented as a married man; his wife and daughter are presented for a few moments when they are allowed to see him in prison before he is led forth to death.

167

Canonge's drama contains many more romantic incidents and is much more melodramatic. As in the case of *Le Comte de Monte Cristo* and *France et Espagne,* he has probably dramatized a novel: this time *Le Comte de Carmagnola* by Molé-Gentilhomme, for in the theatre program for June 6th, 1852, the *Courrier de la Louisiane* announced on June 4th, *Le Comte de Carmagnola,* par MM. Molé-Gentilhomme and Placide Canonge.[4] Canonge introduces Carmagnola in 1419, as a young shepherd, who has come to Milan to say that the child, left when a baby at his father's house by Ericcio, has now reached her fifteenth year. He is witness there to the execution of the duke's wife, Beatrice de Tenda, on a charge of infidelity. Canonge makes a very dramatic incident of this execution: the duchess mounts the scaffold, the man who had sworn that he was her lover is filled with remorse and cries out that he has perjured himself and that the duchess is innocent. He is led off the stage and the sound of the executioner's axe is heard; then the duchess is led away, and the axe is heard again. In the last look of the duchess, Carmagnola thinks he sees Michaela, the young girl whom his father has reared and whom he hopes to make his wife.

Before dying, the duchess learns that her new-born child had been stolen fifteen years before, and a child of the duke and his mistress had been substituted. The duchess reveals this in a parchment which she gives to Captain Bramante, her faithful follower. He, fearing

---

[4] I was unable to obtain a copy of this novel anywhere in New Orleans, nor was I more successful in obtaining it from the Columbia University Library, the New York Public Library, Johns Hopkins, Harvard University, Yale University, Chicago University, or the Library of Congress. I was therefore unable to compare the drama with the novel to see what changes Canonge made in the story.

treachery, instrusts it to Carmagnola. Thus Carmagnola learns that Michaela, instead of Bianci, the substituted child, is the daughter of the duchess and heiress of the duchy of Milan.

In Act II, four years later, Carmagnola is seen again. He has resolved to win for Michaela her rights and, by his prowess as a soldier, to win for himself the rank that would make him worthy of being her husband. For this reason he has become a soldier and has made the Duke of Milan secure on his throne. He now appears before the duke and demands rights for Michaela. The duke's attitude in this matter influences Carmagnola to go over to the side of Venice. To the attempt of the envoys of Milan to poison him, only mentioned in Manzoni's drama, is devoted the whole of Act III in Canonge's play.

The love story is complicated by Bianci's affection for Carmagnola. Thinking that she is the daughter of the duchess and hearing Carmagnola swear before the picture of Beatrice that he will never love any one except her daughter, Bianci believes that her love is returned. She is instrumental in saving Carmagnola's life in a plot contrived against him by her father and Ericcio, but is later used as a tool to accomplish his ruin. Deceived by her father, she writes a letter, dictated by him, welcoming Carmagnola back to Milan. The Duke of Milan causes this letter to fall into the hands of the leaders at Venice. Carmagnola is arrested for treason and condemned by the Council of Ten to be executed. Michaela, in despair, sends for Bianci to intercede. In the meanwhile, the Council advances the time of the execution by twelve hours and Carmagnola is led forth to die. The scene on the scaffold is very dramatic. . Carmagnola recounts to the people all that he has done for them and asks their aid, but they are silent. Then, seizing the

dagger of one of the guards, he stabs himself crying,
" J'échapperai à la hache du bourreau. " Bianci, who
has hastened from Milan, and Michaela both hurry to
save him, but they arrive in time to have a few words
with him before he dies.[5]

Canonge has arranged his drama in acts, divided into
" tableaux ". He has given these tableaux very striking
titles, some of which show the influence of Hugo in
their antitheses: Le Parchemin; L'Echafaud; La voix de
Dieu; Lion et Renard; Le Capitole et la Roche Tar-
péienne; Deux cœurs pour un Amour; and La Couronne
d'Epines. This play was produced in Paris and was
performed one hundred nights.[6]

Canonge continued writing for the papers of New Orleans. He wrote dramatic and musical criticisms in the
" Bulletin Artistique " of L'Abeille; the " Revue de la
Semaine " and " Causeries " in the Courrier de la Louisiane, in 1849; he was editor of L'Entr'Acte in 1850;
collaborated to the Renaissance Louisianaise in 1862;
and was editor of the Epoque in 1869. In the early
seventies, he was director of the French Opera. A
notice in Le Carillon for August 3rd, 1873 spoke of his
skilful directing. He died in New Orleans in 1893.

" SARA LA JUIVE " AND " LA FAMILLE CREOLE "

Auguste Lussan's Sara la Juive with a subtitle, " Chronique Irlandaise ", was performed in New Orleans in
1838 and published in 1839. Long and rather poorly

---

[5] According to history, Carmagnola had a gag placed in his
mouth to prevent his protestation of innocence, and he was
beheaded. J. C. L. de Sismondi: A History of the Italian Republics, p. 219.

[6] Davidson: Living Writers of the South, p. 81.

constructed, it pictures the persecution of the Jews by the Lord Mayor of Dublin. Sara, who had once been the mistress of the Lord Mayor, returns as a sorceress and brings unhappiness to him for the wrongs done her. The drama is very melodramatic in its incidents. Lussan wrote another play, *La famille créole,* which was presented several times at the French Theatre in New Orleans. Its first performance was announced by the *Courrier de la Louisiane* in the program of the French Theatre for February 28th, 1837. It was played on March 9th, April 7th, and May 7th. This might indicate that it was successful, but there was no notice in the papers of the time telling how it was received.[7]

DRAMAS OF MEXICAN HISTORY

In his *Guatimozin,* 1839, Pérennes gives a very sympathetic account of Guatimozin's efforts to defend Mexico against Cortes. When the High Priest announces that the gods demand blood, Zaïna, the fiancée of Guatimozin, wishes to offer herself for the sacrifice, but is prevented from doing so by Guatimozin. The soldiers, in spite of their hunger, fight bravely but vainly to defend the city. Cortes enters as victor. He finally accedes to the demand of his soldiers that Guatimozin be given to them. Eager to know where Guatimozin has his gold, they torture both him and his faithful companion, Namir, with fire. Both die without disclosing the hiding-place. Zaïna comes to share Guatimozin's imprisonment, but finding him dead, she dies too. The soldiers are very much chagrined at their failure to discover the treasure.

[7] I have been unable to find a copy of this drama.

Pérennes gives, in his introduction to this drama, a long appreciation of Guatimozin and his qualities. He does not say much of Cortes since he is well known. The author promises that later, if he has time, he will make a deeper study of Cortes. Pérennes says that he has invented the character Zaïna, not as a creation of mere fancy nor as an innovation from ancient tragedy, but as a local truth, for human sacrifices were common in Mexico. He has fashioned her after the women produced by great catastrophes in all countries and at all times.

Guatimozin is written in Alexandrine verse and observes the unities of time, of action, and to some extent that of place. The scene is an apartment in Guatimozin's palace or a public square near the palace.

Pérennes speaks in the introduction (p. v) of a second drama, *Hicotengal* which, like *Guatimozin,* was inspired by his visit to the Mexican ruins, and was likewise a work of instinct rather than of reflection. Nothing is known of this second drama.

In 1888, *Fortunia,* Dr. Alfred Mercier's only drama, appeared. It discusses the question of fatality and free will. Tiberic evidently expresses the author's own ideas when he says that one can be courageous and still be unable to endure an insult. Instead of being logically developed, events seem to be brought in solely to prove that fate, rather than will, rules over us.

COMEDIES

The comedies of Marie Augustin are for children, and have as subjects *Les vacances de Camille,* and *Le dernier bonnet d'âne.* They are very simple and show little development of plot and very little action. In the former, Camille, who is visiting her aunt, seems incorrigible, and her tricks and pranks disturb every one. Her love for her bird is very strong. Her aunt, realizing this, punishes her through the bird, and quickly—somewhat too quickly to be natural—makes her repent, and all is well. The latter is a scene of school life in which two high-spirited pupils lead a revolt against an unreasonable instructess, who still believes in making the children wear a " Bonnet d'âne ". The director of the school, while instituting a reform and revision of rules, calls on these two leaders to help her, and thus gives them an opportunity to use their energy and executive ability in a constructive way.

The comedies of Felix Voorhies: *Le petit chien de la veuve, Ne pas lâcher la proie pour l'ombre,* and *Les noces d'argent du Couple Néral,* all published in the *Comptes Rendus de l'Athénée Louisianais,* are one-act comedies of intrigue. They are very amusing but have no claim to fame.

In 1877 *L'Ecole du Peuple,* a comedy in one act and in verse, was published by Dr. Charles Deléry. Inspired by the political situation in Louisiana at that time, this comedy shows the poor government as it existed. A character called Demos represents the people and comes in at the end. The author says in the introduction that he merely intended to portray the most hideous figures of the group and let them express on the stage the sentiments they expressed behind closed doors.

Such is the dramatic production in French in Louisiana. Canonge and Lussan, with their companion dramas *France et Espagne,* and *Les Martyrs de la Louisiane,* respectively (see Chapter III) have treated a celebrated event of Louisiana history. They have both written long romantic dramas also; Pérennes has revived ancient Mexican history; Dr. Mercier has contributed his play which studies the question of fate; and three writers, Marie Augustin, Felix Voorhies, and Dr. Charles Deléry have added to the *genre* with their little comedies.

CHAPTER IX

MISCELLANEOUS WRITINGS

There are other writings that might deserve a place in a discussion of French literature in Louisiana: works critical, controversial, autobiographical, biographical, historical, educational, and scientific; works written by lawyers, statesmen, professors, and doctors.

THE WORK OF ALCEE FORTIER

Although Alcée Fortier has produced no drama, no poetry, and only one novel, his name will always be linked with French writings in Louisiana.

Fortier was born in 1856 in St. James Parish, Louisiana, son of Edwige Aime and Florent Fortier.[1] His family, originally from Brittany, came to Louisiana in 1720. He received his early education in New Orleans and then went to the University of Virginia. On account of ill health, he was unable to complete his course. He was, for some time, professor of French in the Boys' High School of New Orleans, and then became principal of the preparatory department of Tulane University. In 1880 he was made professor of French at Tulane University, and in 1894, professor of Romance Languages. His greatest interest was the French language and literature, and wherever he went, he preached his love for them. He did research work in the Acadian and other

---

[1] Facts about his life were obtained from the C. R. A. L., April 1914, pp. 50-63, and also from his wife.

dialects and published some folk tales in dialect form. He won the medal in the first literary contest of the *Athénée Louisianais* in 1878. His subject was *De la puissance de l'éducation et de la nécessité du travail dans toutes les conditions de la vie*. After his prize essay, many of his articles have been published in the *Comptes Rendus* of this organization. Fortier was president of the *Athénée* from 1893 until his death in 1914.

Fortier's other works are historical, critical, or biographical. In 1885 his *Vieux français et la littérature du moyen âge* was published in the *Comptes Rendus de l'Athénée Louisianais*. It explains briefly the changes from Latin to French, discusses the *langue d'oïl et langue d'oc,* and the different works of the Middle Ages. In 1887 he published *Quatre Grands Poètes du dix-neuvième siècle,* lectures given by him at Tulane University on Lamartine, de Vigny, Hugo, and de Musset. These lectures were so favorably received that in 1890 Fortier republished these four and added three others with the title, *Sept grands auteurs du dix-neuvième siècle.* In his preface he expresses the hope that the analyses of several masterpieces and the extracts from the works of these authors will encourage students to read the books mentioned. He intends the volume for use as a literary reader in second-year classes in French, and, for that reason, has made the style simple and easy.

Fortier published an *Histoire de la littérature française* in 1893. The first part of the history is developed in detail, and is much better than the latter part, which does not seem to be well planned. The section called *L'Heure présente* is mainly a list of names under each *genre*. Fortier says, however, at the beginning of Part V that another volume would be necessary to treat of the nineteenth century properly.

In 1899, he published a *Précis de l'histoire de France,* which is also intended for pupils in American schools. It is very clear, leaves out unnecessary details, and is useful for one who wants the main facts of French history. The revised edition (1913) extends to the election of Poincaré in 1913. Fortier has also edited as texts for schools, such works as *Laurette, ou le cachet rouge* and *Les femmes savantes.*

Fortier's desire to make Louisiana better known was the inspiration of a pamphlet by him on *Les planteurs sucriers de l'ancien régime en Louisiane,* a history of the beginnings of the sugar-refining industry in Louisiana. Valcour Aime, Fortier's grandfather, was one of the first to refine sugar on a large scale. This article contains long digressions on the slave question, on the kindness of the planters to the slaves, and on the attachment of the slaves to their masters. (Fortier's *History of Louisiana,* published in 1904, is written in English and is therefore out of place in a discussion of his French works).

Fortier has given, in his *Louisiana Studies,* information about the French language and dialects in Louisiana, but he devotes the greater part of the book to the literature of Louisiana, discussing both the French and English writers. This work, though written in English, is mentioned here, for through it the outside world has learned that Louisiana possesses a French literature, and that the French writers are still loved and remembered by the people of that state. Fortier is very sympathetic towards these French authors, and has, at times, allowed his judgment to be biased by his affections.

Edward Joseph Fortier, son of Alcée Fortier, has also rendered service to the French language and literature of Louisiana. He was born in New Orleans in 1883, received his early education in his native city, and was graduated from Tulane University in 1904. He then went to Johns Hopkins University in Baltimore, Maryland, where he spent two years studying French, Spanish, and Italian. While there, he also taught at the Notre Dame School of Maryland. In 1906—1907, he was instructor of Romance languages at Yale University. Leaving Yale in 1907, he went to the University of Illinois where he was assistant in Romance Languages until 1910. He then went to Columbia University in New York City, and was made instructor, and later, assistant professor. While teaching there he also continued his studies. He contributed articles to the *New International Encyclopedia* and collaborated to the *Cambridge History of American Literature*. In 1912, he was present at the First Congress of French Letters at Quebec, and read a paper on the *Lettres Françaises en Louisiane*. He was planning to write a dissertation for a Ph. D. degree on the subject of the French Literature of Louisiana, which was his favorite topic just as it had been his father's. During his visits to New Orleans, he used to spend a large part of his time in the libraries seeking information about the early French writers. This cherished work of Fortier was interrupted by his death in 1918.[2]

Edward Fortier based his *Lettres Françaises en Louisiane* on the *Louisiana Studies* written by Alcée Fortier. He has, however, added a great number of works to those mentioned by his father, and has represented the subject in more orderly retrospect.

[2] Facts about him were obtained from *Ten Years of the Class of 1904 of Tulane University;* from a memorial issued by Columbia University at the time of his death; from his *Lettres Françaises en Louisiane*, p. 1; and from an interview with Mrs. Fortier.

SHORT ARTICLES BY DR. ALFRED MERCIER

Dr. Alfred Mercier has written articles which are very diverse in subject. His *Etude sur les éclairs, Diamants, Hamlet; son état mental,* and *Rêves, sommeil, somnambulisme* show him to be a man of science; *Dante Alighieri et la Divine Comédie* and *Etienne Viel, sa traduction en vers latins du Télémaque de Fénelon* proclaim him a literary critic; *Excursions dans les Pyrénées, L'Engadine,* and *Alger* reveal a traveler; and his *Etude sur la langue créole en Louisiane* makes him known as a philologist.

WRITINGS, MEDICAL AND OTHERWISE, BY DR. CHARLES DELERY

Among the many prominent physicians of New Orleans who contributed to French literature, was Dr. Charles Deléry. He was born in 1815 on a plantation near New Orleans. In 1829 he was sent to Paris, studied there, received his degree in medicine, and then returned to New Orleans to practice. He was very prominent in his profession, and contributed many articles to the papers of the time on different phases of his work, especially on yellow fever. In 1849, a pamphlet *Etudes sur les passions, suivie d'un aperçu sur l'éducation qu'il convient de donner au peuple,* signed " Un Louisianais " was published in New Orleans. Though it was signed with a *nom de plume,* the contemporaries of Deléry recognized him as the author.[3] In 1859 he wrote *Précis historique de la fièvre jaune,* a discussion of the different theories regarding the origin of yellow fever, its symptoms, and contains some interesting observations he

[3] See Charles Testut's *Portraits Littéraires,* p. 39.

had made on various cases. In 1867 he wrote another pamphlet, *Mémoire sur l'épidémie de la fièvre jaune qui a régné à la Nouvelle Orléans et dans les campagnes pendant l'année 1867.*

About 1878 Dr. Deléry moved from New Orleans to Bay St. Louis, Mississippi, and began, in the *Comptes Rendus de l'Athénée Louisianais,* a series of articles called *Chroniques Indiennes.* On receiving a letter from the *Athénée* congratulating him on these articles, Dr. Deléry answered that it was due to the *Athénée* that his manuscript had seen the light of day, for he had had it buried in a portfolio for several years.[4] After a prologue in verse, instructive as well as interesting prose sketches of Indian life followed. They presented definite information about the character of the Indians, their ideas of the soul, their marriage customs, and their civil and criminal procedure. These *Chroniques* appeared throughout the year 1878. Dr. Deléry died in Bay St. Louis in 1880.[5] In 1911, in accordance with its plan of reviving the works of earlier writers, the *Athénée Louisianais* republished some of Dr. Deléry's poems.

THE YELLOW FEVER EPIDEMICS AND DR. JEAN FAGET

Dr. Jean Charles Faget was born in New Orleans on June 16th, 1818, son of Jean Baptiste Faget, a native of San Domingo. Charles was an only child and was taken by his mother to France to be educated. After finishing his medical studies in Paris in 1844, he came

---

[4] *Comptes Rendus de l'Athénée Louisianais,* September 1878, p. 187.

[5] Facts about him were obtained from his niece, Mrs. Heloise H. Cruzat of New Orleans and from a short preface to some of his poems republished in the *Comptes Rendus de l'Athénée Louisianais in Oct.,* 1911, p. 263.

back to Louisiana and for many years practiced medicine in New Orleans. He was a member of the Anatomical Society, of the Medical Observation Society, corresponding laureate member of the Society of Medicine at Caen, member of the Sanitary Consulting Committee in 1864, and delegate to the 5th National Quarantine and Sanitary Convention in Philadelphia in 1855. In 1855 he published an *Etude sur les bases de la science médicale et exposition sommaire de la doctrine traditionnelle* which, according to its title page, was crowned by the Academy of Medicine at Caen on June 10th, 1853. This work is a long and technical discussion on the possibility of establishing a basis for a doctrine or general system of pathology, to be taught and practiced.

Dr. Faget was greatly interested in the yellow fever question and after the epidemic of 1858, was decorated by the French government for the medical services rendered by him to French citizens in New Orleans. He made some interesting discoveries regarding the differences between yellow and malarial fever, and was the first to observe the lack of correlation between temperature and pulse in yellow fever. In 1864 he published a collection of articles, *Mémoires et lettres sur la fièvre jaune et la fièvre paludéenne,* which had appeared at different intervals in medical journals in Paris and New Orleans.

Dr. Faget and Dr. Deléry carried on heated discussions of yellow fever in letters published in the *Medical Journal* of New Orleans. In 1860 Dr. Deléry wrote *Réplique au mémoire du Dr. Charles Faget publié dans le numéro du 9 mars 1860 du journal de la Société Médicale de la Nouvelle Orléans.* Dr. Faget replied in the journal of July 1860 (pp. 2-16) with his *Cinquième lettre sur la fièvre jaune, ou deuxième réponse au Dr. Deléry.* Again

Dr. Deléry challenged him in the issue of September 1860 (pp. 51-58) with his *Seconde réplique du Dr. Charles Deléry à la cinquième lettre du Dr. Charles Faget*. This controversy must have continued for a number of years, for in 1868, Dr. Deléry published his *Dernière réplique au Dr. Faget*.

Dr. Faget died in New Orleans on December 7th, 1884.[6]

ARTICLES DEFENDING THE CREOLES

Articles of a controversial nature were occasioned by George W. Cable's *Who are the Creoles?* A *Critique du dernier ouvrage de M. Georges W. Cable: Who are the Creoles?* was written in 1884 by John Casimir Delavigne. Delavigne's father, uncle of the Casimir Delavigne of literary fame in France, was a native of France who had left his home city, Havre, and had gone to San Domingo. During the uprising of the negroes, having been warned by a slave, he fled with his wife and children to Cuba. It was there that John Casimir was born. The family later went to New York and then to South Carolina. When John Casimir was 20 years old, he went to Louisiana, where he spent the remainder of his life praticing law. He died in New Orleans on July 14th, 1888 at the age of 82.[7]

Although born under the Spanish flag, Delavigne was an ardent Frenchman. After the first two instalments

[6] Facts about him were obtained from his baptismal record at the Cathedral, from his death record at the City Board of Health office, from his daughter, Mother Faget of the Sacred Heart Convent of New Orleans, and from the title pages of his books.
[7] Facts about him were obtained from his daughter, Miss Emily Delavigne of New Orleans, and from the notice of his death in the *Picayune* of July 15th, 1888.

of G. W. Cable's *Who are the Creoles?* had appeared in the January and February numbers of the *Century Magazine* in 1883, Delavigne answered with his *Critique*. He says that Cable, in his preceding works, *Grandissimes* and *Madame Delphine,* had been treating the Creoles in fiction and that his imagination might have been allowed some sway; however, now that he has entered the domain of history, he should present facts. Delavigne accepts Cable's geographical distribution of the Creoles as practically correct, and also his account of the founding of New Orleans. However, he objects to Cable's statement that the Creoles observe July 4th and, ten days later, celebrate July 14th with far greater enthusiasm. He maintains that the celebration on July 14th is fostered by the people of the French Republic, citizens of France living in New Orleans; that the Creoles, invited to participate, take part as guests, but not with the fervor spoken of by Cable. He also objects to Cable's distinction between the Acadian Creoles and those who, as Cable says, " Try to appropriate for themselves the pure name of Creoles ". Delavigne believes that they are all equally Creoles, and questions Cable's authority for certain statements made regarding the lack of ambition and the imperiousness of temper among the second generation of men in the colony.

After this work of Cable had been published in book form as *The Creoles of Louisiana,* John L. Peytavin raised his voice against it in 1889 with his *Réfutation des erreurs de M. George W. Cable au sujet des Créoles.* Peytavin attacks the statement of the celebration of July 4th and July 14th and makes the same assertions that Delavigne had made: The French residents organize this celebration, and if the Creoles participate, it is only as invited guests. He objects to Cable's statement that the

Creoles call the other citizens of the United States "Americans", and maintains that the Creoles look upon themselves as Americans and are not prevented from doing so by their Latin origin. The Acadian Creoles have the same right to be called Creoles as others of foreign descent. Cable always takes the exceptional cases and accepts them as the general rule, as when he pictures an ignorant, uneducated Creole as the type of all Creoles.

Many years before, in 1848, Bernard de Marigny had published his *Réflexions sur la Campagne du Général Jackson en Louisiane en 1814 et 1815,* a strong defense of the Creoles of Louisiana against the criticisms of their patriotism before and during the War of 1812. Marigny belonged to a family which arrived in Louisiana at the beginning of the founding of the colony. He was born on October 25th, 1785. For many years he was prominent in the politics of Louisiana. At the ceremony of the cession of Louisiana back to France and, shortly after, to the United States in 1803, he was aide-de-camp of Laussat, the colonial prefect. He was on General Jackson's staff, was chairman of the Committee of Defense in 1814—1815, and was a valiant soldier at the Battle of New Orleans. Later he became a member of the legislature several times. On February 4th, 1868, he died from a blow on the head, received when he tripped and fell on the pavement.[8]

In 1822 Marigny published a *Mémoire de Bernard de Marigny, habitant de la Louisiane, adressé à ses concitoyens,* an answer to an attack against him because of his opposition to a certain man nominated for mayor, and also

[8] Facts about him were obtained from Grace King's *Old Creole Families of New Orleans,* MacMillan & Co., New York, 1921.

a defense of his opinions pronounced in the Louisiana Senate on the famous Batture Case. This *Mémoire* and the *Réflexions* mentioned above are well written with clear, definite statements.

AUTOBIOGRAPHY

Quite different from these discussions was the autobiographical work of Mademoiselle Désirée Martin, *Les Veillées d'une sœur, ou le destin d'un brin de mousse,* published in 1877. Mademoiselle Martin tells the story of her life in a very simple and natural way. Her ancestors had come down from Acadia, had endured many hardships, and had settled in the Acadian country of Louisiana where she was born. In her childhood, she helped fill the family purse by serving as " goose girl " to a rich neighbor. To please her mother, who wanted her to be a nun, Désirée took the veil at the age of sixteen. For twenty-seven years she led a life of devotion, and then gave it up. There were many conjectures concerning the reason for her leaving the convent. Her only explanation was that she had entered contrary to her own wishes. She returned to her brother's home and taught a little class at Grande Pointe. In her preface, she relates that while walking one day, she saw a magnolia flower hastening to bloom before the season was over. She asked herself why she should not produce a flower, not a magnolia, but perhaps a *brin de mousse.* This volume, with its story of the life of the early Acadians, of Mademoiselle Martin's family, of herself, and of her forty-seven years of trials and of joy, was the result.

Madame Hélène Allain's *Souvenirs d'Amérique et de France par une Créole,* published in Paris in 1882, is both biographical and autobiographical. In Part I, Madame Allain furnishes a detailed account of her remote ancestors. Her parents—she was of the family of d'Aquin—ruined by the emancipation of their slaves in the English Antilles, went to New Orleans in 1836, when Madame Allain was not yet four years old. In part II she speaks again of her immediate family and of her early days in New Orleans. In Part III she discusses Toulouse and Provençal poetry.

After her marriage, Madame Allain went to France and spent the remainder of her life there.[9] Her book, though well written, does not have a universal appeal because it is too definitely family history and of interest only to her close friends and members of her family.

SKETCHES AND PORTRAITS

Cyprien Dufour's *Esquisses Locales* in 1847 and Charles Testut's *Portraits Littéraires de la Nouvelle Orléans* in 1850 are interesting as biographies of the men of the time by their contemporaries.

Dufour was born in New Orleans on September 16th, 1819. He was a contributor to various papers of New Orleans and in 1862 was collaborator to the *Renaissance Louisianaise*. He died on February 8th, 1871.[10]

The editor who published Dufour's *Esquisses Locales* stated that these sketches had appeared without signature in the columns of one of the papers of New Orleans. The incognito of the writer excited public curiosity, and,

[9] Information about her was obtained from her book, and from her cousin, Miss Margaret Boun of New Orleans.
[10] Facts about him were obtained from the birth and death records of the City Board of Health office, from a copy of the *Renaissance Louisianaise* of 1862, and the notice of his death in the *Abeille* of February 9th, 1871.

when conjectures were made as to his identity, he ceased writing. When Dufour presented his work in book form, he explained (in the preface) that the sketches had been seized on the wing in moments of leisure and were mere reflexions of truth. The sketches are short, some extremely so, but they have a delicacy and sincerity that cause them to be very popular.

Testut dedicated his *Portraits Littéraires* to Madame Emilie Evershed. He refers in his preface to Dufour's work, and hopes that his own will be as successful as that of his predecessor. Dufour had limited his sketches almost exclusively to members of the bar, whereas Testut, as the name *Portraits Littéraires* indicates, assigns first place to the literary men of the day. He pledges himself to forget the man, not to be influenced by any preconceived opinions, and to see only the writer. Most of his portraits are of the directors and editors of the newspapers in New Orleans at the time. He does not limit himself to literary men, however, and many doctors and lawyers are portrayed. He writes of fifty-five men in all, and gives a brief appreciation—sometimes as brief as five lines—of the work done by them. Occasionally he digresses into a didactic or philosophic strain.

TEXT BOOKS

In 1829 Pierre Cherbonnier, whose name appears in the New Orleans directories from 1823 to 1830 as a teacher, published an *Alphabet ou méthode simple et facile de montrer promptement à lire aux enfants ainsi qu'aux étrangers qui veulent apprendre le français, plus principes de grammaire générale appliqués à la langue française, suivis de plusieurs exercices, propres à développer l'intelligence des élèves, orner leur mémoire et former leur jugement,* a text book for the teaching of reading. The title of this work shows that the author wants to make clear to all exactly what he proposes to teach his pupils. A dedicatory epistle to the *Jeunesse Louisianaise* explains more fully his desire to diminish difficulties and awaken a love of study. In the early lessons he uses fourteen tables of letters and combinations of letters, of words with similar sounds or with similar spelling but different sounds. For his rules of grammar he gives a great number of illustrations. He is not a follower of Rousseau, for he uses the fables of La Fontaine for exercises, after having changed the verse to prose. The last part deals with versification and gives many examples of various kinds of verse.[11]

In this same year, 1829, a *Géographie des commençants par demandes et par réponses à l'usage des collèges et écoles de la Louisiane* was published. The copy in the Howard Library has Boimare, New Orleans, as the printer and place, but there is no indication as to who the author was. Another text book of geography called *Précis élémentaire de géographie à l'usage des écoles américaines* was published in 1841, by a certain Dezauche. He explains in the preface that, charged by Louisiana families with the education of their children, he felt that he could not be successful if he did not prepare a geography. He lent the result of his work to other professors who also found the lessons helpful. Encouraged by their report, he decided to publish the book.[12]

L'Abeille of October 6th, 1851, contains an announcement of a collection of songs called *Chansons patrioti-*

---

[11] His name mentioned in the directories was the only trace that could be found of Cherbonnier.

[12] No record could be found anywhere of a Dezauche who was a teacher in New Orleans, nor could any first name be found for him.

ques by Alexander Magnin. The statement is made that Magnin came to this country fleeing the despotism of the Bourbons, and that the Revolution of 1830 inspired some of his best songs. No copy of these songs could be found. Magnin was an attorney in New Orleans for several years until his death in 1836.[13]

In the issues of the *Abeille* from June 11th through June 16th, 1845, a certain G. A. M. advertised a *Histoire pittoresque et curieuse du théâtre français de la Nouvelle Orléans de 1816 à 1846, dédiée aux Louisianais*. The author had been working on it for about thirty years. It would contain the names of all the artists who had appeared at the Théâtre Français, biographical notices of the principal actresses and actors, criticisms taken from the papers of the time regarding the way in which the new plays were given, and anecdotes of the theatre. The price was to be three dollars, but it would be published only if two hundred subscribers were found. Doubtless, G. A. M.—probably Guillaume A. Montmain—was unsuccessful in getting his two hundred subscribers and did not publish his history, for no copy of it can be located and no statement occurs of its having been issued.

Such are some of the important literary productions of French literature in Louisiana. They represent, however, only a part of the total amount, while many names, many classes of work will have to remain unrecorded. The ones mentioned suffice to show the main tendencies and the varities of form, as well as the influences that helped form the literature.[14]

[13] His name appears in the New Orleans directory for 1834 as an attorney and in the death record for 1836 at the City Board of Health office.

[14] For other writers and other works see the Bibliography of Louisiana Writers in the Appendix.

APPENDIX

BIBLIOGRAPHIES

In the bibliographies that follow I have tried to list every work I could find dealing with the Louisiana literature written in French. In bibliography *B*, I have listed only those works which I have been able to locate and examine. I have included with each book, by abbreviations placed after it, the library or private collection where I have found it. All of the places mentioned are in New Orleans unless otherwise indicated. I have named only one place, occasionally two, although I have found copies of some of the books in several places. This list contains works by men and women who, while not all natives of Louisiana, made their homes in that state for two or three years or more and identified themselves with her French writers. There were too many authors to treat each one at any great length; those not specially treated in the previous chapters, I have inserted in the bibliography, adding biographical sketches whenever it was possible. In some instances I was unable to obtain any information; all search for relatives, for friends, for names in the directories, and for names in the birth and death records both at the Cathedral and at the City Board of Health office whereby something might be learned, proved fruitless. I have listed the authors alphabetically; under each author's name I have placed his works chronologically. An asterisk (*) placed before a name indicates that the writer has been treated in detail in the course of this study.

The following is the list of abbreviations used in this bibliography:

A N O....... *Abeille de la Nouvelle Orléans*
C de L....... *Courrier de la Louisiane*
C H A....... City Hall Archives
C R A L.... *Comptes Rendus de l'Athénée Louisianais*
C U L....... Columbia University Library, New York City
H M L....... Howard Memorial Library
L C......... Library of Congress, Washington, D. C.
L H L....... Louisiana Historical Library
L H L CC.... Louisiana Historical Library—Cusachs Collection
L U L....... Loyola University Library
N Y P L..... New York Public Library, New York City
O L......... *Observateur Louisianais*
R L......... *Revue Louisianaise*
Ren. L....... *Renaissance Louisianaise*
S J S........ S. J. Shwartz Collection (now dispersed)
T P T....... T. P. Thompson Collection
T U L....... Tulane University Library

The complete file of the *Comptes Rendues de l'Athénée Louisianais* can be found in the Howard Library.

I have not relisted the newspapers and reviews because I have indicated, in the chapter relating to them, where they are to be found.

A.—*JOURNALS AND ACCOUNTS OF VOYAGES BY EXPLORERS AND TRAVELERS IN EARLY LOUISIANA*

Bossu, N. *Nouveaux voyages aux Indes occidentales; contenant une relation des différents peuples qui habitent les environs du grand fleuve, St. Louis, appelé vulgairement le Mississippi; leurs guerres, leur religion, leur gouvernement, leurs mœurs et leur commerce par M. Bossu, capi-*

taine dans les troupes de la Marine. Paris,
Le Jay MDCCLXIII. (Two parts in one volume.)

— *Nouveaux voyages dans l'Amérique Septentrionale
contenant une collection de lettres écrites sur
les lieux, par l'auteur à son ami, M. Douin,
Chevalier Capitaine dans les troupes du Roi, ci-
devant son camarade dans le nouveau monde,
par M. Bossu, Chevalier de l'Ordre Royal et
Militaire de St. Louis, ancien capitaine d'une
compagnie de la Marine.* Amsterdam, Chan-
guion, MDCCLXXVII.

BUTEL-DUMONT, Georges-Marie. *Mémoires historiques
sur la Louisiane contenant ce qui est arrivé de
plus mémorable depuis l'année 1687 jusqu'à
présent; avec l'établissement de la colonie française dans cette province de l'Amérique Septentrionale sous la direction de la Compagnie des
Indes; le climat, la nature, les productions de ce
pays; l'origine et la religion des sauvages qui
l'habitent, leurs coutumes, composés sur les
mémoires de M. Dumont par M. L. Le Mas-
crier.* Paris, Bauche, 1753, 2 vols. in one.
(Also in French's *Historical Collections*, vol. 5,
p. 1-129.)

CHARLEVOIX, Pierre François Xavier de. *Histoire et
description générale de la Nouvelle France avec
le journal historique d'un voyage fait par ordre
du roi dans l'Amérique Septentrionale (adressé
à Mme. la Duchesse de Lesdiguières).* Paris,
Noyon Fils, MDCCXLIV, 6 vols.

HACHARD, Marie Madeleine. *Relation du voyage des
Dames Religieuses Ursulines de Rouen à la
Nouvelle Orléans.* Rouen, chez Antoine le Pre-
vost, MDCCXXVIII.

HARPE, Bernard de la. *Journal historique de l'établissement des français à la Louisiane tiré des
mémoires de MM. Iberville et Bienville, com-
mandans pour le Roi au dit pays et sur les découvertes et recherches de M. Bernard de la
Harpe.* Nouvelle Orléans, 1831, t. p. w.

(Also in French's *Historical Collections,* vol. III, p. 10-118.)

HENNEPIN, Père Louis. *Description de la Louisiane nouvellement découverte au sud-ouest de la Nouvelle France—avec la carte du pays, les mœurs et la manière de vivre des sauvages.* Paris, Huret, 1683.

JOUTEL, Henri. *Voyage de M. de La Salle dans l'Amérique Septentrionale en l'année 1685 pour y faire un établissement dans la partie qu'il en avait auparavant découverte.* (In Pierre Margry: *Mémoires et documents,* vol. III, p. 91-534. Also in B. F. French: *Historical Collections of Louisiana,* vol. I, p. 85-193.)

PENICAUT, Jean. *Annals of Louisiana from the establishment of the First Colony under M. d'Iberville to the Departure of the Author to France in 1722, including an account of the manners, customs, and religion of the numerous Indian tribes of that country.* (In B. F. French: *Historical Collections of Louisiana and Florida,* vol. 1, p. 37-162. Also in Margry: *Mémoires et documents,* vol. V, p. 375-581.)

PRATZ, Le Page du. *Histoire de la Louisiane contenant la découverte de ce vaste pays; sa description géographique; un voyage dans les Terres; l'histoire naturelle; les mœurs, coutumes et religion des naturels, avec leurs origines; deux voyages dans le nord du Nouveau Mexique, dont un jusqu'à la mer du Sud, ornée de deux cartes et quarante planches en taille douce.* Paris, De Bure, MDCCLVIII, 3 vols.

TONTI, Henri. *Mémoire de Henri Tonti sur la découverte du Mississippi.* (In Margry's *Relations et Mémoires inédits,* p. 1-36. Also in B. F. French: *Historical Collections,* vol. 1, p. 52.)

Three other writings of interest on this early period of Louisiana History are:

BARBÉ-MARBOIS. *Histoire de la Louisiane précédée par un discours sur la constitution et le gouvernement des Etats-Unis.* Paris, Didot, 1829.

VERGENNES, Comte Charles Gravier. *Mémoire historique et politique sur la Louisiane, par M. Vergennes, Ministre de Louis XVI, accompagné d'un précis de la vie de ce ministre et suivi d'autres mémoires sur l'Indostan, St. Domingue, la Corse, et la Guyane.* Paris, Le Petit, 1802.

VILLIERS DU TERRAGE, Marc de. *Histoire de la fondation de la Nouvelle Orléans, 1717-1722, avec une préface de M. Gabriel Hanoteaux.* Paris, Imprimerie Nationale, 1917.

B.—*LOUISIANA WRITERS*

ALEIX, Madame Eulalie. *Les Poésies de Lamartine.* In C R A L, New Orleans, May 1888, p. 89-101.

This article won the prize in the contest of the Athénée Louisianais in 1887. It gives the life of Lamartine and his poems are inserted chronologically.

— *Le Livre d'Or de la Comtesse Diane.* In C R A L, New Orleans, March 1889, p. 269-274.

This is an analysis of this work of the Countess of Beaussay.

— *Maximes de la Vie.* In C R A L, New Orleans, July 1889, p. 358-362.

This article contains a few remarks on the *Maximes de la Vie* by the Countess of Beaussay and quotes from her book.

Madame Aleix, *née* Larocque Turgeau, was a native of New Orleans. She received her education in her native city. At the age of eighteen she married Leopold Aleix. She died at Shreveport, Louisiana, on November 16, 1920. (Information about her was obtained from her daughter, Mrs. W. P. Sparks of Shreveport.)

194

*ALLAIN, Madame Helene d'Aquin. *Souvenirs d'Amérique et de France par une Créole.* Paris, Perisses Frères, 1882. H M L

*ALLARD, Louis. *Les Epaves.* Paris, Hector Bossange; New Orleans, Lelièvre, 1847. H M L.

*ANDRY, Madame Laure Bordelois. *Histoire de la Louisiane racontée aux enfants louisianais.* New Orleans, Imprimerie Franco-Américaine, 1882. H M L   T U L

ANSON, Henry Frederick. *Elégie dédiée aux manes du Grand Napoléon.* In A N O, New Orleans, June 7, 1836.   L H L

— — *Fable: L'Ane et la Chouette.* A N O, New Orleans, June 24, 1836.   L H L

— *Ode à ma chouette.* In *A N O,* New Orleans, June 24, 1836.

— *La Sainte Joseph: Couplets faits à l'occasion de la fête de M. Joseph D. Lambert, Capitaine des Eclaireurs d'Orléans.* In La Réforme, New Orleans, May 31, 1846.

— *Hymne Patriotique à l'occasion de la Guerre des Etats-Unis avec le Mexique.* La Réforme, New Orleans, May 31, 1846. To be sung to the tune of the *Marseillaise.* (Anson's name appears in the New Orleans directories from 1832 through 1837; he is listed as a poet.)

ARMANT, F. *L'Opéra et ses notes, album illustré avec photographies et esquisses biographiques.* New Orleans, du Croissant, 1881.

— *Honni soit qui mal y pense: nouvelles par On-séki.* New Orleans, P. E. Marchand, 1883. H M L

This collection contains seven very short stories. The author signs his name in a postscript to the reader, confessing that he is F. Armant, New Orleans, June 1883.

(I could find no mention of Armant in any of the New Orleans directories, nor any trace of him anywhere else.)

*AUGUSTIN, Marie. *Le Macandal, épisode de l'insurrection des noirs à San Domingue, par Tante Ma-*

rie. Nouvelle Orléans. Imp. George Muller 1892. H M L.

— *Quelques mots sur Paul Bourget*. In C R A L, New Orleans, March 1895, p. 239-247. H M L.

This gives the principal facts of Bourget's life and calls attention to his love of analysing. It discusses some of his novels, such as *Cosmopolis* and *Le Disciple*.

— *Les Vacances de Camille*. In C R A L, New Orleans, July 1896, p. 505-512; September 1896, p. 513-524.

— *Le dernier bonnet d'âne*. In C R A L, New Orleans, January 1898, p. 211-231.

— *Trouvères et Troubadours, ou Cour d'Amour du Romanin*. In C R A L, New Orleans, November 1898, p. 375-390.

— *Les Trois Marguerites*. In C R A L, New Orleans, November 1900, p. 156-163.

This is a very interesting discussion of Marguerite of Provence, Marguerite of Valois, and Marguerite of Navarre.

— *Quelques mots sur Pierre Loti*. In C R A L, New Orleans, October 1904, p. 409-429.

— *Causerie sur le Canada*. In C R A L, New Orleans, October 1906, p. 105-117.

This is an account of a trip taken by the author, and is told in a very interesting manner.

BADOIL, Jean. *Edmond Rostand et son théâtre*. In C R A L, New Orleans, July 1904, p. 378-402.

This was the prize essay in the contest of 1903. It is well constructed with points well chosen and developed. The discussion is confined to *Cyrano de Bergerac* and *L'Aiglon*.

— *A la mémoire d'un de mes amis de collège que je vis mourir*. In C R A L, July 1904, p. 407-408.

Badoil was a young man of promise in the literary world whose premature death in 1905 stopped him at the beginning of his literary career. (C R A L, Jan. 1905, p. 3.)

*BARDE, Alexandre. *La Némésis.* In C de L, New Orleans, January 11, 1845.

— *A Rachel Malade.* In C de L, New Orleans, June 8, 1856.

— *Chant de noces.* In C de L, New Orleans, March 10, 1857.

— *Impressions.* In C de L, New Orleans, November 14, 1858. C H A.

— *Isabelle de St. Victor.* In R. L., New Orleans. Volume II, December 13, 1846.

— *Peppa.* In R. L., New Orleans. Volume II, February 28, 1847, p. 528-529. H M L.

— *Journal d'un candidat.* In R. L., New Orleans, Volume V., Oct. 10, 1847, p. 38-42.

— *L'An 1847,* January 2, 1848. In R. L., New Orleans, p. 329-336.

— *A Béranger.* In R. L., New Orleans, Vol. V, February 27, 1848, p. 520-524.

— *Les Enfants,* March 5, 1848, p. 546-547. In R. L., New Orleans, Volume V.

— *Michel Peyroux.* In R. L., April 30, 1848.

— *Satires du siècle, au Citoyen Barbès.* In R. L., New Orleans, Vol. VII, December 3, 1848, p. 228-233; December 10, p. 259-261.

— *Histoire des comités de vigilance aux Attakapas.* Meschacébé, St. Jean Baptiste, Louisiana, 1861. H M L.

BEAUREGARD, Pierre Gustave Toutant. *Emploi de Torpilles, batteries blindées (flottantes et de terres) et canons rayés à Charleston, Caroline du Sud, pendant la guerre entre les Etats de l'Union de 1861 à 1865.* In C R A L, July 1877, p. 77-80.

This article was read by General Beauregard before the Athénée Louisianais. (He was president of this organization from 1881 to 1892.) This is an interesting account of such means of defense.

General Beauregard was born in New Orleans in 1818 and died in 1893. He is too well known as a General of the Confederate forces during the Civil War to need further information given of him here.

BERJOT, Dr. Eugène. Pamphlets. H M L.
　　These pamphlets contain short stories, some of which offer very vivid descriptions, for the author always gives a definite setting to his stories. They are in the style of the naturalistic writers, showing the sordid side of life.

　　Dr. Berjot was a native of Valence, France. He came to New Orleans where he practiced medicine. He died on November 26, 1898 at the age of 82. (Information from the directories and the death records at the City Board of Health office.)

BERNARD, E. L. *Fleur des Bois.* In C R A L, New Orleans, September 1885, p. 212-226.
　　This is a short story of the attempted settlement of Florida in 1561. (I could find nothing about Bernard.)

BERNARD, Henri. *Souvenir de 1870.* In C R A L, New Orleans, July 1895, p. 301-303.
　　This is a poem in Alexandrine meter which relates an episode of the Franco-Prussian War. The French soldier is shown to suffer death rather than to cry " Vive le roi Guillaume ".

—　*Les vacances.* In C R A L, New Orleans, July 1896, p. 503.
　　This is a poem in well-written Alexandrine verse and reveals a love of nature when its beauties are seen on a vacation trip in the country.

—　*A mon filleul, et neveu.* In C R A L, New Orleans, October 1905, p. 134.
　　The poet almost envies his godchild the joy that he has in his toys on his birthday.

—　*A Mademoiselle.* In C R A L, New Orleans, January 1906, p. 29.

— *A M. le Docteur John S. Thibaut.* In C R A L, New Orleans, January 1906, p. 28.

Henri Bernard was born in New Orleans in 1859. He received his education in the schools of his native city. He loved literature and read extensively. He traveled in America but never made a trip to France, although to visit the country of his ancestors was one of the greatest desires of his life. He died in New Orleans in 1922. (Facts from his brother, Paul E. Bernard.)

BERNARD, Pierre Victor. *Notes sur La Salle.* In C R A L, New Orleans, May 1882, p. 107-109.

This is a very short article. It compares the success of Columbus in finding a new country with the failure of La Salle. The author feels that if Tonti had been with La Salle instead of Beaujeu, the result would have been quite different.

— *Etude sur l'histoire de la Louisiane.* In C R A L, New Orleans, January 1883, p. 297-304.

This is a very short sketch of events after 1752.

— *Un Ancêtre de la Sainte Alliance.* In C R A L, New Orleans, July 1883, p. 405-410.

The attitude of Frederick II of Prussia was the precursor of the Alliance of 1815 which was formed for the purpose of stopping all popular movements.

— *Raison et Sentiment.* In C R A L, New Orleans, November 1883, p. 452-455.

— *Un Début.* In C R A L, New Orleans, March 1884, p. 530-538.

This is a comedy in one act. There is very little plot to it. Marcel Arenil has written a comedy which he has offered for sale. His creditors, tired of waiting for him to pay them, take his bills to his father. The father is grieved at his son's failure to confide in him about his debts. While the question of the

199

bills is being discussed, the purchaser of the comedy enters and pays Marcel $30,000 for the play. There is great joy in the household; the debts are paid; and the engagement of Marcel and his sweetheart, Laure, is announced. The only thing that mars their happiness is the family's fear that such great success may have a bad effect on Marcel.

P. V. Bernard was born in New Orleans on May 26, 1828. He was educated in that city at Orleans College and at Versailles Coliege near Chalmette, Louisiana. He was, for many years, a professor at Guillot's school and at Soule's College in New Orleans. He died on November 15, 1911 at the age of 83. (Facts obtained from his son, Louis L. Bernard of New Orleans.)

BERNARD, Stephen. *La neige*. In C R A L, November 1896, p. 576-578.

This is a poem in Alexandrine verse. Tt pictures the joy that every one derives from snow. It bears the date 1864.

— *A un journaliste*. In C R A L, November 1896, p. 580-581.

The poet here greets Charles Testut, editor, as the standard-bearer of the two nations, America and France. It has the date 1863.

— *A Lamartine*. In C R A L, November 1896, p. 578-579.

This poem praises Lamartine very highly as a patriot.

— *Les deux lapins*. In C R A L, March 1897, p. 62.

This is a fable in verse which the author says was imitated from the Spanish of Thomas de Yriarte. It also bears the date 1863.

Bernard was born in La Rochelle, France, in 1792. He was in the French navy until 1823. He came to Boston in 1824 and later went to Louisiana. In 1848 he was at the head of a boarding school in St. Martinville. He taught for a while in Shreveport, then came to New

Orleans where he kept a private school for
boys. He died in 1872. (Facts from his
grandson, Paul E. Bernard, of New Orleans.)

BERNARD, Theresa. *Joseph de Maistre.* In C R A L,
May 1890, p. 96-103.

This essay won the prize in the contest of
1889. It discusses de Maistre as a statesman,
as a thinker, and as a private citizen.

(I could find nothing about Miss Bernard.)

BEUGNOT, Madame Aimée. *La chanson à travers les
siècles.* In C R A L, July 1900, p. 92-105.

This is a dream in which the « spirit of song »
took the author across centuries and countries
and enabled her to tell of the songs of the different lands.

— *La Bastille.* In C R A L, April 1903, p. 212-
230.

This is a study of the famous prison with
the names of some of its well known prisoners.

— *Alfred de Musset.* In C R A L, January 1908,
p. 282-294.

This is a study of the works and character
of Alfred de Musset.

— *La Comédie Française.* In C R A L, January
1911, p. 160-179.

This is a very interesting account of this
theater with its variety of plays, from Molière
to the present day.

Madame Beugnot (*née* Augustin) was a sister
of Marie Augustin and Madame Louise Augustin Fortier. She was an accomplished musician,
having studied music in Europe where she
traveled extensively. She died on February 9,
1917. (Information from her nephew, L. A.
Augustin, and her sister, Marie Augustin.)

BLANCHIN, Regina. *Les Romans de Pierre Loti.* In
C R A L, July 1912, p. 109-121.

This essay won the prize in the contest of
1911. It gives the life of Loti and analyses
his principal novels.

Mademoiselle Blanchin was born in New Or-

leans on March 15, 1857. Her father was a
native of France and her mother was a native
of New Orleans. She was educated in New
Orleans, Paris, and Bordeaux. She taught
French in New Orleans for many years, both in
private schools and to special pupils. She died
on November 30, 1916. (Information from
her niece, Miss Marguerite McHugh of New
Orleans.)

BLÉTON, Charles. *De la poésie dans l'histoire et de
quelques problèmes sociaux.* In C R A L, November 1877, p. 114-119.

This article is a clear discussion of the part
that poetry and poets have played in history
by inspiring the people to action. The second
part discusses the question of capital and labor
and seems to have no connection with the first
section.

— *La presse libérale.* In C R A L, March 1878,
p. 150-152. May 1878, p. 161-162.

The author here shows that the press has a
great mission in moulding public opinion, and
pleads for the freedom of the press.

— *Des origines du progrès moderne et de la révolution américaine.* In C R A L, July 1878,
p. 183-184; September 1878, p. 187-189; November 1878, p. 207-208.

This is a logical treatment of the development of progress, showing the part played by
the Renaissance, the Reformation, the American Revolution, and the French Revolution.

— *Une prophétie de M. Renan.* In C R A L, March
1881, p. 446-448.

This article remarks on Renan's statement:
" Heureux ceux qui viendront après nous, etc. "

Bléton was born in France in 1822. He
went to Louisiana in 1848 and was for a while
a private teacher. He later entered the field
of journalism and was connected with different
newspapers in New Orleans. In 1848, he was
on the staff of the *Journal de tout le monde;* he

wrote for the *Revue Louisianaise;* from 1856
to 1879 he was connected with the *Courrier de
la Louisiane;* and in 1883, at the time of his
death, he was assistant editor of the *Abeille.*
He died on February 22, 1883 at the age of
61. (Information from the death records at
the City Board of Health office, from the city
directories, and from a notice in the *Abeille*
for February 23, 1883.)

BOISE, Jean. *L'Amant dédaigné,* in *Les Cenelles.*
H M L.

Jean Boise was one of the collaborators of the
Cenelles. He contributed only one poem
which has no value. Nothing is known of his
life.

BOISE, Louis. *Au Printemps, chanson.* In *Les Cenelles.* H M L.

Louis Boise was also a collaborator of the
Cenelles to which he contributed one poem.
This is a song of how spring awakens his heart
and makes him want to tell of the charms of
Cleo.

BREAUX, Joseph A. *Réformateurs judicieux de systèmes
monétaires.* In C R A L, March 1898, p. 252-
255.

Sully, Colbert, and others are given as mod-
els in matters of finance.

— *Notes sur la province et le territoire de la Louisiane.* In C R A L, May 1899, p. 479-485.

This is a brief historical sketch from Crozat
on, dealing primarily with the changes in the
laws.

— *Origines des premières colonies.* In C R A L,
October 1908, p. 384-389.

This was a discourse pronounced at the sixth
Acadian Congress held at St. Balile, Nova
Scotia. It speaks of the close resemblance
between the French of Canada and those of
Louisiana.

— *Congress des Américanistes à Mexico.* In
C R A L, March 1897, p. 41-48.

— *Voyage à l'Ile de Cuba.* In C R A L, January 1904, p. 310-315.
— *Les expositions et les fêtes Hudson-Fulton.* In C R A L, January 1910, p. 8-12.

These three articles are very interesting accounts of trips that were taken by Judge Breaux.

Breaux was born in Bayou Goula in Iberville Parish in 1838. He studied law at the University of Louisiana and at Georgetown University. He was admitted to the bar in 1859. During the Civil War, he served in the Confederate Army. In 1865 he resumed his law practice in New Iberia. He was made Associate Justice of the Supreme Court of Louisiana in 1890. He died in July 1926. (Information from a notice in the New Orleans *Times-Picayune* on July 24, 1926, at the time of his death.)

CALONGNE, Adolphe. *A M. Charles Bléton.* In C de L, September 20, 1857.

When this poem appeared, the *Courrier de la Louisiane* remarked that it was almost the debut of Calongne. It expresses the longing of the poet to calm hearts and to bring sweet thoughts.

— *Bluette.* In C de L, October 17, 1858.

This poem is dedicated " Aux jeunes filles " because, according to the author, when one speaks of the lower one thinks of girls.

— *Ma sœur.* In C de L, February 28, 1858.

This poem, expressing great affection of the author for his sister, is dedicated to Placide Canonge.

— *Marie.* In C de L, October 17, 1858.

This. is a poem with the old theme that the human heart is inconstant.

— *Mon fils, ode à Ewell P. C.* In Ren. L., December 18, 1864. H M L.

Calongne was born in New Orleans in 1836. He received his education in that city and passed his life there. He wrote many poems that were published in the papers of New Orleans. He died in July, 1890. (Information from his son, F. L. Canonge of New Orleans.)

*CANONGE, Louis Placide. *Les Fantômes.* In A N O, February-March 1839. L H L.

— *Christophe.* In A N O, October 16, 1839 ff. L H L.

— *Le maudit passeport, ou les infortunes d'une drogue, vaudeville en un acte.* Gaux & Co., Nouvelle Orléans, 1840. L C.

— Poems in A N O, April 10, May 27, 1840. L H L.

— *Le Comte de Monte Cristo.* In R L, Vol. 1, 1846, p. 145-168; 173-202. H M L.

— *Rires et pleurs.* In R L, Vol. 1, 1846, p. 499-511. H M L.

— *La première et la dernière nuit de Nourrit.* In *La Violette,* March 1849, p. 14-16. T P T.

— *Qui perd gagne, comédie en prose, en un acte.* In C de L, September 20, 22, 25, 1849. Also in H L. C H A.

— *France et Espagne, ou la Louisiane en 1768 et 1769, drame en quatre actes,* n. pub. New Orleans, 1850. Représenté sur le théâtre d'Orléans le 1ᵉʳ juin, 1850. H M L.

— *Un Grand d'Espagne, drame en quatre actes en prose, mêlé de chants.* In L'Orléanais, March 30-April 29, 1851. C H A.

— *Une médaille.* In C de L, June 8, 1856 ff. C H A.

— *Le comte de Carmagnola, drame en cinq actes, dix tableaux et deux époques.* In C de L, Nouvelle Orléans, 1856. H M L.

— *La Louisianaise.* Chassaignac, Nouvelle Orléans, 1861. H M L.

— *Brise du Sud,* n. p. Nouvelle Orléans, 1864. L H L CC.

— *Nojoque; une grave question pour un continent, par Roman Helper de la Caroline du Nord. Traduction française précédée d'une introduc-*

tion avec notes par L. P. Canonge. Plume de
Bronze, New Orleans, 1867. H M L.

CASTELLANOS, John Joseph. *Bouée-signal automatique
de Courtenay*. In C R A L, July 1878, p.
174-177.
This is a detailed description, with illustrations, showing the mechanism of Courtenay's
buoy.

— *Jules César, tragédie de Shakespeare*. In
C R A L, March 1881, p. 444-446.
This is a translation into Alexandrine meter
of the dialogue between Brutus and Cassius,
Act 4, Scene 3 of Julius Caesar.

— *Quién supiera escribir?* In C R A L, November
1885, p. 248-249.
This is a translation of the poem of Ramón
Compoamor.

— *Le Soir*. In C R A L, May 1886, p. 88-91.
This poem in Alexandrine verse is dedicated
to Dr. Alfred Mercier and continues the idea
of Mercier's poem, " *Le Matin* ".

Dr. Castellanos was born in New Orleans on
November 4, 1834. His father was a native
of Cadiz, Spain. He was educated in New
Orleans and at St. Mary's Sulpician College in
Baltimore. He studied medicine in New Or-
leans and began practicing at the age of 21.
He was an enthusiastic member of the Athé-
née Louisianais. He died in 1914. (Informa-
tion from his daughter, Mrs. Edward May of
New Orleans.)

'CHERBONNIER, Pierre. *Alphabet ou méthode simple et
facile de montrer promptement à lire aux enfants ainsi qu'aux étrangers qui veulent apprendre le français, plus principes de grammaire générale appliqués à la langue française, suivis de
plusieurs exercices, propres à développer l'intelligence des élèves, orner leur mémoire et
former leur jugement*. Buisson et Boimare,
Nouvelle Orléans, 1829. H M L.

206

CHOPPIN, Jules.　Dialect poems in C R A L, 1896, 1897, 1898.　H M L.
— *Au Bayou St. Jean.*　In C R A L, September 1898, p. 362.
— *Assis au bord du bayou.*　In C R A L, January 1899, p. 404.
— *Qu'est-ce que l'âme?*　In C R A L, July 1899, p. 506.
— *N'en doutez pas.*　In C R A L, July 1899, p. 506.
— *Encore le vieux bayou.*　In C R A L, July 1899, p. 507.
— *Les singes et le léopard.*　In C R A L, July 1900, p. 113-114.
— *Le chêne de Bienville.*　In A N O, September 23, 1900.　L H L.
— *Le berceau—la tombe.*　In C R A L, November 1900, p. 164-165.
— *Toujours le vieux bayou.*　In C R A L, November 1900, p. 179.　H M L.
— *Les cloches au bayou.*　In C R A L, November 1900, p. 179.
— *Tout passe.*　In C R A L, January 1901, p. 201.
— *La défense de l'âne.*　In C R A L, January 1901, p. 202-203.
— *Jésus sur la croix.*　In C R A L, March 1901, p. 234.
— *La résignation—la mort c'est la vie.*　In C R A L, March 1901, p. 242.
— *Le retour des oiseaux.*　In C R A L, May 1901, p. 264.
— *Stella Matutina.*　In C R A L, May 1901, p. 264.
— *Nos pères.*　In C R A L, January 1902, p. 55.
— *Le signe de la croix.*　In C R A L, January 1902, p. 56.
— *L'arbre du Grand-père.*　In C R A L, July 1902, p. 134.
— *La mère et l'enfant.*　In C R A L, October 1902, p. 173.
— *Une trinité.*　In C R A L, July 1903, p. 269.
— *Mon vieux bayou St. Jean.*　In C R A L, October 1903, p. 289.

— *La grenadine en fleurs-Passiflora.* In C R A L, January 1904, p. 328.
— *L'attendu.* In C R A L, January 1904, p. 329.
— *Elle et lui.* In C R A L, January 1904, p 330.
— *Mon premier coq.* In C R A L, January 1905, p. 27.
— *Trop tard.* In C R A L, July 1905, p. 91-92.
— *Ce petit nid.* In C R A L, July 1905, p. 93-94.

COUSIN, Madame Armand. *La femme louisianaise avant, pendant et après la guerre.* In C R A L, January 1880, p. 330-334.

    This essay won the prize of the contest of 1879. It takes one family as typical and shows the difference in the lives of its members before and after the war.

    Mme. Cousin (*née* Cousin) was born in Bonfouca, Louisiana in July 1846. She was educated at the Ursulines Convent in New Orleans and with private teachers at home. She belonged to a family of poets; she was sister to Maxime and Francis Cousin, and cousin to Adrien and Dominique Rouquette. She died in 1886.

COUSIN, Francis A. *A une amie.* In C R A L, July 1906, p. 104.

    This poem in Alexandrine verse thanks his friend for her missive.

— *Rêverie.* In C R A L, January 1907, p. 159-161.

    This is another poem in Alexandrine verse. It gives a splendid description of Spring and the harmony of its concerts, the songs of the birds and the noises of the insects.

    Cousin was born in Bonfouca, St. Tammany Parish in Louisiana in September 1836. He was educated at the Jesuits' College in Springhill, Alabama. He went to New Orleans and engaged in business there. He died in 1907.

COUSIN, Maxime. *A ma sœur.* In C R A L, September 1886, p. 180.

    This poem in lines of twelve syllables, was

written on the occasion of his sister's death.
H M L.

— *A ma fille.* In C R A L, September 1886,
p. 218.

This poem is an expression of the father's
love for his little three year old daughter.
H M L.

— *La vague.* In C R A L, July 1887, p. 388.

This poem is very much on the order of *Le
Lac* by Lamartine. The wave is associated
with the poet's beloved. H M L.

— *Le feu-follet.* In C R A L, September 1887,
p. 422-423.

This a narrative poem of fifteen stanzas
in which the author claims to give a true story.
It shows the superstition of an old negro and
his fright on seeing a " feu-follet ". H M L.

Cousin was born in Bonfouca on March 13,
1842. He was educated in private schools in
Bonfouca and at Springhill, Alabama. He
served in the Confederate Army during the
Civil War. After the war, he returned to
Bonfouca and lived there until his death in
1924. (Information about the above three was
obtained from E. P. Cousin of New Orleans,
son and nephew respectively.)

CRUZAT, Mme. Héloise. *L'Influence de la France sur
le tempérament louisianais.* In C R A L, July
1915, p. 8.-92.

This article won the prize in the contest of
1914-1915. It is written in clear, concise
style, and the historical facts are well given.
The ideas are also well developed. The author
thinks the French influence is seen in the
women, in the cooking, and in the politeness
which is still proverbial of the Creoles of
Louisiana.

— *Les Martyrs de la Louisiane.* In C R A L, October 1921, p. 88-112.

This is an account of the resistance in 1769,

based on information contained in the French colonial archives of Louisiana.

Madame Cruzat (*née* Hulse) is a native of New Orleans. She is now employed by the Louisiana Historical Museum in indexing and translating the French documents of that organization. (Information from a personal interview.)

CUCULLU, Joseph Salustian, *La vérité sur Miramon et les Etats-Unis*. Imp. Franco-Américain, Nouvelle Orléans, 1860. H M L.

In this pamphlet, the author gives a sketch of the life of Miramon, one of the Mexican generals, and deplores the attitude of the American Press toward him and the Mexican question in general.

Cucullu was born in 1802 on his father's plantation in St. Bernard Parish, Louisiana. He was educated by private tutors and then went to Paris to finish his education. He returned to Louisiana and was a sugar planter. He was a close friend of Maximilian, Emperor of Mexico, and lent him money to run his government. Maximilian visited him on his plantation before going to take possession of Mexico. Cucullu married a Spanish lady from Mexico City. He died in 1893. (Information from Ralph Cucullu of New Orleans.)

*DALCOUR, Pierre. Poems in *Les Cenelles*. H M L.

D'AQUIN, Joseph George. *Pélerinage en Terre-Sainte*. Paris, Gaumes Frères et Dupuy, 1866. H M L.

The author wants to inspire the young people of Louisiana to take a trip to the Holy Land. In this book he gives a detailed account of a journey that he made there with the Easter caravan of 1864.

D'Aquin came, when quite young, to New Orleans in 1836. He was a brother of Madame Hélène D'Aquin Allain. He lived in New Orleans for a number of years. He was

a professor there in 1866. He later went to
France to live, and died there. (Information
from Madame Allain's book, from his cousin,
Miss Margaret Boun of New Orleans, and from
the city directory.)

*D'ARTLYS. *La fille du désert.* In R. L., March 5,
1848, Vol. V, p. 548. H M L.
This poem gives a clear description of the
Arab girl with her flowing hair, her flowing
robe, her necklace of pearls, and her bare feet.
She scorns the young Arab who comes to court
her, and prefers to be proud and free and queen
of the desert.

DAUPHIN, Dessormes. *Adieux.* In *Les Cenelles.*
H M L.
Dauphin was one of the collaborators of the
Cenelles to which he contributed one poem.

*DAUSSIN, Gustave. *Le talisman de Gérard.* In
C R A L, November 1886, p. 241-251.
H M L.

— *Camma.* In C R A L, 1887, p. 272-282, 293-
302.

— *La Sirène.* In C R A L, 1887, p. 365-383, 395-
410.

— *La soirée du Colonel.* In C R A L, 1888, p. 9-
14.

— *Souvenirs.* In C R A L, 1891, p. 343-346.

DAVID, Urbain. *Les Anglais à la Louisiane en 1814
et 1815.* Nouvelle Orléans, Jewell, 1845.
H M L.

— *Au Général Bertrand.* In C de L, September 9,
1843. C H A.
This poem tells of General Bertrand's journey to St. Helena to get Napoleon's body.

— *L'Abbé Perché.* In *L'Union,* August 20, 1857.
C H A.

DE BARONCELLI, Joseph Gabriel. *L'émancipation de la
femme au dix-neuvième siècle.* In O. L., February 2, 1895, Vol. IV, p. 96-103. H M L.
This article advocates freedom for woman

only in so far as it will not interfere with her duties in the home.

— *Le théâtre français à la Nouvelle Orléans, essai historique.* Nouvelle Orléans, Geo. Muller, 1906. H M L.

— *Une colonie française en Louisiane.* Nouvelle Orléans, Geo. Muller, 1909. H M L.

The author states in the preface to this work that it is the result of long and painful research written after a thirty-year stay in New Orleans. It gives information of all kinds on the history of Louisiana and of New Orleans, in all of its activities—opera, theaters, etc.

De Baroncelli was born in France. He came to Louisiana in 1878 and has been connected with various French newspapers in New Orleans. In 1895 he was in charge of the *Observateur Louisianais.* He is now editor of the *Guêpe.* (Facts from a notice in the *Abeille,* March 25, 1917, and in the O. L., Vol. IV, February 1895, p. 103.)

*De Bouchel, Onésime. *Le chien et ses amis.* In C R A L, November 1875, p. 27. H M L.

— *Elmina.* In C R A L, January 1877, p. 40.

— *Rêverie.* In C R A L, July 1877, p. 84.

— *La violette.* In C R A L, May 1877, p. 66.

— *La louve et la brebis.* In C R A L, September 1877, p. 98.

*De Bouchel, Victor. *Histoire de la Louisiane depuis les premières découvertes jusqu'en 1840.* Nouvelle Orléans, J. F. Lelièvre, 1841. H M L.

— *Napoléon.* In A N O, March 20, 1841.

*De Chatillon, Auguste. *La Toussaint de la Nouvelle Orléans.* In C de L, November 8, 1848. C H A.

— *L'Eglise.* In C de L, January 31, 1849. C H A.

— *A mon ami, Eugène Chassaignac.* In C de L, July 25, 1849.

— *Le Cavalier.* In C de L, August 9, 1849. C H A.
— *Michel Ange.* In C de L, August 18, 1849. C H A.
— *Amaranthin.* In C de L, August 30, 1849. C H A.
— *Je suis le sort.* In C de L, September 13, 1849. C H A.
— *A mon ami, Placide Canonge.* In C de L, October 24, 1849.

*De Courmont, Felix. *Le Taenarion, revue littéraire-Recueil de douze livraisons, satires, épîtres, joyeusetés.* July 15, 1846-January 1, 1847, Nouvelle Orléans, S J S.

*Dejacque, Joseph. *Les Lazarréennes; fables, chansons, poésies sociales.* Nouvelle Orléans, J. Lamarre, 1857. H M L.

*De la Houssaye, Madame Sidonie. *Le mari de Marguerite.* In A N O, August 26-December 18, 1883. C H A.
This story tells of a proud girl whose true character was shown in her battle with adversity during the Civil War and after.

— *Pouponne et Balthasar, Nouvelle Acadienne.* Librairie de l'Opinion, Nouvelle Orléans, 1888. H M L.

— *La fauvette et le poète, allégorie.* In C R A L, May 1890, p. 104-108.
The author tells that this story was suggested to her by the marriage of a charming young music teacher who had refused many advantageous offers in order to marry a poor poet.

—— *L'Amour qui renferme en lui seul tous les amours.* In C R A L, May 1890, p. 108-112.
This story shows how the devotion of a lover can lessen one's grief at the loss of one's family.

— *Amis et Fortune, roman louisianais.* Imp. du Meschacébé, Bonnet Carré, 1893. L. B. Tarlton's book.

213

— *Quarteronnes de la Nouvelle Orléans,* Bonnet
Carré, 1894. L. B. Tarlton.
— *Mythologie des petits enfants.* Manuscript of
128 closely written pages, 8 × 10. (It is in
the possession of L. B. Tarlton, Franklin, La.)
The author dedicates this " A mes petits
enfants" and says that she has promised to
write for them a course in mythology which
they could understand. She says that she will
narrate in the simplest manner possible. She
gives twenty chapters that tell the stories of the
outstanding characters in mythology.

*DELAVIGNE, John Casimir. *Critique du dernier ou-
vrage de M. Geo. W. Cable,* " Who are the
Creoles? ". In C R A L, March 1883, p. 319-
327.

*DELÉRY, Dr. Charles. *Questions sur diverses bran-
ches de sciences médicales.* Rignoux, Paris,
1842.
This was his thesis for a doctorate in medicine, received at Paris in 1842. It is found
in Volume I of a collection of " Thèses de médecine N. Orléanais " from 1836-1844.
H M L.

— *Essai sur la liberté.* New Orleans, Sollée, 1847.
S J S.
— *Etude sur les passions, suivie d'un aperçu sur
l'éducation qu'il convient de donner au peuple,
par un Louisianais.* Meridier, New Orleans,
1849. H M L.
— *Précis historique de la fièvre jaune.* Imp. Franco-
Américaine, Nouvelle Orléans, 1859. H M L.
— *Réplique au mémoire du Dr. Charles Faget publié dans le numéro du 9 mars 1860 du journal de la société médicale de la Nouvelle Orléans.* Imp. Franco-Américaine, N. O., 1860.
— *Seconde réplique du Dr. Charles Deléry à la
5e lettre du Dr. Charles Faget.* In *Journal de
la Société Médicale de la N. O.,* September
1860, Vol. II, number 3, p. 51 ff.
— *Le dernier chant du guerrier orateur, à la mémoire*

du lieutenant-colonel C. D. Dreux. Nouvelle
Orléans, n. p., 1861. T P T.
> Also in C R A L, October 1911, p. 268-
> 272. H M L.

— *Mémoire sur l'épidémie de la fièvre jaune qui a
régné à la Nouvelle Orléans et dans les campagnes pendant l'année 1867.* Nouvelle Orléans,
n. p., 1867. H M L.

— *Dernière réplique au Dr. Faget.* L. Marchand,
Nouvelle Orléans, 1868. H M L.

— *Le spectre noir ou le radicalisme aux Etats-Unis.*
L. Marchand, N. O., 1868. H M L.

— *L'Ecole du peuple, comédie en un acte et en vers.*
Imp. du Propagateur Catholique, 1877.
H M L.

— *Chroniques Indiennes.* In C R A L, 1878,
p. 129-131, 146-148, 158-161, 197-204, 217-
219, 225-228.

— Poems reprinted. In C R A L, October 1911,
p. 264-267, 275.

DELL'ORTO, Dr. John. *Immigration et colonisation en
Louisiane.* In C R A L, 1887, p. 35-39, 41-
49.
> The author believes that the development of
> the Louisiana plantations must come from
> within the state and not from foreign capital-
> ists.

— *Le roman d'un ouistiti.* In C R A L, January
1890, p. 21-23.

— *Gorilla affinis hominis?* In C R A L, January
1887, p. 282-288.
> The above two are stories translated from the
> Italian.

> Dr. John Dell'orto was born in Italy in 1834.
> He went to Louisiana after the Civil War to
> practice medicine. He won for himself a warm
> place in the hearts of the physicians there and
> distinguished himself by his services during the
> yellow fever epidemics. For this service he
> was decorated by the King of Italy with the
> Distinguished Service Cross. On account of ill

health, he went back to Italy where he died. (Information from his nephew, Arturo Dell'-Orto of New Orleans.)

DELPIT, Albert, was born in New Orleans in 1849, but left there when quite young and spent the remainder of his life in France. Hence, he will not be given further notice among Louisiana writers. (Information from a notice in the *Abeille* for January 24, 1893, the time of his death.)

DERON, Elie Etienne. *Anniversaire de la naissance de Washington.* In C de L, February 21, 1848.

This is a long poem of nine stanzas in which the author gives great praise to Washington as a hero above heroes and above Napoleon especially. It called forth remonstrances from the ardent admirers of Napoleon.

Deron was a Frenchman who came to Louisiana where he established a school. While going on a vist to France he died July 30, 1851, on board the American ship, Franklin. (Information from the death record at the City Board of Health office.)

DESBROSSES, Nelson. *Le retour aux villages aux perles.* In *Les Cenelles.* H M L.

Desbrosses was one of the collaborators of *Les Cenelles.* He contributed one poem which bears the date, March 1828. He died in New Orleans in 1853. (Information from his death record at the Cathedral.)

DESDUNES, Rodolphe L. *Nos hommes et notre histoire, notices biographiques accompagnées de réflexions et de souvenirs personnels.* Arbour et Dupont, Montreal, 1911.

In this book the author tells of three classes of colored men in Louisiana: those born there, those from Martinique, and those from San Domingo. He tells of the part played by these in the campaign of 1814-1815, and also of their work in various professions. H M L.

(Nothing is known of him except that the

directory as late as 1911 gives him as assistant weigher at the Custom House.)

*Dessommes, Edward. *Femme et statue.* Alphonse Lemerre, Paris, 1869. H M L.

— *Madeleine et Berthe.* In C R A L, 1891, p. 245-252.

— *Artiste et virtuose.* In C R A L, 1901, p. 352-353; 1902, 42-55, 91-100, 138-142, 148-166; 1903, 196-203, 231-238, 259-289.

Dessommes, Georges. *A une jeune fille.* In C R A L, July, 1876, p. 7. H M L.

— *Mes poètes.* In C R A L, July 1877, p. 81. H M L.

— *Subtilité.* In C R A L, September 1877, p. 97. H M L.

— *L'Auberge.* In C R A L, November 1878, p. 219. H M L.

— *Sonnet du jour de l'an.* In C R A L, January 1882, p. 3. H M L.

— *Le Désir.* In C R A L, September 1885, p. 228. H M L.

— *Sonnets câlins (3).* In C R A L, May 1891, p. 326-327. H M L.

— *A la mémoire du Dr. Alfred Mercier.* In C R A L, July 1894, p. 109. H M L.

— *Mandeville, paysage louisianais.* In C R A L, July 1876, p. 7.

— *Un Soir à Jackson Square.* In C R A L, July 1880, p. 376-378.

— *Berceuse.* In C R A L, January 1882, p. 41.

— *L'Orage.* In C R A L, March 1882, p. 81.

— *Afternoon.* In C R A L, July 1885, p. 198.

— *A deux morts.* In C R A L, May 1887, p. 361.

— Poems (no names). In C R A L, January 1891, p. 254; January 1892, p. 35-36.

— *Geoffroy le Troubadour.* In C R A L, March 1877, p. 50-52.

— *Fleurs des prés.* In C R A L, May 1890, p. 114.

— *Le nid aux baisers.* In C R A L, July 1878, p. 178-180.

— *Obsession.* In C R A L, September 1879, p. 297-300.

— *Tante Cydette, nouvelle louisianaise.* Imp. Franco-Américaine, Nouvelle Orléans, 1888. H M L.

— *La légende d'Oreste dans Eschyle, Sophocle, et Euripide.* In C R A L, 1890, p. 122-134, 151-169.
This article brings out the differences in the ideas of these three dramatists as seen in their treatment of the Orestes story.

DEVRON, Dr. Gustave. *Le Calendrier Mexicain-Monté-zuma.* In C R A L, November 1885, p. 238-247.
This article was occasioned by reading in a Mexican paper that this sun dial of Montezuma was going to be moved. It is a history and description of it.

— *Les Portraits de Colomb.* In C R A L, May 1893, p. 384-396.
This article shows the great doubt that still exists about authentic portraits of Columbus. The author speaks of one painted in New Orleans which is supposed to be genuine. He adds that he knew the artist who executed this portrait and also the model who was certainly not Columbus.

— *Pierre Margry.* In C R A L, July 1895, p. 295-299.
The writer here gives information about Margry's important work of compiling documents and his genius for this kind of work.

— *Deux documents inédits.* In C R A L, July 1897, p. 120-128.
These documents relate to Aubry, the last French governor of Louisiana. One is a declaration of his leaving New Orleans, and is signed Cabarn de Trepis, the other is a declaration of the loss of his vessel, and is signed Carrere.

— *Deux lettres inédites du Révérend Père N. I. de Beaubois, S. J. fondateur de la mission des Jésuites en Louisiane et premier directeur des Ur-*

218

sulines de la Nouvelle Orléans. In C R A L, September 1897, p. 142-149.

These two letters, supposed to be written to the secretary of the East India Company, tell about affairs in the colony.

— *François Etienne Bernard Alexandre Viel.* In C R A L, July 1899, p. 490-501.

The author gives here a full account of this great scholar and lists his translations.

Dr. Devron was born in New Orleans in 1835 and died there in March 1900. He was very much interested in History and contributed many articles to the *Comptes Rendus de l'Athénée Louisianais.* (Information obtained from the C R A L, May 1900, p. 73-76, and an account of a short talk on him at the time of his death.)

*DEZAUCHE. *Précis élémentaire de géographie à l'usage des écoles Américaines, par Dezauche.* J. F. Lelievre, New Orleans, 1841.

DIAZ, Josephine. *Les Romans de Pierre Loti.* In C R A L, July 1912, p. 80-108.

This essay won the prize in the contest of 1911-1912. It gives an analysis of the novels and criticizes them from the point of view of ideas and style.

Mlle. Diaz was, for a while, a student in New Orleans. She came there from Mexico at the age of 7 and was for ten years a student at the Guillot school. After graduating, she attended Newcomb College and was graduated from there in 1909. (Information from Miss Guillot and from the Newcomb Registrar.)

DIETZ, Ambrose P. *Coup d'œil sur les écoles publiques.* In C de L, August 8, 1849. C H A.

— *Rêveries.* In *L'Orléanais,* January 17, 1852. C H A.

Dietz was for several years a teacher in the public schools of New Orleans. He wrote poems that were published in the papers of that city. (Information from the directories from 1851 to 1855.)

DOMENECH, J. Passama. *Le Mexique et la Monarchie, questions d'histoire et d'actualité.* Imp. de Zornoza, Mexico, 1866. H M L.

This is an article which is very outspoken in its sympathy for Mexico.

— *L'empire mexicain, la paix et les intérêts du monde.* Mexico, n. p., 1866. H M L.

The author is writing here for the benefit of the Europeans in Mexico. He says that what has been known of Mexican history is far from true. He feels that Mexico needs an absolute monarchy.

— *La France et la civilisation.* L. Marchand, Nouvelle Orléans, 1870. H M L.

The author gives a short history of France, of her deeds, and of her sufferings. A statement at the beginning says that the book is to be sold for funds for the wounded and for victims of the war in France.

Domenech was in New Orleans in the early 70's and was an assistant on the staff of the *Abeille.* He was one of the founders of the French Union and was president of it from 1872 to 1873. He left New Orleans in about 1875, and nothing further is known of him. (Information from the directories 1870-1875, and from Biographical and Historical Memoirs of Louisiana, p. 188.)

DOUSSAN, Gaston. *Lafayette en Amérique.* In C R A L, May 1887, p. 340-356.

This was the prize essay in the contest of 1886. The author received a letter from the grandson of General Lafayette complimenting him on this essay. This letter was printed in C R A L, November 1887, p. 453.

— *Etude sur la Révolution Française.* In C R A L, November 1887, p. 430-441.

— *Les derniers jours d'un philosophe.* In C R A L, Sept. 1888, p. 137-157.

— *Etude sur Robert Edward Lee—Généralissime des troupes confédérées pendant la guerre de sécession 1861-1865.* In C R A L, January 1890, p. 5-20; March 1890, p. 41-57.

— *Paul Morphy (1837-1884).* In C R A L, Jan. 1892, p. 4-24.
A study of the great chess player, his genius, his triumphs at home and abroad.

— *Louis XIII et Richelieu.* In C R A L, 1893, p. 257-272, 297-313.
This is an analysis of the historical study of Marius Topin, who believes that Louis XIII, instead of being a mediocre person, was a great king like Henry IV.

— *Causeries du lundi de Sainte Beuve.* In C R A L, January 1894, p. 1-8.

— *Vauvenargues.* In C R A L, September 1894, p. 141-148.

— *Honneur! Patrie!* In C R A L, Nov. 1896, p. 573-575.

— *De l'honneur, Réflexions sur Montaigne.* In C R A L, January 1898, p. 201-204.

— *De l'amitié, De l'âme.* In C R A L, November 1898, p. 366-373.

— *Abraham Lincoln.* In C. R A L, January 1900, p. 13-18.

— *Théodore-Jouffroy—Etude philosophique.* In C R A L, September 1895, p. 321-327.
Doussan was born on a plantation near Port Allen, Louisiana, on September 21, 1855. When one year old, he was taken to France. He was in school in Nice until 1867 when his family went to New Orleans. There he attended the Jesuit's College. He went into the business world and was employed for 42 years by the firm of D. H. Holmes, & Company. He is now retired on a pension because of faithful service. (Information from Mr. Doussan.)

DREUX, Charles Didier. *Au Général Zachary Taylor.* R. L., Vol. VI, September 17, 1848, p. 594-596. H M L.

These verses were read at the distribution of prizes at the Lycée d'Orléans. Although the author was quite young at the time he wrote it, this poem is worthy of praise both for its form and contents. It relates the brave deeds of General Taylor and his self-sacrifice.

Dreux was born in New Orleans in 1832. His parents removed to Paris when he was quite young, and he received his early education there. They later returned to Louisiana. He was graduated in law from Transylvania Law University in Kentucky and practiced law in New Orleans. When the Civil War began, he immediately answered the call to arms and was killed only a short time after enlisting.

(Information about Dreux was obtained from the pamphlet: *Life and Military Services of Col. Charles Didier Dreux,* by Arthur Meynier Jr., published by E. A. Brandao & Co. in New Orleans.)

DUBOS, Henri. *Monographie du ténor.* In C R A L, January 1883, p. 281-297.

— *Avantages de la culture des arts.* In C R A L, January 1889, p. 245-261.

— *Le théâtre de Molière.* In C R A L, July 1901, p. 283-293.

Dubos was a professor of music and also a journalist for a while in New Orleans. He was a Frenchman by birth. He was first collaborator on the staff of the *Abeille,* and in 1894 he became editor. (Information from the directory from 1874-1885)

DUCROCQ, Henry L. *Femme et Fleur.* In C R A L, July 1893, p. 417-434.

This is a story, very simply told, of the love of two young people, the death of the girl, and the retirement of the boy to a religious life.

Ducrocq was a teacher in a classical and commercial institute in New Orleans for a few years. He left the city, however, in 1896.

(Information from the city directories before
1896, and the C R A L, May 1896, p. 449.)

*DUFOUR, Cyprien. *Esquisses Locales, par un Inconnu.*
Nouvelle Orléans, J. L. Sollée, 1847. H M L.

*DUGUE, Charles Oscar. *Essais poétiques.* Imp. de
A. Fortier, Nouvelle Orléans, 1847. H M L.

— *Mila, ou la mort de La Salle.* J. L. Sollée, Nouvelle Orléans, 1852. H M L.
(Reprint, C R A L, Oct. 1907, p. 250-
264; 1908, 320-338.)

— *Homo, poème philosophique.* Librairie Paul Duf-
fis, Paris, 1872. H M L.

— Poems. In C de L, August 22, 1842; May 29,
1846; February 14, 1857; September 19,
1858.

DUMESTRE, Marie. *De tous les écrivains français du dix-
neuvième siècle prosateurs ou poètes, quel est
celui qui vous plaît le plus et pour quelles rai-
sons.* In C R A L, May 1894, p. 75-87.
This essay won the prize in the contest of
1893. The author has chosen Hugo as her
favorite.

— *Le parfum et le souvenir.* In C R A L, July
1895, p. 303-307.

— *La fleur du prisonnier.* In C R A L, March
1896, p. 438-446.

— *Causerie.* In C R A L, March 1899, p. 424-
430.

— *Le Roitelet et l'Aigle de St. Malo.* In C R A L,
Oct. 1912, p. 132-139.
This is the story of the little wren that revived the courage of Chateaubriand.
Mlle. Dumestre is a native of New Orleans.
Her father was a Frenchman, René Dumestre,
and her grandfather was Joseph Girod. She
is related to Nicolas Girod, whose home is
still known as the Napoleon House, because of
a plan to rescue Napoleon and bring him to
New Orleans to occupy this house. She is
known in educational circles in her city, and

is now director of the School of the French Union. (Information from her.)

DUPAQUIER, Dr. Auguste. *Les Doryphores.* In C R A L, September 1877, p. 94-95.

— *De l'H dite aspirée.* In C R A L, January 1878, p. 134.

— *La Machine gramme et ses applications comme génératrice de l'électricité, à l'éclairage et à la galvanoplastie.* In C R A L, September 1878, p. 190-193.

— *Les Xylophages.* In C R A L, September 1878, p. 212-214.

— *Faune et flore de la Louisiane.* In C R A L, November 1878, p. 215-217.

Dr. Dupaquier was born in Paris. He attended the public schools there until his family came to America in 1852. After his arrival in Louisiana, he studied engineering and was employed by the city of New Orleans. He later studied medicine and began to practice that profession. He was untiring in his work during the yellow fever epidemics. He devoted so much of his energy and strength in the terrible epidemic of 1878 that he died on April 6, 1879. He was one of the charter members of the Athénée Louisianais and contributed many scientific articles to its meetings. (Information from his son, Dr. Edward Dupaquier of New Orleans, and from the death records at the City Board of Health office.)

*DUPERRON, Jean. Poems. In A N O, November 13, 1827; December 5, 1827; June 21, 1828; July 29, 1828; March 5, 1829; July 21, 1829; October 18, 1832.

DUPORT, Marguerite. *Frédéric Mistral.* In C R A L, 1910, p. 86-94, 121-134.

This essay won the prize in the contest of 1909. It discusses the works of Mistral and his desire to write in his own language.

— *Paul Bourget et ses œuvres.* In C R A L, 1917, p. 12-22, 45-48, 75-78, 96-100.

This is a discussion of Bourget under the divisions of how he conceives the novel and the new bearing he gives to it, his style, and his philosophy.

Mlle. Duport came to America from Paris in 1907 with Mrs. F. C. Robertson of New Orleans. She spent a while in New Orleans and then went with the Robertson family to Los Angeles, California, where she is now living. (Information from Mrs. Ben Waldo, sister of Mrs. Robertson.)

*Du Quesney, Adolphe Lemercier. *Essais littéraires et dramatiques; le mal d'Oreste, poème dramatique; nouvelles, Sursum Corda! Chant d'Ipomoea, Un été à la Grand'Ile.* Imprimeries Réunies, Paris, 1892. (Book lent me by his brother, Albert.)

— *Sursum Corda!* In A N O, September 20, 1891.

— *Un été à la Grand'Ile.* In A N O, September 25, 1898.

Durand, Abel. *Ce qu'il doit faire.* In A N O, December 3, 1914. L H L.

— *Le Remède.* In A N O, February 5, 1915. L H L.

— *La Note.* In A N O, August 15, 1915.

These poems are all short and treat of Kaiser Wilhelm's efforts to enter Paris by Christmas 1914.

Durand was born in France. In 1906 he came to Louisiana with the intention of becoming a farmer and settled near Lafayette. About 1916, he went to Haiti in the service of the government. He died there in 1918. (Information from his brother-in-law, Pierre Doucet of Lafayette.)

Durel, Lionel. *François Coppée et ses œuvres.* In C R A L, 1909, 482-506, 507-528.

This essay won the prize in the contest of 1908-1909. It gives a short biography of Coppée and then speaks of the diversity of his talent.

— *Baudelaire, poète.* In C R A L, 1915, p. 22-29, 54-64.

    The author thinks that this poet can not be reproached regarding his technique, but a " choice " of his poems should be read if real enjoyment is desired.

— *Molière.* In C R A L, January 1923, p. 9-24.

    This was a lecture given at the Athénée Louisianais. It discusses Molière the man, his life, his works, and his portrayal of life.

    Durel was born in New Orleans in 1884. He began to study law but soon gave it up. He was teacher for a time in the high school and later in Newcomb College in New Orleans. He is still professor of French at Newcomb. (Information from his mother, Mrs. Gus Durel, and from Bussiere Rouen.)

*Duvallon, Berquin. *Un recueil de poésies d'un colon de Saint Domingue.* De l'Imprimerie Expéditive, Paris, 1803. H M L.

— *Vue de la colonie espagnole du Mississippi ou des provinces de Louisiane et Floride occidentale en l'année 1802 par un observateur résident sur les lieux.* L'Imprimerie, rue St. Benoist, Paris, 1803. H M L.

*Evershed, Madame Emilie. *Eglantine ou le secret.* Hector Bossange, Paris, 1843. L H L.

— *Essais poétiques.* Hector Bossange, Paris, 1843. H M L.

— *Esquisses poétiques.* Hector Bossange, Paris, 1846. H M L.

— *Une couronne blanche.* Hector Bossange, Paris, 1850. H M L.

*Faget, Dr. Jean Charles. *Etude sur les bases de la science médicale et exposition sommaire de la doctrine traditionnelle.* Méridier, Nouvelle Orléans, 1855. H M L.

— *Cinquième lettre sur la fièvre jaune, ou deuxième réponse au Dr. Deléry.* In *Journal de la Société Médicale de la Nouvelle Orléans,* July 1860, Vol. II, Number I, p. 2-16.

— *Mémoires et lettres sur la fièvre jaune et la fièvre paludéenne.* Propagateur Catholique, Nouvelle Orléans, 1864.

FERRAN, Paul. *La Fontaine et ses fables.* In C R A L, July 1913, p. 230-247.

This essay won the prize in the contest of 1912-1913. The author shows a keen understanding of the fables of La Fontaine.

(I could find nothing about Ferran.)

*FORTIER, Alcée. *De la puissance de l'éducation et de la nécessité du travail dans toutes les conditions de la vie.* In C R A L, March 1879, p. 240-243.

— *Le vieux français et la littérature du moyen âge.* Franco-Américain, Nouvelle Orléans, 1885. H M L.

— *Gabriel d'Ennérich.* Franco-Américain, Nouvelle Orléans, 1886. H M L.

(Also C R A L, 1886, p. 91-105, 151-164, 181-199, 222-239.)

— *Contes Louisianais en patois créole.* In C R A L, September 1900, p. 142-147. H M L.

— *Quatre grands poètes du dix-neuvième siècle.* Imp. Franco-Américaine, Nouvelle Orléans, 1887. H M L.

— *Sept grands auteurs du dix-neuvième siècle.* D. C. Heath & Co., Boston, 1890. H M L.

— *Histoire de la littérature française.* Henry Holt & Co., New York, 1893 (Revised 1913). H M L.

— *Hommage à la mémoire du Dr. Alfred Mercier, secrétaire perpétuel. Séance spéciale de l'Athénée Louisianais, 18 mai, 1894.* Nouvelle Orléans, 1894. H M L.

— *Les créoles de la Louisiane.* In C R A L, September 1901, p. 317-328. H M L.

— *La politique française contemporaine jugée par les étudiants américains. Rapport sur le fonctionnement des prix annuels fondés, par M. le Baron Pierre du Coubertin dans les Universités américaines de Harvard, Princeton, Johns Hop-*

kins, Tulane, Palo Alto, et Californie. Nouvelle Orléans, n. pub., 1902. H M L.

— *Précis de l'histoire de France avec des notes explicatives en anglais.* New and revised edition. MacMillan Co., New York, 1913 (First edition, 1899). H M L.

— *Les planteurs sucriers de l'ancien régime en Louisiane.* Extrait de la *Revue de Synthèse Historique,* Paris, 1906. H M L.

— Many articles in C R A L as follows: 1882, p. 197-205; 1884, 484-506; 1888, 14-22; 1890, 24-32; 147-149; 1894, p. 38-60; 88-96; 121-128; 129-140; 147-149; 1895, 216-224; 230-238; 353, 386, 427, 467, 487, 525; 1897, 49-57; 129-141; 1899, 397-402; 517-522; 1900, 45-57; 1901, 257-262; 1903, 290-296; 1904, 429-438; 1905, 6-22; 1906, 4-22.

— Translations in C R A L:

Se taire pendant la vie et pardonner à la mort, 1884, p. 548-571. F. Caballero : *Callar en vida, y perdonar en muerte.*

Le Baromètre, an anonymous comedy found in W. I. Knapp's, *Spanish Grammar,* November 1897, p. 169-185.

Casilda, conte populaire par Antonio Trueba, November 1897, p. 185-190.

Ferdinand VII par Emilio Gastelar, Jan. 1898, p. 205-210.

L'Arrabiata par Paul Heyse, traduite de l'allemand, July 1898, p. 310-332.

Le miroir de Matsuyama, conte japonais de l'espagnol de Juan Valera, March 1899, p. 433-437.

Peppa et Gramigna, de l'italiano de Giovanni Verga, October 1905, p. 97-108.

(*Louisiana Studies.* Literature, customs, and dialects, history, and education. Hansell, New Orleans, 1894.) H M L.

*FORTIER, Edward Joseph. *Lettres françaises en Louisiane.* Imp. l'Action Sociale limitée, Québec, 1915. H M L.

FORTIER, Florent. *La Salle*. In C R A L, March 1882, p. 94.

This poem speaks of La Salle as the discoverer of Louisiana and tells how his name is still held in veneration by the descendants of the French there.

Fortier was born in Louisiana on a plantation in St. Charles Parish in 1811. He received his education in France. He was the father of Alcée Fortier. He died in 1886. (Information from C. P. Dimitry: Louisiana Families, *Times-Democrat*, March 27, 1892, p. 14.)

*FORTIER, Madame Louise Augustin. *Le bon vieux temps*. In C R A L, March 1900, p. 224-234.

— *Chronique du vieux temps—La folie aux roses*. In C R A L, October 1902, p. 167-172.

— *Chronique du vieux temps—Un incident de la Guerre Confédérée*. In C R A L, April 1905, p. 39-49.

— *Les grands artistes français*. In C R A L, April 1911, p. 187-204.

— *Les orateurs de la révolution française*. In C R A L, July 1914, p. 88-104.

FORTIN, Madame Aménaïde Le Carpentier. *La Musique*. In C R A L, May 1882, p. 130-132.

This essay won the prize given to women in the contest of 1881. It considers music from the point of view of its practical, intellectual, and moral usefulness.

Mme. Fortin was born in New Orleans on September 22, 1814, daughter of Joseph Le Carpentier and Modeste Blache. She was educated by private tutors and was a fine musician. She was left a widow when quite young, and when reverses came after the Civil War, she bravely went to work. For a number of years she had a position in the New Orleans mint. In 1887 she went with her daughter, Mrs. Marie Fortin Buck, to Birmingham, Alabama. She died there in 1896. (Information from her granddaughter, Miss Mina Buck of

Evanston, Illinois, and from her baptismal record in the Cathedral.)

FOUCHÉ, Louis Nelson. *Nouveau recueil de pensées, opinions, sentences et maximes de différents écrivains, philosophes et orateurs, anciens, modernes et contemporains.* Imp. de M. Capo, Nouvelle Orléans, 1882. T P T.

This volume is only a collection of quotations on various subjects. There is nothing original in it.

Fouché was a native of New Orleans and was for many years an architect there. He died May 20, 1886, at the age of 62. (Information from city directories for 1858 ff. and from the Cathedral death record.

FRIES, Frédéric. *De la puissance de l'éducation.* In C R A L, March 1879, p. 243-247.

This essay won second prize in the contest of 1878.

— *Eloge de Bienville.* In C R A L, January 1880, p. 328-330.

This essay won first prize in the contest of 1879. It speaks of Bienville's wise dealings with the savages, the injustice done him, and the great love of the people of Louisiana for him.

Fries was an Alsatian who came to New Orleans in about 1866 and taught there until his death in 1883. (Information from the city directories 1886 ff. and from C R A L, 1883, p. 410, a notice of his death, and from the death record at the City Board of Health office.)

GARREAU, Armand. *Louisiana.* In *Les Veillées Louisianaises,* Vol. I, p. 159-396, Meridier, Nouvelle Orléans, 1849. H M L.

— *L'Idiote.* In Ren. L., May 15, 1864, p. 12-19. H M L.

*GAYARRÉ, Charles Etienne Arthur. *Discours adressé à la législature en réfutation du rapport de M. Livingston sur l'abolition de la peine de mort.* 1826. H M L.

— *Discours prononcé dans la cathédrale à l'occasion*

de la fête du 8 janvier. In A N O, January 11, 1830. L H L.

— *Essai Historique sur la Louisiane.* Benjamin Levy, Nouvelle Orléans, 1830. H M L, T U L.

— *Histoire de la Louisiane.* Magne et Weisse, Nouvelle Orléans, 1846-1847, two volumes. H M L.

— *Esquisse biographique de John Rutledge.* In C R A L, November 1877, p. 102-108.
This sketch gives Rutledge special credit for his part in the creation of the constitution.

— *La race latine en Louisiane.* In C R A L, March 1885, p. 79-100.
This is a sketch of the history of the French in Louisiana, a eulogy of the French language, and praise of the Athenée for its desire to perpetuate this language.

— *Cession de la Louisiane aux Etats-Unis.* In C R A L, 1877, p. 58-60, 71-73.
The author here sets forth that this was not a sale of Louisiana to the United States, and the money question was not the only interest. France had a right to interfere until Louisiana became a state. Her becoming a state was one of the terms of the sale.

GENELLA, Asenath Louise. *Victor Hugo, auteur dramatique.* In C R A L, July 1902, p. 116-134.
This essay won the prize in the contest of 1901. It speaks of Hugo's *Préface de Cromwell* and his revolt against the classic drama, and also of his love of antithesis which, the author thinks, Hugo carried to excess in *Le roi s'amuse.*

Mlle. Genella was born in New Orleans. Her father was a native of Switzerland. After finishing the course in the high school in New Orleans, she went to Paris where she studied from 1889 to 1891. On her return to Louisiana, she entered Newcomb College and was graduated from there, *magna cum laude,* in

1894.   After traveling in Europe for a number
of years, she returned to her native city.   She
received her M. A. degree from Tulane University in 1901 and has done some work towards her Ph. D.   She married George S.
Dodds in 1904, and is now living in Brookha-
ven, Mississippi.   (Facts from her.)

*GENTIL, Jules.   Poems.   In A N O, June 3, 1900;
June 10, 17, 24, 1900; August 18, 25, 1901;
September 29, October 6, 1901.   H M L.

— Poems.   In C R A L, May 1879, p. 268; September 1880, p. 400.

GERARD, Aristide.   *Sur les dangers relatifs à la naviga-
tion et sur les moyens propres à les prévenir.*
In C R A L, May 1877, p. 54-56.

— *A un Athée.*   In C R A L, September 1877,
p. 99.
This is a short three-stanza poem in which
the author is led to moralize when he sees
a hen dividing the grain for her chicks.
Gerard was a native of Bordeaux.   He came
to New Orleans, married, and lived there
during the remainder of his life.   He died on
August 26, 1890 at the age of 60.   (Information from Board of Health record and an account of his death in the *Picayune* of August
27, 1890.)

GIRARD, Madame Marie Drivon.   *Histoire des Etats-
Unis suivie de l'histoire de la Louisiane.*   Antoine, Nouvelle Orléans, 1881.   H M L.

*GRIMA, Edgar.   *Pour un nickel.*   In C R A L, November 1889, p. 416-418.   H M L.

— *La veille de Noël.*   In C R A L, January 1890,
p. 23-24.

— *Pourquoi Jean est garçon.*   In C R A L, May
1890, p. 113.

— *A ma mie (élégie sur la mort de son sérin).*   In
C R A L, November 1890, p. 219.

— *Stances sur la mort d'une jeune fille.*   In
C R A L, Jan. 1891, p. 253.

- *Une défaite en amour,* idylle serio-comique. In C R A L, May 1891, 327 ff.
- *Lettre à mon ami.* In C R A L, July 1892, p. 127-129.
- *Au bois.* In C R A L, January 1893, p. 296.
- *Quand j'étais petit.* In C R A L, March 1894, p. 37.
- *Sans mère.* In C R A L, November 1894, p. 192.
- *Notre ami Bob.* In C R A L, March 1895, p. 257.
- *L'arbre de Noël.* In C R A L, January 1896, p. 420-421.
- *L'arbre mort.* In C R A L, July 1896, p. 501-502.
- *Le chien de l'aveugle.* In C R A L, September 1898, p. 342.
- *La cigale et la fourmi.* In C R A L, March 1899, p. 453-454.
- *Mon premier testament.* In C R A L, May 1900, p. 76-79.
- *Les deux siècles.* In C R A L, July 1902, p. 135-137.
- *Le baiser.* In C R A L, April 1905, p. 50.
- *Conte de Noël.* In C R A L, January 1906, p. 29-32.
- *Chantecler fils.* In C R A L, October 1910, p. 117-120.
- *Fidélité.* In C R A L, January 1913, p. 164-165.
- *Ne m'en veux pas.* In C R A L, April 1916, p. 79.
- *Les miséreux.* In C R A L, May 1922, p. 33-34.
- *Le fiancé de Marguerite.* Story, in C R A L, May 1892, 84-94.
- *Edmond Rostand.* In C R A L, January 1901, p. 186-196.

GUIROT, A. J. *Epître à M. Alexandre Latil* (in *Les Ephémères* of Latil.)

Racked with pain and discouraged, Latil had

thought of writing no more poems. Guirot tries in this poem to persuade him not to break his pen nor to silence his lyre. H M L.

— *A Tullius St. Céran* (in *Les Louisianaises* of St. Céran).

The author here expresses his pleasure in reading the verses of St. Céran and urges him to continue his poems in exaltation of liberty.

Guirot was a native of Santiago de Cuba, born 1803. He came to New Orleans where he was employed in the mint. He ran for mayor in 1846 but was defeated. He died on December 11, 1871 at the age of 68. (Information from the city directory for 1858; from *La Réforme*, March 29, 1846; and from the death record at the Cathedral.)

GUTIÉRREZ-NÁJERA, Margarita. *Ronsard, Poète lyrique.*

This was one of the essays that won the medal in the contest of 1926. It will be published in the next issue of the *Comptes Rendus de l'Athénée Louisianais.*

Mlle. Gutiérrez-Nájera is a native of Mexico who came to New Orleans in 1917, leaving Mexico on account of the conditions there. Her maternal grandfather was French, and she was educated in the French convent, St. Joseph, in Mexico City. Her father was Manuel Gutiérrez-Nájera, poet, writer, and editor of the *Revista Azul* of Mexico City. She is now employed in the business world in New Orleans.

HARRISON, Madame Jeanne Dupuy. *Les pionniers français dans la vallée du Mississippi.* In C R A L, July 1905, p. 73-91.

This essay won the prize in the contest of 1904. It is serious and well written, and treats principally of La Salle.

Mme. Harrison was born in New Orleans and was educated at the Sacred Heart Convent. She studied voice and piano with such teachers as Mme. Julie Calvé Boudousquié, Miss Adèle Henrionnet, and others. She is now a teacher of voice and piano, and is well known in the world of her profession. She is president of the Musical Club, Cercle Lyrique, vice-president of the New Orleans Music Teacher's Association, and chairman of many music committees. (Facts obtained from her.)

HART, Noelie. *Madame de Staël; sa vie et ses œuvres.* In C R A L, May 1884, p. 595-602.

This essay won the prize in the contest of 1883. As its name indicates, it gives the main facts of the life of Madame de Staël and discusses her works.

Mlle. Hart was born in Reserve, Louisiana. She received her education at the Sacred Heart Convent in New Orleans and also at the Louisiana State University. She was graduated from the latter with a degree of B. A. She has spent her life teaching French in the high schools of New Orleans, in L. S. U., at the State Normal at Natchitoches, Louisiana, and at the University of Texas. She is now living at Alexandria, Louisiana trying to regain her health in order to resume her work in the teaching profession. (Facts obtained from her.)

HAVA, Dr. John. *La nécessité d'avoir une médecine légale en Louisiane.* In C R A L, July 1876, p. 4-7, Sept. 1876, p. 1-11.

The author laments the absence of legal medicine in his state, and the fact that the town doctor is the sole witness at the coroner's inquest, when the law should require at least two experts. He cites instances where medico-legal advice has changed verdicts.

— *Emigration espagnole en Louisiane.* In C R A L, January 1881, p. 418-423.

Immigration agents having gone to Spain to find immigrants, the Spanish consul in New Orleans wrote to his country discouraging their coming and saying that the climate was unhealthy. This article was written in answer to that letter and speaks in favor of Louisiana.

— *Causerie sur la tarentule.* In C R A L, May
1881, p. 461-466.
>   The author makes many observations on spi-
>   ders in general and on other stinging insects.
— *Souvenir d'enfance.* In C R A L, July 1881,
p. 475-483.
>   This is a short story of two little boys who
>   were greatly incensed at the sight of a cruel
>   slave owner and also of a cruel officer in charge
>   of some boys in training as soldiers.

>   Dr. Hava was a native of Cuba. He died in
>   New Orleans on January 15, 1894, at the age
>   of 60 years. (Facts obtained from the death
>   record at the Cathedral.)

HERBELIN, Jules. *De l'élevage des vers à soie.* Philippe, Nouvelle Orléans, 1883. H M L.
>   Herbelin was in New Orleans for a short
>   while and was employed as a dyer and as pro-
>   prietor of the Louisiana silk mills. (Informa-
>   tion from the directories of 1880-1888.)

HOSMER, James Stonewall. *Donner une idée générale
des principaux romanciers des Etats-Unis
d'Amérique.* In C R A L, May 1881, p. 458-
460.
>   This essay won the prize in the contest of
>   1880. The author devotes his study to Charles
>   Brockden Brown, James F. Cooper, and Natha-
>   niel Hawthorne.
— *George Eliot.* In C R A L, September 1881,
p. 492-494.
>   The author discusses *Mr. Gilfil's Love Story*
>   and *Romola* as extreme examples of the genius
>   of George Eliot.
— *Longfellow.* In C R A L, July 1882, p. 161-
171.
>   This article was inspired by the death of
>   Longfellow and expresses great admiration for
>   the poet. The author analyses briefly Long-
>   fellow's principal works.

>   Hosmer was born July 21, 1862. He was

graduated from Mt. St. Mary's College, Emmitsburg, Maryland. He was studying law when he died in September 1884. (Facts obtained from his uncle, Charles Vatinel.)

HUARD, Dr. Octave. *De l'utilité de la langue française aux Etats-Unis.* In C R A L, May 1882, p. 117-130.

This essay won the prize in the contest of 1881. It tries to show that the influence of France and of the French language should not effect the Old World alone but the American Union as well.

— *Le triomphe d'une femme.* In C R A L, 1883, p. 464-467; 1884, p. 507-526.

This is a story of a Louisiana family before, during, and after the Civil War, and shows how the Creole women were undaunted by the hardships that came after the War.

Dr. Huard was born March 19, 1838. He was the son of Jules Huard, who came to New Orleans from San Domingo. After graduating in medicine in New Orleans, he went to Paris where he spent twelve years in the hospitals. He received the Geneva medal. He returned to New Orleans and opened an office. He was instructor for many years in the Charity Hospital. He was always interested in preserving the French language in Louisiana, and refused to serve on the board of examiners in 1880 if French were not taught in the schools. He died in 1896. (Facts obtained from his baptismal record at the Cathedral; from C R A L, November 1880, p. 402-404; from the *Renaissance Louisianaise,* September 25, 1864, p. 14; and from Mrs. Octave Huard of New Orleans.)

JAUBERT, Irma. *Les Américains, défenseurs du droit de la liberté.* In C R A L, April 1919, p. 58-62; July 1919, p. 86-94.

This essay won the prize in the contest for

1917-1918. It is a brief statement of the part that America played in the war.

Mlle. Jaubert is a native of New Orleans. She was educated first at the Sacred Heart Convent at St. Michael's in St. James Parish, and later at the Ursulines Convent in New Orleans. She has written several stories and articles in English that have been published in various magazines. The first of these was an installment for a continued story published in the *Woman's World* (McClure Publishing Co.) for which she won the prize of $ 100.00. Besides her great love for literature and for writing, she is very much interested in vocal music and devotes a great part of her time to singing. She is now Mrs. L. E. Kenney of New Orleans. (Facts were obtained from her.)

LAFARGUE, André. *Rouen et la tour de Jeanne d'Arc.* In C R A L, January 1916, p. 8-21.

This was a lecture given by the author in the Athénée Louisianais. He speaks of the importance of Rouen and describes the tower, which is not, as some think, the one in whose dungeons Jeanne d'Arc was imprisoned.

— *Conférence sur le pacifisme.* In C R A L, October 1913, p. 253-276.

This article gives the history of the efforts that have been made toward universal peace, making mention of the " Œuvre de Concilia- tion Internationale. "

— *La Chapelle Expiatoire.* In C R A L, October 1914, p. 111-128.

The author gives a description of this chapel in memory of Louis XVI and Marie Antoinette, and tells of his impression on seeing it.

Lafargue was born in New Orleans on July 17, 1878. He received the degrees of A. B., A. M., and Ph. B. from the college of the Immaculate Conception. He received his train- ing in law at Tulane University and began to practice in New Orleans in 1902. In 1910 he was appointed Counsellor of the French Consulate General at New Orleans and has been acting as the legal adviser of the French Government ever since. In 1917, he was chairman of the delegation sent by the city of New Orleans to Paris to commemorate the 200th anniversary of the founding of New Orleans. In 1921 he represented his city at the ceremonies held at Orleans in honor of Joan of Arc, and represented Louisiana at the exercises held at Napoleon's tomb celebrating the anniversary of his death. He has received many honors from the French government and in 1922 was made Officer de la Légion d'Honneur. He holds many important offices in his city. (Information from Mr. Lafargue.)

LAFFITTE, Justina. *L'Influence de Napoléon Ier sur les destinées de la France*. In C R A L, May 1896, p. 458-467.

This essay won the prize in the contest of 1895. It is rather short, but gives a logical treatment of Napoleon's influence on France internally in education and fine arts, and externally in her well organized army. Napoleon was harmful to France in that he turned all the other countries against her and left her smaller than he had found her.

(I could get no information about her.)

*LAFRÉNIÈRE, Nicholas Chauvin. *Mémoires des négociants et habitants de la Louisiane sur l'événement du 29 octobre 1768*.

The original of this memorial is in the Bibliothèque Nationale in Paris. A photostat copy is in the New York Public Library. N Y P L.

LA MESLÉE, Alphonse Marin. *Le monument de la Grande Armée*. In C R A L, October 1919, p. 100-128.

The author tells the story of the American woman who wanted to rent the Arch of Triump for a big fete one night. Her request was refused because the monument was not to be used that way. He explains some of the uses that have been made of this arch, such as serving as the gate of entrance to Paris when there is a reception of a sovereign. He asserts that it is, above all, really a memorial to Napoleon and his soldiers.

La Meslée was born in Nantes in 1865. In 1888 he came to America and lived in St. Martinville, Louisiana. He was a teacher and taught in several of the large colleges of America. In 1914 he went to New Orleans and became professor of French at Tulane University after the death of Alcée Fortier. He died there in 1921. (Information from C R A L, Jan. 1922, p. 9-10, and from the registers of Tulane University, 1915-1921.)

*Lanusse, Armand. *Les Cenelles, choix de poésies indigènes.* H. Lauve et Compagnie, Nouvelle Orléans, 1845. H M L.

Lanusse, Numa, was the brother of Armand Lanusse, and like him, was born in New Orleans. He was one of the collaborators of the *Cenelles* to which he contributed two short poems. (Information from Armand Lanusse's poem " *Un Frère au tombeau de son frère* ", p. 62-63 of *Les Cenelles* in which he speaks of Numa's death at the age of 26.)

Larue, Ferdinand. *La quarantaine contre les rats.* In C R A L, May 1901, p. 262-263.

This is a poem burlesquing the board of health's decree against the rats that came on vessels from Brazil, and picturing the reception that will be accorded to these rats if they try to immigrate.

Larue is a native of New Orleans. He was educated in England and Paris. His father was a native of San Domingo who came to New Orleans. He has been for many years in the cotton business in New Orleans. (Facts from Mrs. Larue.)

*Latil, Alexandre. *Les Ephémères, essais poétiques.*

Alfred Mout, Nouvelle Orléans, 1841.   H M L.

LAYTON, Dr. Thomas.   *Etudes cliniques sur l'influence des causes qui altèrent le poids corporel de l'homme adulte malade.*   In Vol. II, *Thèses de Médecine N. Orléanais,* Paris, Parent, 1868.

This is a thesis prepared and sustained before the Faculté de Médecine de Paris for the degree of Doctor in medicine.   H M L.

— *Jubilat d'or de l'épiscopat de Sa Sainteté le Pape Pie IX.*   Propagateur Catholique, Nouvelle Orléans, 1877.

Discourse pronounced at the Great Catholic Assembly of the Catholics of New Orleans, May 13, 1877.   H M L.

Dr. Layton was a native of New Orleans. He went to Paris to study, and received his M. D. degree there in 1868.   He returned to Orleans and practiced medicine until his death. He died on May 7, 1889 at the age of 44.   (Information from his thesis, from the death record in the Board of Health office, and from a notice in the *Picayune* for May 8, 1889.)

LE BEUF, Dr. Louis.   *Etude sur Chateaubriand.*   In C R A L, May 1899, p. 466-477.

This essay won the prize in the contest of 1898.   It gives Chateaubriand's life including his works, but does not discuss his works in detail.

— *Le Bayou Ouiski, une légende indienne.*   In C R A L, March 1900, p. 35-39.

This is a legend telling how an Indian tribe was slain after having been given enough brandy to intoxicate them. Their lands were taken from them.   The daughter of the chief hid under the bodies of her brothers and escaped being slain.   She jumped into the bayou where, according to the legend, her soul still sleeps.

Dr. Le Beuf was born on a plantation in Louisiana in 1866.   He received his medical training at Tulane University, then known as the

Louisiana State University. He died in May 1913. (Information from Mrs. Le Beuf.)

LE BLANC, Eugène. *Essais poétiques.* Alfred Moret, Nouvelle Orléans, Colomb des Batines, 1842. S J S.

This collection of poems shows that the author is filled with love for humanity and faith in God.

Le Blanc was born in New Orleans on February 17, 1817. He was a teacher there for several years. He published some poems in the *Abeille* and the *Courrier de la Louisiane.* Some of these were later republished in a volume. (Information from the baptismal record at the Cathedral, from the city directories for 1838 ff., and from the C de L, December 5, 30, 1840, A N O, Feb. and April 1841.)

LE BRETON, Dagmar Adélaïde. *Pascal.* In C R A L, January 1925, p. 6-24.

This essay won one of the prizes in the contest of 1924. It is a psychological study of Pascal and is well worked out with quotations from his " Pensées " to confirm the statements made.

Mme Le Breton (*née* Renshaw) was born in New Orleans, daughter of Marie E. Deynoodt and Henry Renshaw. After her graduation from Picard Institute, she attended Newcomb College and was graduated from the Normal Art Course there in 1912. She married that same year, Edmond Jules Le Breton, nephew of Alcée Fortier of Tulane University. Her son, Edmond Jules Le Breton, was born in November 1913. After the death of her husband in 1914, Madame Le Breton resumed her studies and obtained from Tulane University the degrees of Bachelor of Design and Master of Arts. She has taught for a number of years and is at present a member of the faculty of Newcomb College. (Facts from her sister, Marguerite Renshaw.)

LECLERC, Joseph. *Chant Patriotique.* In C R A L,
November 1895, p. 373-374.

This poem is dedicated to the New Orleans
militia and to the brave defenders of the city.
It is another commemoration of the Battle of
New Orleans in 1815. In publishing it, the
editor of the *Comptes Rendus* says that it was
composed shortly after the victory of 1815,
but had probably never been published before.
It was due to H. L. Favrot that it was lent to be
published then.

Leclerc came to Louisiana from San Domingo
and was in charge of the publication of *L'Ami
des Lois* from 1813 to 1819. In 1822 he was
a teacher. He died in April 1827. (Information from the city directories, from *L'Ami des
Lois,* February 22, 1819, and from the death
record at the Cathedral.)

LE FRANC, Emile. *La vérité sur l'esclavage et l'union
(suivie d'un résumé de la statistique et de l'histoire des Etats-Unis.* Imp. Franco-Américaine,
Nouvelle Orléans, 1861.

This work contains letters from a business
man in New York to a Frenchman traveling in
the South, May 1861. The Frenchman in his
answers, wishes to clear up the ideas of the
New Yorker.

Le Franc was a Frenchman who came to New
Orleans about 1860. He was for a number of
years editor and proprietor of *La Renaissance
Louisianaise.* He also taught there for several
years and then returned to France. (Information from the directories through 1880.)

LEJEUNE, Mme. Emilie. *Jean Richepin, sa vie, son caractère, sa lutte avec les ennuis, et la misère.*
In C R A L, January 1914, p. 26-36.

This was a lecture delivered before the Athénée Louisianais. The author chose Richepin
because he is the defender of the heritage of
Latin civilization.

243

— *La Roumanie.* In C R A L, October 1917,
p. 82-95.
This article speaks of the songs of Rouma-
nia and offers some of them translated into
French.
— *Eugène Brieux.* In C R A L, January 1915,
p. 10-19.
The author here quotes the different opinions of Brieux and discusses his plays according
to the groupings given by Barret H. Clark
in the *Bookman* in 1913.
Mme Lejeune (*née* Mercier) is a native of
New Orleans, niece of Drs. Armand and Alfred Mercier. She was very much interested
in music, and received musical training from
Madame Julie Calvé Boudousquié. She was
fond of travelling and also studied in Europe.
She is now living in Porto Rico. (Information
from Mr. Rouen and from *Some Notables of
New Orleans Biographical and Descriptive
Sketches of the Artists of New Orleans and
their Work,* by May Mount, n. p., New Orleans, 1896, p. 205.
*LEMAITRE, Charles. *Rodolphe de Branchelièvre.* Sollée, Nouvelle Orléans, 1851.
*LEPOUZÉ, Constant. *Poésies diverses.* Bruslé et Les-
seps, Nouvelle Orléans, 1838.
LIMET, Félix. *Aperçus généraux sur les mariages con-
sanguins.* In C R A L, May 1878, p. 164-
168.
The author of this article does not claim to
give anything new. He cites numerous examples of marriages of this kind among such people as the Tartans, Scythians, Egyptians, and
others.
— *Duels et attentats politiques aux Etats-Unis.* In
C R A L, January 1882, p 23-32.
This is a reprint of an article by Limet published in the *Revue Britannique* in Paris. It
gives a history of the duel in which Andrew
Jackson killed Charles Dickinson in 1806.

Limet was a Frenchman who came to New
Orleans and was engaged in the newspaper
business. In 1861 he became one of the
editors of the *Abeille* and was connected with
this paper until he sold his interests in 1881
and returned to France. He was always
interested in furthering the study of French in
Louisiana, and was vice president of the Athénée Louisianais when he left for Europe. He
continued to be a corresponding member. He
died in 1896. (Information from the *Abeille*,
which names him editor, and from the C R A L,
May 1881, p. 461, and January 1897, p. 3.)

*LIOTAU, Mirtil Ferdinand. Poems in *Les Cenelles*.
H M L.

*LUSSAN, Auguste. *Les martyrs de la Louisiane, tragé-
die en cinq actes et en vers, précédée d'un prologue.* Martin et Proe, Donaldsonville, 1839.
H M L.

    (Reprint—C R A L, 1912, p. 7-32, 140-154;
1913, p. 181-186, 202-220.)

— *Sara la Juive, ou la nuit de Noël, drame en cinq
actes, représenté pour la première fois sur le
Théâtre Français de la Nouvelle Orléans le
5 juin 1838.* Donaldsonville, Johnson &
Phelps, 1839. H M L.

— *Les Impériales.* New Orleans, Gaux a Co., 1841.

— *Cantate, dédiée au Général Jackson.* C de L,
January 9, 1840. C H A.

MALTRAIT, Joseph A. *Louis XIV et son siècle.* In
C R A L, May 1898, p. 278-290.

    This essay won the prize in the contest of
1897. It is a picture of that century, its great
great men in all branches of literature and art,
men in all branches of literature and art, its
splendor at Versailles, and its great women.

— *Les Nez.* In C R A L, September 1898, p. 349-
350.

    This is a humorous poem of a Chinaman who,
having sold one man a nose for a large sum of
money, thought it a good business. He made a

supply of noses and set out to sell them in Gascony. He found that the Gascons had noses with which they were perfectly satisfied.

— *La Chatte et les chatons.* In C R A L, September 1898, p. 348-349.
This is a fable in verse of the old cat who taught her kittens to be kind but did not follow her precepts. She excused herself with the old refrain " I did not mean to do it ".

— *Le Melon.* In C R A L, January 1899, p. 403.
This poem tells the story of the man who put poison in a fine melon in his patch in order to catch the thief who had been stealing his melons. The next day, he found his only son dead.

— *Ballade à l'Horizon.* In C R A L, March 1899, p. 430-432.
The Rev. Maltrait is a Frenchman who came to Louisiana and for nearly twenty-five years was parish priest at Kaplan, Louisiana. He finally resigned and returned to France to live. (Information from J. R. Bollard, Rector of St. Magdelen's Church, Abbeville, Louisiana.)

*MARIGNY, Bernard de. *Mémoire de Bernard de Marigny, habitant de la Louisiane, adressé à ses concitoyens.* Trouve, Paris, 1822. H M L.

— *Réflexions sur la campagne du Général Jackson en Louisiane en 1814 et 1816.* Sollée, New Orleans, 1848. H M L.

— *Réflexions sur la politique des Etats-Unis depuis 1784 jusqu'à l'avènement de Franklin Pierce au pouvoir; statistique de l'Espagne et de l'Ile de Cuba.* Sollée, New Orleans, 1854. H M L.

*MARINONI, Ulisse. *Récit d'un père, une page d'histoire.* In C R A L, July 1901, p. 298-316.

— *Ma Tante Louise.* In C R A L, January 1911, p. 150-159.

— *Mon Oncle Jacques.* In C R A L, July 1916, p. 107-120.

— *L'Ombrie.* In C R A L, January 1912, p. 38-55.

— *Le caractère français pendant la guerre.* In C R A L, 1918, p. 70-82, 86-98.

— *Dante et son Temps.* In C R A L, May 1922, p. 46-55.

*MARTIN, Désirée. *Les Veillées d'une sœur, ou le destin d'un brin de mousse.* Cosmopolite, Nouvelle Orléans, 1877. H M L.

MAZÉRAT, Sélika. *1815, 1915—Comparison.* In C R A L, 1916, p. 98-106, 124-140.

This essay won the prize in the contest of 1915-1916. It compares Napoleon's return in 1815 with the arrival of Kaiser Wilhelm at the Marne in 1915. It also compares the military operations of 1815 with those of 1915.

Mlle Mazerat is a native of New Orleans and was educated at the Sacred Heart Convent there. She is now employed in the business world of her native city. (Facts from her sister.)

MCCLOSKY, Adèle. *Faible hommage à la France et à sa langue.* In C R A L, July 1917, p. 73-74.

The author of this poem of twelve stanzas expresses great faith in France and in her power to repulse Germany. She extols the language of the troubadours and of the " siècle du Grand roi ".

Mme. McClosky (*née* Mérilh) is a native of New Orleans. She was educated at the Sacred Heart Convent and has studied also at Tulane University. She is now Mrs. Harry B. McClosky of New Orleans. (Information from her.)

*MERCIER. Dr. Alfred. *La Rose de Smyrne; l'ermite du Niagara : Erato Labitte.* Paris, 1840. H M L.

— *Biographie de Pierre Soulé, Sénateur à Washington.* Dentu, Paris, 1848.

— *De la fièvre typhoïde dans ses rapports avec la phtisie aiguë.* Rignoux, Paris, 1855. H M L, *Thèses de Médecine,* Vol. II.

- *Le fou de Palerme, nouvelle sicilienne.* Nouvelle Orléans, 1873. H M L, T U L.
- *La fille du prêtre, récit social.* Cosmopolite, Nouvelle Orléans, 1877, 3 vols. H M L, T U L.
- *Etude sur la langue créole en Louisiane.* C R A L, 1880, p. 378-383. Pamphlet also. H M L.
- *L'Habitation St. Ybars, ou maîtres et esclaves en Louisiane.* Imp. Franco-Américaine, Nouvelle Orléans, 1888. H M L, T U L.
- *Lidia.* Imp. Franco-Américaine, Nouvelle Orléans, 1887. H M L.
- *Fortunia, drame en cinq actes.* Imp. Franco-Américaine, Nouvelle Orléans, 1888. H M L. (Also C R A L, November 1888, p. 179-234.)
- *Réditus et Ascalaphos.* 1890, New Orleans, J. L. Gerig's book.
- *Paracelse.* In C R A L, November 1890, p. 190-218.
- *Johnelle.* Antoine, Nouvelle Orléans, 1891. H M L.
- *Emile des Ormiers.* New Orleans, 1891, n. p. H M L.
- *Hénoch Jédésias.* In C R A L, March 1892-November 1893. H M L.
- *L'Anémique.* New Orleans, n. p., n. d.
- Articles in C R A L as follows: September, November 1876; July 1878; May, November 1879; May 1880; July, November 1883; July 1884; January 1886; March 1887; March, July, September, November 1889; July 1890; May 1893.
- *La fleur et le sylphe.* In C R A L, September 1877, p. 100.
- *Amour et foi, rêverie.* In C R A L, January 1882, p. 42.
- *Le Matin.* In C R A L, March 1883, p. 342.
- *Vieux Barde et jeunes filles.* In C R A L, May 1883, p. 373.
- *Du Panlatinisme-Nécessité d'une alliance entre la*

France et la Confédération du Sud.   Paris, n.d.
  H M L.
— *Esprit charmant.*   In C R A L, November 1885,
  p. 260.
— *L'Etranger.*   In C R A L, November 1885,
  p. 261-262.
— *La Houle.*   In C R A L, November 1885, p. 260.
— *Lolotte.*   In C R A L, September 1886, p. 216.
— *Gentille Suzette.*   In C R A L, September 1886,
  p. 217.
— *La curée.*   In C R A L, November 1886, p. 253-
  254.
— *L'homme-l'araignée.*   In C R A L, July 1887,
  p. 389.
— *Tawanta.*   In C R A L, November 1887, p. 451-
  452.
— *Dans la rue.*   In C R A L, January 1888, p. 22-
  24.
— *Message.*   In C R A L, September 1888, p. 158.
— *Où sont-ils?*   In C R A L, September 1888,
  p. 158-160.
— *Soleil couchant.*   In C R A L, January 1889,
  p. 264-265.
— *Les Soleils.*   In C R A L, March 1889, p. 295-
  296.
— *La nuit.*   In C R A L, March 1889, p. 296.
MÉRILH, Mathilde.   *Pascal.*   In C R A L, January 1925,
  p. 24-42.
      This essay won one of the prizes in the con-
  test of 1924.   The author sketches the life of
  Pascal and comments on his works in
  chronological order.
      Mlle. Mérilh is a native of New Orleans.
  She is an artist and still dwells in New Or-
  leans.   (Facts from her sister, Mrs. Adele
  McClosky of New Orleans.)
MÉRY, Gaston Etienne, was born in Baton Rouge, Loui-
  siana in 1793.   He died in France in 1844.
  His work was all written in France, hence he
  will not be given further consideration here.
  (Facts from *Library of Southern Literature,*

Vol. XV, Biographical Dictionary of Authors,
p. 300.)

MONTMAIN, Guillaume A. *Couplets de Circonstance.*
In A N O, February 24, 1832.

This *chanson* was sung at a celebration on
Washington's birthday, and gives full praise to
this hero.

— *Les Immortelles ou les trois journées de juillet
1830.* In A N O, July 29, 1833.

These verses exalt the French love of liberty. They were read by Montmain at a
dinner in celebration of the " Trois Journées ".

— *Aux gardes d'Orléans.* In A N O, October 28,
1837.

This is a poem to commemorate the anniversary of the Orleans Guard.

— *Charles Cuvellier.* In C de L, November 10,
1845.

This poem is in honor of General Cuvellier
who had wanted to die in battle, but, like Cyrano de Bergerac, had not died so.

— *Declouet et Kenner.* In A N O, September 29,
1849.

This is a poem in honor of two candidates,
one for governor and one for lieutenant-gover-
nor.

Montmain was a resident of New Orleans
from the year 1823 to 1851. Many poems by
him were printed in the *Abeille* and the *Courrier de la Louisiane.*

*MOREL, Amadéo. *Récit sur l'ouragan de la Dernière
Isle.* Imp. du Pionnier de l'Assomption, Napoleonville, 1858. H M L.

PERCHÉ, Napoléon Joseph. *De l'importance du mariage
sous le rapport social et religieux.* Méridier,
Nouvelle Orléans, 1846. H M L.

This is a series of articles which were first
published in the *Propagateur Catholique.* A
request to have them printed together caused
them to be reproduced in pamphlet form.

Perché was born in Angers, France, in 1805.

He came to New Orleans in 1841. In 1842
he was appointed chaplain of the Ursulines
Convent. He was later made Archbishop of
New Orleans, which position he held for
14 years. He established a paper, *Le Propagateur Catholique* in 1844, which continued only
a few years after his death in 1883. (Information from *Biographical and Historical Memoirs,* Vol. II, p. 136-137; Chapter VI, History of Louisiana Churches.)

*Pérennes, P. *A Victor Hugo sur son désir d'être
admis à l'Institut.* In A N O, September 11,
1838. L H L.
— *Une fleur au désert.* In A N O, October 30,
1838. L H L.
— *La conquête du Mexique, 1521.* In A N O, December 11, 1838.
— *Les Morts.* In C de L, October 31, 1840.
— *Funérailles de Napoléon.* In C de L, February 8,
1841.
— *Guatimozin, ou le dernier jour de l'Empire Mexicain, tragédie en cinq actes.* Sollée, Nouvelle
Orléans, 1839.

*Peytavin, John L. *La Louisiane; analyse historique.*
In C R A L, November 1884, p. 674-685.
This is a rapid sketch of its history from the
time of La Salle's first visit through the Civil
War and through reconstruction days.
— *Albert Dupont, Nouvelle Louisianaise.* In
C R A L, 1885, p. 254-259; 1886, p. 41-48,
67-76, 106-120, 170-180, 200-213; 1887,
288-290, 316-321, 356-361.
— *Réfutation des erreurs de M. Geo. W. Cable au
sujet des Créoles.* In C R A L, July 1888,
p. 125-133.
— *Traité sur l'éducation au dix-neuvième siècle.* In
C R A L, September 1894, p. 149-159; No-
vember 1894, p. 163-170.
— *Le théâtre pendant la Confédération.* In C R A L,
September 1890, p. 178-185.
This article tells of the efforts of the theaters

to continue in operation and their improvisations
and inventions for costumes during the war.
— *Mélange des langues.* In C R A L, January 1891,
p. 260-274.

PICHOT, H. Léonie. *Souvenir d'un épisode de l'histoire
de la Louisiane.* In C R A L, September
1883, p. 420-427.
This is a short sketch of Louisiana history
from La Salle through 1769 with special em-
phasis on 1763-1769.

— *Une page d'histoire.* In C R A L, March 1885,
p. 71-78.
This is a short article referring to the third
part, recently published, of the work of the
Count of Paris on the war in America. The
Count of Paris and the Duke of Chartres took
sides with the Union in the Civil War. The
writer of this article wants to correct some of
the errors that she believes the Count had
made in his book.
Mlle. Pichot was a native of New Orleans.
She died there on June 30, 1898 at the age
of 55. (Facts from the death record at the
Cathedral.)

POPULUS, August. *A mon ami P. qui demandait mon
opinion sur le mariage.* In *Les Cenelles.*
H M L.
The author explains in a note that this poem
has a double significance. If the first and third,
then the second and fourth lines of each stanza
are read, the second meaning can be obtained.
Populus was one of the collaborators of the
Cenelles. His name appears in the city directory up to 1854.

*POYDRAS, Julien. *La prise du morne du Baton Rouge
par Monseigneur de Galvez, Chevalier, pen-
sionné de l'ordre Royal distingué de Charles
Trois, Brigadier des armées de Sa Majesté, In-
tendant, Inspecteur et Gouverneur Général de
la Province de la Louisiane.* Imp. Antoine Boudousquié, Nouvelle Orléans, MDCCLXXIX.

(Reprinted in the account given of Poydras in
Alcée Fortier's *Louisiana Studies*, p. 7-23.)
H M L.

QUESTY, Joanni. *Vision, Une larme sur William Stephen. Causerie.* In *Les Cenelles.* H M L.
Questy was one of the collaborators of *Les
Cenelles* to which he contributed three poems.
He was a teacher in New Orleans where he
died in April 1869. (Facts from the death record in the Cathedral and from the city directory for 1860 ff.)

*QUEYROUSE, Léona. *Vision.* In C R A L, January
1885, p. 40-42.
— *Le désir.* In C R A L, March 1885, p. 132.
— *Le regret.* In C R A L, September 1885, p. 227-
228.
— *A ma mère.* In C R A L, September 1885,
p. 215-216.
— *Palpitans.* In C R A L, November 1886, p. 252.
— *Sonnet.* In C R A L, November 1886, p. 252.
— *Au Docteur Charles Turpin.* In C R A L, March
1887, p. 321.
— *Sonnet, sur une pensée donnée.* In C R A L,
March 1887, p. 322.
— *Fantôme d'Occident.* In A N O, December 23,
1894.
— *Sonnet: Ad incognitum.* In A N O, December
23, 1894.
— *Sonnet: Hommage et remerciement à l'illustre
auteur du Méfistole, Arrigo Boito.* In A N O,
December 23, 1894.
— *La Lyre brisée.* In A N O, September 10, 1899.
— *Exil.* In A N O, September 24, 1899.
— *Idylle.* In A N O, October 1, 1899.
— *Samson.* In A N O, December 24, 1899.
— *L'âme du poète.* In A N O, December 22, 1901.
— *In Graeciam.* In A N O, September 1, 1908.
— *Resurge* (Sonnet). In A N O, December 25,
1908.
— *Etude sur Racine.* In C R A L, November 1880,
p. 406-411.

— *Conférence sur l'indulgence.* In C R A L, November 1884, p. 694-713.

QUEYROUSE, Maxime. *Influence d'un grand caractère en bien ou en mal sur la destinée des différents peuples.* In C R A L, May 1885, p. 147-157.

This article won the prize in the contest of 1884. It is a well developed discussion of the place held by each great character in history, and shows that each one had his own place and that no one of the others could have filled it.

(This has been published in pamphlet form also.) H M L.

Queyrouse is a native of New Orleans and received his education in that city. He is now attorney there. (Information from him.)

REINECKE, J. Alfred. *Les frères Rouquette.* In C R A L, 1920, p. 12-30, 37-62, 70-84. (January, April, July issues.) H M L.

This article won the prize in the contest of 1919. It gives a clear and full account of the two brothers and their works.

Reinecke was born in New Orleans on September 1, 1891. He was educated in the public schools of that city and at Tulane University. He received his A. B. degree from Tulane in 1913 and his A. M. in 1914. He is now a teacher of French in the New Orleans Academy.

*REMY, Henri. *Histoire de la Louisiane.* St. Michel, 1854-1855 (part of it). (Manuscript, part of it.) H. P. Dart's possession.

— *Le Hamac.* In A N O, May 9, 1840.

This poem gives a fine pen picture of a young girl in a hammock, dreaming of love.

RENSHAW, Gladys Anne. *Ronsard, poète lyrique.*

This essay was one of those that won the prize in the contest of 1926. It will be published in the next issue of the *Comptes Rendus de l'Athénée Louisianais.*

— *S'instruire en s'amusant.* Allyn & Bacon, 1926.

This is a book of cross word puzzles and

games for clubs. It was published in collaboration with Simone de la Souchère Deléry.

— *La Française* (Brieux), New York and London, Century Co., 1927.

This is an edition of Brieux' comedy with introduction, notes, and vocabulary by G. A. Renshaw and Simone de la Souchère Deléry.

Mlle Renshaw is a native of New Orleans, daughter of Henry Renshaw. She received her education there and is now a teacher. She is a member of the faculty of Newcomb College in New Orleans.

RILLIEUX, Victor Ernest. *Le Timide*. In *Nos hommes et notre histoire*, p. 81-82 by R. D. Desdunes. H M L.

As this name indicates, the poem is the outcry of a timid lover who cannot express his love to the lady of his choice.

— *Hojas secas*. (*Les feuilles mortes*), *Daily Crusader*, N. O. 1895.

This is a metrical arrangment of a translation of Becquer's poem into prose. The poet follows the translation closely except for a few necessary changes and for a certain amount of padding in order to fill out the lines. The prose translation was made by Mrs. Corinne Castellanos Mellen.

Rillieux was a native of New Orleans. He was born about 1845 and died on December 5, 1898, at the age of 53.

RIQUET, Nicol. *Rondeau redoublé: aux francs amis* (*Cenelles*). H M L.

Riquet was one of the collaborators of the *Cenelles* to which he contributed one poem only.

ROBERI, Dr. H. *Parallèle des langues*. In C R A L, July 1878, p. 182-183.

This is a comparison of Latin, French, Italian, and English in order to show that French is superior to all of them in clearness.

— *Parallèle entre Démosthènes et Cicéron.* In
C R A L, January 1881, p. 423-424.
The author prefers the sweetness and charm
of Cicero to the vehemence of Demosthenes.
— *Parallèle entre Corneille, Racine, et Voltaire.* In
C R A L, May 1881, p. 466-467.
The author thinks that each one of these
writers has his own characteristics of greatness,
and it is not necessary to state which is greatest.
— *La Phrénologie.* In C R A L, September 1881,
p. 491-492.
The author thinks phrenology is of great use
and should be studied. He thinks it recognizes
intelligence as well as instincts in animals.
Dr. Roberi was a native of Piémont. He came
to Louisiana and lived in St. Landry Parish.
He was a corresponding member of the Athénée Louisianais until his death in 1883. (Information from C R A L, July 1883, p. 410.)
ROBERT, Ermance. *La femme dans la littérature française comme auteur au dix-neuvième siècle.*
In C R A L, May 1886, p. 131-142.
This essay won the prize in the contest of
1885. Madame de Staël is the woman who
receives special mention.
— *Elizabeth d'Autriche.* In C R A L, May 1901,
p. 246-256.
This is a very clear account of the principal
events in the life of Elisabeth.
— *François Coppée.* In C R A L, January 1903,
p. 189-195.
The author speaks of Coppée only as a poet
in this article. She discusses some of his
collections and speaks of his glorification of the
poor and feeble.
— *Le savant.* In C R A L, April 1906, p. 50-61.
This is a biographical sketch of Louis Pas-
teur.
— *Jeanne d'Arc.* In C R A L, April 1911, p. 205-
216.
This is a simple account of the events in the

life of the young peasant of Lorraine and of her canonization by Pius X.

Mlle Robert was born in New Orleans on October 30, 1848. She received her education at the Ursulines Convent. She taught for four years as principal of the School of the French Union. In 1888 she opened a private school where she taught until her death in August 1919. (Facts from Miss Clara Garidel, who worked with her for nearly 17 years.)

*ROQUIGNY, Jacques de. *Les amours d'Hélène, ou deux cœurs brisés.* La Sère et Cie., Nouvelle Orléans, 1854. H M L.

ROST, Emile. *Voyage aux mines d'argent.* In C R A L, September 1896, p. 533-536.

— *Voyage en Savoie.* In C R A L, March 1900, p. 39-45.

The two sketches above are accounts of trips made by the author.

— *Souvenirs sur le barreau de la Nouvelle Orléans.* In C R A L, July 1899, p. 502-505.

These souvenirs were occasioned by the death of Mr. Semmes. Several noted lawyers are named: Alfred Hennen, Christian Roselius, Pierre Soulé, and Randall Hunt.

— *Poésie coloniale.* In C R A L, March 1901, p. 215-223.

After a few general observations, the author quotes from the works of Berquin Duvallon.

— *La grande revue de Béthény.* In C R A L, January 1902, p. 5-9.

This article tells of the grand review at the little village of Béthény near Reims on the occasion of the visit of the Czar Nicholas II and the Czarina.

Rost was born June 17, 1839. His father was a native of Paris and his mother was a native of Louisiana. He received his early education in private schools in New Orleans and then attended Georgetown University at Washington. He was graduated from there in 1858.

He received his law degree from Harvard in
1859. During the Civil War, he visited the
courts of Spain and France, accompanying his
father, who was one of the commissioners sent
by the Confederate States to foreign powers.
After the war, he practiced law in New Orleans
until 1869 when he went to manage his plantation in St. Charles Parish. He died on January 2, 1913. (Facts from the notice in the
Picayune for January 3, 1913, at the time of
his death.)

*ROUEN, Bussière. *Nécessité des études élémentaires
pour le choix d'une profession, d'un art ou d'un
métier*. In C R A L, May 1883, p. 349-359.
    This essay won the prize for men in the con-
test of 1882. The author chooses medicine,
painting, music, architecture, and teaching as illustrations to show the necessity of the elementary studies.

— *Rêveries—Du berceau à la tombe*. In C R A L,
November 1883, p. 455-458.

— *Cent huit ans*. In C R A L, May 1884, p. 574-
589.
    This is a rapid sketch of the history of the
United States from the Declaration of Indepen-
dence to 1883.

— *L'enfant et l'image*. In C R A L, March 1886,
p. 57-62.

— *Rayon de soleil*. In C R A L, March 1887,
p. 310-316.

— *Réflexions*. In C R A L, January 1895, p. 206-
216.

— *Fin du siècle*. In C R A L, January 1901,
p. 197-201.

— *1918?* In C R A L, January 1918, p. 11-12.

— *Les poètes louisianais*. In C R A L, 1921, 7-26,
37-50.
    This was a lecture given at the Athénée Loui-
sianais. The author uses the *Louisiana Studies* of Fortier as his chief source. He quotes
from a great many of these poets.

*ROUQUETTE, Adrien. *Les savanes, poésies américai-*

nes. In H M L, Labitte, Paris, 1841. A. Moret, Nouvelle Orléans.

— *Discours prononcé à la Cathédrale de St. Louis, Nouvelle Orléans, à l'occasion de l'anniversaire du 8 janvier.* Sauvaignat, Paris, 1846. H M L.

— *La Thébaïde en Amérique ou l'apologie de la vie solitaire et contemplative.* Méridier, Nouvelle Orléans, 1852. N Y P L.

— *L'Antoniade ou la solitude avec Dieu, poème érémitique.* E. Marchand, Nouvelle Orléans, 1860. H M L.

— *La nouvelle Atala, ou la fille de l'Esprit, légende indienne.* Imp. du Propagateur Catholique, Nouvelle Orléans, 1879. H M L.

*ROUQUETTE, Dominique. *Les Meschacébéennes.* Sauvaignat, Paris, 1839. H M L.

— *Fleurs d'Amérique, poésies nouvelles.* Méridier, Nouvelle Orléans, 1856. H M L. In C R A L, poems (reprint), April 1905, p. 51-59.

*ST. CÉRAN, Tullius. *Rien-ou-moi.* Imp. de Gaston Bruslé, Nouvelle Orléans, 1837. H M L.

— *Mil huit cent quatorze et mil huit cent quinze, ou les combats et la victoire des fils de la Louisiane.* Gaux et Cie., Nouvelle Orléans, 1838. H M L.

— *Les Louisianaises.* J. L. Sollée, Nouvelle Orléans, 1840. H M L.

— *Chansons.* (Page with date, publisher, place, etc. missing.) H M L.

ST. PIERRE, Michel. *Le Changement; La jeune fille mourante; A une demoiselle qui me demandait des vers pour son album; Deux ans après; Couplet contre une demoiselle sur qui on avait tiré un coup de pistolet; Tu m'as dit: " Je t'aime ".* In *Les Cenelles.*

St. Pierre was one of the collaborators of *Les Cenelles,* to which he contributed six poems.

*SÉJOUR, Victor. *Le retour de Napoléon* (in *Les Cenelles*). H M L.

SENNÉGY, René de. *Une paroisse louisianaise—St. Michel*. Capo, Nouvelle Orléans, 1877. L U.
This little book is addressed to the Catholics of the parish. It speaks of the different Catholic priests who have served there, of the convents, of Jefferson College, and of the different societies.

Sennégy was a native of France. He came to Louisiana in the fall of 1873 and taught French at Jefferson College in Convent, Louisiana, from 1873 through the session of 1878-1879. When *Le Foyer Créole* was first established, he was connected with it and wrote many articles for it. He was with it from 1880-1883. He left Louisiana and went to Africa. He died in Algeria. His real name was A. M. J. de la Peichardière. (Facts from Father Rapier of Jefferson College, Convent, Louisiana, and B. J. Dicharry, editor of the *Intérim* of Convent.)

*SHELDON, Madame W. J. *Edmond Rostand et son théâtre*. In C R A L, April 1904, p. 349-374.
This essay won the prize in the contest of 1903. It tells that Rostand was the favorite of the gods from birth; he was wealthy enough not to have to be mercenary, and wrote from inspiration rather than from necessity.

— *Le farfadet, conte rustique*. In C R A L, September 1922, p. 78-89.

— *Une rêverie, conte semi-rustique*. In C R A L, September 1923, p. 20-27.

— *A travers les siècles*. In C R A L, Jan. 1904, p. 320-328.

— *Loin*. In C R A L, January 1908, p. 274-276.

— *Les colombes blanches*. In C R A L, April 1909, p. 466.

— *Le groupe des barques*. In C R A L, April 1909, p. 465.

— *Sonnet à un artiste*. In C R A L, July 1909, p. 506.

— *Sonnet à François Coppée.* In C R A L, July 1911, p. 245.
— *Réponse à l'auteur de " Jérusalem ".* In C R A L, Oct. 1912, p. 129-131.
— *Avril.* In C R A L, April 1912, p. 63.
— *Réflexion.* In C R A L, April 1912, p. 64.
— *L'écho des pêcheurs de lune.* In C R A L, October 1912, p. 126-127.
— *Les deux drapeaux.* In C R A L, October 1912, p. 125-126.
— *Les lys dans les vallées.* In C R A L, October 1912, p. 128.
— *Guynemer.* In C R A L, October 1919, p. 98-100.
— *L'idéal.* In C R A L, January 1922, p. 22-24.
— *Chant en l'honneur de Virgile.* In C R A L, May 1924, p. 24-25.
— *France, fille de Dieu.* In C R A L, May 1924, p. 25.
*SHOENFELD, Madame Gabrielle. *Poésies et nouvelles.* F. C. Philippe Jr., Nouvelle Orléans, 1910. T P T.
— *La question du jour.* In C R A L, April 1910, p. 59-62.
— *Le vase de Sèvres, Mon pays.* In C R A L, April 1910, p. 55-57.
SONIAT, Gustave Valérien. *Histoire de l'agriculture en Louisiane.* In C R A L, July 1894, p. 111-121.
  This article begins with the simple agriculture of the Indians and then tells of the different products that the Louisiana planter tried to raise: wheat, indigo, tobacco, sugar-cane, and later rice.
— *Quelques réflexions sur le système de loi en Louisiane.* In C R A L, July 1897, p. 108-119.
— *De la mémoire et de la mnémonique.* In C R A L, March 1898, p. 237-251.
  The author shows himself a firm believer in memory training.
— *De l'influence des éléments sur l'agriculture en*

Louisiane. In C R A L, January 1900, p. 4-13.

Soniat was born July 1856, on a plantation near New Orleans. He was a great-grandson of Guy Soniat du Fossat. He was a sugar planter for a while, but later moved to New Orleans where he practiced law. He died in 1903. (Information from *Biographical and Historical Memoirs of Louisiana,* Vol. II, p. 398.)

*Soniat Du Fossat, Guy. *Synopsis of the History of Louisiana from the Founding of the Colony to the end of 1791.* (Translation in 1903 by Charles T. Soniat for the Louisiana Historical Society.) H M L.

Souchère, Simone de la. *Les maîtres du théâtre français contemporain.* In C R A L, January 1924, p. 5-34.

This essay won the prize in the contest of 1923. The author discusses such authors as Dumas Fils, Augier, Rostand, Hervieu, Brieux, and others.

— *S'instruire en s'amusant.* Allyn & Bacon, 1926.

This book was prepared in collaboration with Gladys Anne Renshaw. It consists partly of cross word puzzles and partly of games and rules for French clubs.

— *La Française* (Brieux), Century Co., New York and London, 1927.

This is a text book arrangement of Brieux's comedy. It was also written in collaboration with Gladys Anne Renshaw.

Mlle. de la Souchère was born in Bourganeuf, France. When a child, she was sent to Paris. She studied at the Lycée Fénelon, at the Ecole Normale Supérieure de Sèvres, and at the Sorbonne. She received from the Sorbonne a " Certificat d'aptitude à l'enseignement des lettres ". She prepared the " Agrégation d'histoire " and taught at the Collège de Sens. She was offered a " bourse d'études " by Bryn Mawr College, Pennsylvania, where she spent the year 1919-1920 doing post-graduate work. She taught one year at Middlebury College in Vermont and then went to Newcomb College in New Orleans. She is now Mrs. Frank Deléry of New Orleans. (Facts were obtained from her.)

SYLVA, Manuel. *Soudain, Le rêve, essai littéraire.* In *Les Cenelles.* H M L.

Sylva was one of the collaborators of *Les Cenelles* to which he contributed two exercises in rhyming.

TARLTON, Gabrielle. *Rose Blanche.* In C R A L, May 1891, p. 301-325.

This story won the prize in the contest of 1890. It is one which deals with the private life of one particular family. The reader is introduced to them and shown their different emotions: joy, sorrow, grief.

Mlle. Tarlton is a native of Franklin, Louisiana. Her grandmother was Mrs. Sidonie de la Houssaye, who is well known for her stories of Acadian life in Louisiana. She is now Mrs. L. B. Cross of New Orleans. (Facts from her.)

TESSON, L. *Chœur d'Indiennes.* In C R A L, July 1877, p. 82.

A poem of four stanzas treats of the prayer to the Great Spirit to stop the fratricidal struggles between the whites and the Indians. It admonishes Indian warriors to seek other glory than that of scalps at the belt.

(I could find nothing about Tesson.)

*TESTUT, Charles. *Les Echos.* Nouvelle Orléans, 1849, n. p.

— *St. Denis.* In *Les Veillées Louisianaises,* Vol. I, 1849. H M L.

— *Calisto.* In *Les Veillées Louisianaises,* Vol. II, 1849. T P T.

— *Portraits littéraires de la Nouvelle Orléans.* Imp.

des Veillées Louisianaises, Nouvelle Orléans,
1850. H M L.
— *Fleurs d'été*. Nouvelle Orléans, 1851, n. p.
H M L.
— *Le vieux Salomon, ou une famille d'esclaves au
dix-huitième siècle*. Nouvelle Orléans, rue de
Chartres, 1872. H M L.

THÉARD, Cyrille Charles. *Poésie à Mme. Eugénie de
Montijo, ex-impératrice de France, veuve de Sa
Majesté Napoléon III, qui régna de 1852 à
1870*. Imp. Philippe, Nouvelle Orléans, 1896.
H M L.

This poem is divided into two parts. Part I
treats of Empress Eugenia, her Spanish traits,
her Scotch ways, her ease in adapting herself
to French ways in Paris, her love for the people, their grief at her fall. Part II treats of the
two Napoleons and their destinies.

Théard was a native of Louisiana, son of Thomas Théard and Clémentine Larocque-Turgeau.
His father was a brilliant journalist and Cyrille
inherited his literary tastes. Cyrille was a
teacher in New Orleans, and was for many
years principal of the Bayou Road School.
(Facts were obtained from Charles J. Théard
and from the city directories up to 1902.)

THIBERGE, Marie. *Jeanne d'Arc dans l'histoire et dans
la littérature*. In C R A L, May 1895, p. 267-
290.

This essay won the prize of the contest of
1894. It is a well developed presentation of
Joan of Arc as given in history and contains a
list of works, beginning with Christane de
Pisan's *La Pucelle*, and treating of her and her
part in French history.

Mlle. Thiberge is the daughter of the late
Henry R. Thiberge, architect from Paris,
France, and Emma Druilhet de Flaville, de-
scendant of French Colonists of Louisiana. She
was born in St. James Parish, Louisiana on her
ancestral plantation. She was educated at the

Sacred Heart Academy in New Orleans. She
is a member of the Athénée Louisianais and of
the Louisiana Colonials of which she is secretary. She is now living in New Orleans. She
has now and then been successful in drawing
and painting, both in oil and in water colors.
(Facts obtained from her.)

*Thierry, Camille. *Poems in Les Cenelles.* H M L.
— Poems in the *Orléanais,* 1850. C H A.
— *Les Vagabondes,* Paris, 1874. S J S.

Tujague, François. *Le Premier pas, essais littéraires.*
Imp. de L. E. Marchand, Nouvelle Orléans,
1863. H M L.
— *Utilité des langues vivantes.* In C R A L, Nov.
1889, p. 408-415.
— *Une ouvrière.* In C R A L, November 1891,
p. 408-416.
— *A travers l'océan.* In O L, Vol. II, May 6, 1893,
p. 210 ff.
— Articles in O L , Vol. I, p. 348-355; Vol. II,
p. 162-171, 356-369, 260-269, 501-520, 553-
571. H M L.
— *Les forêts de la Louisiane.* In O L, Vol. II,
p. 123-134.
— *Les chasseurs de crocodiles en Louisiane.* In
O L, Vol. II, p. 401-414. H M L.
— *Les prairies tremblantes de la Louisiane.* In O L,
Vol. III, 11-22.
— *Chroniques louisianaises :*
Lafrénière. In O L, Vol. III, p. 59-71, 107-118.
Le pirate Lafitte. In O L, Vol. III, p. 168-178.
Le navire Charles. In O L, Vol. III, p. 220-
225.
Sous les " Chênes Verts ". In O L, Vol. III,
p. 271-281.

Turpin, Dr. Charles. *Etude sur Alfred de Musset.* In
C R A L, Nov. 1876, p. 22-27.
This articles is a very frank study of de Mus-
set, the man.
— *Du mouvement et de ses transformations dans la
société.* In C R A L, May 1877, p. 61-62.

This article states that restlessness and tendencies toward variability cause development and progress.

— *Du mouvement et de ses transformations dans l'hérédité.* In C R A L, September 1877, p. 89-92.

This article shows the necessity for man to recognize and try to counteract the fatality of heredity.

— *Liquéfaction et solidification du gaz.* In C R A L, Nov. 1878, p. 208-212.

— *Souvenir.* In C R A L, July 1879, p. 275-276.

The author's memories were awakened by thoughts of the Indians. He tells the story of an old Indian woman who was going to walk twenty miles with the dead body of her little grandchild in order to bury it beside its mother.

— *De l'interjection Ah! Ha!* In C R A L, Nov. 1880, p. 405-406.

In this very short article, the author shows that this interjection is more eloquent than a long discourse. It is the first cry of grief and the last breath of man. It expresses the movement, noise, and passions of life.

— *Le Bouvreuil.* In C R A L, January 1886, p. 35-40.

This is a rather pathetic story of a mother's grief at her daughter's death and the comfort she was able to derive from the pet bird.

Dr. Turpin was born on September 19, 1816 in New Orleans. His father was a native of Bordeaux. Charles studied in Paris and received his M. D. degree there. He returned to New Orleans in about 1844 and began his practice of medicine. He was always greatly interested in art and in literature. (Facts were obtained from his baptismal record in the Cathedral, from the city directories, and from a short biographical sketch in C R A L, May 1886, p. 52-57.)

Tusson, Dr. Walter. *A ..... pour ses vingt ans*. In
C R A L, July 1907, p. 232-233.

    The poet is led to philosophize on the happiness of a woman whose heart is awakening to love at the age of twenty.

— *L'amour dans un grenier*. In C R A L, October 1907, p. 246.

    The woman in this poem tells the story of her hardships in getting food for her family.

— *Chantecler*. In C R A L, October 1910, p. 97-116.

    This is a *causerie* in which the author admits his great admiration for Rostand. He calls attention to Rostand's lyrical verses such as the " *Hymn to the Sun* ". He quotes passages to show the nobility of Chantecler's character. To him, there is something pure and refreshing in this drama.

    Dr. Tusson was born in New Orleans on April 23, 1873. He was graduated in medicine from Tulane University in 1899. He practiced for a while in the country towns of Louisiana, and then went to Guatemala in 1905. He soon returned to Louisiana. He died there in 1917. (Facts were obtained from Mrs. Tusson who still resides in New Orleans.)

Valcour B., was one of the collaborators of *Les Cenelles*. His most important poem is his " *Epître à Constant Lepouzé* " in which he thanks Lepouzé for his inspiration. He claims to be an admirer, like Lepouzé, of Horace and Vergil. This poem bears the date 1828.

    Poems in *Les Cenelles*. H M L.

Védrenne, Louis H. Nicholas. *A mon chien fidèle*. *La Réforme*, April 11, 1846.

— *Allégorie*. *La Réforme*, April 23, 1846.

— *Romance*. *La Réforme*, May 10, 1846.

— *Le papillon du soir*. *La Réforme*, May 3, 1846.

— *Vers à Mlle. E. A. D*. *La Réforme*, April 19, 1846.

— *Tout fuit. La réforme,* April 26, 1846.

Védrenne was a native of France who came to Louisiana and taught in New Orleans. He died there on May 3, 1854 at the age of 45. He published some poems in *La Réforme,* the majority of which are love poems. (Information from the city directories and from his death record in the Board of Health office.)

VIEL, Etienne Bernard Alexander, was born in New Orleans in 1736 and died in France in 1821. Although he has no rightful place in a discussion of the French Literature of Louisiana, he is mentioned here because of the great pride taken by his native state in his translation of Fénelon's *Télémaque* into Latin verse. (Facts were obtained from *Louisiana Biographies,* Vol. I, p. 11, February 18, 1882, and C R A L, July 1899, p. 490-501.)

VIGNAUD, Henri, was born in New Orleans and was educated there. He was engaged in journalistic work and was connected with the *Renaissance Louisianaise* and the *Courrier de la Louisiane.* He was literary editor of the former paper when he was appointed on a diplomatic commission to France in 1862. He went there in 1863 and made his home there until his death in 1922. He wrote *La lettre et la carte de Toscanelli sur la route des Indes par l'ouest* and *Etudes sur la vie de Colomb avant ses découvertes.* These were written after his departure for France, hence they will not be discussed here. (Facts were obtained from the *Louisiana Historical Quarterly,* Vol. V, 1922, p. 63-75, and from the *Renaissance Louisianaise.*)

*VILLENEUFVE, Paul Leblanc de. *La fête du Petit-blé, ou l'héroïsme de Poucha-Houmma, tragédie en cinq actes; fait historique pris chez une nation sauvage.* Imp. du Courrier de la Nouvelle Orléans, 1814. (Reprinted in C R A L, 1909,

p. 421-432, 443-464, 529-536; 1910, p. 13-30, 41-55.) H M L.

VILLERÉ, Arcadie. *De l'influence de la femme dans la famille*. In C R A L, November 1883, p. 359-363.

This essay won the prize given to women in the contest of 1882. It exalts family life and praises the wife as the soul of the family circle.

— *De l'amitié*. In C R A L, November 1883, p. 458-460.

The author speaks of the foundations of friendship and asserts that there can be no discouragement for any one who knows how to understand this word.

Mlle Villeré is a native of New Orleans and received her education there. About 1884, she went to Chicago and taught for a while in Madame Von Ende's school. She is still living in Chicago where she now gives private French lessons. (Facts from her cousin, Paul Villeré, and from C R A L, July 1885, p. 179-181.)

VILLERÉ, Paul. *La propagande allemande*. In C R A L, July 1919, p. 23-32.

— *Le Créole*. In C R A L, July 1921, p. 65-85.

This is a story of Jacques Landrey given as a type of Creole who felt his French blood awaken at the time of the World War. Jacques' service in France is described.

Villeré is a native of New Orleans. He was educated there at the Jesuits' College. For the past thirty years he has been connected with the Hibernia Bank and Trust Company. He is now vice-president, which place he has held for six or seven years. He was helper on the staff of the *Abeille* in its last days.

*VOORHIES, Felix. *Le petit chien de la veuve, comédie en un acte*. In C R A L, January 1891, p. 227-244.

— *Ne pas lâcher la proie pour l'ombre, proverbe en*

un acte. In C R A L, October 1905, p. 108-133.

— *Au coin du feu*. In C R A L, April 1906, p. 43-50.

— *Les noces d'argent du couple Néral*. In C R A L, January 1918, p. 12-26.

— *Une nuit parmi les Jay-hawkers*. In C R A L, August 1907, p. 172-183.

— *Un cochon de lait féroce*. In C R A L, January 1908, p. 294-302.

— *Idylle en prose*. In C R A L, January 1911, p. 145-150.

WOGAN, Clara. *La chanson-chansonniers*. In C R A L, Jan. 1913. p. 171-180.

   In this article the author limits her discussion to Béranger and Gustave Nadaud. She quotes several *chansons* by Beranger.

— *Voyage aux châteaux de France*. In C R A L, April 1919, p. 48-57.

   This article gives descriptions of the chateaux of Blois, Amboise, Chenonceaux, Chambord, Chinon, Loches, and Pau.

— *La femme à travers les âges*. In C R A L, July 1920, p. 85-96, Oct. 1920, p. 98-102.

   This is a discussion of Joan of Arc, Isabelle of Castille, Mme. de Sévigny, Mlle. de Scudéry, and Florence Nightingale.

— *Clémenceau*. In C R A L, May 1923, p. 21-23.

   This is a short study of Clémenceau's political life, especially during the war.

   Mme. Vogan (*née* Beugnot) is a native of France, born in Paris where she lived until she was seven years of age. She went to New Orleans and was educated there. Later, she returned to Paris and studied music. She was a pupil of Dr. Guiseppe Sariate with whom she completed her musical studies. She is now Mrs. Jules Wogan of New Orleans.

C.—WORKS OF WHICH NO COPIES WERE FOUND

BROUSSARD, ?: Poem on the Defeat of the English at Chalmette. (Mentionned in the notes left by Edward Fortier.)

CANONGE, L. Placide: *Gaston de St. Elme: drame en 5 actes et en prose.*

— *Jean, ou une histoire sous Charles Quint.*

— *L'Ambassadeur d'Autriche.*

CHAUMETTE, Dr. J.: Poème: *Les droits de l'homme*, New Orleans, Tribune, 1865.

D'ARTLYS, ?: *Le Soulier Rouge.*

DELERY, Dr. Charles: *Les Némésiennes confédérées, Mobile*, 1863.

— *Les Yankées fondateurs de l'esclavage aux Etats-Unis et initiateurs du droit de sécession*, Paris, 1864.

DESSOMMES, Edward: *Jacques Morel.*

DUGUÉ, Dr. Charles Oscar: *Le Cynge, ou Mingo*, 1852.

DUPERRON, Jean: *Recueil complet des poésies fugitives, érotiques et politiques.*

LAMULONIÈRE, E.: *Organisation de l'enseignement en Louisiane*, 1854.

— *Une Vocation.* (Mentioned in notes left by E. J. Fortier.)

LAUC-MARYAT, E. de: *La Femme en loterie: vaudeville en un acte*, 1850. (Mentioned in notes left by E. J. Fortier.)

LUSSAN, Auguste: *La famille créole, drame en cinq actes et en prose*, New Orleans, 1837.

MAGNIN, Alexandre: *Chansons Patriotiques*, 1831?

MONTMAIN, G. A.: *Mes Bulles de savon.* (Mentioned by Cyprien Dufour in his *Esquisses locales.*)

M., G. A.: *Histoire pittoresque et curieuse du théâtre français à la Nouvelle Orléans de 1816 à 1846.*

MOREL, Amadéo: *L'Esclavage aux Etats-Unis du Sud*, Paris, 1862.

PERENNES, P.: *Hicotengal.*

ROUQUETTE, Adrien: *Le vingt-cinquième anniversaire du Pontificat de Pio Nono*, Propagateur Catho-

que, Nouvelle Orléans, 1871. (Mentioned in
notes left by E. J. Fortier.)

SEGHERS, Julien: *Le Louisianais, recueil de poésies.*

TESTUT, Charles: *L'Album poétique de la Louisiane.*

— *Les Mystères de la Nouvelle Orléans,* New Orleans, 1852-54.

— *Les Filles de Monte Cristo,* 1876.

TRUDEAU, James: *Considérations sur la défence de l'état
de la Louisiane,* 1861.

The above works that have not already been
spoken about in the body of this book were
listed in the *Cambridge History of American
Literature.* That list was prepared by Edward
J. Fortier.

D.—*SOURCES OF INFORMATION ON FRENCH WRITERS
OF LOUISIANA*

Cambridge History of American Literature, vol. IV.

Comptes Rendus de l'Athénée Louisianais.

DAVIDSON, James Wood: *Living Writers of the South,*
Carlton N. Y., S. Low & Son, 1869.

DE MENIL, Alexander: *Literature of the Louisiana Territory,* St. Louis News, 1904.

*FORTIER, Alcée: *Louisiana Studies,* New Orleans,
Hansell, 1894.

*FORTIER, Edward Joseph: *Lettres françaises en Loui-
siane,* Québec, l'Action Sociale, 1915.

GILL, Henry M.: *The South in Prose and Poetry,* New
Orleans, Hansell, 1916.

MANLY, Louise: *Southern Literature,* from 1759-1895,
Richmond, Va.; Johnson, 1895.

Library of Southern Literature, vol. XV.

M'CALEB, Thomas: *The Louisiana Book, Selections
from Literature of the South,* New Orleans,
R. F. Straughan, 1894.

*Most important.

E.—WORKS ON CREOLE DIALECT AND SONGS

ALLEN, William Francis, Charles Pickard Ware, Lucy
    McKim Garrison: *Slave Songs of the United
    States*, New York, A. Simpson and Co., 1867.
CABLE, George Washington: *Creole Slave Songs* in
    Century Magazine, April 1886.
FORTIER, Alcée: *Louisiana Studies*, New Orleans, Han-
    sell, 1894.
HEARN, Lafcadio: *Gombo Zhèbes, Little Dictionary of
    Creole Proverbs*, New York, Will H. Cole-
    man, 1885.
LEJEUNE, Emilie: *Creole Folk Songs* in *Louisiana Histo-
    rical Quarterly*, October 1919.
MERCIER, Alfred: *Etude sur la langue créole en Loui-
    siane*, New Orleans, 1880.
PETERSON, Clara Gottschalk: *Creole Songs from New
    Orleans* (sheet music), New Orleans, Grune-
    wald, 1902.
SCARBOROUGH, Dorothy: *On the Trail of Negro Folk
    Songs*, Harvard University Press, 1925.

F.— WORKS CONSULTED, OTHER THAN THOSE
BY LOUISIANA WRITERS

CHAMPIGNY, Chevalier de: *Memoir of the Present State
    of Louisiana*. (In B. F. French's *Historical
    Memoirs of Louisiana*, vol. 5, p. 194 ff.)
CLARK, Daniel: *Proofs of the Corruption of Gen. James
    Wilkinson, and his connexion with Aaron Burr,
    with a full refutation of his slanderous allega-
    tions in relation to the principal witness
    against him*. Philadelphia, Hall & Piérie,
    1809.
COXE, Daniel: *Description of the English Province of
    Carolina, by the Spaniards called Florida and
    by the French La Louisiane, as also of the great
    and famous river Meschacébé or Mississippi*.
    London, Crows, 1741.

DARBY, William: *Geographical description of the State of Louisiana.* New York, Olmstead, 1817.

DART, H. P.: *Remy's Lost History.* (In *Louisiana Historical Quarterly*, vol. 5, January 1922, p. 1-17).

DAVIDSON, James Wood: *Living Writers of the South.* Carlton, New York; S. Low & Son, London, 1869.

EATON, John Henry: *Life of Major General Jackson, comprising a history of the war in the South from the commencement of the Creek Campaign to the termination of hostilities before New Orleans. Addenda containing a brief history of the Seminole War and cession and government of Florida.* 3rd edition revised and corrected. Philadelphia, McCarty, 1828.

FRENCH, B. F.: *Historical Collections of Louisiana embracing many rare and valuable documents relating to the natural, civil, and political history of that state, compiled with historical notes and biographical notes and an introduction by B. F. French.* 1846-1853. 5 vols.

— *Historical Collections of Louisiana and Florida, including translations of original manuscripts relating to their discovery and settlement with numerous historical and biographical notes by B. F. French.* New series. Vol. I, II. New York, J. Sabin & Sons, 1869.

FORSTALL, Edward J.: *Analytical Index of the whole of the public documents relative to Louisiana deposited in the Archives of the Department " De la Marine et des Colonies " at Paris; containing matters of great interest, many of which are unknown to the present generation, in relation to the early history of this country and showing that Louisiana was the first province upon the continent of America to raise the standard of liberty, carefully drawn from the above named archives by a Louisianan.* E. Johns & Co., New Orleans, 1841.

GAYARRÉ, Charles: *History of Louisiana. French Domi-*

nation, 2 vols. in one. New York, Redfield, 1854. *Spanish Domination*, New York, Redfield, 1854. *American Domination*. New York, 1866.

— *History of Louisiana*. 1903 edition, 2 vols. New Orleans, Hansell and Brother, 1903.

HALDEN, Charles ab der: *Etudes de littérature canadienne-française*, Paris, F. R. de Rudeval, 1904.

JONES, Howard Mumford : *America and French Culture, 1750-1848*. Chapel Hill, N. C. The University of North Carolina Press, 1927.

KENDALL, John Smith: *History of New Orleans*. Lewis Publishing Co., New York and Chicago, 1922. 2 vols.

KING, Grace: *An Old French Teacher of New Orleans*. (*Yale Review*, January 1922, p. 380-392.)

— *Old Creole Families of New Orleans*. McMillan & Co., New York, 1921.

LATOUR, Arsène Lacarrière: *Historical Memoir of the War in West Florida in 1814-1815 with an atlas*. Originally in French. Philadelphia, Conrad, 1816.

MARGRY, Pierre: *Relations et mémoires inédits pour servir à l'histoire de la France dans les pays d'outre-mer, tirés des archives du ministre de la Marine et des Colonies*. Paris, Chalamel, 1867.

— *Mémoires et documents pour servir à l'histoire des origines françaises des pays d'outre-mer. Découvertes et établissements des Français dans l'ouest et dans le sud de l'Amérique septentrionale (1614-1698)*. Paris, Maisonneuve et Cie. 6 vols. MDCCCLXXIX.

MARTIN, Francis Xavier: *History of Louisiana from the Earliest Period*. New Orleans, Lyman, 1827. 2 vols.

— *History of Louisiana*. 1882 edition. New Orleans, James Gresham, 1882.

MEYNIER, Arthur Jr.: *Life and Military Service of Col. Charles Didier Dreux*. E. A. Brandao & Co., New Orleans.

MOUNT, May: *Some Notables of New Orleans, Biographical and Descriptive. Sketches of the Artists of New Orleans, and their Work.* New Orleans, 1896.

ROUEN, Bussière: *L'Abeille de la Nouvelle Orléans* (*Louisiana Historical Quarterly*, vol. 8, October 1925, p. 587 ff).

SISMONDI, J. C. de: *A History of the Italian Republics being a View of the Origin, Progress, and Fall of Italian Freedom,* London, Longman, Brown, Green, & Longmans, 1832.

STODDARD, Major Amos: *Sketches Historical and Descriptive of Louisiana.* Philadelphia, Matthew Cary, 1812.

VEGA, Garcilaso de la: *Histoire de la conquête de la Floride; ou relation de ce qui s'est passé dans la découverte de ce pays par Ferdinand de Soto, traduite en français* par Pierre Michelet, Leide, Pierre Vander, MDCCXXXI.

WELLBORN, Alfred: *History of New Orleans City Park.*

WHITE, Joseph M.: New *Collection of laws, charters, and local ordinances of governments of Great Britain, France, and Spain relating to the concessions of land in their respective colonies, together with the laws of Mexico and Texas on the same subject.* Philadelphia, Johnson, 1839, 2 vols.

WILKINSON, General James: *Memoirs of My Own Times.* Philadelphia, Abraham Small, 1816.

BULLETINS AND GENERAL WORKS OF REFERENCE

Bibliography of American Newspapers, 1690-1820 compiled by Clarence S. Brigham in *Proceedings of the American Antiquarian Society,* New Series, volumes 23, 24 (1913, 1914). Published by the Society, Worcester Mass.

Biographical and Historical Memoirs of Louisiana embracing an authentic and comprehensive account of the chief events in the history of the State and a special sketch of every parish and a record of the lives of many of the most worthy and illustrious families and individuals. Chicago, Goodspeed Publishing Co., 1892, 2 vols.

Bulletin of Tulane University, College of Arts and Sciences.

Cambridge History of American Literature.

Catalogue of Newspaper Files in the Library of State Historical Society of Wisconsin, compiled by Ada Tyng Griswold, Madison, Published by the Society, 1911.

Check List of American Newspapers in the Library of Congress, compiled under direction of Allan B. Slausson, Chief of Periodical Division, Washington, Government Printing Office, 1901.

Larousse, Grand Dictionnaire Universel.

Histoire de la Presse Franco-Américaine, Alexander Bélisle, Worcester, Mass., Ateliers Typographiques de " l'Opinion Publique ", 1911.

Library of Southern Literature, vol. XV.

Memorial, issued by Columbia University at the time of the death of Edward Joseph Fortier, 1918.

Newspapers and Periodical Press, S. D. North, Washington, Government Printing Office, 1884.

(Notes toward a) History of the American Newspaper, William Nelson, New York, Charles F. Heartman, 1918.

Southwest Louisiana, Biographical and Historical, New Orleans, Gulf Publishing Co., 1891.

Ten Years of the Class of 1904 of Tulane University.

DOCUMENTS AND STATUTES

Acts of the State of Louisiana, 1868, Act 8, sec. 10.

Louisiana Constitution of 1879, Articles 154 and 226.

Record 38 (January 23, 1845-May 18, 1846) in Conveyance Office in New Orleans.

All the French Newspapers as quoted.

The Picayune, The Times Democrat, The Times-Picayune, The Item of New Orleans.

Printed in the United States
707900001B